PRAISE FOR CHARLIE N. HOLMBERG

STAR MOTHER

"Readers will find entertainment and hope in this sweeping, mythic tale."

—*Publishers Weekly*

"In this stunning example of amazing worldbuilding, Holmberg (*Spellbreaker*) features incredible creatures, a love story, and twists no one could see coming. This beautiful novel will be enjoyed by fantasy and romance readers alike."

—*Library Journal*

"Gods and men mingle in this fantasy tale of celestial beings, battling gods, and time travel. Fans of Neil Gaiman's *Stardust* (2008) will appreciate the unique characters in this fantasy adventure."

—*Booklist*

THE SPELLBREAKER SERIES

"Romantic and electrifying . . . the fast-paced plot and fully realized world will have readers eager for the next installment. Fans of Victorian-influenced fantasy won't want to put this down."

—*Publishers Weekly*

"Those who enjoy gentle romance, cozy mysteries, or Victorian fantasy will love this first half of a duology. The cliff-hanger ending will keep readers breathless waiting for the second half."

—*Library Journal* (starred review)

"Powerful magic, indulgent Victoriana, and a slow-burn romance make this genre-bending romp utterly delightful."

—*Kirkus Reviews*

THE NUMINA SERIES

"[An] enthralling fantasy . . . The story is gripping from the start, with a surprising plot and a lush, beautifully realized setting. Holmberg knows just how to please fantasy fans."

—*Publishers Weekly*

"With scads of action, clear explanations of how supernatural elements function, and appealing characters with smart backstories, this first in a series will draw in fans of Cassandra Clare, Leigh Bardugo, or Brandon Sanderson."

—*Library Journal*

"Holmberg is a genius at world building; she provides just enough information to set the scene without overwhelming the reader. She also creates captivating characters worth rooting for and puts them in unique situations. Readers will be eager for the second installment in the Numina series."

—*Booklist*

THE PAPER MAGICIAN SERIES

"Charlie is a vibrant writer with an excellent voice and great world building. I thoroughly enjoyed *The Paper Magician*."

—Brandon Sanderson, author of *Mistborn* and *The Way of Kings*

"Harry Potter fans will likely enjoy this story for its glimpses of another structured magical world, and fans of Erin Morgenstern's *The Night Circus* will enjoy the whimsical romance element . . . So if you're looking for a story with some unique magic, romantic gestures, and the inherent darkness that accompanies power all steeped in a yet to be fully explored magical world, then this could be your next read."

—Amanda Lowery, *Thinking Out Loud*

THE WILL AND THE WILDS

"An immersive, dangerous fantasy world. Holmberg draws readers in with a fast-moving plot, rich details, and a surprisingly sweet human-monster romance. This is a lovely, memorable fairy tale."

—*Publishers Weekly*

"Holmberg ably builds her latest fantasy world, and her brisk narrative and the romance at its heart will please fans of her previous magical tales."

—*Booklist*

THE FIFTH DOLL

Winner of the 2017 Whitney Award for Speculative Fiction

"*The Fifth Doll* is told in a charming, folklore-ish voice that's reminiscent of a good old-fashioned tale spun in front of the fireplace on a cold winter night. I particularly enjoyed the contrast of the small-town village atmosphere—full of simple townspeople with simple dreams and worries—set against the complex and eerie backdrop of the village that's not what it seems. The fact that there are motivations and forces shaping the lives of the villagers on a daily basis that they're completely unaware of adds layers and textures to the story and makes it a very interesting read."

—*San Francisco Book Review*

KEEPER

of

ENCHANTED
ROOMS

ALSO BY CHARLIE N. HOLMBERG

The Star Mother Series

Star Mother
Star Father

The Spellbreaker Series

Spellbreaker
Spellmaker

The Numina Series

Smoke and Summons
Myths and Mortals
Siege and Sacrifice

The Paper Magician Series

The Paper Magician
The Glass Magician
The Master Magician
The Plastic Magician

Other Novels

The Fifth Doll
Magic Bitter, Magic Sweet
Followed by Frost
Veins of Gold
The Will and the Wilds

KEEPER

of

ENCHANTED ROOMS

CHARLIE N. HOLMBERG

47N⬤RTH

Text copyright © 2022 by Charlie N. Holmberg
All rights reserved.

Published by 47North, Seattle

www.apub.com

Amazon, the Amazon logo, and 47North are trademarks of Amazon.com, Inc., or its affiliates.

ISBN-13: 9781662500343 (paperback)
ISBN-13: 9781662500336 (digital)

Cover design by Faceout Studio, Lindy Martin

Cover illustration by Christina Chung

Printed in the United States of America

To Jeff Wheeler.
Thank you for the help, the charisma,
the opportunities, and the
permission to be a diva
once a week.

FIRST FLOOR

ENCLOSED PORCH

KITCHEN

TOILET

SUNROOM

LIVING ROOM

BREAKFAST ROOM

RECEPTION HALL

DINING ROOM

SECOND FLOOR

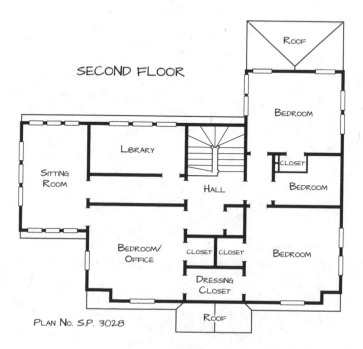

ROOF

BEDROOM

LIBRARY

CLOSET

BEDROOM

SITTING ROOM

HALL

BEDROOM/ OFFICE

CLOSET CLOSET

BEDROOM

DRESSING CLOSET

ROOF

PLAN No. S.P. 3028

DOCTRINES OF MAGIC

Augury • Soothsaying, fortune-telling, divination, luck
1. Repercussion: forgetfulness
2. Associated mineral: amethyst

Psychometry • Mind reading, hallucination, empathy, intuition
3. Repercussion: dulling of senses
4. Associated mineral: azurite

Conjury • Creation, summoning of natural components
5. Repercussion: loss of equal worth to summoned object
6. Associated mineral: pyrite

Necromancy • Death/life magic, life force, disease/healing
7. Repercussion: nausea
8. Associated mineral: turquoise

Wardship • Shielding, protection, spell-turning
9. Repercussion: weakening of physical body
10. Associated mineral: tourmaline

Element • Manipulation of fire, water, earth, or air
11. Repercussion: fire, chill; water, dryness; earth, vertigo; air, shortness of breath
12. Associated mineral: clear quartz

Alteration • Shape-shifting, changing, metamorphosis
13. Repercussion: temporary physical mutation
14. Associated mineral: opal

Communion • Translation, communication with plants/animals
15. Repercussion: muteness, tinnitus
16. Associated mineral: selenite

Hysteria • Manipulation of emotions, pain
17. Repercussion: physical pain, apathy
18. Associated mineral: carnelian

Kinetic • Movement, force
19. Repercussion: stiffness, lack of mobility
20. Associated mineral: bloodstone

Chaocracy • Manipulation of chaos/order, destruction, restoration
21. Repercussion: confusion
22. Associated mineral: obsidian

Prologue

May 17, 1818, London, England

Silas took up the brush and started smoothing Marybelle's coat, even though the stable hands had already tended her. It was late, the sun long since set, and most of the servants had already turned in. But Silas liked being out in the stables. He'd gotten used to the smell. There was something peaceful about the animals, who stood and endured their confined spaces with little complaint. Just as he did.

The horse in the next stall nosed the back of his head, blowing warm air over his neck. Smiling, Silas reached back and stroked the velvet between the animal's nostrils. "I'll get you next." He ran the short-bristled brush over Marybelle's flank. Inhaled the scents of horseflesh and hay. Relaxed as much as his sixteen-year-old frame would let him. A few lights still shined through the house windows; he imagined his mother was having her hair wound into curling papers right about now. He should turn in, too. His new arithmetic tutor would be arriving early tomorrow to train him for Oxford, or maybe Cambridge.

He heard the sound of another horse walking before he picked up the stuttering gait of the man leading it. His stomach tightened. He glanced to the back of Marybelle's stall. Enough room to squat down and hide, but if he was seen, there'd be no opportunity to escape. Instead, Silas set the brush aside and carefully unlatched the stall door, hoping to sneak around back and enter the house through the servants' door.

He'd almost made it into the shadows when his father's voice called, "Who goes there?"

Silas cringed at the slurred words. His father was drunk. But if he kept walking, his father might think him one of the staff—

"Silas!" he barked.

Dread filled Silas's gut as he turned. "Want me to help you with the horse?" He had a sliver of luck in his blood, inherited from his grandmother. He prayed it would cooperate with him now.

His father had a lead on the animal, but the mare seemed to be all that held him up. He had a bottle in his hand, and his cheeks slouched like he'd aged himself into jowls. He was *never* this drunk. Silas couldn't tell if that was a good thing or a bad one.

Not taking his eyes from Silas, his father crooked a finger. The bolt on the nearest empty stall *clicked*, and the door swung open. Silas couldn't blame his father for using magic; in his condition, it was probably easier than stabling the horse physically.

But his father didn't put the horse away. An invisible hand shoved against Silas's back, drawing him close enough to smell the whiskey wafting off his father like mist off the sea. And when the hand shoved him into the stall, Silas's nerves lit up, every last one of them, until his blood raced and his skin burned.

"L-Let me get you to bed," he said.

His father stepped into the stall and closed the door, leaning heavily on it for the stiffness the magic had left in his legs. "Excused me," he rumbled. "They *excused* me. For"—he laughed—"drunken behavior."

Silas peered beyond the stable, praying a servant, his mother, his brother, *anyone* would come by. "Who excused you?"

"King's League."

His stomach plummeted. "You were dismissed?" No wonder he was so drunk. Both of Silas's parents were members of the King's League of Magicians. They'd practically been groomed for it from birth.

Oh no. This wasn't going to be good for him. Silas held his hands up, palms out, as though calming a rabid dog. "Let's get food in your stomach—"

His father threw the bottle. It collided with Silas's shoulder. A spell—the same one his father had used to pull him in here—burned in Silas's blood, begging to be released, but he didn't use it. It *always* made his father angrier when he used magic. His father hated that Silas had more magic than he did, thanks to the added pedigree of his mother.

Silas didn't defend himself when the first fist struck, nor the second. This was habitual, for them. It passed quicker when he took it. Another blow, another. Any moment now, his father would be done, and he'd sneak back inside, find something to nurse the bruises—

The kick to his ribs cracked bone and ripped air from his lungs.

His weakest spell, luck, was not with him today.

Silas slammed into the back wall. *This is wrong.* His father had never broken a bone before, and—

Dizziness engulfed him. A blow to the head. Silas didn't remember falling to his knees. His skull radiated pain. Had he been hit with the bottle, or a kinetic pulse?

"Father—" he tried, but a fist hit the side of his mouth, cutting his cheek on his teeth. Silas couldn't help it; he covered his head. He had to.

"You think you're better than me?" his father raged, slamming the toe of his shoe into Silas's hip. "You think you . . . can take my place?"

"No!" Silas cried, fire radiating up his spine. His father stumbled back but shot out a kinetic blast that attempted to crush Silas's entire body. Blood spilled from his lips. Stars danced across his eyelids. Something snapped and ached.

His father had never hurt him this badly before. Never.

"Please!" Silas begged.

A second magical blast had bile coursing up Silas's throat. Acid splattered over his shirt.

I'm going to die. I'm going to die.

"I'll show you—"

Silas's blood lit white hot.

Kinesis blasted from his body and slammed his father into the stall door. Broke it off its hinges. Sent man and door skidding across the manicured lawn. The horses whinnied and reared in their stalls as Silas's bloody fingers clambered for a grip. His joints seized with the use of power, but he worked his hands, knuckles popping, and strained to stand. Wheezing, he lifted his head and peered through the sweaty locks covering his eyes.

His father didn't move.

Limping, holding his middle, Silas crossed the distance between them, the stiffness gradually easing. His father's chest still rose. His breathing was loud in the quiet night. Had no one heard them? Or did the staff merely not *want* to hear, knowing they could do nothing to stop the master of the house? They'd never once stepped in to save Silas or his brother.

His father's hand gripped grass as he lifted his head, eyes finding Silas. "I'll . . . kill . . . you . . ."

The invisible hand wrapped around Silas's throat.

Silas didn't even think. Had he thought, maybe he could have coaxed the spell from his neck. Maybe he could have lulled his father into sleep and passed another day in his shadow. But he didn't.

His necromancy came from his mother's side. It seemed eager to serve, to penetrate his drunken father's skin and mix with his soul. To drain him until the kinetic spell broke and his head thumped back against the ground. But the other spells grew jealous, and they rode along the path, merging with the first, stretching unseen lines between father and son—

Silas woke with his face pressed into the lawn. When had he . . . ? His ribs stung with every breath. The left side of his body, where he'd taken the kinetic blows, burned and pulsed with new bruises. Iron slicked his teeth. Scabs matted his hair.

Beside him, his father still breathed as though drawn into the deepest of slumbers.

But despite the injuries, despite the misery entangling his body and screaming in his bones, Silas felt . . . different. He felt . . . strong, somehow. Not in a physical sense but a metaphysical one. His magic . . . His magic felt like a thousand brilliant candles within him. Like it had . . . grown?

He stared at his father's face. His slow breaths still reeked of alcohol.

Using a hand unattached to himself, Silas let the fingers pinch over his father's windpipe. *No more.*

The breaths stopped.

And the surge of strength snuffed out. So suddenly that Silas found himself gasping for its loss. He gaped at his father's corpse. Had he taken . . . but he couldn't have . . . could he?

One thing was certain, as Silas carefully, joint by joint, pulled himself upright once more.

No one would ever have power over him *again.*

Chapter 1

September 4, 1846, Baltimore, Maryland

The reading of a will was far more exciting when one hadn't been disinherited thirteen years prior. Indeed, Merritt Fernsby was not sure why the lawyer had contacted him at all.

He hadn't come with his family, of course. He hadn't spoken to them in a decade. Hadn't been allowed to. There were letters in the beginning, all from him—the start of his writing career, in a melancholy sort of way, but melancholy things always made for great fiction. The coddled and content seldom told good stories. And though he was thirty-one years of age as of last March, he had yet to start a family of his own, for various reasons he could get into but never did.

And so he was very interested to receive a telegram from Mr. Allen, his maternal grandmother's estate lawyer. Interested and confused, he'd made the trip out to Baltimore to satiate his curiosity. If nothing else, it might make good fodder for an article, or perhaps his work in progress.

"I'll get to the point, Mr. Fernsby." Mr. Allen leaned casually against his desk with papers in hand. He seemed to loom over Merritt and the well-worn chair he sat in, like a vulture sniffing out a fresh carcass, which was a somewhat harsh metaphor given that, thus far, Mr. Allen had been nothing but polite and professional.

Merritt wondered if his parents and siblings had been called into this office as well, or if Mr. Allen had made the trip out to New York to read the will to them there. Admittedly—and Merritt loathed to admit it, even to himself—he'd hoped they'd be here. Death often brought people together, and—

He swallowed hard, keeping his tongue at the back of his throat, until the familiar disappointment burned up in his stomach.

He pushed objectivity into his thoughts. Perhaps they had all come to Baltimore to see Grandmother before she passed. Then again, Merritt had, at best, only seen his grandmother once a year during his childhood, and he couldn't quite remember the scale of sentimentality between her and his mother.

He wondered what his mother looked like now. Did she have lines in the corners of her eyes? Did she wear her hair differently, and had it started turning gray? Perhaps she had gained weight or lost it. Wincing, Merritt shut off the wondering early; the more he wondered, the less he could remember.

He realized then that Mr. Allen was still talking.

"—weren't included in the rest," he was saying, "but an addition was made some time ago."

Merritt put two and two together. "How long ago?"

He checked his papers. "About twenty-five years."

Before the disowning, then. He wondered if his grandmother had forgotten to take him off. Then again, the break had been his father's doing. Perhaps Grandmother had, despite never trying to contact him, still cared for him. He preferred that explanation to the other. Of course, there was always a third possibility: guilt might have prevented her from removing his name.

"To my grandson Merritt Fernsby, I leave Whimbrel House and anything that might be left within it, along with its land."

Merritt sat straighter in his chair. "Whimbrel House?" When Mr. Allen didn't reply quickly enough, he added, "That's it?"

8

Mr. Allen nodded.

Merritt wasn't sure what he'd expected, but the mention of a *house* had him distracted. "I've never heard of it. A real house?"

"I don't believe false ones can be inherited." Mr. Allen put the papers down. "But I looked into the matter myself; it's all in order."

"How did my grandmother own a second house?"

Mr. Allen leaned back to open a drawer in his desk. He shuffled a few things around before pulling out a large envelope. Withdrawing a new set of documents, he said, "The property came into the Nichols line some time ago. Before that . . . Well, it hasn't had a tenant in a very long time."

"How long is very long?"

He flipped a paper. "Last *recorded* resident was 1737."

Merritt blinked. That was over a century ago.

"Understandable," Mr. Allen went on. "The place is out of the way, on Blaugdone Island in the Narragansett Bay." He glanced up. "Rhode Island."

Which meant marshland. "I'm aware of it." A house abandoned for a hundred years in the middle of a marshy island . . . It must be in terrible repair.

"Commuting would be difficult. Unless you own an enchanted watercraft."

Merritt shook his head. "Fortunately, I don't have need to commute." Although he'd made his name in journalism, Merritt had recently sold his second novel to his publisher—the first having been a moderate success—and one could write novels anywhere there were ink and paper available.

He rubbed his chin, noting he'd forgotten to shave that morning. Having been on his own since he was eighteen, he'd learned how to shingle roofs, place floorboards, grease hinges, the lot of it. There would be a great amount of work ahead of him, but he might be able to fix up the place.

It would be nice not to share walls or pay rent. And finally break away from the Culdwells.

Mr. Culdwell was Merritt's landlord. He was a crochety moose of a man who was grisly even on his best days. And though Merritt was always timely with his rent, the bloke's grandson had recently moved to the city for school. Culdwell, of course, wanted to house him in Merritt's space. When Merritt refused to move out in exchange for a month's returned rent, Culdwell had blatantly said there would be no renewal of contract come October. Which, obviously, put Merritt in something of a bind.

Plus, Culdwell's wife was nosy and smelled like broccoli.

So the pertinent questions were, how poor was the condition of Whimbrel House, and how much did Merritt actually care?

"I . . . might divulge one other thing listed here." Mr. Allen's mouth skewed to the side almost in distaste. A thick line formed between his eyebrows.

"Oh?"

He shrugged. "I'm not one for superstition, Mr. Fernsby, but it does state here that the previous tenant claimed the place was haunted."

Merritt laughed. "Haunted? This is Rhode Island, not Germany."

"Agreed." While it *was* possible for magic to root itself in inanimate objects, it had become so rare—especially in a place as new as the States—that the claim felt incredible. "But haunted or not, the parcel is yours."

Merritt knit his hands together. "How large of a parcel is it?"

Mr. Allen glanced at the papers. "I believe it's the entire island. Roughly eighteen acres."

"Eighteen," Merritt exhaled.

"Marshland, mind you."

"Yes, yes." He waved his hand. "But wasn't Jamestown built on the same? Folk are always multiplying and expanding. If the house is unsalvageable, there's the land. I could sell the land."

"You could, with the right buyer." Mr. Allen didn't hide his skepticism as he handed over the papers. "Congratulations, Mr. Fernsby. You're now a homeowner."

⁓

Despite his ever-growing curiosity, Merritt did not spend the extra money to take the kinetic tram out to Rhode Island; he took a train, a wagon, and then a boat. By the time he crossed a good portion of the Narragansett Bay and reached Blaugdone Island, he understood why no one had bothered to live there. It was vastly out of the way. There was something uncomfortable yet incredibly appealing about how out of the way it was.

Because after the hired boat dropped off Merritt and the one bag he'd packed, he heard a beautiful thing.

Silence.

Now, Merritt did not hate noise. He'd been raised in a sizable town and lived in a bustling city for over a decade. He was used to it. It was familiar. But the only time cities got quiet was during heavy snowfall. So it was strange for a place to be both quiet *and* warm. There was something about the hush that made him realize he was completely alone, on an island that may have been untouched by humankind for . . . years. *A century*, even. But it didn't bother him, not precisely. After all, Merritt had been alone a long time.

The cry of a bird broke the silence momentarily, announcing Merritt's arrival to others. Shading his eyes from the sun, he spied what he believed to be a heron off in some tall grass between trees. The leaves had not yet changed on the elms and oaks spotting the land, but they were certainly thinking about it. Just beyond that was a nub of a shadow—the house, most likely. He walked toward it, and the heron took off, long legs trailing behind.

The earth was moist beneath his shoes, the local plant life wild and untouched. He recognized some of it: weeping cherries, golden aster, autumn olive. He thought he smelled chrysanthemums as well, which had the effect of relaxing his shoulders. He hadn't realized they'd been tense. Crouching, he pinched some soil between his fingers. It looked rich; if he started a garden now, he might be able to wheedle some garlic, onions, and carrots out of it before the frost hit.

A cottontail thumped and darted from his path—he'd have to cut down some of this grass—and a flock of swallows watched him from a slippery elm. The house grew in size, enough to garner some color— was that a blue roof? Blue shingles were a surprise, given the age of the house. Time faded colors. That, and most of the early roofs in the States were thatched.

The house continued to grow to two stories, and its sides took on a yellow hue. Merritt's steps quickened, startling a feeding bird—a whimbrel—from a puddle. He'd half expected the house to be slanting one way, to have gaps between weathered boarding, to shelter large families of mice. Hence his decision to pack a single bag. It wasn't his intent to stay; this visit was exploratory.

He approached the house from the north; it faced east. When he came around to the front, his lips parted as sea-scented air puffed his hair back.

The house was . . . fine.

It was perfectly fine. In fantastic condition, at least from the outside. No weathering, no missing shingles, no broken windows. The nature around it was wild, but surely *someone* lived here for the place to be so pristine. It could almost be brand new, though the style was certainly colonial.

"I'll be," he said, and followed it with a whistle, which seemed appropriate. He squinted at the windows but couldn't see much within. So feeling strange, he approached his front door and knocked. He didn't know how to feel when no one answered. Had he expected someone to answer?

"Surely someone has been keeping it up . . ." Perhaps they had vacated the premises after the place was bequeathed to him, but Mr. Allen had said there had been no recent tenants. Squatters, perhaps? Very handy squatters?

There was a key in the lawyerly envelope in his bag, but when Merritt tried the handle, the door opened with only the slightest creak of its hinges. It was early afternoon, so sun shined through the windows, which were only lightly pocked with trails of rain. The moderate reception hall looked every bit as fine and put together as the exterior. At the end was a set of intact stairs and a door. Leaving the front door open, Merritt stepped in, marveling. He'd intended to open that second door, but his attention was diverted by the rooms stemming off either side of the reception hall—a dining room on the right, with a table *already set* for a party of eight, and a living room on the left, fully furnished in burgundy and forest green.

Merritt gaped. He *had* considered that his grandmother's will was set to dump an unwanted parcel on him, leaving it to him to let it rot or try to sell it, but this house already looked . . . amazing. More than he could afford, unless he managed to pull an Alexandre Dumas and make a fortune from his publisher.

"Thank you, Anita," he murmured, reaching out and touching the wall. There was a portrait there of a British woman, though nothing else to denote who she might have been. She seemed to look at him, wondering about the transition of ownership just as much as he did.

He turned to the living room, stepping reverently. Everything was in order, like it'd been prepared for him, though a heavy coat of dust lined every available surface, and the furniture had some wear. But no sign of rodents, or even a fly. He ran his hand over the back of a settee before peering through the next doorway, which led to a sunroom. The plants there were either dead or overgrown, as though whoever had been caring for this house lacked a green thumb. But Merritt owned a *sunroom*. The thought put a weird pressure in his chest he didn't quite understand.

Turning back, he was a quarter of the way through the living room when something caught his eye. Turning toward the window, his gaze fell upon a burgundy armchair, upholstered in velvet, maple leaves carved into the armrest and legs.

And it was melting.

Merritt squinted. Rubbed his eyes. Inched closer.

It was . . . most definitely melting. Like a candle under too hot a flame. The seat dripped onto the carpet, though the carpet didn't absorb or repel it. The drips simply ceased to be. Meanwhile, the wood glistened with perspiration and wobbled, ready to break under the lightest touch.

"Good Lord," Merritt mumbled, stepping away. He caught himself on the settee, and his hand pushed through its soupy exterior.

Yelping, he wrenched back, toppling onto the carpet, quick to get his legs under him again. Drips of settee clung to his fingers, then puffed away as though they never were. Once the walls began warping, Merritt sprinted back into the hall, his breath coming fast, his previously gooped hand to his chest.

"What on earth?" he asked, spinning about.

The portrait's eyes followed him.

Something thumped up the stairs.

Swallowing, Merritt bolted for the front door.

It swung shut and locked just before he reached it.

Chapter 2

Hulda Larkin sat in the smaller foyer in the back of the Bright Bay Hotel, which was specifically sectioned off for the Boston Institute for the Keeping of Enchanted Rooms, or BIKER for short. The bench was backless, but pushed up against a wall to compensate for it, and had a false rosebush off to one side and a real potted fern off to the other. She was going through her latest purchase—a receipt book full of seafood recipes—inserting tabs on the most sensible meals. She had just returned to Boston yesterday after a six-week assignment in Canada, overseeing the preservation of a well-warded longhouse off the shore of Lake Ontario. She'd been called down to the office only an hour prior.

She didn't have to wait long. Miss Steverus, the young receptionist, bounced in as Hulda placed the third tab, announcing, "Ms. Haigh will see you now."

Closing her book and stowing it away, Hulda stood and shook out the ruching on her skirt before offering a polite nod and heading into the office. It was a fairly large room with expansive windows backlighting a heavy desk and the petite, elegant woman who sat behind it. One wall was covered in shelves like a library, while the other was completely bare.

"Myra," Hulda said with a nod and smile.

"The timing is perfect." Myra Haigh stood from her chair and walked over, swiping a folder off the corner of her desk with the grace of a ballerina. Her black hair was curled and pinned meticulously, crowning lightly tanned skin, one of the few things that gave away her Spanish heritage. Although she was nearing her fiftieth year, she looked younger, perhaps because she was always at the ready, always available, and always aware. She never went on holiday or rested when ill, save for a bout of fever in 1841 that had had the institute pleading for her quick recovery. Myra Haigh *was* BIKER, more than any library or office space ever could be.

"I have a new assignment for you," Myra declared.

Hulda blinked. "Already? Overseas?" Her trunks had only arrived that morning. Though BIKER was based in Boston, they often took on international work, especially when their parent organization, LIKER—the *London* Institute for the Keeping of Enchanted Rooms—was shorthanded. Magicked homes were far more common in Europe than the States.

"No, actually. A new resident has inherited Whimbrel House." She opened the folder and handed it to her. "My sources say he moved in yesterday."

Blueprints and a single sheet of information stared up at her. "Whimbrel House? I'm not familiar with it." She read. "Rhode Island?"

"Indeed. It's long abandoned for obvious reasons. Used to be a safe-house for necromancers during the mess with Salem." She clucked her tongue in distaste. "I got the telegram late last night. The new owner's name is Merritt Fernsby."

Hulda scanned the information sheet. The house had been inherited from an Anita Nichols.

"It looks to be a raw trade," Myra added.

Hulda let out a long breath. "Oh dear. Those are always interesting." A nonwizard moving into an enchanted house was a delicate situation. She turned back a page. "This is a very thin file."

"I'll credit that to my predecessor," she said with a tone of apology. "It's a lone house out of the way, sparsely inhabited over the years, and its denizens hardly carved their names into the walls." She knit her fingers together. "I know you've only just returned, but could you leave today? It's only two hours by tram and boat. I'd rather not let it sit."

Sit and risk the resident damaging the house, or the house damaging the resident. Hulda nodded. "My things are still packed away, so it's no bother." Though for the initial review, she'd just bring her handy black bag. She never went anywhere without it.

Myra clapped her hands. "God bless you. I couldn't send anyone else, Hulda. You really are our best."

Hulda rolled her eyes, though the praise warmed her. "Only because Mrs. Thornton is still in Denmark."

"Pah." Myra set her hand on her shoulder. "It's a bit out of the way. Take the kinetic line into Providence. BIKER will reimburse you."

Nodding, Hulda turned toward the door, still poring over the small file.

"And, Hulda."

She paused.

Myra knit her fingers together. "Do be careful."

Pushing her spectacles higher on her nose, Hulda said, "I always am."

❧

Whimbrel House was rather charming. Enchanted buildings tended to be, but this one's appeal was amplified because it was swathed in nature, wild grasses tipped with afternoon sunlight, an unseen egret crying in the distance. The smell of the ocean clung to everything, and it cooled the breeze, which would be very pleasant in the height of summer. Granted, it was already September, and Hulda would not be here long enough for the year to turn and come back to July, but it was a nice enough thought.

The place had a steeply gabled roof and a variety of windows, big and small, circular, circle topped, and rectangular. Oak shades stained darkly, blue shingles that glimmered teal beneath the direct sun. It wasn't a particularly large house, which meant it would require a smaller staff. In truth, that would make matters easier, both for hiring and for the new owner's pocketbook. It was hard enough for BIKER to find people adequately familiar with magic to hire, let alone ones who were employable.

Approaching the door, heavy tool bag hanging off her shoulder, she took up the brass knocker and rapped four times. Loudly. Hulda preferred not to repeat herself.

For a moment, all was silent. Then she heard the sound of something thick crashing onto the floor—several somethings—followed by a brief shriek. Pulling out her folder, she glanced at her information one last time, just to be sure. *Merritt Fernsby.*

"Hello?" His voice was pitched high on the other side of the door, and desperation leaked through the wooden fibers.

Hulda pushed up her glasses. "Mr. Fernsby?"

"Please help me!" he cried. "It won't let me out!"

Oh dear. Hulda opened her bag. "How long have you been in residence?"

The doorknob jiggled. "Who are you? I tried breaking a window, but—oh God, it's looking at me again."

"Please refrain from damaging the premises." She pulled out her crowbar. "*What* is looking at you?"

"The woman in the portrait!"

Hulda sighed. Houses like this really should be run through BIKER before they were handed out to average citizens. "Stand back, Mr. Fernsby." She wedged the crowbar between door and jamb, then murmured, "Really, little house. He'll never take care of you if you behave like a child."

She tugged a few times before the latch gave and the door swung in, and then she returned the crowbar to her bag.

Four fingers wrapped around the door and wrenched it open.

He stood just shy of six feet. The document said he was thirty-one years old—three years Hulda's junior—though with the bags under his eyes, he looked older. He had light-brown hair that hung unfashionably about his shoulders and was in need of combing. His nose was straight save for a slight widening in the center of the bridge. His clothes were of good make, but he wore a multicolor scarf instead of an ascot, and the scarf had certainly seen better days. The first two buttons of his pale-yellow shirt were undone—no, all the buttons were off by one, something that niggled at Hulda's brain, demanding to be fixed, but she was a housekeeper, not a valet. The poor man had one foot bare and one socked, and his panicked blue eyes looked at her with an eagerness that suggested he hadn't seen another human being in years.

Not entirely unexpected.

"Hello, Mr. Fernsby." She extended her hand. "My name is Hulda Larkin. I've been sent here on behalf of BIKER, or the Boston Institute for the Keeping of Enchanted Rooms. As you have recently inherited an enchanted home—"

"Oh thank God." Mr. Fernsby tried to shake her hand, but the moment his fingers reached the doorway, part of the doorjamb detached and bent, barring his path. Closing his eyes, he slumped against wood. "It won't let me leave."

"I see that," Hulda remarked. She reached forward herself, her hand passing easily into the house.

"I wouldn't, if you want to be able to go home," he warned.

She offered him a firm smile. "I am a professional, I assure you. May I come in?"

He gaped at her. "You want to come *in*? By all means, it's yours! Just *get. Me. Out.*"

"I'm afraid I won't be able to do that until I've done an assessment of the abode."

He blinked like *she* was the one going mad. "Assessment of the abode? Just"—he thrust his hand at her—"pull me out!"

She frowned. "I'm assuming you paid enough attention in school to know magic doesn't work like that."

He blinked at her. "What school did you attend?"

Hulda frowned. It was true that most education boards in the United States included instruction only on magic's historical importance, not the craft itself, such as the seizing of British kinetic ships during the infamous Boston Tea Party. Hulda had spent several years studying abroad in England, where the categorization and use of magic was much more prevalent, both in the schoolhouse and in the country at large.

Mr. Fernsby scrubbed his eyes. "It's haunted—"

"Possibly, likely not," she interjected. "Haunting is only one possibility for an enchanted—"

"Blazes, woman." He pinched the bridge of his nose. "Fine! Come in, and see how it treats *you*." He stepped aside, allowing her entrance, but cast a wary glance at a portrait on the north wall.

The house groaned as she strode in, her shoes clacking against the hardwood floor. Whether or not the house would keep her confined had yet to be determined. She glanced around—it was light outside, but the sun struggled to permeate the windows. Shadows clung to the stairs and walls, casting the rooms—as far as she could see—in incomplete swathes of darkness. The eyes of the portrait to her right were following her, she noticed, so she nodded a greeting. "It seems to be in very good repair, considering its history. Granted, that is typical for strongly spelled structures."

Mr. Fernsby wiped a hand down his face. "A-And how do you know about this place?"

"It is our business to know." Reaching into her pocket, she retrieved a card and handed it to him. The information for BIKER—save its address, which was seldom given out—had been stamped upon it, along with her name.

"Has the house spoken to you?" she asked.

He gaped. "*Spoken* to me?"

She pulled off her gloves. "You need not be so aghast, Mr. Fernsby. Magic is uncommon in today's age, but hardly unheard of. I took the kinetic tram to get here." A tram powered by kinesis, one of eleven schools of magic.

"Yes, yes." He rubbed his eyes. Likely hadn't slept last night, assuming he'd stayed the night. "I am aware, but it is particularly"—he waved his hand, trying to find a suitable word—"*dense* here."

"Indeed. As is the case with domiciles. Enchantments existing outside a flesh body do not receive the normal backlash from the constant casting of spells."

He shifted. "Pardon?"

"I will need to take a tour if you would like it diagnosed," she continued. "An enchanted house cannot be well kept without a thorough diagnosis."

Mr. Fernsby ran a hand back through his hair. No wonder it looked so unkempt.

"You mean diagnosing the type of magic?"

"Among other things. There are several reasons for a house to be enchanted." She pushed up her glasses. "It could simply be under a spell, or built on a site where an abnormal amount of magic was expelled. It could have specifically been built to be enchanted, which is common. Or there could be half a dozen other explanations. Perhaps the materials used were magicked, or a wizard possesses it, or it is very old and gained sentience on its own, which is unlikely given the colonial style. Sometimes homes are just unhappy with their floorplans and choose to enchant themselves, merely so they can amend—"

Something thudded upstairs. Mr. Fernsby jumped.

Tilting her head, Hulda listened, but heard nothing more. "Is anyone else in residence?"

He shook his head.

Clearing her throat, Hulda finished, "It would be best for me to see the house and determine the source of the magic, if you don't mind."

Mr. Fernsby looked through the house, almost as though frightened by it. Hulda couldn't blame him; the walls of the reception hall were beginning to melt. Chaocracy, most likely. The eleventh school of magic.

"Anything to get me out," he muttered.

"It is my goal to see you well situated. Enchanted houses can be tamed." When he gave her an incredulous, bloodshot expression, she gestured to the right. "Perhaps we'll start in the dining room?"

Mr. Fernsby shifted. "T-The dining room table ate my wallet. That must sound utterly absurd to you—"

"Not at all."

"It nearly ate *me*."

Fishing through her bag, she pulled out a string necklace with a red embroidered sack hanging from it and handed it to him. "This is a ward." She pulled out a second for herself. "Wear it, and it should offer some protection as we move through the house—"

"*Some* protection?"

"Nothing is foolproof." She slipped her own ward over her head before meeting his eyes. "They're dangerous to keep on the person for too long; portable spells like these can have strange effects on the body, but it's safe to keep in-house, otherwise."

Mr. Fernsby picked up the sack in his hand and turned it over. "How does it work?"

"This is first-rate magic. *Very* expensive." She gave him a look that hopefully said, *Please don't break it.* "This ward in particular is a chaocracy ward. Order and restoration, specifically. Very few people are at risk of having too much order in their lives, so I doubt the house will wield it against us." They were packed with obsidian dust, but each sack also contained some blood and a fingernail from the wizard who had created them. Mr. Fernsby seemed an excitable sort, however, and she determined it would be better not to mention that.

"May I?" She gestured toward the dining room.

Mr. Fernsby nodded and followed her. The shadows darkened significantly as she entered, trying to choke out the light coming from the large window on the east wall. They did a decent job of it.

"It wasn't like this when I first arrived," Mr. Fernsby said as she approached the table.

"What was it like?"

"Like a normal house."

"Hm." She set her hands on the back of the chair—eight total. It was a small dining room, though a host could sit twelve if he was in dire straits. The table was already set, though dusty.

Rapping her knuckles on the surface, she said, "Come now, give it up. What is the point? You certainly can't do anything with his wallet, now can you?"

The floor creaked like they stood on the deck of a ship sailing into troubled waters.

Reaching into her bag, Hulda pulled out a stethoscope, inserted the earpieces into her ears, and pressed the drum into the tabletop. She shifted it around a few places, tapping with her free hand, until she found a spot where the wood sounded compact. Pulling out a smaller ward, she dropped it on the table, and the furniture belched up a well-used leather wallet.

"You're a saint." Mr. Fernsby snatched up the wallet before the table could consume it once more.

Gesturing to the west door, Hulda asked, "And through there?"

Mr. Fernsby wrapped his free hand around the ward hanging from his neck. "Admittedly, I haven't explored that way yet."

That didn't surprise her. The doorway was completely dark.

Retrieving the ward and slipping it into her pocket, Hulda pulled free a small lamp. She twisted a dial on it, and it illuminated.

"What is that?" Mr. Fernsby asked.

"Enchanted lamp. Conjury and elemental. Fire." She held it before them and led the way.

"Without even a match? Why don't they have those lining the streets?"

"Because they're expensive, Mr. Fernsby."

"Isn't everything."

Hulda approached the door, holding her light high. According to the blueprints, the breakfasting room was through here—

The door swung for her. She jumped back, but not quite far enough—

Two hands seized her waist and hauled her into the dining room, the door just narrowly missing her lamp. It would have shattered the glass—and the spells—completely.

Mr. Fernsby released her, but that did not stop embarrassment from burning in her cheeks. She held the light away from her face to conceal it, then smoothed her skirt. "Thank you, Mr. Fernsby."

He nodded, scowling at the door. "Nearly lost my nose to one upstairs."

This house was proving more troublesome than Hulda had anticipated. She set the small ward on the floor by the door. She'd only brought eight with her, which had seemed like an overindulgence at the time.

The door did not resist her when she walked through this time, though she stepped quickly, and Mr. Fernsby followed suit. The breakfast room was about half the size of the dining room and had another set table that sat four. Walking its perimeter, Hulda said, "You could knock out that wall if you want to host a larger party."

The house grumbled, like it was a stomach and they the food.

"I don't intend to even host myself." He turned suddenly, searching the shadows for something. "This place is unlivable."

"It would be a great loss to you, to give up so quickly," Hulda warned. "Whimbrel House hasn't been inhabited for some time, which may be why the place acts so poorly. You couldn't even sell it in this state. If nothing else, it would be a financial loss."

He seemed to consider that.

She stopped at the next door. "I presume the kitchen is through here." The door did not resist her. It was a little brighter in this room, since flame flickered from an iron chandelier overhead. The kitchen had both a hearth and a woodsmoke stove, as well as good counterspace and a pump-operated sink. "Very nice. Do you have a stool?"

"Nice?" Mr. Fernsby repeated. "Are we in the same house?" He peered around and found a three-legged stool on the other side of the hearth. He brought it over, but had crossed only half the distance when he started shrieking.

"Get it off, *get it off*!" He flung his hands out, but the stool's seat sucked onto them, melting and climbing up his arm. It couldn't seem to get past his elbow, though, which meant the ward he wore was working.

"And how does this benefit you?" Hulda asked the ceiling.

The lights on the chandelier flickered.

Sighing, Hulda went to Mr. Fernsby and grasped his shoulder. "Try to calm down."

"It's *eating* me!"

"It's simply having a tantrum." She grabbed one of the stool's legs, though it was soft as warm wax, and pulled. Despite its liquid state, the stool was still one *thing*, and it gradually slid off Mr. Fernsby's arm. When Hulda released it, it plopped onto the floor like a mud pie. She reached into her bag for a ward, but the stool reshaped itself on its own.

Before it could change its mind, she placed it beneath the chandelier. "If you could spot me, Mr. Fernsby." She didn't want the thing deliquescing while she stood atop it.

He stepped to her side, eyeing the stool. "You're very cavalier about this, Miss Larkin."

"Mrs. Larkin will do." She stepped up.

He glanced at her bare left hand. "You're married, then?"

She focused on the chandelier. "It is proper to call a housekeeper by *Mrs.* regardless of her matrimonial state." She pulled out her magnifying glass and ran a finger around its rim. It, too, was enchanted, and refocused itself to suit her needs. Mr. Fernsby inched behind her to get a better look, letting out a weak whistle.

Ignoring him, Hulda focused on the flames. "See how they're not actually extinguishing? Likely Whimbrel House does not possess elemental magic." She made a mental note and stepped off the stool. There was an enclosed porch just behind the kitchen, but with the floor bubbling like tar, she determined it best not to explore it at this time.

The house creaked significantly as they returned to the reception hall. Wielding her lamp, Hulda opened the door by the stairs to find the toilet. She stepped inside, examining the mirror, but found it ordinary.

When she moved to the far corner, Mr. Fernsby following behind, the door slammed shut, startling her, and all six walls, including the floor and ceiling, began to crush inward, warping the toilet and sink as though they were made of clay. Piping shoved Hulda into Mr. Fernsby, who caught her by the shoulders as the wall behind them grew spikes.

For the first time since arriving, fear curdled in her stomach.

"Stop this at once!" she shouted, but the house had already proven itself unreasonable. The sink pushed the two of them together; she tried to wrench back, but the room gave her little space to do so, and it was still shrinking, forcing Mr. Fernsby to stoop as the ceiling buffed his hair.

Fresh spikes formed on the opposite wall, catching the edge of Hulda's bag, inching closer, closer—

Mr. Fernsby hissed through his teeth as one pressed into his backside. He desperately tried to open the door. The lock jammed. He threw his shoulder into it once, twice—

The door grew spikes fine as needles.

"Mr. Fernsby!" Hulda shouted.

He reeled back before puncturing himself—reeled back into *her*. Spikes whispered against her neck.

Think, think! She took a deep breath, trying to calm herself, noting that Mr. Fernsby smelled of ink, cloves, and the light, floral addition of petitgrain.

She searched through her bag, her knees threatening to buckle as the floor pressed upward. A spike jabbed her elbow, and—

She'd forgotten she'd packed that.

Yanking her hand out, she shouted, "Hold on, Mr. Fernsby!"

And threw her bomb at one of the spiked walls.

The lavatory *erupted*. False smoke filled the space. The walls, floor, and ceiling all snapped into place, the force of which expelled both Hulda and Mr. Fernsby from the room. She landed hard on the reception floor, but with little injury other than a bruised knee. Coughing, she dropped her bag and checked her hair. Darkness or no, she would not look frumpy while performing her job.

Mr. Fernsby was slower to rise. He blinked rapidly and puffed hair from his face. "What the hell was *that*?"

Given their circumstances, Hulda did not rebuke him for his language. "A chaocracy mine. Very—"

"Expensive," he finished for her, shaking out his shirt and finding his feet. He offered her a hand, which she took, then glanced back toward the lavatory. The lamp, still lit, lay on the floor just outside the door, illuminating a very normal-looking space and toilet.

He shook his head. "Chaocracy . . . It should be in shambles."

"A common misconception." She cleared her throat, forcing the slight tremble in it to smooth. "Chaos is disorder, but if something is *already* in chaos, then its disorder is order."

He glanced at her. "Where did you say you were from again?"

"BIKER. It's on my card."

He fished the card from his pocket as Hulda retrieved her lamp. She took a moment to steady herself. Perhaps she should go back to Boston and get a second opinion . . . but no, she could finish this. Enchanted houses were rarely malicious, and this was hardly the worst she'd come by.

It was simply a challenge. And she'd never convince Mr. Fernsby to give the place a chance if she couldn't do the same.

So she pulled out her stethoscope and listened to the outer wall of the lavatory.

"What does that do?" Mr. Fernsby asked. "Commune with the wall?"

"Communion only works with flora and fauna, Mr. Fernsby." It was the eighth school of magic. "This tool is noetic—imbued with psychometry. Also generally reserved for the living, but enchanted houses do meet one or two of the qualifications."

Indeed, she could almost make out a heartbeat. Stowing the stethoscope away, Hulda strode past him, moving into the reception hall and then the living room.

Whimbrel House insisted on keeping its shadows and creaks, but this time it added cobwebs.

"The furniture was melting yesterday." Merritt prodded a settee quickly and jerked back, as though it might attack him as the kitchen stool had.

Hulda hoisted her light.

"I am more concerned about the color scheme." She clucked her tongue, taking in the space. Everything was in deep hues of red and green, like a sad Christmas. If the client's budget allowed it, she would see some of this updated. In her peripheral vision, she caught the slight tic of a grin from Mr. Fernsby and ignored it.

She started for the next door, then paused when something dropped from the ceiling.

A rope, made of cobwebs. Or more specifically—

"A noose," Merritt croaked. Then, in false humor, he added, "At least there isn't anyone in it."

"Yet," Hulda said, and couldn't help but smile at Mr. Fernsby's widening eyes. Internally, she chided herself. Dark jocularity would not help her, nor would it reflect well on BIKER.

The rope was made of cobwebs, so it disintegrated when she swiped her hand through it. "I have never heard of a house killing a man, if that settles you," she offered.

"How about maiming him?" he countered.

She marched for the next door, listening for any new surprises. Mr. Fernsby said, "The sunroom is through there."

The door was locked.

"I didn't lock it," he added.

Hulda sighed. "Do you have a key?"

He felt at his stomach, perhaps forgetting he wasn't wearing a vest, then his slacks, pulling out a simple key ring from the right pocket. Approaching the door, he put in a small key.

The lock spit it out.

"Come now," Hulda chided the house.

Mr. Fernsby tried again. This time, he couldn't even fit in the tip of the key. The house was changing the lock.

Hulda rapped at the door. "Will we need to do this all day?"

The house didn't respond.

Rolling her eyes, though she ought not to, Hulda fished around in her pack and pulled out a crowbar.

"And what spell does that have on it?" Mr. Fernsby nearly sounded entertained.

"It is a crowbar, Mr. Fernsby. Simple as that." She wedged the claw between the door and its jamb and, with a solid thump from her hip, forced the door open. The space beyond was well lit—the house hadn't darkened the windows—and narrow, filled with dead and overgrown plants. Hulda waited for something to happen, then breathed easily when nothing did.

"The plants aren't attacking, which is a good sign," she offered.

"Oh good. I wouldn't want to fall asleep fearing I'll be strangled by daffodils." He mussed his hair again. "I don't want to *worry* about it at all, Miss—Mrs.—Larkin. But the place won't let me leave . . ."

Stepping back into the living room, Hulda waited until his eyes met hers. "There has never been a house I haven't gotten into working order. I guarantee this place will be worth your investment."

He sighed, looking genuinely hopeless, and Hulda wondered what his story was. "Can you, though?"

"I can." She shifted her bag to her other arm. "Let's see the upstairs—"

Her mind registered the splintering of wood and the *thumping* of something soft before she thought to use her light to inspect it. She did so, and a shiver coursed up her spine. Mr. Fernsby gagged.

The house had dropped dead rats on the floor.

The back of her mind connected patterns between the corpses, and Hulda shuddered as her own small magic took over. Augury did that from time to time, divining without her wishing it to. Behind her eyes, she saw the shadow of a great animal, as though lit by moonlight. A dog, maybe a wolf.

Perhaps thinking her faint, Mr. Fernsby grasped her elbow and pulled her from the dead rats. They seemed relatively fresh. Like the house had been collecting them for this very moment.

Her stomach tightened at the thought. *Collections. Bodies.*

Now was *not* the time to reflect on that horror. For goodness's sake, she would stroll through dead rats every day if it meant forgetting that . . .

"Mrs. Larkin?"

Mr. Fernsby was studying her, brows tight together. Pulling away from him, she nodded to her health and walked briskly toward the stairs.

The nosing on the first step separated from the riser and snapped at her.

Pulling out another ward, she hung it on the newel cap, and the impromptu mouth clapped shut. She turned back to Mr. Fernsby, who stared at the wooden mouth with wide eyes. Stiffening her spine to lend them both courage, she said, "Move quickly."

And they did, but upon reaching the second floor, Mr. Fernsby nearly toppled back down the stairs. His face paled in the magicked light of her lantern. "Not this again."

Blood dripped from the hall's ceiling.

Hulda sighed, grateful to see something familiar. "This is an old trick."

Mr. Fernsby gaped. "How can you be so complacent about all of this?"

"I told you, Mr. Fernsby." She crouched and held out her light, watching as the "blood" hit the carpet and fizzled out of existence. "I'm a professional."

He mumbled something under his breath that she couldn't discern. Standing, she held the lamp higher. "I believe it's paint. The house would need to have conjury to produce actual blood, and despite the rats, I doubt it does. Else this is by far the most impressive house I've had the pleasure of trespassing."

The house groaned and clicked, sounding much like the lavatory had before closing in on them. She ignored the gooseflesh parading up and down her arms.

Mr. Fernsby reached out and let some of the paint plop on his hand. "Is it?"

"Is there anything painted this shade of red in this house? It could be moved from that, then 'melted,' as the furniture was."

He glanced at her like he was seeing her for the first time. "I . . . I'm not sure. It's been . . . dark."

She offered him what she called a "business smile," and his shoulders relaxed. "I will know for sure when I finish my report. How many bedrooms?" Reaching into her bag, she withdrew her umbrella and unfurled it over their heads before heading left.

"F-Four, I think."

The first of which, fortunately, had an open door. It was fortunate because it had no floor.

Hulda held up her light, but the seemingly bottomless pit sucked it up.

Mr. Fernsby stumbled back. She closed her umbrella. "I'm sure the floor will return. Houses dislike being incomplete."

"Do they now?" Sarcasm punctuated the question, which Hulda disregarded.

They moved toward the next room, and again the house slammed the door, though Hulda had expected that. She moved on. The room at the end of the hall was presumably where the central bedchamber lay.

Ensuring the door would not take off her head, Hulda peeked inside. At first glance, it looked like a perfectly ordinary bedchamber. No shadows, no cobwebs, no *rats* . . . one of them would need to clean those up, because based on the smell, Hulda was certain they weren't illusionary, which would fall under the second school of magic: psychometry. Indeed, the space looked quite pleasant. The sun shined through a rain-spotted window, the bed was made, the floor relatively clean—

Mr. Fernsby cursed, startling Hulda.

"Whatever is the matter?"

He strode into the room, a much more confident man than the one who had answered the door. "My notebooks were right here on this side table!" He ran his hand over the furniture. Opened a drawer, revealing some sort of pistol within. Searched the four-post bed and swept his hand beneath it, revealing a musket. Goodness, how many firearms did a man need? And he hadn't even moved in yet! "I know they were. I was writing in one shortly before you arrived."

Fishing into her bag, Hulda retrieved her dowsing rods and held them before her gently, keeping her fingers steady. She walked heel to toe, first toward Mr. Fernsby, then toward the other side of the room. The rods slowly pulled apart.

She prodded a lump in the carpet with her toe. "I believe they are here."

Merritt stared at the lump like he was missing his spectacles, then marched over and inspected it. "But . . . how? The carpet is nailed in! How am I supposed to retrieve them?"

"I believe you have three choices. Pull up the carpet, cut them out, or wait for the house to return them."

He gaped at her, but before he opened his mouth, she added, "I would recommend restraint when it comes to disparaging the house. We need it to be our ally."

"Right. Ally." He rubbed his palms into his eyes. Let out a long puff of air.

She gave him a moment to collect himself before asking, "And the rest of the house? Other than the fourth bedroom."

He slowly stepped away from the books. "Um. Bedrooms, yes. Sitting area. Library. Be careful of the library."

"What happened there?"

"It threw books at me."

Hulda bit down on a smile. When Mr. Fernsby saw it, he did the same. At least there was still some humor left in the poor man.

"Threw them at you?" She headed back into the dark and dreary hallway. "Or did you simply get in the way of the throwing?"

Mr. Fernsby did not answer.

Utilizing the umbrella, they passed through the dripping hallway again, past the stairs, and headed straight into the library. Indeed, books flew from shelf to shelf, seeming to pick up speed under Hulda's scrutiny. More portraits hung on the walls here; one with a sailboat in the bay appeared to be leaking water. The one of a poppy field had the flowers swaying in the breeze, but the only "wind" came from the flying books. Another sign the house likely didn't possess any elemental spells.

Attempting reason one last time, Hulda said, "Come now." She rubbed the interior wall of the library. "Settle down. This is no way to treat a guest."

The books continued flying.

She toed into the room. "You may not like him, but I am reasonable, am I not?"

For just a moment, it seemed the books slowed. Only a moment, but that was a win in Hulda's book.

Mr. Fernsby also noticed, for he said, "I take offense."

The fourth bedroom's door was open, revealing a bubbling carpet. "This would make an excellent office."

"I wish I had your optimism."

"Soon enough." She turned to the final door. "Then I suppose this is the sitting room?"

"I only had a glance."

"Only a glance?" She tested the knob.

"You may recall my story about nearly losing my nose—"

It took her last few wards, but Hulda got the door open. The sitting room was as dark as the rest of the house, though not from shadows.

"The windows are gone," Mr. Fernsby said astutely.

"Indeed." Handing him the light, she retrieved her stethoscope and a small hammer and then traced the wall, lightly tapping here and there. She never heard the tinkle of glass, which confirmed this wasn't an illusion. Likely alteration, the seventh school of magic. Which would also explain much of the house's other . . . quirks.

Pulling a ward from the door, Hulda gestured to two chairs in the sitting room. The door slammed shut in protest as they sat down. Hulda set the ward beside them, then took off the one she wore around her neck and set it at their feet. Mr. Fernsby hesitantly followed suit, placing his ward behind them.

"That should stultify the area for a moment." She took the lamp from him and turned it all the way up, revealing a simply decorated room with oak panels that matched the shutters, an Indian rug, a full blush sofa, and a smattering of matching armchairs. A white-painted fireplace took up the opposite wall, along with the bust of a bored child. Hulda wondered if that was the artist's original sculpture or if the house was trying to tell her something.

Setting down her tool bag, Hulda pulled out Mr. Fernsby's file, a pad of paper, and a pencil.

"All right, Mr. Fernsby, let us discuss your house."

Chapter 3

"A letter for you, Lord Hogwood."

Silas blinked from the snowy, gray scene outside his window. He didn't remember standing from his chair and walking over here, but he'd brought his tea with him, and it had cooled to lukewarm. Turning, he saw his butler, once his father's butler, awaiting his reply, a cream-colored envelope on a silver tray before him. He'd turned it so Silas could see the seal. The royal seal.

Silas took the letter and set his cup on the tray, nodding his thanks. The butler left without word. Alone in the study, Silas turned the letter over in his hands twice before breaking the seal and reading it, confirming his suspicions.

It was from the regent himself, who, being the active ruler of Britain, was also the leader of the King's League of Magicians. The same league his mother had belonged to, before her illness forced her to retire. The same league that had expelled his father that fateful night.

"Personally invited," he read aloud. He was eighteen now. In truth, he was surprised the invitation hadn't been extended on his birthday. His family's pedigree was almost as impressive as the regent's. Spells of chaocracy, alteration, necromancy, augury, and kinesis ran through Silas's veins. And for the briefest moment, he'd possessed even more. He *knew* he had, but his father's death had taken those borrowed abilities away.

There was no research on such a phenomenon—Silas had sought it with diligence. Subtly, for he didn't want to draw unwanted attention to himself. It was easy for family, friends, and authorities to believe that Henry Hogwood had overdrunk himself after the dismissal of his career, beaten his son, and then succumbed to alcohol poisoning. But Christian, Silas's younger brother, suspected something was amiss. That, or Silas was unreasonably suspicious. But better suspicious than unprepared.

He considered it, for half a heartbeat. The King's League might have literature the rest of them didn't. It might lead him to the answers he sought.

And yet Silas strode to the blazing fire beneath the mantel and tossed the letter in, envelope and all. He loomed, watching the wax seal melt and sizzle, until it was indiscernible among the ash.

"You'll never have me," he whispered to the flames. He still bore the scars his father had given him, inside and out. Scars that reminded him of what had been—and what would *never again be*.

Because no one, even old King George himself, would have authority over Silas. No one would overpower him again.

And Silas was willing to do anything to keep that true.

Chapter 4

Merritt sunk into his armchair opposite Hulda—Miss Larkin—*Mrs.* Larkin, wondering at her as he did so. Two days ago, he would have thought it very peculiar to have a stranger suddenly appear at his door, show herself in, and give *him* a tour of the place. But that was before Merritt had been more or less swallowed by an evil enchanted house that rained fake blood and real rats, and whose lavatory had nearly skewered him in multiple places.

Things seemed calm now. At least, he could pretend they were calm, with these wards sitting about him and an obviously competent wizardly housekeeper making the floorless rooms and cobweb nooses appear commonplace. And she had a card. Who was he to question her? He was desperate for help. Besides, she'd gotten his wallet back.

He might have seen all of this as excellent story fodder if it weren't for his commandeered notebooks.

And the lavatory. God help him, he was never going to defecate again.

Hulda Larkin was writing something by the light of her lantern, giving him time to study the room around him. And, when he finished that, to study *her*. She seemed to be in her midthirties, and she had a sort of schoolmarm air, what with the high collar of her sage-colored dress and the severity of her aquiline nose, which was, perhaps, her most prominent feature. A delicate pair of silver-rimmed glasses perched upon it—the most delicate Merritt had ever seen, as though chosen specifically to be as invisible as possible. Her dark-brown hair was pulled up simply while still hitting the beat of fashion, and a few curls brushed her cheekbones. They were high cheekbones, which lent to her upturned eyes, while also mirroring the square shape of her jaw.

She looked up at him. Her eyes were either brown or green; he wasn't close enough to tell, and her irises had been the least of his concerns during their adventure in the lavatory.

"I've determined the house persists on spells of alteration and chaocracy, which explains the"—she gestured to open air—"*severity* of the enchantments."

"Shape-shifting and destruction. What a delight." Magic had not been a part of his life up until now, though he remembered enough from his school days. Alteration involved changing of some sort, whether objects, one's physical self, or other spells. And chaocracy was simply a mess.

"More or less," Hulda agreed. "Now, there is the matter of hiring staff."

Merritt held up a hand, stalling her, and retrieved her card once more, examining its simple, crisp black lettering. "So your institute, *BIKER*"—*strange acronym*—"are magic tamers?"

A slight line formed between Hulda's eyes. "BIKER trains adroit individuals in service who are specifically sanctioned for the caring and operating of enchanted buildings."

His lip ticked. "You talk like a dictionary, *Mrs.* Larkin. A British dictionary, though the accent's wrong."

She turned her nose up at the sentiment. "I will not apologize for being well educated."

"In London?"

"Perhaps."

In truth, speaking to another person, about *anything*, was making him feel better about the situation. And perhaps he was mad to consider staying, but he *did* want the situation to improve. This place would make for a fantastic novel, for one thing, and he didn't have much to go back to. His apartment in New York was being swept out from beneath him, and he'd have to devote all his time to finding housing elsewhere. He'd prefer to be writing. "And what makes you *adroit*? Which you are, don't get me wrong." He stowed the card away. "But are you a wizard or something?"

She let out a long breath through her nose. "If you must know, I am an augurist."

He blinked. He'd half meant it as a joke—magic had been so diluted over the years it was rare to find anyone with special ability. Most historians agreed that magic had come about at the "turning of the world," associated with the life of Christ, given that there were eleven schools—equal to eleven apostles, minus Judas. Magic passed down through blood, but it diluted every time, splitting spells and abilities until there was barely anything left to split. Only targeted breeding had kept it alive in medieval times, mainly in aristocratic societies. Indeed, the English monarchs were some of the strongest wizards in the world.

Magic builds upon magic, so a wizardly mother and a wizardly father could increase their enchanted line with wizardly offspring. The dilution was such, however, that most magical users either came by their abilities as the result of an arranged marriage or pure luck. This day and age, both sets had limited abilities.

If he recalled correctly, augury was the first school of magic.

"So are you going to read my fortune?" he asked.

Hulda only looked at him like a tired governess. "About the house, Mr. Fernsby, I strongly recommend a staff. To successfully run such a house, you will need a maid and a cook, at the very least."

He leaned back in his chair. "Don't you cook?"

Resting her hands atop her file, she retorted, "Mr. Fernsby, were we in England, I might have had a mind to gasp at such presumption."

He grinned at that, though Hulda gave no such expression of mirth.

"Staff will be trained specifically for this house," she went on. "The more staff you have managing the magic, the more enjoyable the abode will be."

He frowned.

"This is unacceptable?" she asked.

He considered his response. "I am well aware that I don't know how to maintain . . . this"—he gestured to the far wall, where a shadow passed, creaking the wood as it went—"but . . . I've taken care of myself for well over a decade. I know how to do laundry and cook a meal. It would be . . . odd, to have strangers about doing that for me. On the presumption that I could actually afford it."

She eyed him over the silver rim of her spectacles. "And when, since your arrival, have you been able to do any of those things?"

He paused. "I . . . have not." He hadn't even really slept.

"The care of this house will be BIKER's priority, including the majority of its pecuniary consolations," she continued. "We want to see that it thrives for generations to come. Enchanted homes are a dying breed."

The home and not the tenant, Merritt almost said, but decided to hold his tongue. He sighed. "Let's say I humor you with this staff nonsense. I do well for myself, but I'm hardly a wealthy man."

She opened the file again. "And what is your employment?"

"I'm a writer."

She simply nodded and jotted it down. Funny. He was used to getting follow-up questions when he stated his profession. Questions like, *What do you write? Are you published? You're not a political columnist, are you?*

"The keeping and protection of enchanted residences is very important to BIKER," Hulda repeated. "The institution will accommodate you in regard to my services while you require them. My diagnosis will help with the rampant enchantments. Given the size of the house, a large staff may be unnecessary."

The downstairs groaned, and Merritt quickly reassessed. Trying to ignore the shadows, he asked, "Do you work on many small houses?"

"This is the second-smallest permanent structure I've personally overseen." She looked up then, not at him, but at a spot on the carpet, or beyond it. A wistful expression washed over her face before flitting away. He wondered what she was remembering.

"And the largest?"

She straightened, as though having momentarily forgotten he was there. "An estate near Liverpool" was all she said. Pulling a sheet of paper from the file, she closed the folder and tucked it away, then handed the paper to Merritt.

He leaned forward to grab it. "What is this?"

"My résumé. I am willing to personally oversee this house until you have your feet under you. A housekeeper should be included in your staff unless you find an adept maid of all work."

The résumé was very long, with letters penned very small.

"While BIKER absorbs my fees, I do require room and board."

He lowered the résumé. "You're moving in?"

"Only if you wish it, Mr. Fernsby, but I come highly recommended."

He glanced from her to the résumé and back. "I'm sorry, I'm still coming to terms with the idea of this place being livable."

She quirked an eyebrow. "Do you doubt my abilities?"

He shook his head. "Hardly. But I don't know how you'll bring your things here if the house won't let you leave."

"We'll see about that."

He nodded. "But yes, if you can keep this beast in line . . . of course I'll take the help. I . . . am about to be in a housing predicament—goodness, I *am* in a housing predicament"—he eyed the walls and ignored the gooseflesh pebbling his arms—"and . . . well, I don't want to see the house and land go to waste."

Admittedly, if the spells hadn't kept him indoors, he might have burned the place down and fled back to New York. But seeing Hulda's ability to control the place, and her calm demeanor while doing it, had sparked hope for the future. Maybe this *was* a blessing. Maybe it *could* turn into something great.

To think, he'd be a homeowner. A landowner. He could increase his fortunes and make a good life for himself. Write his next book and then another after it.

The floor shuddered. He gripped his armrest.

"Excellent choice." She recovered the wards and stood, putting hers over her neck and handing the other two to Merritt. "You may hold on to these. Be careful with them. They're expensive."

He nodded.

She walked with confidence to the door, though she had to utilize the crowbar once more to see it open, and then out came the umbrella as they passed through the . . . paint. The ward on the stairs held the banister in place. Merritt focused on the back of Hulda's head so he wouldn't see the portrait in the reception hall watching him.

To his surprise, the house allowed Hulda to open the door, revealing late-afternoon sun . . . beautiful sun. It filled the reception hall and banished the shadows, and Merritt breathed easily for the first time since he'd arrived.

Hulda poked through the doorway with her umbrella first, then, clasping her ward, stepped through.

And nothing happened.

He let out a deep sigh. "Thank goodness." But the moment he tried to follow her, the doorway snapped and shrunk to the size of his torso, barring him from leaving.

A sob threatened to leave the base of his throat. "You blasted thing!" He pushed one of the wards against the wood. It didn't budge.

"Do not antagonize the house, Mr. Fernsby," Hulda warned, running a hand over the shrunken doorway. "There's a great deal of magic in these walls, and for whatever reason, it does not want you to exit." She patted the warped door. "I also would not suggest crawling through this."

He had the grisly image of his body pinching in half, and shuddered.

"The thing is," Hulda continued, "I came out only to give the place a gander. I don't have my belongings with me, just a small suitcase." She tapped her chin. "I have your current address in New York on file. I will see your things brought in. Between making those arrangements and packing up more of my own things, I will need two days."

Two days. "I can't survive that long."

"Be kind to the house," she said. "And keep your wards." She considered. "Perhaps one day. Do you have enough to eat?"

His shoulders slackened as he recounted what he brought. "I've some cheese and gingersnaps." He wouldn't starve to death, at least. Merritt paused. "Wait, can you post something for me?" He'd started a letter to his friend Fletcher, currently living in Boston, in his notebook, but that was currently under the carpet . . .

"Of course."

When he didn't move, she retrieved her notebook from her bag and flipped to a clean page before handing it to him. He was tempted to read what she'd written in there, but . . . priorities.

Leaning on the doorway, he penned a hasty letter informing his friend of his predicament, though he made it sound lighthearted. Bad habit of his. He signed it, folded it, and handed everything back to Hulda.

"Please hurry," he begged.

"I do not dawdle," she said, lifting her nose. But her eyes softened. "And of course. I will aim to return by tomorrow evening."

She turned to leave, paused, and turned back, rummaging through her sack until she pulled out a tin lunchbox. She passed it through the shrunken door without word, then started for the coast.

Inside was an apple and a ham sandwich.

Merritt sat down to eat, and the front door slammed shut.

Chapter 5

Silas's mother was dying.

She hadn't opened her eyes for two days. Her breathing was raspy and shallow, her face sunken and pale.

It wasn't a surprise. She'd been steadily declining for years. Her light had become so dim Silas wondered if he'd notice when it snuffed out completely.

Deep down, he knew he would.

Clenching and unclenching his hands, he glanced to his mother's door. Christian had just left the bedchamber. Silas had already turned the servants away and locked up behind them. His mother wouldn't make it to the end of the week. Maybe not even the end of the day.

It was, in a way, a mercy to test this on her.

In January, Silas had found an enchanted cottage in the Cotswolds, a simple house imbued with the elemental spell of controlling water, inhabited by an aging owner who didn't mind, or didn't notice, Silas's snooping about. Reliving that night with his father, Silas had worked through the spells in his blood—spells he'd learned were just the right combination to *take*. Necromancy to connect to life force . . . a house wasn't a *living* thing, of course, but magic was. Chaocracy to break up the magic and reorder it. Kinesis to move it from vessel to vessel—house to him. The process with his father had been angry and quick. With the house, it was calculated and careful.

And it had *worked*.

A house wasn't a living thing, which meant it couldn't die. That cottage in the Cotswolds still stood and would continue to do so for some time. So while his father's death had zapped his spells from Silas, nothing could take the elemental water spell from his person. As for the resident . . . modern plumbing or a housemaid would replace what he had lost.

Now, one of the most powerful necromancers in England lay dying in bed before him. And when she died, her magic, carefully bred and cultivated, would die with her.

Unless Silas's new theory proved correct.

Silas possessed one alteration spell from his paternal line—the ability to condense, to shrink. The cottage had given him the ability to control water. He'd tested it again and again, alone, and felt confident he could use it here.

Magic was tied to the body. So if he could *preserve* the body, the magic would live. In a sense, his mother would live on. In him.

He glanced to the door again. Listened. No sound of anyone coming or going. He glanced at the old clock on the mantel. The second hand seemed too loud.

Removing his gloves, Silas took one last long look at his mother before laying his hands on her, one on her forehead and the other on her chest. Necromancy first. He carefully wound the spell down, finding her magic, gathering it, holding it. It took much longer than it had with his father. Because there was more to be had, perhaps, but in his experimentation with the cottage, he'd also realized he'd stolen only a fraction of his father's magic that night outside the stables. To collect all of his mother's ability would take time.

He glanced at the door as nausea curled through him—the counterbalance to necromancy. Would someone come by, despite his orders? Test the lock? If it was Christian, how would he explain?

Focus. The second hand *tick, tick, ticked.* He shifted to chaocracy and broke his mother's spells apart—he'd inherited a portion of most of them, which made it easier. He truly had to *focus* here, for chaocracy caused confusion, and if he faltered, he might lose her magic forever. Too much time passed before he felt ready to shift to kinesis to transfer the magic, his joints stiffening the longer he pushed the spell. Sweat beaded on his forehead from the exertion, but—

Yes. His body trembled as new magic burned within him, strengthening existing spells, lending him new ones that hadn't been inherited. The nausea intensified. Where was he? *Focus.* He had to finish. He had to—

Mother. But she was dying, anyway. He reminded himself she was already good as dead.

Water. Shrink. Condense. His mouth dried as he worked, and a strained mewing escaped his mother's throat. He felt his shoulders mutate as his mother's body gradually warped and shriveled, taking on a dark-green cast. His bones enlarged and pushed against skin as hers waned and withered, until the spells could pull nothing more out of her.

Blinking dry eyes, Silas grounded himself. Remembered where he was. What he was doing. The clock on the mantel said . . . but surely two hours hadn't passed . . .

His mother was unrecognizable. Not only as herself, but as a *human.* Her body was dark and ghastly, about the length of Silas's forearm, and wrinkled as a fingertip after an hours-long bath. Her limbs had sucked into her body, leaving little flaps behind. Her face had caved into itself until there was no longer a face at all.

And the new spells, her magic, still burned brilliantly within him. He'd done it. A sharp chuckle ripped up his throat. *He'd done it.*

Footsteps in the hallway brought him back to himself. He grasped his mother and wrapped her in one of the clean towels left by the side of the bed. Loosened the buttons of his coat to hide his malformed shoulders—that side effect would pass in time, but any who saw it would know he'd done something. Timing his escape carefully, he fled the room for the wine cellar, where he could stow away his mother and better preserve her.

Once he returned, he would need to act shocked and confused that the body was gone. He could never explain to anyone what he had done.

No one would understand.

Chapter 6

While Merritt waited, his wards arranged around him—not on his person, as they'd begun making him queasy when he wore them—he told himself all the benefits of staying on Blaugdone Island.

No more rent. No more landlords. No more pestersome neighbors. An office to write in. Lots of space. Lots of reading available, once the books stopped hurling themselves at him. And the island was beautiful, not that Whimbrel House was allowing him to enjoy it.

And he certainly wouldn't be *bored*.

Essentially, this house was a challenge, and besting a challenge was progress, and progress was success, as far as Merritt was concerned. Progress was something he could achieve all on his own, regardless of what he had lost—or who had abandoned him—along the way.

Something *shifted* upstairs. He wondered if the breakfast room had dropped down. It had moved last night, replacing the bottomless pit of the first bedroom.

Merritt had slept in the reception hall.

Wards now on his person, he shuffled through the kitchen for a knife, hoping dearly that the house could not somehow wield it against him, and was surprised by how calm the place was being. Shadows still lurked in the corners and snuffed light from the windows, but otherwise it was . . . he dared not say *peaceful*, but tolerable.

And yet, as Merritt ventured up the stairs, he felt like the place was watching him.

Deep breaths. She'll be back today. It felt better facing this place with another person, especially one who understood it far better than he did. But it was . . . interesting to think Hulda Larkin would essentially be his roommate.

He wouldn't call her a roommate, of course. Not to her face. He imagined he'd be scolded for that.

Entering the largest bedroom, he paused, adjusting to the sunbeams streaming through the window, the light smell of dust, and the overall pleasantness of the space.

"You know," he said to the ceiling, standing clear of the door in case it slammed again, "we would get on swimmingly if you could make everything like this. I'd even weed the foundation outside."

The house didn't respond.

Swallowing, Merritt approached the lump in the carpet. "I need the books back." Hulda had spoken to the house, so why shouldn't he? "It's very important that I get them back. I have a manuscript and notes in there." He knelt. "I'm going to cut it very cleanly, all right? Nice and easy."

He touched the knife tip to the carpet. Held his breath. Waited. Gripped the ward around his neck with his other hand. Hulda had said not to wear it long, but he also liked living.

So.

Pushing the knife into the carpet, he sawed a slit just long enough to pull the books out. He felt like he was helping a cow give birth, trying to wedge the things out. It was a worthy metaphor, because he *had* helped a cow give birth once. In Cattlecorn, after he'd moved in with Fletcher's folks.

A sigh escaped him as he retrieved the last book and flattened the carpet down. You could hardly tell he'd cut into it in the first place.

He didn't notice the drawer of the dresser inching toward him until it was nearly under his chin.

Shrieking, Merritt whipped back at the same time the drawer snapped shut, missing his face but snatching the scarf around his neck. It was loosely tied, so instead of choking him, it came clean off.

Merritt's blood steamed.

Not. The. Scarf.

"Give it back!" He lunged at the dresser, which danced away from him on suddenly mobile bracketed feet. Forgetting the notebooks, Merritt surged up and took chase. The dresser couldn't fit through the doorway, so he—

The doorway expanded like the mouth of a snake, allowing the furniture passage.

"No!" he barked, grasping its top. It pulled him into the hallway. "Please, stop! Take anything else! Take back the notebooks! Just *give me the scarf*!"

The drawer with the scarf popped free. For a sliver of a second, Merritt thought the blasted house was going to listen to him.

But the drawer merely skidded off, using its handle like a clam's tongue, and raced for the stairs, leaving the dresser blocking Merritt.

"HOUSE!" He shoved the dresser down and vaulted over it. "I mean it! Give it back!"

The drawer toppled down the ward-frozen stairs.

Merritt's eyes stung as he grabbed the banister and charged after it, nearly tripping on the steps.

The drawer scooted through the reception hall and into the dining room.

Panic suffocated him. *Notthescarfnotthescarfnotthescarf.*

"Please!" he shouted, bursting into the dining room as the drawer slid into the breakfast room. "It's all I have of her. I'll do anything! I'll leave! Back to New York!"

He dove into the now well-lit breakfast room, smashing his ribs into the floor. His fingertips brushed the drawer, but it slid from his grip. Merritt hit his shoulder on the table as he stood and ran after it, into the kitchen.

"House, *stop*—"

The windowsill separated from the wall, and the drawer tossed the multicolored knit scarf into the separation, which swallowed it like a mouth.

For a long moment, Merritt didn't do anything. He stood there, near the three-legged stool, chest heaving, eyes wide. Staring.

Then he bellowed like a Viking and lunged for the window, slamming bodily into it.

"Give it back! *Give it back!*"

He dug his fingernails into the sill and tried to lift it, but the house didn't budge. Grabbed the ward around his neck and pressed it to the glass, but the house still didn't move. The spell was over. There was nothing to undo.

Vision tunneling, Merritt turned toward the cupboards and flung them open, rifling through them. A jar hit the floor and shattered. Empty flour sack. Spoons flew into the air, matches and an acid vial, an old lamp, a meat mallet—

He took the last thing and slammed its head into the windowsill, trying to break it off. And while a meat mallet was not made for hammering wood, he did a decent job of it.

The wall shuddered and rebuffed him, sending him flying back. He landed hard on his hip, and the meat mallet arced from his fingers toward the hearth.

Wincing, Merritt pushed himself up, eyes going to the nearly empty vial of sulfuric acid.

Acid used to light the chlorate of potash on the ends of the matches.

He grabbed both, then snatched up the empty flour sack. "You want to challenge me?" he seethed. *"Fine."*

He dipped the matches, lighting them. The flames caught easily on the flour sack.

Which he then threw into the empty cupboard.

Fire licked the cupboard walls. For a heartbeat, it seemed it wouldn't catch.

Until it did.

The entire house bucked. Sounds of shattering glass and warping metal penetrated his ears. The floor rumbled and *split*, sending a gush of marsh water up into the kitchen, dowsing—and mudding—the cupboards.

But the house didn't stop there. Because why would it?

The great chasm in the kitchen jerked apart, widening, and swallowed Merritt whole.

⁓

Merritt groaned. Cold seeped through his clothes and into his skin. His head and back ached, and . . . No, he was still breathing. Just took a moment to remember how.

His hand brushed moist, dark soil. His other brushed the ward still secure around his neck. He lay supine, staring up at the hole in the floor of his kitchen. Wondered why it was still open at all. Maybe his ward prevented the house from closing over him. Maybe the house was reeling from its own injuries.

Maybe Merritt didn't care.

Grunting, he pushed himself to sitting. His pulse thumped painfully beneath his skull. Prodding his hair, then his neck, he checked for injuries. Just bruises, he guessed. Bad bruises, but bruises had never killed him.

None of it had ever *killed* him.

Propping his elbows on his knees, he dropped his head into his palms. Focused on his breathing. *In, out. In, out.* He sat like that for a long time, trying to tamp down the anger and the hurt. Just when he thought it was finally done, that he was *finally* cured, it came bubbling up again. Something always brought it up, and he hated it, because it never hurt any less, even so many years later.

He breathed until his throat wasn't tight anymore. Until his lungs felt a little lighter. Then he stood slowly, testing for other injuries, fortunately finding only bruises. He'd fallen about . . . eleven or twelve feet.

Good news, his house had a root cellar.

At that thought, he glanced around, searching for bodies. Human, rat, or other. But there was nothing here but dirt, roots, and some dripping water.

"Okay, then," he murmured to himself. "Step one, get back into the house."

If it didn't kill him on the way up.

Unfortunately, there wasn't a lot for Merritt to use to climb back up. There were some boards in the foundation, but none were beneath the hole. Not enough stones to build a tower. And Merritt most certainly could not jump that high. He was a writer, not an athlete.

Sighing, he ran his hand back through his hair, then grimaced at the slick sensation of mud on his forehead. He walked the perimeter of the dark space—which would only get darker after sunset—searching for something to help him. He found the meat mallet and two matches, useless to him without the acid vial.

He tried to climb. He really did. Using the wood of the foundation, he dug his shoes into the mud and attempted to shimmy across the knobs and crevices under the floor. He tried, and he fell. He tried again, and he fell harder, earning himself a new bruise. After the fourth time, he didn't get back up. He sat, elbows on his knees, and breathed.

"Can you lower something?" he asked the house, his voice strained. "I'm sorry I lit you on fire. I just wanted it back. I need it back."

The house didn't respond.

A lump formed in his throat. "If you're going to keep me down here, can't I have it back?"

It was stupid to bargain with a magical house he'd just tried to set on fire. He *knew* it was stupid. The scarf was old. Starting to fray. But it was all he had of her. His sister Scarlet had knitted it for him the Christmas before . . . before all of it had happened, and he hadn't seen her since. He'd accepted he'd never see her again.

He'd never gotten to say goodbye. To any of them.

Ignoring the mud, Merritt pressed his knuckles into his eyes. *Exhale. Inhale. Exhale.* It was all he had left of her. He had nothing of Beatrice. Would he even recognize her now? She was probably married with kids. *Kids.* He had nieces and nephews who might not know he existed. And he didn't know them. And damnation, he should look for them, because they were still *his*, weren't they?

But what if . . . what if Beatrice hated him, too?

He laughed. He pressed his knuckles in harder and laughed. It wasn't funny. It was mad, if anything. But he preferred laughing to crying. Always had.

This was a dark moment. He recognized that. But it wasn't his darkest, which made him feel a little better. Only a little, but he would take it.

He sat like that awhile, thinking and trying not to think, trying to let go of the scarf, trying to figure his way out. He tried climbing again. Still didn't work.

Maybe there weren't any skeletons down here because he was meant to be the first.

Somehow, Merritt had managed to doze. Doze, not sleep, because he didn't think he'd hear the creaking if he'd been unconscious.

Sitting up, Merritt registered that the sun was casting burnt-orange light through the kitchen above, suggesting the day was growing late. He listened eagerly and then slumped when he realized the house was likely up to its tricks again, creaking and shadowing and moving the walls. But the creaks turned into steps, coming toward *him*, and he leapt to his feet at the same time he heard a woman gasp overhead.

"What on God's good earth *happened?*"

His eyes rolled back as utter relief washed over him. "Mrs. Larkin, you have the voice of an angel."

The creaks and steps neared, slower this time. Then they stopped. A new light burned overhead, likely that enchanted lamp of hers, and two sets of fingers curled around one of the splintered floorboards. Hulda's face peeked over next.

Her eyes widened. "Mr. Fernsby! What are you doing down there?"

Exhaling relief, he shoved his dirty hands into his dirty pockets. "The house and I got into a bit of a tiff, you see. I believe I'm being disciplined."

She blinked. Pushed up her glasses. "Care to explain what happened?"

He didn't, but he did it, anyway, keeping the tale as surface level as possible.

Hulda clucked her tongue. "I see the drawer. Really, Mr. Fernsby. I told you not to antagonize the place."

The house groaned as if in agreement.

"In my defense," Merritt tried to keep his tone light, "it antagonized me first."

The housekeeper's nails drummed against the floor. "Let me see if I can get you up." She vanished.

Cupping his hands around his mouth, Merritt shouted, "Can't you ward it or something?"

Farther away, she said, "You're *beneath* the house now, Mr. Fernsby. The *beneath* is not enchanted, and I cannot compel the place to lend you a hand. Or a . . . floorboard, I suppose."

Her voice grew quieter and quieter, until he couldn't hear her at all. He waited a quarter hour before she returned.

She sat down near the hole. "Unfortunately, I did not think to bring a length of rope with me." Her tone was such that Merritt could not determine if she thought the whole thing farcical or if she was taking it very seriously. "Even so, I don't know whether I could pull you up. I hope you can climb."

His shoulders and elbows ached from previous attempts. "I've certainly tried."

A sheet dipped over the hole, tied to another, then another. The woman must have stripped the beds upstairs. A wonder that the house had let her instead of merely pushing her into the cellar, too.

The sheets reached him, and he waited while Hulda found something to tie the other end to. However, Merritt quickly learned that climbing up sheets was *very* difficult. Rappelling down them might have been possible, but there was nothing to really grip except the knots, and by the time he managed to scramble to the first one, out of breath, it came undone and dropped him back into the mud.

"Bother," Hulda muttered.

"Let me try," he offered.

Hulda lowered the sheets until he could reach the second, and he tied the fallen one to it with a water knot. It held much better, but he just couldn't pull himself up those damnable sheets, and though she tried, Hulda could not haul him up.

Merritt stood in the cellar, hands on his hips, digging a shallow grave for his mounting despair and burying it messily. "It was a good effort."

Hulda sighed. "I feel I am to blame. I should have sent a message ahead instead of leaving."

"Then we might both be down here."

She snorted. "As if I would have let you near matches under my watch. Oh." She vanished again, only for a moment this time. "Here."

She lowered down a wrapped cloth. Merritt hadn't realized how hungry he was until he saw the sandwich within it.

He ate it quickly. "Thank you."

"I brought groceries as well, and a receipt for the collection and delivery of your things. Your landlord was rather compliant. The rest of my things are being delivered tomorrow. Trunks and such." She worked her jaw. "Perhaps if you set the wards aside, we could—"

"No."

She frowned at him. "I'm beginning to fear that only magic will get you out of this, Mr. Fernsby. And as I said, the house has no power outside of itself, and you are outside of the house. It might not be able to do anything."

"And it might drop one of these support beams on my head and finish the job," he countered.

Shaking her head, Hulda said, "At least you see the importance of good staff, hm?"

"Yes." His tone hardened. "As I plan on falling into pits regularly, it would be good to have some wizards-in-servitude available to fetch me out."

"You needn't say it like that," she protested. "Servitude is the best way for the unfortunate to rise in their station and procure good wages for themselves and their families."

Merritt chucked the sandwich cloth at the dirt. "You talk like a politician."

"You seem to enjoy pointing out my idiosyncrasies." She pulled her tool bag over and rummaged through it, but Merritt already knew there would be nothing in there to help him. "Despite our current conundrum," she went on, "we *will* fetch you out. In the interim, I'll lower down a blanket and food. My movers will arrive tomorrow, and we'll enlist their help."

"Can they also break down the front door?"

She closed her bag. "The place merely requires a firm hand. I assure you that with some time and effort it will be quite livable—"

"Mrs. Larkin."

She eyed him.

Pulling on the ends of his hair, Merritt asked, "Why is it so important to you?"

She hesitated. "Why is what so important to me?"

"This house. My staying. All of"—he waved his hands—"this."

She opened her mouth as though to deliver a smart retort, then closed it again, thinking. The orange of the sun dimmed, and the enchanted lamp cast shadows on the walls—the parts Merritt could see.

"Magic," she began carefully, "is a dying art. Magicked homes even more so. They're crucial to our history. They preserve what we cannot, spells long lost to the whims of genealogy, for when magic has no fallible body, it cannot fade or dissipate. In the modern world, magicked homes provide endless study for scholars, wizards, and historians alike. They are museums of the craft."

Merritt folded his arms. "That's why they're important, yes. Not why *this* house is important to *you*."

She hesitated. Shifted. For a moment, Merritt thought she was going to leave, but she didn't. She smoothed her skirts. Adjusted her glasses. Smoothed her hair.

"Because this is my life, Mr. Fernsby," she said, softer. "And because I do not have and will never have anything else."

His arms loosened. "That's a dreary thing to say."

"Hardly. It's realistic."

His lips quirked. "Don't you think someone with magic powers should, I don't know, *not* believe in realism?"

"Just because magic is rare does not make it unreal," she countered.

They were both quiet for several seconds.

"I have made a career of caring for these wonders." She gestured to the kitchen. "And when the wonders stop, so will my career. I enjoy what I do, Mr. Fernsby. I'm good at it. I would not give you the guarantee if I weren't."

"I don't doubt your abilities."

"Don't you?" she questioned, and Merritt shifted his weight from foot to foot. "You wish to know why I care about this house? I see opportunity here. Opportunity that can be seized and tamed and made into progress."

That last word caught his attention. Hadn't he been thinking of that very thing?

She considered a moment. "If you leave this house behind, Mr. Fernsby, what would your next step be?"

He shrugged. "I could donate it to BIKER."

"You could, I suppose. We might find a good curator for it. And then what?"

He met her eyes as best as he could, from the cellar. "I don't know. I suppose I'd search for another apartment, perhaps in Boston this time. My publisher is in Boston. Find a quiet place to write my book." Go on as he had before. Yet why did the idea unsettle him?

"Buy a home?"

"I don't know." He didn't really want to think about it, not while he was cold and out of sorts. "Have to save up a little longer to do that. Could build for cheaper, but I'd have to head west for that, and country life doesn't really suit me. There's no kinetic rails heading out there, either. Be hard to go back and forth." His enthusiasm evaporated a little more with each word.

"Give us a chance, Mr. Fernsby," she said, her mouth curving upward ever so slightly. "Imagine a future where you own a home flush with magic, on an island teeming with life. Imagine—"

She cut off abruptly, and Merritt craned to better see her. "Mrs. Larkin?"

"Pardon me. I just saw something in the debris."

He paused. "A spider?"

She rolled her eyes. "A vision, Mr. Fernsby. By chance, do you know a well-dressed Black man with short hair? Someone who might have reason to come to the island?"

Relief bubbled up, easing the stress in his body. "Yes, I do, Mrs. Larkin. And God grant that he's coming *now*."

Chapter 7

"Is this a zero or a six?" Silas asked, tilting the ledger toward his steward.

Lidgett adjusted his spectacles. "A zero, sir. My apologies. I was writing quickly."

Silas nodded and turned the page. "And how is the—"

The door to the study flung open and filled with the body of Silas's disheveled brother. He wasn't even wearing a cravat, which made Silas wonder what he'd been doing before barging in. He'd been expecting this confrontation for days now.

"Is it true?" Christian asked.

Closing the ledger, Silas waved to his steward, who immediately gathered his things under his arm, bowed, and left the room, though Christian didn't give him much space to do so.

Playing along, Silas leaned back in his chair and asked, "Is what true?"

"That you're *selling the estate*!" Christian strode in, crossing the distance between door and desk swiftly.

Silas pushed an ink vial away. "You seem to be sure of the answer, given your conduct."

A vein pulsed in his brother's forehead. "You're selling it for less than it's worth! Taking it from the family! What about your future sons, Silas? What about *mine*? And why not tell me?"

Silas retained his composure. "Given the nature of this conversation, is that really a surprise?"

Christian's jaw slackened. "You're impossible. I would have stepped up. Taken on your role. You never even gave me a chance."

Redipping his quill, Silas opened the ledger he'd been reviewing to a clean page to write down the numbers still in his head. "I'm not leaving us homeless. I intend to purchase another estate better suited to our needs."

"Better suited." Christian flung up his hands. "How? Where?"

"It's called Gorse End. In Liverpool."

"Liverpool!" He paced toward the bookshelf. "That's away from . . . from everything!"

Silas waited for the numbers to dry before turning to the shelf behind his desk, finding the plans for the newly purchased estate tucked safely between volumes of his encyclopedias. "I've reviewed everything myself—"

Christian stomped back and snatched the plans, unfolding them on his side of the desk. Blew hair from his eyes as he looked them over. The study was painfully silent for nearly a minute.

"It's smaller." He shook his head. "It's *older*. How is this a fair trade?"

Reaching over, Silas calmly collected the papers, ensuring he folded them along the proper creases. "It's an enchanted house."

"So what?"

So what? Such a simple question. Gorse End was an enchanted home with spells he had previously never even dreamed of possessing. Spells he feared simply taking, for while the place wasn't among the holdings of the King's League of Magicians, it was documented by the London Institute for the Keeping of Enchanted Rooms, an institution with which the previous tenant had been friendly. If Silas wanted those spells, his best bet was to reside at the estate so he could feign its magical ability should the law ever come around to check. Besides, he had to live somewhere, did he not? There would be no snooping soldiers in Liverpool, and the estate was away from everything, a perfect hideaway for him as he sorted out his future and built his invisible walls. It was a place he could tuck into and rest. A place he would feel *safe*. A place that would let him move on and forget, for his father's presence still haunted the shadows here. And, sometimes, his mother's.

He eyed his brother. The King's League had been working hard to recruit Christian as well. Now that his brother's studies were finished, it was only a matter of time before he joined. Before he unwittingly became another chain Silas would have to break.

Frustrated by Silas's lack of answer, Christian kicked the desk, jolting it.

"Really, Chris." Silas sighed.

"A portion of the estate belongs to me." His brother's voice took on a dark edge. "It's in father's will. I'll get a solicitor and block the sale."

Silas's stomach clenched. "You will do no such thing."

"You don't lord over me, *Lord* Hogwood." His nose creased like he smelled something disgusting. "You are not the sole benefactor. You are not—"

Silas stood abruptly, causing his chair to skid over the hardwood. Collecting his ledger, he headed for the door. "Keep your portion, then," he said. "You can hunker down in your precious little cottage on the south end and suck up to the King's League for your maintenance."

He had nearly reached the door when a kinetic pulse clipped his shoulder and slammed it shut.

His father shoved him into the wall, screaming obscenities so slurred together Silas couldn't determine what they were. The next blow hit his stomach so hard, he vomited.

Silas whirled around.

Christian lowered his hand, the fingers stiff. "I am not finished."

"Oh yes, you are," Silas growled. "You *dare* to use our father's magic against me? I haven't felt that sting for fifteen years."

"I didn't mean to—" Christian slashed away the words with a swipe of his hand. Paused. "What really happened to him, Silas?" A shadow spawned on his face. "What really happened to *Mother*?"

"Why do you keep. Asking. Me." He spoke through clenched teeth. "Why do you think I know? I wasn't there. Her body was never recovered. It doesn't matter. She was—"

"Dying anyway. So you always say."

"So you always question!" Silas countered. "You discovered her missing first. Why don't *you* tell me what happened to her, hm? How a servant snuck her away under your nose?"

"You always turn it around on me."

"You always point the finger first!"

"You were the last to see her!" Christian shouted.

"In a house that employs seventy-eight, you fool!" Silas didn't often raise his voice, but it ricocheted off the oak walls. "And what does it matter? She's at peace. Stop digging up the dead—"

"At peace?" Christian marched toward him. "At *peace*? How would you know?"

His jaw worked so tightly Silas thought he might break a tooth. Getting right into his brother's face, he said, "I. Don't." And he turned for the door.

"You *do*."

Silas ignored the accusations. Wrenched the door open.

"You *do*!" Christian shouted, and another kinetic blast ripped the door from Silas's hand and slammed it shut.

"I *don't*!" Silas screamed as he whirled around, sending out a kinetic blast of his own. It struck Christian in the chest and sent him hurtling backward, toward the fireplace.

Silas's stomach lurched into his throat, but his body couldn't move fast enough to stop it.

His brother crashed into the mantel, smashing his head onto the marble. He crumpled to the floor, leaving a bloody streak above the embers.

For a moment, Silas just stood there, watching.

Then he ran to his brother's side. "Christian. *Christian.*"

His brother didn't respond. He was breathing, but his eyes wouldn't open. Silas patted, then slapped, Christian's cheeks. Peeled back his lids to see rolling eyes and dilated pupils.

"Blazes." He shook his brother, but he didn't respond. How would he explain . . .

He looked toward the desk. Gorse End. It had taken so long to find that estate, and now his brother was going to . . .

Unless he . . .

Silas hesitated. His mouth went dry while his palms moistened. Chills ran up his arms and down his back.

Unless.

Silas didn't remember committing to the decision. Nor did he remember using kinesis to lock the door. The idea surfaced in his mind, and then it was happening, just as it had with his mother. Necromancy, chaocracy, kinesis, alteration, element. Time became moot as his brother sucked down into a warped, peanut-shaped *thing*, and his powers rebirthed inside Silas, strengthening those abilities they shared and adding the one they didn't—because while Silas had been born with his grandmother's augury spell of luck, Christian had inherited their granduncle's wardship magic of spell-turning.

Silas had never considered . . . but now it was too late . . .

The sun had sunk, darkening the room. He stared down at his brother. What *had been* his brother. The confusion left by the chaocracy wafted away like steam, clearing his head too slowly.

His strength returned by drops.

Stoking the fire, Silas burned the clothes. Moved his tongue around his dry mouth as he summoned the water in the glass on his desk to wash away the blood. Tucked his brother—*his brother!*—in his shirt and dashed from the study, avoiding the servants, speeding through the house, not truly *seeing* anything until he went down, down, down to the wine cellar, then to the little hidden door to the second cellar he'd carved out, where his mother rested in a locked iron box, safe from prying hands and worms and rats.

Silas fumbled for the key. He always kept it on him. No one else could find it, use it. He found the key and dropped it. Picked it up and opened the box and slid his brother inside.

His brother.

His brother.

Grabbing fistfuls of hair, Silas keeled over and screamed through closed lips, strangling himself. His pulse rocketed, skin sweated, limbs trembled. He was too hot and too cold, and *his brother was in the box.*

Pushing himself back, he vomited on the cold stone and mortar. Tears and snot streamed from his face. He bit his lip badly trying to keep the sounds in. The despair, the outrage, the disbelief. All the while, power curled and pumped through him, welcoming him, greeting him. Magic that had been just as alive as his brother had been, not simmering in a soon-to-be corpse.

Murderer.

He retched a second time, and a third, then curled in on himself, smearing vomit up his pant leg and into his hair.

‿◦

It had to be done.

Yes, it *had* to be done, hadn't it?

He'd been defending himself. Just as he'd defended himself against his father. He'd *protected* himself. The rest was happenstance. No, it was fate. Silas hadn't pushed Christian into the mantel. Destiny had.

Christian Hogwood had the ability to overpower Silas. He'd forbidden him from leaving the room and, worse, from making his escape to Liverpool. Haunted his steps ever since their mother's body had disappeared. Christian had lorded over Silas, just as their father had. He would have hurt him, eventually.

Silas had simply struck first.

Now Gorse End would be his, with no trouble. It would be *theirs*, because Christian was part of Silas now. Just as his mother was. They were together, combined, protecting each other. Safe. Silas was keeping them *safe*. Keeping himself safe.

And no one would stop him now. A little farther, a few more steps . . . no one would be able to hurt him again.

Never again. Never again.

He'd report his brother missing in the morning.

Chapter 8

God did grant, for the man from Hulda's vision—whom she knew only as "Fletcher"—arrived just as the last tendril of sunlight slipped over the western horizon.

As there was no butler at hand and Mr. Fernsby was preoccupied, Hulda greeted him at the door, holding a new ward to the hinges. It would look very poor on them if slamming took off some of their guest's fingers.

Fletcher held up a lantern. "Hello . . . are you Mrs. Larkin?"

"I am indeed. And you are Fletcher, though I am remiss of your surname, Mr. . . . ?"

"Portendorfer." The lantern light illuminated a smile. "It's a mouthful, I know. Forgive my late arrival, but the letter I received . . . Merritt didn't sound like he was in good spirit. It was . . . well, full of puns far more terrible than usual."

Indeed, Mr. Portendorfer carried a suitcase in his other hand. He intended to stay the night. Hulda sighed inwardly that there would be no way to properly prepare a bedroom for him, let alone for herself, but in cases such as these, etiquette had to be stretched, if not packed away entirely.

"We could use your assistance. Come in, please." She eyed the doorframe. "Quickly."

Stepping aside, she allowed the man in. He was roughly the same height as Mr. Fernsby, though a little broader in the shoulders.

Mr. Portendorfer froze just two steps inside the reception hall and held his lantern higher.

"Is it really . . . enchanted?" he asked. He was studying the portrait. It must have, oh, winked at him or something.

"It is, indeed." Hulda pulled out another ward on a string and offered it to him. "Might I suggest you wear this? Not for too long, mind you. There are side effects to wearing such wards on one's person for an extended period of time. But it will help." She turned to the dining room. "And I beg you to take care, Mr. Portendorfer. Those wards are expensive."

He mouthed, *Wards,* and slipped it over his neck.

"Now, if I could please have your assistance hefting Mr. Fernsby out of the pit in the kitchen, I'm sure we would both be much obliged."

༄

The hour was late, but there were things to be done. It would be a long night for the three of them.

Hulda left Mr. Fernsby and Mr. Portendorfer chatting in the kitchen as she went through the house and set up all the wards she'd managed to borrow from BIKER, which weren't as many as she would have liked. She was, essentially, drugging the house into submission until she could understand it better. She didn't have enough wards for every room, so she placed them in the dining room, the unfortunately split kitchen, the lavatory, the reception hall and upper hall, and two of the bedrooms upstairs, reserving the first for herself. Mr. Fernsby had requested that Mr. Portendorfer stay with him, which suited Hulda just fine. For now.

71

Once that was finished, Hulda brought her two bags upstairs and began unpacking her necessities. "Terribly sorry about the kitchen," she said to the house as she shook out dresses and hung them in the closet. "I will ensure such atrocities do not repeat themselves, but I would greatly appreciate your cooperation."

The house didn't reply, which meant the wards were working.

Mr. Fernsby knocked at the door after she'd finished with the first of her two suitcases. "I wanted to . . . thank you, for your haste."

Hulda nodded. "I said I would return in short order. I am a woman of my word." She glanced over. "How is it that you know Mr. Portendorfer?"

"Fletcher's my oldest friend." He leaned wearily on the doorframe. "We grew up together in New York."

She took in his appearance. He was a right mess. Mud streaking his hands, face, hair, and clothes. He looked utterly exhausted, which somehow made his blue eyes brighter in the candlelight. "Might I suggest a bath and a change of clothes, Mr. Fernsby? Did you bring that much? Your things won't arrive until tomorrow."

Posture stooping, he nodded solemnly. After covering a yawn with his fist, he said, "I think I saw a tub in the kitchen."

"Pray that you don't tumble in again." Opening her other suitcase, Hulda pulled out a thick folder stuffed with papers and handed it to him. "These are the résumés of several BIKER-endorsed persons for employment. You'll see applications there for maids, chefs, and stewards."

"Stewards?" Mr. Fernsby thumbed through the papers, his forehead wrinkling a little more with each one.

"Yes, someone to look over the financial aspects of the house and land—"

"I don't need a steward." He stifled another yawn.

"Then you may start with the maids. I will see myself settled in. I brought several things of use for taming the manor, and intend to begin work on diagnosing the house first thing in the morning."

He closed the folder. "Finding the source of magic, you mean."

"Precisely." It usually wasn't too hard of a task—most homes were not secretive about the sources of their power. Gorse End had been tricky, as the old magic had *changed* in her interim as housekeeper, but that had been Mr. Hogwood's interference—

Closing her eyes, Hulda reoriented her thoughts. The less she thought of Gorse End, the better off she was, even all these years later.

Mr. Fernsby left, muttering to himself—or perhaps over the folder—as he went. Hulda unpacked her second suitcase quickly; she was well practiced at it. As the room smelled of dust, she went to open the window and found it stuck, though she imagined that was the house's doing, not the window's. A ward couldn't muffle the place entirely.

"Do you want to smell musty?" she asked, rapping on the window. "Don't be silly. Let me open it."

When she tried again, the pane slid upward. She smiled. Whimbrel House wasn't a terrible house, just an immature one. "Surprising, given your age," she murmured, and she rested her elbows on the sill, looking out over the island, trusting the place not to bring the pane down on her. Tomorrow her trunks would arrive, and she would stock the pantry, and the challenge of bringing the house to working order would begin in earnest.

A swarm of gnats flew past the window, forming odd patterns with their tiny bodies. A chill crept down her spine, though she couldn't quite tell if it was the breeze or her augury. Beyond the passing swarm, she thought she spied two golden orbs in the distance. Eyes. She squinted, making out the silhouette of a wolf against the fading twilight, its form almost indistinguishable from the shadows and trees around it.

She furrowed her brow. Wolves didn't live in this bay, did they? She hadn't heard a single howl. Removing her glasses, she wiped them on her sleeve and replaced them.

The wolf was gone, leaving her wondering if it had been a premonition or a shifting shadow, and with no means to be certain of either.

❧

The next morning, Hulda carefully worked about the splintered kitchen and made breakfast. She had it set on the table before the two men roused. When Mr. Fernsby toed into the dining room, as though fearful it might eat him up, he paused. "I thought you didn't cook."

Hulda folded her arms. "I am *able* to cook, Mr. Fernsby, but it is not in my job description. Considering the night you had, I thought it would be appropriate to provide sustenance in the form of legumes and pease porridge."

Mr. Fernsby's lips quirked.

That made her eye twitch. "Pray tell what is so humorous."

"Sustenance," he repeated, pulling out a chair as Mr. Portendorfer came up behind him.

"Thank you, Mrs. Larkin," Mr. Portendorfer said. "I was in such a rush last night I didn't eat dinner, and this smells delicious."

"You're quite welcome."

Mr. Portendorfer offered grace, and the two gentlemen ate. Hulda couldn't help but feel a little vindicated when Mr. Fernsby's eyebrows rose. "This is good. Are you sure you don't want to be my chef?"

"Quite," she quipped.

Mr. Fernsby paused. "Are you not eating?"

"I already had my fill, thank you. It's not appropriate for staff to dine with the family."

Merritt shrugged. "Hardly any family here."

"The rule still stands, Mr. Fernsby."

He swallowed another bite before saying, "Please call me Merritt."

"I prefer formal designations."

Smirking, Mr. Portendorfer said, "You best do as she says. This one is serious. Don't let her walk out on you. Don't look a gift horse in the mouth."

"Gift horse? I'm paying for her."

"BIKER pays for me, Mr. Fernsby," Hulda corrected. "You will be supplying salary for the chef and maid you hire."

"BIKER?" Mr. Portendorfer repeated.

"That Bostonian place I mentioned," said Mr. Fernsby.

Hulda departed to let the men eat, using her dowsing rods in the reception hall and the lavatory in the meantime. She hadn't put any wards in the living room or adjoining sunroom, and dark shadows roiled within, as though the house were having a tirrivee at having been forced into order. When Hulda approached the doorway, her dowsing rods parted, but that was to be expected, as magic was condensed in this part of the house. If she couldn't find the magical source in the warded rooms, she'd start moving the wards around to better search.

When she returned to the dining room, she caught the men midconversation.

"—is doing real well. Real well," Mr. Portendorfer was saying as Hulda slipped in and gathered dinner dishes. "Think she'll be getting married soon."

"Married?" Mr. Fernsby leaned forward. "Isn't she, what, fifteen?"

Mr. Portendorfer laughed. "Serious, Merritt? She's twenty-three!"

Mr. Fernsby whistled, as he was wont to do. "Twenty-three. In my head, she's forever twelve."

"For a man who's based his life on collecting facts, you sure lose the easy ones." Mr. Portendorfer glanced Hulda's way. "Did you know this man once got himself hired by the Reese Brothers' Steel Company just so he could write an accurate story on their illegal business practices?"

Hulda rested her hand on the doorframe. "I was not aware."

Mr. Portendorfer clapped his hands. "Four months you worked there, wasn't it?"

"Only three. It was miserable."

"Your arms sure got big, though."

Hulda interrupted, "I intend to make another list for groceries this afternoon, Mr. Fernsby. We're in need of meat, if you have a preference."

Mr. Fernsby breathed out slowly—it seemed to be a motion of relief. "Any kind is fine, as long as it's reasonably priced. Thank you."

She nodded. "And do you have a preference of spirits?"

He smiled then, but it didn't fit the rest of his expression. "I, uh, don't. That is, no need to stock them on my account."

"Still dry?" asked Mr. Portendorfer.

Mr. Fernsby shrugged. "I avoid things that might get me into trouble."

The soberness of the statement caught Hulda's attention; it could also be seen in Mr. Portendorfer's expression. As though the friends shared a secret they did not dare utter between these enchanted walls.

And however etiquette was being stretched, it was not yet broken enough for Hulda to ask.

◠◡

Four days after inheriting Whimbrel House, after Merritt's New York apartment was emptied courtesy of a Boston institute he'd never heard of, his things brought to a remote island in the Narragansett Bay, Merritt got out the tools he'd collected over the last thirteen years and hesitantly entered the kitchen that had more or less tried to kill him.

Hulda had placed little red sacks around the place—wards from BIKER. Ever since placing them, the house had seemed . . . like a house. Shadows and creaking had kept to a minimum, so long as he stayed within the boundaries of the wards. He'd slept more soundly than he had in days. It almost felt normal.

The kitchen, however, was a mess. Beside him, Fletcher whistled, as though he had heard the thought and meant to punctuate it.

The house might have been able to repair itself if the wards were taken down. Merritt wasn't sure. Or perhaps it would open the floor again, suck him *and* Fletcher in, and trap them for good, turning the root cellar into a grave. That made him swallow. He really didn't want to go into the pit again. For multiple reasons. And Fletcher had to return to that agricultural wholesaler he worked for. Not sure how his employer would take "eaten by a house" as an excuse for not showing up to work.

As it were, the floor was still split, opening for about two paces at its widest part and the length of his foot at the smallest. The edges of the floorboards were splintered, and the second cupboard from where he stood was singed, the door hanging uneasily on its hinges, possibly warped from exposure to water.

But the oven was fine, so there was that.

"Floor first?" Fletcher asked.

Merritt nodded and approached with caution, stepping over the narrowest part of the gap, waiting for the floor to buck and knock him in again. The house rumbled slightly. It knew he was here.

"All right." Unsurety danced in his voice. "I'm making an attempt, all right?"

"Done floors before," Fletcher said.

"I'm talking to the house."

Merritt set the tools down on the counter, his attention lifting to the cabinets. He examined the hinges. Couldn't replace them without a trip into town, but he could tighten and oil them, shave off the bottom of the door so it closed better.

And it just so happened the movers who'd delivered his things had loaded them into two large wooden crates. Possibly just enough raw material to patch the floor.

"Mind fetching those crates?" he asked, never taking his eyes from the kitchen's maw. He imagined Fletcher nodded, for his footsteps toed out, and a moment later, the front door opened and shut. Like Hulda,

Fletcher had been granted freedom to come and go as he pleased. Only Merritt was prohibited from leaving.

Frowning, Merritt knelt gradually, as though the hearth were a bull ready to charge. Holding his breath, he touched the first splintered board.

The house rumbled like the belly of a dragon. But it didn't buck or twist or drop rats on him.

And so, very carefully, Merritt pulled out a handsaw and got to work.

∽

Hulda's augury was essentially useless.

She had *some* control over it, and she used that word delicately. Her only augury spell was divination, or the ability to see one's future specifically through patterns he or she created. In the case of the house, she wished it would show her the precise moment she discovered its secrets, thus revealing them to her early. But then that would change the future, and her augury seldom gave her the opportunity to do something so substantial. Otherwise, she certainly would have taken advantage of it by now. Thus far, all her augury had done was inform her of Mr. Portendorfer's coming arrival, which she would have learned about, anyway, and the possible presence of a wolf, which, while peculiar, hardly seemed relevant.

Her dowsing rods, likewise, hadn't told her much about the house, so she'd carefully collected the wards from her bedroom and set them up in the library so she could search it instead. She made modest use of the wards, hoping that if the books began flying again, they might form a pattern, which would in turn show her something relating to the house's magical source. She needed to prove herself capable here, for both the health of the house and Mr. Fernsby.

After three-quarters of an hour, however, all she'd found were a few interesting titles on old spines. She noted their location for the future, though she predicted without the aid of magic that the house would likely move them before she got around to cracking open a cover.

She'd just packed up her things when Mr. Portendorfer appeared in the doorway. "Can I be of assistance to you, Mrs. Larkin? Merritt's up to his elbows in sawdust downstairs, and given the shortage of tools, I only seem to be getting in the way."

She paused. "He's making the repairs?" She'd thought those grinding and hammering sounds were the house complaining to her.

He nodded as he stepped into the space, holding his hands up to shield himself from possible projectiles.

Hulda hefted her bag onto her shoulder. "I assure you it's safe enough for the time being." She eyed the wards. "At least, it won't throw anything with dynamism."

Mr. Portendorfer relaxed and spun, taking in the rows of books. "It would take a lifetime to read all of these."

"I suppose that depends on how fast of a reader you are compared to how long you intend to live."

Mr. Portendorfer pointed a finger at her. "You're a funny one."

Was she? "It's unintentional, I assure you."

He pulled a book off the shelf and tilted it toward Hulda's lantern. Then did the same with another title, and another one. "I've never heard of these."

"I haven't looked at even a fraction yet, but many are missing title pages and dates. They're quite old."

"Perhaps a librarian in Portsmouth could look them up."

"Perhaps." It wasn't a bad idea, to research some of these titles. She would, if she failed to find clues elsewhere.

His smile grew. "You know, in Cattlecorn, back when Merritt lived with us, we would get so bored in the winters we'd stow away to a small, locally run library when the weather wasn't too bad. It was four and a half miles away, but it was worth the walk to get out of the house. We'd pretend those shelves were just about anything. Monsters, mountains, the British army . . . you name it." He laughed. "Not so much reading."

It was a quaint image, but that wasn't what caught Hulda's attention. "When Mr. Fernsby *lived* with you?"

The mirth faded a fraction. "Oh, well . . ."

What reason would Mr. Fernsby have to live with another family? Did he have no relatives? "Were you at a . . . boarding school?"

Mr. Portendorfer returned the book to the shelf. "Something like that."

Now, augury did not pertain to the mind, not like psychometry did, but Hulda rarely needed magic to detect a lie. "Something like that," she repeated, perhaps a little too deadpan.

Mr. Portendorfer sighed. "I mean, we *did* meet in school. Merritt . . . he and his father . . ." He paused, lifting hands in surrender. "You know, Mrs. Larkin, it's not my story to tell. Merritt is my best friend; I would be doing him a disservice sharing his history when he's here to tell it. But"—he lowered his hands—"I will say there are few men out there better than he is. He's got a good heart. I think you two, and whoever else comes along, will get on real nice."

She nodded, and Mr. Portendorfer departed, venturing down the hallway toward Merritt's room. Hulda lingered in the doorway, wondering. It wasn't *so* odd that a man—a boy—might stay with another family for a time. She could fathom a dozen reasons for it. But the manner in which Mr. Portendorfer defended the history made her curious.

What issues did Mr. Fernsby have with his father? Why didn't he keep spirits? And why had he inherited this forgotten house, left on an island in the middle of Narragansett Bay?

In truth, it wasn't Hulda's business to know. But staying out of clients' business had hurt her in the past. Not that she thought this would be another Gorse End catastrophe, but she wanted to know.

Seemed discovering the source of this place's magic wasn't the only secret Hulda had to unwind.

⁓

Merritt needed wood glue and more nails, but considering his limitations, the work was coming along nicely.

He'd been in the kitchen half the day, hardly remembering to eat, measuring and cutting and sanding floorboards. When he got sore, he worked on the cabinet door, then buffed away as much of the scorch as he could, which was most of it—the house hadn't let him get far with the matches. He stopped once, and only once, to glance at the windowsill that had eaten Scarlet's scarf, but he didn't want to dwell on it. Wasn't anything he could do about it at this point.

Hulda checked on him a couple of times, but she never said anything, just peeked in. Fletcher came by, too, chatting with him while he worked, forcing him to eat. Merritt was grateful his friend had up and left home to help him. It was a sort of cycle of theirs, though neither of them had ever pointed it out.

As the day eased on, Merritt pushed the darkness back little by little, like an overgrown cuticle, until he felt more himself again. Fletcher was due back to Boston and his accounting work tomorrow morning, but Merritt . . . Merritt could do this. This life. This house. This change. He was nothing if not adaptable.

The sun was half-set when Merritt stood and stretched his back. The repairs weren't perfect. The wood didn't match. Part of the gap still showed. But the cupboards looked unscathed, and no one was going to break their legs walking across the floor, so that was success.

Progress.

Hulda's and Fletcher's voices sounded softly from the dining room. In the kitchen, there were three wards total, including the one on his person, which Hulda had reminded him hours ago he should take off.

What are the side effects if I don't? he'd asked.

Indigestion and stubbornness, one of which you're not accustomed to, she'd retorted.

Merritt smirked and stepped back, ensuring he hadn't missed anything. Picked up a bent nail and pocketed it. Glanced to the forearm-long crack he hadn't been able to patch, down into the dark cellar below.

He wished he understood this house, but even the expert hadn't wrapped her head around it. And he wished the house understood *him.* Was it even capable of such a thing? Hulda seemed to think so; otherwise she wouldn't talk to it.

He crossed the floor. Closed the toolbox.

The house was old. His lawyer had said there'd been no known residents for a hundred years. What a long time for a house to stay empty.

He glanced back to that crack, mulling it all over. Remembered one of the suggestions Hulda had made when he was stuck in the root cellar. Pausing, he listened to the walls, the ceiling, the glass.

It creaked slightly, though there was no sign of wind outside and no people upstairs.

No people.

Merritt's idea solidified, sticking to him like a briar on his shirt, just uncomfortable enough to notice. He chewed his lip and tried to peel it off, only to find another briar beside it.

He'd always considered himself good with metaphors.

He slipped from the kitchen, not too concerned that the doors would slam on him, and passed through the darkening breakfast room to the dining room, where Hulda's enchanted lamp beamed from the center of the table. Fletcher leaned back in a chair, facing the window and not Merritt, watching the elms in the illumination of the purple-hued sunset. Hulda had her nose in a cupboard and a receipt book in the crook of her arm.

Merritt slipped by both of them, into the reception hall. Past the ward on the stairs and up. The way to the left was safe and warded. The way to the right—

A few smoky shadows curled in the hallway. The library was silent. Perhaps Hulda had tamed it, or maybe it was merely waiting for a target before it started hurling books again.

Steeling himself, Merritt walked right, past the bedroom and the library, to the sitting room door. He opened it.

The windows had returned, letting in violet, orange, and red sun rays. They fell over chairs and sofas, a dark fireplace, a scenic portrait on the wall, and an empty corner that might have once borne a piano-forte or a harp. Seemed the right size. As Merritt watched, those smoky curls reformed themselves in the corner, muting the sunset. The ceiling warped like it was being stretched by a torrent of rain water. The carpet ruffled like the fur of a threatened cat.

Gooseflesh rose on Merritt's arms. One by one, he removed his fingers from the doorknob.

And stepped inside.

The door didn't slam shut behind him, but as he moved to the center of the room, it creaked on its hinges, easing shut with the practice of an experienced lover. The floorboards creaked and the baseboards popped. It was angry, and Merritt felt it. He could almost . . . hear it.

Then, with cold fingers, Merritt took the ward off his neck and tossed it behind him.

The far wall broke from the others and rushed forward, knocking furniture from its path, upturning the carpet, charging for a body-shattering blow—

Merritt closed his eyes and formed fists with his hands—

The wall stopped short, sending a gust of air over him, blowing his hair back. When Merritt opened his eyes, it was an inch from his nose.

He waited for the house to do more. To grow spikes, to buck, to crush him.

It waited. It *breathed*.

When his heart settled back into his chest, Merritt whispered, "Aren't you lonely?"

The wall rippled before him. He didn't step back. Neither did the house.

"That's the point of being a house, isn't it?" he asked, nails digging into his palms. "To be lived in. Last resident was in the 1730s, wasn't it? So aren't you lonely?"

Patterns of light and dark danced over the wall as shadows slipped across the window.

"I am." His voice was barely audible, but he knew the place heard it. "I've been lonely for a long time. Sure, I've had friends, colleagues, so I'm not isolated. But I still *feel* it. It's the deep, lasting kind of loneliness. The hollow kind that settles in your bones."

His muscles were so stiff his arm jerked when he moved it. Carefully he pressed fingertips, then fingers, then palm to the wall, his knuckles sore from clenching.

"I'll be good to you if you're good to me," he promised. "Maybe . . . Maybe we could *both* use a fresh start."

The room stilled.

He waited. Swallowed. Waited some more.

"I'll admit"—a coarse chuckle worked up his throat—"that the rats were a nice touch."

The room creaked. Merritt's pulse picked up, but the wall shifted backward, away from his touch. Back, back, back, until it *clicked* back into place. The furniture jellied and reoriented itself, though the carpet remained overturned. Cautiously, Merritt picked up its end and smoothed it down. When he looked up, he saw a multicolored knitted scarf lying on the floor.

And the shadows disappeared.

Chapter 9

Silas felt like he could finally breathe.

He'd left it all behind. The house, the staff, the city, the memories. The transition had been smooth, nearly without conflict. These walls held no portraits of lords past, nor of the lost. No painted eyes followed him, and the walls sang with magic that he would incorporate into himself. Yes, he'd left it all behind, except for the bodies. They were stowed away safely now, where no one would ever find them.

And that included the staff the London Institute for the Keeping of Enchanted Rooms had insisted on inflicting on him. He'd accepted the bare minimum of staff, for if he'd refused any help, it would be deemed peculiar. Gorse End was a notable estate registered with LIKER, so it would look well to play by their rules. For now.

He strode down a hall with east-facing windows, taking in the crisp autumn morning, the bright white of the sky. Hands clasped behind his back, he smiled, breathing in the cool air seeping through open panes.

He was at home here.

The sound of approaching footsteps gave him pause. Turning, he saw Stanley Lidgett, his steward, approaching. Lidgett was the only staff member he'd kept from Henspeak—he'd discharged the rest into the city. He wanted a skeleton staff here, only those whose presence was absolutely necessary. And Lidgett—he'd always trusted Lidgett. He understood more than others did.

When the steward reached him, he bowed. "Sorry to disturb you, but the housekeeper from Boston arrived early."

"Oh?" Silas gestured with a hand, and the two men walked back the way Lidgett had come. He knew LIKER had a child company in the States—they must have been overburdened to bring in someone from Boston. Silas hid a smile—all the better for his purposes, to have a housekeeper who wasn't local. He wasn't entirely put off by the obligation; aspects of Gorse End were still unfamiliar to him. Once he fully understood the nature of the house's magic and had resided there for the required length of time, as established per LIKER's regulations, he would carefully dismiss their employee. He didn't want any nosy would-be wizards detecting that the spells had suddenly vanished from the house and embedded themselves in Silas's person.

They went down the stairs to the morning room. No footman waited to open the door, which made Silas smile inwardly. Stepping inside the white-and-green-furnished room, his eyes fell upon a young woman on the settee.

She immediately rose, but before Lidgett could make the introduction, Silas said, "You're a little young for a housekeeper, are you not?" Early twenties, mid at most. Another blessing—she was inexperienced.

The woman gave him a patient smile. "I assure you I am well trained both in housekeeping duties and in enchantments, Lord Hogwood."

Lidgett cleared his throat. "The housekeeper, Lord Hogwood. Mrs. Hulda Larkin."

Silas nodded, inspecting the woman. She was a little on the tall side, with her hair pulled back into a severe knot. She had sharp eyes and a square jaw, with spectacles resting on a too-large nose.

Utterly average.

"I'm aware of the faux pas," Silas added, "but given your employer, I presume you've magic of your own?"

A rosy glow took to her cheeks. She pushed her shoulders back. "As I will be working under you, Lord Hogwood, it is a fair question. I am an augurist."

It took a great deal of effort to keep his face smooth. An augurist could prove tricky, unless she happened to have a simple spell of luck, like his own. "Intriguing! What is your specialty?"

The flush remained as she answered, "I do not wish to get your hopes up, my lord. My skills are weak at best, and I've only the ability of divination."

He considered this a moment. Divination was tied to patterns—tea leaves, dice, even clipped nails. Weak though she may be, if this woman saw something of his and peeked into his future, it might ruin everything.

Turning her away would cast suspicion on him, however, and with the disappearance of both his mother and brother, he could not risk further suspicion.

Besides . . . keeping her around would do the opposite, wouldn't it? Only a man innocent of wrongdoing would keep an augurist in the house. If he subtly circulated news of his new staff member, it would boost his reputation.

At least she wasn't a psychometrist, or he might already be found out.

"Welcome aboard, Mrs. Larkin." He smiled. "My steward will show you the house." Turning about, he clasped a hand on Lidgett's shoulder and leaned close to his ear. "Tell the maids I will speak with them in my study. As soon as possible."

The steward nodded, and Silas left the room. Yes, the maids would be his protection. He would keep Gorse End immaculate, not a stray hair or stirring of dust to be seen. Nothing to give a floundering diviner any chance of spying into his future.

It belonged to no one but him.

Chapter 10

The next morning, Merritt stepped *outside*.

He'd had his doubts, though the scarf was once again securely around his neck despite the balmy weather. But he opened the door, and he stepped outside, and nothing stopped him from doing so.

He laughed. It was a strange laugh, like something deep in his soul had bubbled and burst halfway up his throat. Hoarse yet relieving, and as he took a second and third step, it repeated itself.

"Very well done, Mr. Fernsby," Hulda remarked from the doorway, a pencil in one hand and a notebook in the other. "Admittedly, I had my doubts, but—"

He whirled around. "This is the first time I've walked this direction across the porch."

She blinked at him, and Merritt laughed again, this time twirling on the ball of his foot. "It's utterly *pleasant* out here!"

Leaping off the porch, he landed in a weedy patch of wild grass. "I will pull these!" he exclaimed, half to Hulda and half to the house. "I will weed the entire foundation. And over there, that's the perfect spot for a garden!" He nearly skipped out to survey the area. A breeze carrying the scent of chrysanthemum rolled by, one of the last whispers of summer, and Merritt sighed in ecstasy. "I never realized how entirely beautiful the outdoors is." He turned slowly, taking in the island, its weeping cherries and golden aster. A couple of shorebirds groomed themselves in the distance, half covered by reeds. He peered past them to the ocean.

He felt like he'd missed an entire lifetime, locked in that house. And now he desperately wanted to reclaim it.

Grinning hard enough to hurt, he whirled back to Hulda. "Go on a walk with me, won't you, Mrs. Larkin?"

His housekeeper both smirked and rolled her eyes. "Thank you for the invitation, but despite this new solidarity between you and this abode, there are many things that still need to be organized. Such as the *staff*, Mr. Fernsby."

"Do call me Merritt."

"Thank you, but no."

He shrugged. "Would you mind terribly if I asked you to take charge of that? I don't know heads or tails of maids and cooks. Perhaps you could choose those you'd get along with. I trust you would do it justice. In a sense, they would be *your* staff, no?"

He knew by the way she tilted her head to the side that she was considering it.

"The résumés are on my dresser." He'd moved it back last night.

She nodded. "Very well. I'll see it done."

He bowed his thanks. "And I, Mrs. Larkin, am going to run like a fool."

Turning, he took off across the island, barely hearing Hulda call out "As long as you come back!" over the wind whistling past his ears.

When was the last time he'd run?

Well, he'd done so when he was late to an appointment with his editor, but city running wasn't the same. This . . . He felt like he was ten years old again.

He ran, leaping reeds and trampling goosefoot, ducking under slippery elm branches and startling rabbits and mice alike. He tripped once on a narrow stream hidden by grass, then again on an uplifted tree root, but he didn't care. He laughed, then shouted, then did what he considered a very good imitation of a seagull—a party trick he'd discovered in his adolescence.

He ran until his lungs burned, until the house was a lump in the distance. He faced west, toward the mainland, and considered. He was out. Free. He could go back to the city if he wanted to. His things were here, yes, but he could get them shipped out before the house knew what was happening.

And yet, though he'd promised nothing, he felt as if he would be breaking a trust, not only with Whimbrel House, but with Hulda and BIKER as well. That, and . . . what precisely did he have to go back *to*?

Homeowner, he reminded himself. *Progress.*

He could do this. See it through. And the place really was lovely. What better environment to give him inspiration for his book?

I should really work on that. He chewed his lip as he strolled, watching his foot placement a little better now, though if he *were* to break an ankle, best he do it while Fletcher was still here. The thought reminded him that he couldn't take too long if he wanted to see his friend off.

He walked until he reached the north coast, which was rocky and uneven, high in some places, low in others. More stones than seashells, but he picked a few up as he went, turning their smooth sides over in his hands, skipping flatter ones into the bay. He grinned, listening to the salty breeze rustle leafy shrubs. It almost sounded like a song.

As he came around a boulder, he paused, seeing a dark shape on the other side. Upon closer inspection, he discovered it was an old two-person boat lashed to a rusted spike, its rope worn and filthy and hanging on its last thread. The boat was badly weathered, but when he freed it from its binds and inspected it, he found no holes. In fact, its hull bore a barely there seal of two loose spirals intersecting. The same seal that stamped every single kinetic tram he'd ever ridden.

Curious, and without an oar, he pushed the boat into the water and pressed the kinetic seal. The boat moved of its own volition, inciting a startled laugh from Merritt. He quickly shut off the magic and, with some effort, got the boat back to shore. "This will be fantastic," he said to no one in particular, "for getting to and from Portsmouth."

There was no public transportation between Blaugdone Island and the mainland for resupplying. He, Hulda, and Fletcher had all hired private boats to get here. Return voyages had to be scheduled ahead of time, as Fletcher had done, unless one had a communion stone, windsource pigeon, flare, or another sort of signal to summon transportation. Or, perhaps, to alert the nearest lightkeeper you were in need of aid. There were two lighthouses between Blaugdone Island and the mainland. Merritt would have to introduce himself and get on their keepers' good sides.

As Merritt dragged the boat farther ashore to keep the tide from lapping at it, he wondered if resupplying was something this staff would do. And how much it would cost to pay them. Easier to just do it himself, really. But Whimbrel House was wild, and a magically inclined staff would admittedly prove handy. Especially since Merritt had a book deadline coming up and hadn't written a word of it since arriving.

Patting the boat goodbye, he traipsed back to the house, outlining the next two chapters in his head as he went, and, after waiting with Fletcher for his ride back, came up with a couple of splendid ideas for a third.

∽◎∽

Two days after Mr. Portendorfer departed, Hulda learned something terribly grievous about her new client.

He was . . . *messy.*

Mr. Fernsby had moved from a small apartment to Whimbrel House, so he did not yet possess enough belongings to fill its rooms.

And yet.

Hulda was making rounds with her dowsing rods, stethoscope, and other tools, trying to get to the heart of the home's magical source. She'd brought a feather duster along as well; efficiency was a godly gift.

In his office, Mr. Fernsby had multiple pens and pencils strewn about, as though every time he set one writing implement down, he retrieved another instead of picking up the first. The floor was littered with half-filled papers, some crumpled, some flat, others in between. Worse, his dinner plate was *sitting next to the notebooks*, and *there was still food on it.*

Frowning, Hulda picked up the plate and carried it downstairs. Where she found his breakfast dishes had not quite made it to the sink, his fork was on the floor, and the eggs were not put away.

And the most atrocious of them all, she later discovered, was that *Mr. Fernsby did not make his bed.*

She stared at the disheveled monstrosity in his room, blankets askew, pillows flat, one forgotten on the floor. For goodness's sake, she understood the library being a mess, the house was what the house was. But this was ghastly. Expected from aristocracy, yes, but this was the United States, and Mr. Fernsby was not accustomed to staff. He had no excuses.

She blanched. *What if he doesn't wash his sheets?*

Tucking her tools away, she marched downstairs, excusing herself outside for some fresh air and a rejuvenation of her sanity. She walked the perimeter of the house with her dowsing rods, finding little of interest, then listened to the foundation and corner posts. "I don't think you're built of magicked materials," she said to the house, which did not respond. She made a note in her ledger and determined she might as well conduct a full inspection of the exterior while outside. Walking around the house, Hulda noted panels and buttresses, then examined the structure again from farther out, taking notes on the shingles and shutters. She hadn't previously noticed the house had a weather vane.

Perhaps that was something to investigate . . . though climbing up there would be a challenge in and of itself. Her dresses were not made for such adventure, and she did not own a pair of trousers.

Next she studied the windows, listening to them with her stethoscope and testing them with dowsing rods. She took her time because she didn't want to perform the task twice. Indeed, by the time she had finished her inspection, the sun was beginning to sink.

Mr. Fernsby was writing by candlelight in his office when she returned indoors. She desperately wanted a long and thorough bath, but for decency's sake, she would wait until after he had turned in for the night.

His door was open, and he must have heard her, for his fingers stilled and he turned in his chair. "Ah! Hulda, I have a question for you."

Masking a frown, Hulda stepped into the room and said, "Mrs. Larkin, if you please."

"Right! My apologies." A flash of embarrassment swept his face, which was quickly replaced with nonchalance. "I want your opinion on something I'm writing."

Hands on hips, she retorted, "I am not an expert on—"

"Everyone reads, do they not?" he interrupted. "You see, I'm writing an adventure story, taking place in New York. My protagonist is a young woman named Elise Downs, and she's a Scottish immigrant—though I might change that. Either way, she's just arrived in the city for the reading of a will, only to find the address for her lodgings is wrong. Then she witnesses a murder in a nearby alley."

Hulda stiffened. "Good heavens."

"Excellent response." He grinned, and something about the motion—or perhaps it was the candlelight—made his eyes look green. "But I have a quandary. I would think any sensible woman would run, and Elise needs to be sensible to be likable. But I also need her to see the timepiece one of the murderers has on his person, so I think she should go in and try to save the bloke . . . What do you think?"

She frowned. "I think I would not be venturing into alleyways on my own in the dark. I assume it's dark."

"I don't think murderers function as well in the day."

Pushing her glasses up her nose, she said, "I must confess that I don't read much in the way of fiction. I won't be a great help to you."

Mr. Fernsby reeled back. "What? Who doesn't read fiction? What else is there to read?"

"Receipt books, histories, the newspaper—"

"All of them hogwash, the last one most of all."

Hulda folded her arms. "Did you not work for the press, Mr. Fernsby?"

He smiled. "How else would I know? Now, about Elise—"

Hulda rolled her eyes. "I don't know. Does it have to be a murder?"

"Why shouldn't it be a murder?"

"Because murders are frightening."

"They're *exciting*. In fiction, that is. I had two in my first book, and it did rather well."

She rubbed the bridge of her nose. "Perhaps if it were a mugging, it would still be *exciting*, but not so dire that a brave young woman wouldn't run in and try to startle the thieves. Or perhaps there is another witness with her, someone who emboldens her."

He considered a moment, tapping his index finger against his lower lip. "I suppose they could meet earlier . . ."

"They?"

He snapped his fingers. "That might just work. Thank you, Mrs. Larkin. You've been a great help."

He turned back to his notebook and tore the paper he was working on from its spine, then began anew, scrawling at a speed Hulda couldn't help but be impressed by.

Leaving him to his work, she ventured downstairs to find something to eat and search for a tub for a bath. "Now, where did I put the cured duck?"

The farthest kitchen cupboard opened.

She smiled. "Thank you." She pulled the wrapped meat free, then turned around, scanning the kitchen, the floor of which had been polished and fully resewn by the house. "I don't suppose you know where the tub is?"

A great belch emitted from the hearth, sending a cloud of soot into the air. Hulda shielded her eyes as the tub, covered in grime, fell from the chimney.

She coughed and waved her hand to dissipate the cloud. "Really, Whimbrel House!"

The window opened.

"Thank you." She stifled another cough and crossed to the tub. Goodness, it would take her the better part of an hour to scour the thing!

Ultimately, however, the scouring wasn't at all an issue, for Mr. Fernsby did not go to bed for a very long time.

Chapter 11

October 16, 1835, Liverpool, England

Silas burst into the manor from the rain. He'd only run from the carriage to the door, but the weather was torrential, and his coat and hat were already dripping. He had a spell that could whisk the water away—the ensuing cost of dehydration was manageable—but he wasn't supposed to *have* that spell, and thus would not perform it where anyone might see him, such as the maid running up to take his sopping things.

Giving her his coat and hat, Silas continued down the hallway, leaving wet boot prints in his wake and shaking water from his curling hair. His latest outing had been successful in ways he hadn't expected. He'd been dreading the evening's activities, for he'd had to spend it at his neighbor's ball to keep up appearances, and being a wealthy bachelor always brought unwanted attention. *But* he'd since learned the step-mother of a Miss Adelaide Walker possessed an incredibly rare hysteria spell, one she'd been sanctioned *not* to use by the King's League of Magicians, for its danger. The spell that could inflict pain on another person, just with a thought!

If Silas could get his hands on that spell, his grisly work could finally end.

He'd collected a number of spells since relocating from humans and houses alike, bolstering himself and his defenses, assuring his freedom and welfare. To add such magic to his person would surely put him above all those who might seek to overthrow him. He didn't want much—he didn't desire the crown or political merit, didn't seek land or prestige. He just wanted assurance.

After Miss Walker, he could be done. No more killing, no more hiding. He didn't entirely mind using Adelaide Walker to reach his end, either—if anything, having a woman of the house would give him an excellent reason to dismiss LIKER's housekeeper a year earlier than her contract demanded, which would then allow him ample opportunity to absorb the rest of Gorse End's spells. He'd already taken its fire elemental spell, though he'd had to stage occasional magical manifestations of that power to keep the staff from noticing.

Simply put, the end was in sight.

As he headed for the basement, he spied his housekeeper down an adjoining hallway. "Mrs. Larkin!" he called. "I think I will invite the Walkers over for dinner this weekend. Could you see the place prepared?"

Mrs. Larkin stopped abruptly. "I . . . Yes. I will."

She seemed intimidated by the very idea—Mrs. Larkin was always so sure of herself, so stiff and resolute. Silas smiled as he went on. He'd likely caught her off guard. He so rarely invited guests over, and when he did, it was only for appearances.

Slowing his step as he reached the back of the house, he glanced around once, checking for watching eyes—the basement was hardly secret, and the staff knew they were not allowed in it, but he still preferred privacy. Seeing no one, he descended the stairs, taking a lantern off the wall as he went and lighting it with the twitch of a finger. The sensation of ice shot up his hand, but it dissipated by the time he reached the last step.

He didn't bother lighting the sconces on the wall here; instead, he continued to the trapdoor hidden in the stone beneath a rug, to the second basement he'd carved out with his own hands, his own magic. There, he lit lamps and candles, illuminating the small space in an orange glow.

This was where he kept them.

He visited often, ensuring the place didn't get too cold or damp, ensuring his donors didn't spot with mold or show odd symptoms. They were well preserved, but Silas wasn't foolish enough to believe them immortal. His newest ones sat on a shelf, tied up like cured meat, ensuring they dried out entirely and didn't bruise. The others were kept away behind a hidden and vaulted door. No one would ever find them without Silas's help.

"One more," he whispered to them, touching the closest, the one that had given him clairvoyance. "One more, and we'll be complete."

He cut the string of the first and delicately unwrapped it, cradling it as if it were more fragile than china. As he began working on the second, however, he heard a noise.

He paused, held his breath. Listened.

That noise was . . .

His blood drained from his body and pooled at his feet.

Someone had opened the hidden basement door.

Panic flooded him so suddenly he momentarily forgot himself.

Footsteps thundered on the stairs. Too many footsteps.

Snapping to wakefulness, he cut the strings binding the second and third donors and grabbed them. He didn't have time to go to the vault, he had to hide them—

Policemen burst into the room, so many they could barely fit. A dozen, at least. Nowhere to hide the donors, nowhere to—

"Lord Hogwood! You're under arrest!"

No.

One of the men grabbed him. Tried to bind his hands.

"No!" he bellowed as he shot out a kinetic blast at the fool, sending him barreling into a second officer. "Unhand me!"

He whipped around to strike another officer, only to hit an invisible shield. A wardship spell. His pulse throbbed in his head. *King's League.* They had King's League men here.

But . . . how did they know? How could they possibly have *known*?

Silas dropped the donors and retreated from the wall, shooting off a blast of fire, forcing the officers to give him a wide berth. There was no other exit than the stairs. How would he escape? He'd have to kill them all—

He smacked into another wardship spell, hard enough to loosen teeth. It dazed him for half a heartbeat, but that was enough time for his worst fears to come to fruition. A chaocracy spell of breaking shot out from his hands, only to be spell-turned by another of the king's men.

The officers piled onto him, wrenching back his arms, binding his wrists and knees, mouth and ankles. Wardship spells pressed in like the walls of an invisible coffin. Overpowering him. Just like his father had.

Silas screamed into the gag, cursing them all. They shoved a bag over his head and hauled him up the stairs of his own home . . . *Who had let them in?* He tried to use magic, but a King's Leaguer was at his feet, keeping him inside a wardship box so strong the wizard would undoubtedly be left sick and weak for a fortnight.

Still, Silas didn't give up. He pulled at the ropes until his skin tore and bled. He pushed magic outward until his still, dry, and cold body shuddered with exhaustion. He writhed and pulled, managing to move the bag off his head—

He saw her there, standing by the front door, her mouth pressed into a hard line, her eyes resolute, her posture that of granite. Watching as the officers carried him out.

The woman with all the keys of the house. The one he'd thought *perfect* for her position.

As magic drained from his body, shocking him like a dagger sheathed in ice, he knew his donors were being destroyed. That Hulda Larkin had found his secret hideaway. She had known, and she had informed the King's League. The woman had opened the doors to these men, when Silas was *so close* to peace.

And he would never forgive her.

Chapter 12

That Sunday, Merritt could not determine why Hulda was so remarkably angry with him. She'd been stiff—stiffer than usual, that was—all day. Curt—more curt than usual, again—in her responses to him. Was it because he hadn't gone to church? Did she not realize how far away *church* was, even with an enchanted boat? And he was just on the cusp of breaking into the next act in his novel.

The truth came out when he sat down in the dining room to eat a snack.

Hulda stormed in from the direction of the kitchen. "Socks in the kitchen, Mr. Fernsby? Must we live like we're . . . we're . . . *mountain men?*"

Merritt paused, an apple halfway to his mouth. "Do mountain men have kitchens?"

The question seemed to stoke the fire lighting the housekeeper from toe to head. She held up his dress socks like they were bloody rags—dress socks he'd left at the edge of the sink. "Why are these here?"

He'd honestly forgotten about them. It had been many years since he'd last shared living space with someone. "Because they were dirty. They're drying."

She looked sick. Merritt tried very hard not to laugh at the expression—they were mere socks, and they were clean.

"Genteel people do not *wash their socks* in the same bin as they wash their dishes! And I hung a drying line outside. Did you not see it?"

"I did see it." He'd run into it once, actually. Nearly lost an eye. "But it was late."

"And therefore you could not step outside to hang up your socks."

She had him there. Taking a bite of apple, he chewed, shoved it into his cheek, and added, "It was dark?"

Hulda's eyes nearly rolled, but she stopped them before the irises reached their peak. "Really, Mr. Fernsby!"

The ceiling shifted from white to blue overhead. Merritt rather liked the color, though he wondered what the house was getting at. He pushed his attention to Hulda. "The maid is coming today, yes? Will she be gathering the laundry?"

"Thank the Lord for that." She stormed to the window and peered out. "And yes, she will do the laundry, though you will have to leave it in the basket in your bedroom if you want her to be able to find it."

"They're just socks, Mrs. Larkin."

"And your coat is in the living room. Your shoes in the reception hall."

His guilt warred with defensiveness. He wasn't a child, for heaven's sake, and this was his home. "Why not leave shoes in the reception hall? Otherwise I'll drag dirt all over the place."

"I agree with you." She turned from the window. "But in that case, shoes can be left *neatly along the wall*, not thrown across the floor like they were attacked by a dog."

Merritt nodded. "I've always wanted a dog."

A funny little choking sound emitted from Hulda's lips. She started for the door, but as she reached for it, it shifted to the right.

Merritt bit down on a chuckle. "What did you say the maid's name was again?" He was still unsure about a maid—not only living with yet another strange woman. Merritt hoped that the more nonchalant he acted about the arrangement, the more normal it would feel.

"For the third time, it is Beth Taylor."

"You know, since I'm your employer"—the corners of his eyes wrinkled at the tease—"you could be a little sweeter to me."

She gave him a withering look. "I am sweet on kittens and lemon drops only, Mr. Fernsby. And as I've said before, you are BIKER's client, not my employer. However, once a permanent housekeeper is brought on board, you may disparage her and her temperament as thoroughly as you see fit."

Setting down his apple, Merritt spun in his chair. "What do you mean, a permanent housekeeper? You're not staying?"

"I am staying long enough to sort out the issues with this house; then I will move on to wherever BIKER has need of me."

Merritt felt two things at the forward statement: disappointment and surprise. Disappointment that Hulda would be leaving, and surprise that the fact disappointed him. Everything was going so . . . well. The house had settled down into occasional pranks and calls for attention, instead of death threats and dead vermin.

"But what if I don't like my new housekeeper?" he protested.

Her lip twitched toward a smile. "Well, if you had reviewed the résumés as you were supposed to, you would have gotten to handpick one. But since you've left it up to me, I've sent inquiries to the nastiest and most expensive women of my acquaintance."

He narrowed his gaze. "You didn't."

Hulda didn't reply, beyond a smug look. Snatching the door handle, she jammed her foot into the frame so it wouldn't move again, then promptly left.

Merritt turned back to his apple, noting almost subconsciously that the bite he'd taken out of it looked a lot like France.

Beth arrived at 4:00 p.m. sharp. Merritt knew this because she knocked at the same time he checked his watch. Had he not been expecting her, he might not have heard the sound—it was a timid rapping, not purposeful and demanding like Hulda's.

"Please be kind to her," he whispered to the walls of the living room. "We're in this together, are we not?"

The house responded by allowing the sofa to sink halfway into the floor. Merritt departed before the sudden sinkhole could devour him as well.

Hulda, unsurprisingly, beat him to the door. "Miss Taylor! Wonderful to see you. Was it much trouble arriving?"

"Your directions were good, Mrs. Larkin. My thanks."

Hulda stepped aside to let in a dark, petite woman, her black hair pulled into a tight knot at the crown of her head. She had large, attractive eyes and a round face. Like Hulda, she wore a dress that covered her chin to toe, although hers was a comfortable pale-blue day dress to Hulda's gray. Her umber eyes found Merritt immediately, and before Merritt could offer his own welcome, she said, "Are you a writer, Mr. Fernsby?"

He paused. "I . . . Yes." Perhaps that was in his file, but if it was, she shouldn't need to ask.

Beth nodded. "That's interesting. Never worked for a writer before. I like it when people earn their own way and their own things."

"Well, thank you." He wouldn't mention that the house had been *given* to him.

Something *thumped* upstairs. Turning about, Merritt muttered, "Please don't be my model ship."

"That's just the house," Hulda explained. "In much better constitution than it was in the beginning. I'll see you situated, then give you the tour."

Stepping forward, Merritt reached out. "May I?"

Beth paused, eyeing her suitcase before hesitantly handing it over. After Merritt grasped it—the thing was rather light—she said, "I think I'll like it here just fine."

"And you're also from BIKER?" Merritt asked as he led the way up the stairs, leaving Hulda to take up the caboose.

Beth nodded. "I'm a contractor with them."

"Does one have to have magic to work with BIKER?"

"Of course." Beth didn't even blink when the stairway flashed bright red. "But my talents are small. I'm only eight percent."

"Eight . . . what?" he asked.

"Miss Taylor, it's distasteful to share your ancestral composition with your employer," Hulda chided.

Merritt paused at the top of the stairs, wary of the ceiling, which remained dry at present. "Ancestral composition?"

"Really, Mr. Fernsby." Hulda pushed past both of them. "As you will now be dealing with magic on a regular basis, you should educate yourself on the matter."

"I'll educate myself when and if I decide to write a book on it," he countered. "But since the distaste has passed"—he offered Miss Taylor a smile—"what do you mean eight percent?"

Miss Taylor glanced to Hulda.

Hulda sighed. "It is an estimation, based on genealogy, of what percentage of your ancestry was magical. The higher the percentage, the more magic—or stronger magic—one is likely to have."

Merritt leaned on one foot. "What's the difference?"

"It's in the spells, Mr. Fernsby," Beth chimed in. "Sometimes a person might possess only one spell, but they have a lot of it, so they can do that one thing very well. Sometimes a person has many spells but only a little of each, so they do a lot of things poorly. Most times, families with a history of magic get their children tested for it."

Merritt nodded. "Isn't it just a case of math, then?"

Hulda shook her head. "Genetics are a tricky thing, Mr. Fernsby, and magic is recessive. My sister, for example, hasn't an iota of magic in her, but our parentage is the same."

Merritt processed this. "Interesting. So what percentage are you, Mrs. Larkin?"

She frowned. "As I said, it is distasteful to discuss. This way. You're in the second room here, next to mine. If you have any questions, don't hesitate to knock. But given that Mr. Fernsby is the sole occupant of Whimbrel House, your duties will be simple."

"Is it on your résumé?" Merritt pressed as he followed. "Can I see it?"

Hulda ignored him. "I've already turned down the bed for you. Mr. Fernsby tends to sleep in late, so you may visit his room last in the mornings."

"I'll tell you mine," Merritt continued. "Zero. Now you go."

Beth chuckled. Perhaps it *was* beneficial to have others about the house.

Hulda cast both of them a withering look. "If it is so important to you, Mr. Fernsby, BIKER calculated me to be a twelve. High percentages are very rare among common folk."

He nodded. "What do you think the queen is, then? Fifty?"

Rolling her eyes, Hulda took the suitcase and laid it on the bed. "Miss Taylor, let's start in the library."

Merritt followed them down the hallway. "Sixty? Goodness, it's not *seventy*, is it?"

Hulda ignored him again, opening the door to the library, where books were flying. He highly doubted she would do anything to stop him from being whapped in the side of the head by a soaring volume, so he begrudgingly left the women to their business.

It wasn't until he returned to his notebooks—thankfully all in one piece—that he realized he'd forgotten to ask what *kind* of magic Beth had.

Pulling out a new piece of paper, he wrote himself a note to visit the closest public library the next time he left the island. He was going to check out a few books on magic.

 ⁓

Miss Taylor toured the house, asking appropriate questions, and set to work the moment she was done, stating, "I can unpack when everything is clean."

Truly, Hulda had not heard more beautiful words in some time.

Thankfully, Miss Taylor had basic kitchen skills, which was one of the reasons Hulda had hired her, Myra's recommendation being the other. Later that evening, she prepared dinner with minimal assistance from Hulda and announced that she would venture to Portsmouth in the morning to gather a new batch of supplies. Everything was beginning to run smoothly.

With the dishes tucked away and both Miss Taylor and Mr. Fernsby retiring to their rooms, Hulda took the opportunity to tour the house once more, trying to pass through its spaces in different patterns than was customary. Her dowsing rods were in her bag, but her stethoscope remained around her neck. She studied each charm to see if it had changed—none of them had—and even purposefully knocked over a few things in hopes her divination spell might give her a hint, but of course the fickle magic rarely worked that way. If anything, she'd only get a glimpse of her own future.

She was nearly at the point where she might need a candle when she started back down the hallway from the direction of the bedrooms. Paint began dripping—though this time it was gray—so she opened her umbrella and walked slowly, searching the corners of the space, trying to peer through its walls, so to speak. As she stepped into the library, as expected, books started flying. Today, the house was flinging black-spined volumes, of which there were many.

Hulda nudged a single foot into the room, not wanting to risk being struck, though the house had thus far spared her physical harm. But as she was about to brave her other foot, she happened to glance over her shoulder to the hall.

The paint rain had ceased.

She paused. Glanced into the library. Pulled her first foot out but left the door open.

Within seconds, the paint began again, pattering as it had before, vanishing into the carpeting like it had never been.

"Hmm," she said aloud, stepping fully into the library. Books began flying. She peeked into the hallway. No drips.

She stepped back into the hallway. Drips.

Facing the hallway, Hulda walked backward until she passed into the sitting room. One step, two steps, three—

The furniture began rumbling as though coming to life. And the paint drips stopped.

A smile lifted her mouth. *Well, there you have it.*

"Mrs. Larkin." Mr. Fernsby exited his bedroom at the other end of the house, holding a piece of paper in his hand. "This is going to make me sound like an imbecile, but how do you spell *privilege*? Is there not a *d* in it? I swear . . ." He glanced up, likely noting her expression. "What have you done now?"

"It's spelled p-r-i-v-i-l-e-g-e, Mr. Fernsby." She put a hand on her hip. "And I have discovered Whimbrel House's source of magic."

The furniture stopped rumbling.

Mr. Fernsby smirked. "I don't suppose my lawyer was right and it's haunted."

"Why yes, Mr. Fernsby," she replied in all seriousness. It fit. A single ghost could only do so much at once, and the magic hopped from room to room, as though trying to impress her. "I am quite positive that the spirit of a wizard is in possession of the facilities."

Chapter 13

Silas quite liked America. It was a bit backward and unrefined, yes, but there was a sort of *freedom* here that he appreciated. Not freedom to vote, or to worship, or to venture west and claim land . . . none of that mattered to him. No, his *freedom* came from the purged slate on which this place had been built. There was no royalty in the United States. No generations-old families inbreeding their sons and daughters to cling to the ladder of prestige, power, and aristocracy. No blood built upon blood built upon blood to preserve magical ties. The people here were as ordinary as they came, dregs from other countries with little to no importance, clamoring together to make a better life for themselves. Which meant that Silas was very likely the most powerful person here.

He savored the feeling that no one could quell him, not with spells and not with bars. And he'd do what needed to be done to keep it that way. His first order of business was to restore the power he had lost in England, when several of his prized dolls had been destroyed, along with the spells they'd lent him.

Which brought Silas to another excellent aspect of America: there were no castles.

In England, important things were always secured in castles, which were dastardly things to break into, even with magic.

The hotel where BIKER kept its files was much more easily penetrated. The luck spell that ran through Silas's veins was feeble, but today it cooperated, leading him to the room he needed without a single stumble.

He didn't use a candle or lantern as he browsed their files. His eyes had adjusted well enough to the light coming through the room's two narrow windows. Each file was devoted to an enchanted house.

Houses were prime for building his magic. *Houses* could not be killed, and thus did not require preservation. Not only would Silas be acting within the bounds of the law, but he wouldn't have to drag any poor souls into the little cavern he'd dug out for himself. That, and he might be able to get some bartering chips for future negotiations with his new allies.

He opened the file on Willow Creek, a thatched cottage in New York, and wrote the address on his forearm with a grease pencil, along with the magic it possessed. Stowing that file away, he moved to the next, a mansion near the Hudson . . . but it had been exorcised. *Damn.* Such a waste. The next was a house in Connecticut, which had several residents, something that would make his work harder. But he smeared the address onto his skin all the same.

Sidestepping, Silas pulled out the last file on this shelf. A place called Whimbrel House in Rhode Island. His brow quirked as he saw a newly added list of spells. This would do *very* nicely, and—

He paused, staring. The person in charge . . . Could it be? *Hulda Larkin. So we meet again.*

He'd thought of her often, while he was trapped in Lancaster. Wouldn't it be fun to see her again? She'd never interested him before, but . . .

Silas snapped the folder closed and smiled. Things seemed to be going his way again, weren't they?

To be sure.

Chapter 14

"I am quite positive that the spirit of a wizard is in possession of the facilities," she said.

Merritt paused. Everything *paused*. His blinking, his breathing, his mental faculties.

Forcing a smile, he spoke through clenched teeth. "Mrs. Larkin. Might I speak to you outside for a moment?"

He pushed past her without waiting for an answer. The hall ceiling started dripping, *red* again, and he found it very difficult to believe it was paint. He darted past the problem area, down the stairs, and across the reception hall, practically leaping outside. Part of him feared the front door would not open—that the house could read his mind—but he made it outside in one piece, recalling as he stepped outside that psychometry had not been included in Hulda's report.

He did not stop until he was some distance from the house, ensuring it would not hear him. Hulda followed behind, closing up her umbrella as she walked.

"Is there a problem, Mr. Fernsby?" she asked once she caught up.

"Problem?" He kept his voice low. "There is a *ghost* living in my house!"

She didn't respond right away. Like she expected further explanation. "And?"

"And?" He stalked away, then back. "And *why are you so calm about this?*"

"Because, Mr. Fernsby"—she planted hands on hips—"this is not the first possessed house I've been acquainted with, nor will it be the last. You of all people should know that *fiction* is just that. Do not lean on the ghost stories of your childhood."

"Ghost stories have origins," he hissed.

"From superstitious witch hunters, perhaps," she countered, two lines forming a Y between her eyebrows. "I assure you, the house is just the same as it was before. The only thing that has changed is that we have now identified where the magic comes from!"

"From a *poltergeist.*"

She frowned. "Do you think all of the dead are malevolent ghouls waiting to feast on the flesh of the living?"

Merritt paused. Considered. "That was a good line, Mrs. Larkin. You should write a book."

She rolled her eyes.

"Listen." He put up his hands, as though illustrating with them might help him make his point. "It was kind of cute, when I thought I was dealing with a half-sentient kitchen or armoire. It is utterly horrid that there is an *actual* walking spirit from the grave floating around, watching me dress, breathing down my neck, and dropping me into pits!"

Hulda breathed deeply but nodded, which made him relax a hair. "It is simply that, on occasion, a person of magic does not wish to pass on to the world beyond, and instead finds a new body. Houses are large, made from natural materials, and often social, without a preexisting soul. It's a rational choice."

Merritt breathed out, long and slow, through his mouth. Grabbed some of his hair at the roots. Released it. Glanced back at the house.

It *seemed* so normal from out here. Then again, he'd thought the same when he first arrived, before it trapped him inside and tried to murder him in the lavatory.

They'd reached a truce, hadn't they?

But how trustworthy was an ancient soul?

"Whatever is haunting this place," he spoke nearly at a whisper because all the goodwill they'd built with Whimbrel House might very well be lost if the ghost overheard them, "it's been haunting it a long while. And it *obviously* has issues."

"I believe," she said carefully, "it's merely forgotten standard decorum."

"Standard decorum." He grabbed his hair again. "Forgive me if a slip of *standard decorum* is not enough to balm . . . this." He made a general gesture toward the place. "I mean . . . can't we make him . . . go away?"

Hulda's face fell. Only a fraction, before she covered it up, but Merritt saw it nonetheless, and it transported him back to the hole in the kitchen, where she confessed her reasons for preserving the house as is.

"Shouldn't it, I don't know," he tried, "be laid to rest? Houses can't really die, right? What if he doesn't even want to be here anymore?"

"Or her," Hulda remarked.

"For the sake of my sanity, let's choose one pronoun to work with. How do we make *him* go away?"

She sighed and folded her arms, though it looked more like she was hugging herself. "I cannot legally stop you from pursuing that route. But if you do so, the magic will be stripped away. Lost."

Merritt frowned, hating the worm of guilt in his chest. "And you'll be unemployed."

"If I may remind you yet again, Mr. Fernsby, I am BIKER's employee. Should you choose to proceed with the exorcism, they would see to my vocational direction, as well as Miss Taylor's." Hulda's usual rigidness returned in full force. "In the meantime, removing the wizard will take some work."

Absently picking at lint in his pocket, he asked, "Like what?"

"Like learning the identity of the soul within these walls." Turning, Hulda took in the house like she was seeing it for the first time. "We cannot call him out if we don't know his name."

"I see. And how do we do that?"

"Research, Mr. Fernsby." Hulda loosened her arms and gripped the umbrella's handle. "A great deal of research."

⟨∾⟩

Beth walked into Merritt's office with a feather duster in one hand and the mail in the other. She'd taken his little kinetic boat across the bay to Portsmouth this morning to post mail—all of which was Hulda's—and pick up supplies.

"Some missives from the post office, Mr. Fernsby," she said, handing him three letters.

Merritt hesitantly plucked them from her fingers. Now that he knew the truth about the house's magic, he was very aware of everything he did, like the wizard in residence was watching him. Supposedly he could only haunt one room at a time, but he could be *lurking*, and the awareness of that made Merritt fidget. He thought to utilize the wards again, but he didn't want to make the haunter angry. "I don't have a box at the Portsmouth post office."

Beth shrugged. "You do. Comes with the house, I guess. Any forwarding was handled by BIKER."

Turning the letters over, he saw the first addressed to him in elegant handwriting, without a return address. Shifting it to the back, he lit up as he recognized the stamp of the *Albany Sunrise Journal*, which he'd published three articles in earlier that year, and tore open the envelope to find an acceptance of a satirical article he'd written about how one could tell a Democrat from a Whig based on how he buttoned his coat, along with a paycheck that certainly didn't hurt his financial situation. To further bolster him, the second letter was from Mr. McFarland, his editor, and it contained a substantial check for a portion of his contracted advance.

"Praise the Lord and all that be," he murmured, setting the two letters aside.

Beth had already set to dusting. "Good news?"

"Good news! The world is right, and we shall continue forward in comfort." He chuckled before turning back to the last letter. Curious, he ripped open the envelope with his thumb and pulled out a single piece of parchment, which was signed at the bottom by a Maurice Watson.

"Never heard of the fellow," he muttered. He read over the message, back straightening when he got to the meat of it.

What was in the air today? Not that Merritt was complaining, but this last letter could very well be a solution to his ghostly problem, not to mention the financial boost it promised . . . and yet his stomach felt oddly ill at the thought of accepting the offer. Had he grown so attached already? In truth, he wasn't sure what to do with the sentiment. In his experience, it was always better to adopt an attitude of nonchalance, to keep feelings shallow so that they couldn't grow teeth. He'd have to be careful moving forward.

"Mrs. Larkin!" he bellowed. When she did not reply, he raised his voice further. "Mrs. Larkin!"

Shuffling sounded down the hallway. Hulda appeared in the same green dress she'd worn upon first arriving, and it swished around her as she turned into the room. "I am not a dog, Mr. Fernsby." She eyed the letter. "What is it?"

"A Watson fellow is inquiring about purchasing the house."

Her eyes widened. "What?" Crossing the room, she snatched up the letter and read it herself, adjusting her glasses as she did so.

It was a simple letter, merely asking if Merritt would be willing to sell his property and, if so, to name his price.

How high a price could he name?

"How strange," she murmured. "The house is so obscure even I hadn't heard of it, and it's not listed. How would he know?"

Merritt folded his arms. He *had* intended to stay, but . . . "Perhaps he would be willing to keep it . . . as is."

Hulda pressed her lips together. "Perhaps," she repeated. "But Whimbrel House is . . ." She eyed the walls, perhaps trying to sense for the resident wizard. "Well, undesirable by the general populace, given the location and the enchantments. It hasn't had a buyer in ages. Why now?"

"Mr. Fernsby?"

Merritt nearly jumped out of his chair at Beth's quiet voice behind him. He smacked his hand to his chest to keep his heart in place. "Good heavens, Beth. Do step more loudly in the future."

She smiled. "May I see it?"

Hulda passed over the letter. Beth closed her eyes, holding the page gingerly in her hand.

Hulda whispered, "Are you reading it?"

Merritt frowned. "She obviously isn't."

Hulda shushed him, and he folded his arms, feeling every bit an indignant child.

Beth's eyes opened. "Odd feeling about this one. Can't explain what, but . . . doesn't sit right with me."

Hulda frowned. "Odder and odder."

Hesitant, Merritt pulled the missive from Beth's fingers. "What were you doing just now?"

Beth swept back a few strands of hair. "My talents lie in psychometry, Mr. Fernsby. I'm clairvoyant. A little, at least. Get ideas and feelings that aren't my own, at times. Felt strange about that letter from the beginning but didn't want to overstep."

"Oh. Like Hul—Mrs. Larkin, then."

Clicking her tongue, Hulda said, "Clairvoyancy is in the school of psychometry, Mr. Fernsby. Seership is augury. They are quite different."

He hesitated. "Are they?"

The housekeeper stifled a sigh.

"What Mrs. Larkin means," Beth said with care, "is that augury involves future-telling and fortune. Psychometry occupies the mind. Mind reading, hallucination, empathy. I specifically possess the power of discernment." She gave him a patient smile. "I might sense you sneaking up on me, no matter how clandestine you're trying to be. Or suppose you were pretending to be a Turk, I would know you were not."

"Oh. Well. There goes that scheme." He glanced at the refined handwriting. Obviously this Maurice Watson was educated. He might have a pretty penny to his name. But if Beth had a bad feeling about him, particularly one prompted by magic, he might not be the easy answer to their predicament after all.

Merritt thought about the weeping cherries and whimbrels and Beth and Hulda . . . then opened a drawer and slipped the letter inside. "I suppose I've only just gotten here. I should see through the mystery with the"—he swallowed—"ghost." He shrugged without even thinking to, the movement was so practiced.

A soft smile touched Hulda's lips. Some of her features were severe, accentuated by the way she carried herself, but she was pretty when she smiled. "Excellent choice, Mr. Fernsby."

He certainly hoped so.

❧

The file BIKER had on Whimbrel House was indeed sparse—it listed Mr. Fernsby's maternal grandmother, who'd won it from a Mr. Sutcliffe, who'd inherited it from his father, who'd taken the deed from his brother. That was it, and none of those listed on the deed had ever actually *lived* at Whimbrel House, or in Rhode Island, for that matter, and therefore none of them could be the house's haunter. It seemed evident that the house had been built—and abandoned—in the early settling of the colonies, given the style and lack of documentation, then picked up again before the finalizing of US law. It was really quite a mess.

And so, in order to update the file and get the information Hulda needed on the wizard's identity, the most obvious place to start the search was the library.

The library wasn't large in the way of noble houses, but the side walls were stacked with shelves reaching floor to ceiling, most of them full, which made for a good deal of books. They were also vastly unorganized, thanks to the house's habit of book throwing.

Hulda started on the far end of the south shelf, and Mr. Fernsby started on the close end of the north, and they proceeded with their search while Miss Taylor occupied herself in the kitchen. Hulda would contact BIKER as well, though if the history of the house wasn't in the file Myra had initially given her, Hulda doubted the institution knew anything else.

"Search for journals, biographies, wedged newspapers," Hulda murmured as she put one hardcover back and selected another, "anything of the like. Even a name printed on the inside cover."

"*The Anatomy of Galapagos Sea Turtles*," Mr. Fernsby read. "You don't suppose our ghost is a turtle, do you?"

Hulda snorted. "He is a very intelligent turtle if so." The book in her hands proved to be a receipt book with no helpful markings.

The next book was an old sketchbook used by an artist of little talent, only an eighth full at best. No names or dates, just birds, trees, and monsters. That was followed by *Utopia* by Thomas More and volume 3 of *Shakespeare*. Hulda wondered who the bookworm was who'd stocked these shelves, or if the collection had been built over time since the invention of the printing press. She highly doubted the spirit wizard was a reader, the way he treated these spines.

A book near her shoulder started to wiggle free on its own. Hulda shoved it back into place and said, "Not now. Do you want us to help you or not?"

Whether the wizard *wanted* to be parted from the house was another question entirely, but Hulda had yet to clarify her purpose where the being could hear. Regardless, the book stayed put.

Mr. Fernsby chuckled softly.

She glanced over the rim of her glasses, which made his edges fuzzy. "What?"

He flipped a page in the small book in his hand, closed it, and held it up. "Something called *Hills of Heather*. Looks to be an Irish romance." He turned the book over in his hands. "My sister loved to read things like this."

Mention of his sister sparked something uncomfortable in Hulda's chest, like she'd swallowed the burr atop a long blade of grass. "Mr. Fernsby, if I may ask you a personal question."

He met her eyes, but she didn't utter a word until his head dipped in consent.

"Why did you live with Mr. Portendorfer? Are you . . . estranged from your family?"

"Oh. Ha." He returned the book, moving his gaze squarely to the shelf in front of him. "We are that, yes. Family politics, really. You know. General nonsense." He shifted for the door. "Say, where is Miss Taylor? I wanted her opinion on something. Be right back to do"—he waved his hand broadly—"this."

And with that, he slipped into the hallway, evading the conversation entirely.

Hulda wondered if it would have been better not to have asked.

Chapter 15

September 15, 1846, Blaugdone Island, Rhode Island

The following morning, Merritt and Hulda took the enchanted skiff across the Narragansett Bay at speed. Although cramped for two, it got them safely to shore. From there, they hopped an unenchanted coach, as most were, to Portsmouth, where they would look into the matter of the unwanted ghost. All in all, the trip took about an hour.

Merritt helped Hulda off the coach and guided her to the edge of the busy street. "Nearly forgot the rest of the world exists, being out on that island." Hands in his trouser pockets, he took in the tall buildings and the numerous faces, the smell of horses and something sweet baking nearby, the sight of cobbled roads.

"And much more of it outside Portsmouth." Hulda tugged on the hem of her gloves, securing them to her fingers, looking even more like a faux Englishwoman. "Best for you to start at the city building and then move on to the local library. I'll accompany you to the first."

Merritt frowned and moved in step with her. "You make it sound like you're not attending."

She peeked at him over her glasses. "I told you I was visiting BIKER today."

"I thought that was *after*."

Hulda clicked her tongue. "Two birds with one stone, Mr. Fernsby. I hardly think you need me holding your hand while you inquire about your property."

Merritt grinned. "Mrs. Larkin, are you flirting with me?" The morbid shock that covered her face made him laugh out loud. "Offering to hold my hand in a public place—"

She whapped him with her umbrella, which had been hanging off her forearm. "*Do* be appropriate, Mr. Fernsby!" She blew out a puff of air. "I shall have to warn any future replacement that you have a tendency to go rogue."

He tripped over his own feet. "Replacement? Already?"

They paused on a corner. A wagon passed by. "Of course, Mr. Fernsby. I'm not intended as a permanent employee. My specialties lie with identifying and taming an enchanted home's magic and training staff to maintain it. Then I move on to the next project—wherever it is BIKER needs me. Besides, once this business with the wizard is complete, it will be up to you whether or not you want to continue on with a routine housekeeper, maid of all work, or not. BIKER won't be involved once the enchantments are moot." Her voice dipped with disappointment. "There *are* relevant résumés in the documents I gave you." She raised one eyebrow before crossing the street.

Merritt hurried to keep up with her, his stomach sinking. "B-But I don't want a new housekeeper or maid of whatever. I've just gotten used to you. You want me to do this horrid dance all over again?"

"I don't recall dancing." But her lip ticked up, which was always a good sign.

"Oh please, Mrs. Larkin." They reached the next corner, and he grasped both her hands and dropped to his knees. Her eyes went wide as dollars. "Please stay!"

She jerked from his grip. "Mr. Fernsby! People are looking!"

The utter horror that painted her features had him popping up off the sidewalk immediately. "I suppose I can't embarrass you into staying on longer?"

She gave him a stern look. "I beg you to keep your gregarious disposition to yourself." Her mouth worked. "I *suppose* I could speak to BIKER about *temporarily* extending my stay."

He grinned. "Then you *didn't* request the nastiest and most expensive of your acquaintances to assail my house?"

Her mouth was hesitant to smile, but he got a decent arc out of it. "Obviously that was an exaggeration."

She started walking, so he fell into step behind her. "Means we're good friends, that," he teased, trying to irk a smile from her. "I'm thinking, given your inevitable abandonment of—"

Hulda stopped midstride, causing Merritt to bump into her shoulder. He expected her to whirl around and scold him, but her eyes remained fixed on something across the street, in the direction of a clock shop. Her stance was stiff, her face pale, like she was going to be sick.

Merritt gingerly touched her arm. "Hulda?"

She stepped back, nearly colliding with him, into a narrow alley between buildings, never taking her eyes off . . .

Merritt couldn't tell. He squinted, examining the shop, the people next to it, passing by—

Hulda let out a long breath.

"Are you all right?" he pressed.

She shook herself. Smoothed her skirt. "I . . . am perfectly fine, thank you."

"What were you looking at?"

"It's nothing, Mr. Fernsby."

"It's obviously something." He stepped in front of her, blocking both her view and her way out. The muscles in his arms and chest twitched, like he was ready for a physical confrontation.

But she shook her head. "You need not concern yourself."

A spike of offense shot through him. "Why would I not concern myself with you?"

She paused. Glanced up at him. Away. Adjusted her glasses. Took a deep breath.

"Hulda—"

"I thought I saw someone is all," she finally answered, staring at the alley wall. "An old employer of mine. It surprised me."

Merritt contemplated this. "Was he . . . unkind?"

She chewed on the inside of her lip. "In truth, he's supposed to be in prison."

"Oh." He turned, scanning the street again. "Perhaps just a doppelgänger—"

"Yes, perhaps." But she didn't sound like she believed it. She was shaken. Merritt had never seen anything disturb Hulda before, and he lived in a damnable enchanted house with her.

She took a steadying breath. "I think I should get to Boston, Mr. Fernsby. The city building is just three blocks that way." She pointed.

"I'll walk you to the tram." He stepped onto the street.

"Unnecessary, but thank—"

"Please." His voice was low and resolute. He held out his elbow. "Let me walk you to the tram."

She hesitated a heartbeat before nodding. "If you insist. I might be a while, so don't wait up for me." She took his arm.

He thought he heard a faint *thank you* under her breath, but it might have been the passing of a carriage.

∽

Silas Hogwood.

That was who Hulda had seen.

Her thoughts lingered on him as the kinetic tram followed its track north, fueled by magic nearly as old as the country. It was a wide sort of bus without seats, save for a few chairs along the south wall. Everyone else held on to poles and railings. Hulda stood near the doors, her bag under one arm, her other snaked securely around a pole as the tram gently jostled her back and forth, back and forth.

Silas had been the owner of Gorse End, an enchanted mansion Hulda had worked at shortly after joining BIKER, near Liverpool in England. He was a charismatic man and a fair employer.

He was also a murderer and a thief.

Hulda closed her eyes, pushing against surfacing memories that were a decade old. Memories of disappearing guests; of crazed eyes; of shrunken, mutated bodies, dry and crinkled as old raisins.

Her stomach clenched, and a shiver crossed the span of her shoulders. Silas Hogwood was the most powerful wizard she knew, because *somehow* he had learned to extract the magic out of others. She was sure that's what he'd done, though *how* was another question entirely. He'd never seemed overly interested in *her* abilities, but then again, they were negligible.

Silas Hogwood was supposed to be in prison. Hulda knew, because she had been the one to put him there.

Mr. Fernsby is right. It's probably just someone with similar features. She squeezed the pole tighter. *Why would he be free, let alone across the Atlantic and in Portsmouth? Be reasonable, Hulda.*

But it had looked so much like him. *So much* like him. And Hulda didn't think of him too often, not anymore. Surely it wasn't a mere projection of her mind.

She was grateful for Mr. Fernsby's interference, even if he had only escorted her to the tram. There was still a slight tremor in her fingers.

It was a good thing she was visiting BIKER. Myra would know what to do.

Hulda could not seem to keep her stride at a reasonable pace. She hastened from the tram, she speed-walked down the Boston streets, and she speed-walked to the back of the Bright Bay Hotel and up the stairs to BIKER's offices.

Miss Steverus looked up from her reception desk as Hulda blustered in. "Mrs. Larkin! What a surprise!" She glanced down at some notes. "I don't have you written down for today. Everything all right?"

"Just fine, thank you." She patted her hair, hoping it wasn't too much of a mess. "Is Myra in?" She started for the office.

Miss Steverus flipped through some notes. "I don't see any appointments—"

Hulda gripped the knob and opened the door.

Myra, sitting at her desk, startled, hand flying to her breast. "Hulda! My goodness, you startled me!" She paused. "Whatever is the matter?"

Hulda shut the door behind her and dropped her bag on the nearest chair. "A few things to discuss. To start, Whimbrel House is possessed by a wizard, and—"

"Possession! I'm not surprised." Myra tapped a pencil to her lip. "And how is the owner liking it? Mr. . . . ." She pulled out a ledger.

"Fernsby. He seems to be taking to the house and our administrations well, but he's not fond of ghosts." Her thoughts were spinning, and she desperately tried to organize them. Sucked in a deep breath through her nose to steady herself. *One thing at a time, Hulda.* "He wants the spirit exorcised." *Stop fidgeting.*

Myra's face fell. "Does he? He won't be convinced otherwise?"

Hulda rolled her lips together, considering, bossing her thoughts into a single row so she could process one at a time. "He . . . may be convinced yet. I think he's becoming fond of the place; he turned down an interested buyer, for the time being."

Myra looked a little stiff. "I see."

"But I'm doing the necessary research, regardless of the outcome."

"As you should."

Hulda nodded. "On that errand, I did want to see if BIKER had any information on Whimbrel House not included in the initial file."

Her employer's lips pulled into a frown. She stood and paced to the window. "I'm afraid not—that was everything I could easily pull when the news came in. But I could have Sadie check the library downstairs, just to be sure."

"I don't mind checking it myself. I would like to return to the island tonight."

Myra waved her permission. "Is that all? You could have sent a note, Hulda." A slight smile curled her lips. "Always so thorough. That's what makes you invaluable."

Hulda bit back a smile of her own. "A few other matters." Another deep breath. "That is, we've only hired a single staff member, thus far—"

"How is Miss Taylor faring?"

"Quite well. She's a good find."

Myra rubbed her chin. "Indeed. She has quite the story, if you ever care to ask her."

"I will have to do that."

"I might as well tell you while I'm thinking of it—that request you sent in for a cook? She already hired out and is on her way to Connecticut."

"Of course she is." Hulda removed her glasses and rubbed the bridge of her nose. "I'll ask Miss Steverus for some other leads." She reached for her bag handle to occupy her hands, then recalled she'd discarded it. "While I'll see through the exorcism, Mr. Fernsby has also requested that I stay on longer. He is unaccustomed to staff and believes my leaving would be jarring. If there is nothing in BIKER's queue, an extension would be relatively harmless."

Myra raised an eyebrow. "Oh? Not an uncommon request. What are your thoughts on Mr. Fernsby?"

"He is an interesting character," she answered truthfully. "A little eccentric at times, but friendly. He manages stress well. He has a creative mind that often gets caught up in his stories. He's also a clutterbug."

Myra laughed. "I'm sure that has been a challenge for you."

Hulda paused, thinking again of the tram and the alleyway. *Why would I not concern myself with you?*

"But he is kind," she amended, voice softer. Her stiffness dissipated a little. "And considerate."

Myra paced to the desk, gripping the back of the chair and leaning her weight on it. "That is good. You are, of course, welcome to stay until I've an assignment for you elsewhere."

Hulda nodded. "That would benefit the client."

Drumming her fingers on the chair back, Myra asked, "Anything else? You swept in here like a storm."

"I . . ." Hulda fidgeted. Seized an empty chair and brought it over. Sat. Myra followed her lead and sat as well. "I have a problem. Or I might have a problem."

Concerned, Myra leaned forward. "What?"

Hulda appreciated being given the time to put it into her own words, knowing very well that Myra could simply pluck memories of the incident from her mind. "I . . . that is, in Portsmouth just two hours ago . . . I believe I saw Silas Hogwood."

Myra reeled, paling. "Silas Hogwood?" Her mouth worked. "From Gorse End?"

Clasping her hands together, Hulda said, "Yes."

Myra leaned against her backrest and folded her arms. She deliberated for several seconds. "That's just not possible. Are you sure?"

"As sure as I can be with two eyes." She explained where she had been, where he had been, what he had been wearing.

Myra pinched her lips together. Leaned forward. Took up her pencil and began rapping its blunt end against the desk. "May I?"

Nodding, Hulda pulled up the image as crisply as she could. Although she didn't feel Myra's intrusion into her thoughts, she knew she was there, seeing what Hulda had seen. Myra sighed, marking her retreat.

"Mr. Fernsby is not a bad-looking fellow," she commented.

Hulda's face warmed. "Myra, really!"

The woman responded with an uneasy smile, blinking rapidly—a common side effect for psychometry was the dulling of other senses. All magic had countereffects, though most people had so little magic in their blood, they were rarely severe. "They do look similar, I'll give you that," Myra agreed. "But I don't think it was Mr. Hogwood."

"Truly?" Hulda knit her fingers. "Even his manner of dress—"

"You haven't seen him for eleven years," she pressed, gentle. "Mr. Hogwood is locked away. And even if he got out, what would he be doing in Rhode Island, of all places?"

Hulda sank into her chair. "I have told myself that very thing." She knew Mr. Hogwood reasonably well; after all, she'd been in his employ for two years, back when she was a full-time housekeeper. One learned a lot about a person by being their housekeeper. She knew he was terribly tidy. He was kind to those close to him but didn't like meeting new people. He'd kept entire wings of the house to himself because he savored privacy . . . and not just to hide the malevolent crimes he was committing. He was certainly a man set in his ways, and his ways were set in England. Never in all her time knowing him had he even hinted at a desire to leave home.

She offered a sympathetic nod. "Sleep on it. Seeing a fellow who favors him in appearance must have been a shock to the system. Those were . . . unfortunate times, and you were caught in the middle of them. Such memories can't ever truly be put to rest."

Hulda forced herself to relax. "All true, of course. I half wish you could just pluck them from my skull and let me live in blissful nescience."

Myra chuckled. "Unfortunately, not something I can do."

Sighing, Hulda got to her feet. "I'd best go."

"Be sure to ask Miss Steverus for your mail."

Hulda paused. She didn't often get mail sent to BIKER, but it wasn't unheard of. "Thank you, Myra."

"Keep me updated, Hulda. Please." She offered a warm expression.

Hulda returned it, grabbed her bag, and saw herself out. Before she even had a chance to ask, Miss Steverus turned about in her desk and said, "Pulled this for you!" and handed her a crisp envelope. "Looks important."

"Indeed it does." She turned it over in her hand. There was a return address she didn't recognize. "Would you put in a request for a pair of communion stones?"

"Right on it; need to pull some files, anyway." Standing, the receptionist moved down an adjoining hallway to the records room. Hulda sat on one of the available chairs. Might as well read this missive before applying herself to a fruitless hunt in the small BIKER library. Breaking the seal and pulling out the letter, she read,

> *Dear Miss Hulda Larkin,*
> *My name is Elijah Clarke, and I'm the chair for the Genealogical Society for the Advancement of Magic.*

Hulda rolled her eyes. Of course she was being solicited. Still, she read on.

> *We discovered you through your great-grandmother Charlotte "Lottie" Dankworth. As you know, she was a famous carnival diviner and astrologist along the East Coast. We were very excited to see she had descendants! If you're not familiar with GSAM, let me take a moment to introduce the organization.*

Hulda was well aware of what the society did.

Our goal is to study the heritage of magically capable people in hopes of pairing them together to form magically beneficial unions. We believe you have a significant portion of your great-grandmother's talents, given your pedigree, and would love to speak with you further on the matter of propagating magic for generations to come. It is a needful and blessed resource that continues to rapidly decline; we want those of the future to benefit from it as we have.

Please send your reply at the below address. I would love to speak to you about your abilities, options, and future. You will be compensated for your efforts, of course.

Sincerely and with great hope,

Elijah Clarke

Hulda rolled her eyes again—a bad habit she'd formed as a child and was hard pressed to overcome. While the Genealogical Society for the Advancement of Magic had the most magnificent ancestry records in the Western Hemisphere, it was also a glorified organization for arranged marriages. Groups like it had existed for centuries, ever since mankind had realized magic wasn't an unlimited resource. Ultimately, their mission was noble. Yes, the world *would* prosper from the continuation of magic. It provided energy, pushed public transport, grew crops . . . where it still existed, anyway. It was simply unfortunate that the only way to increase its presence in the world was through selective bedding.

Still, perhaps it was hasty of Hulda to dismiss the letter so readily. It felt somewhat invasive to be traced on her great-grandmother's pedigree, but it wasn't like Hulda would ever make a match on her own. She was thirty-four years old and had never even been kissed by a man, let alone courted by one. Peradventure she should hear this Mr. Clarke out, while her body was still capable of creating offspring.

"I don't know," she murmured aloud. "It's just so . . . awkward." And the process would likely be rife with disappointment. She couldn't stand the thought of being paired with a man who would regard her with disgust or disdain. Her heart might shatter.

"My goodness, has someone died?"

Hulda stiffened, smoothing her face and folding up the letter at the sound of Myra's inquiry. "Not at all. I was just thinking."

"Glad I caught you. I have a free hour; would you like help in the library?"

Hulda smiled. "Yes, I would. Thank you."

"Not a problem at all." Myra turned, but Miss Steverus was coming their way, and Hulda didn't have time to warn either of them. The women crashed into one another, sending papers flying.

"Ms. Haigh!" Miss Steverus exclaimed. "I'm so sorry!"

Hulda quickly stood from her chair. "It's all right, let's pick them up."

Myra laughed. "You'd think I'd be able to 'hear' you coming, Sadie." She bent down to pick up papers.

Hulda crouched to reach for one, but her mind registered an odd pattern in the parchments. Before any of them could pick up the first document, a vision flashed through Hulda's mind.

A wolf. A wolf in a . . . library?

Miss Steverus grabbed several papers, destroying the premonition before it had fully manifested. Hulda blinked, trying to recall the shapes and colors. The animal had appeared large, black in color . . . not unlike the wolf she had seen on Blaugdone Island. Then again, wolves didn't have a lot of variety among them, did they? But what on earth would a wolf be doing in a library? Her premonitions were finnicky, but they were unambiguous. She was no dream reader; what she saw was what would be seen, in some indeterminate amount of time. But this was just outlandish. Perhaps, had the papers gone undisturbed, it would have made sense.

Now . . . what had she been doing? Ah, yes, the paperwork. Such a meddlesome thing, to experience the side effects of far-seeing when she hadn't intentionally used her ability. Forgetfulness loved to accompany divination. But what did the vision mean? Her augury was usually more . . . concise . . . than this. And this wasn't the first time it had shown her a large dog.

Was the reading for Myra or Miss Steverus?

"Could you pass me that one, Mrs. Larkin?"

Flashing to the present, Hulda grabbed the paper closest to her and handed it over. "Yes, sorry."

Myra glanced at her. "Did you . . . see something?"

Hulda shook her head. "Nothing important." And it often wasn't.

But after the events of the day, Hulda wasn't comforted by that fact.

Chapter 16

The history of Whimbrel House was so obscure it took Merritt two hours to find the records he sought, which included colonial census records, deed records, and recorded deaths from the Salem witch trials, since the latter had been mentioned in Hulda's file. Still, he cautioned himself not to be too optimistic. Records that old were often spotty, with gaps in the timeline, and the Narragansett Bay tended to be lumped together as a whole without individual islands, when it was bothered to be mentioned apart from Rhode Island itself.

Merritt would have called it a successful enough day, but someone very official looking stopped him on his way out to tell him he couldn't just *take* the records. If he wanted the information, he would have to copy them by hand.

Damnation. "You don't have a secretary on lend, do you?"

The official-looking person merely raised an eyebrow and walked away, glancing back to make sure Merritt didn't make a run for it with the pages. Which he considered, but the man had long legs and could probably outrun him. So with a sigh, Merritt took up a seat by a window and laid out the paperwork. He could already feel the muscle beneath his right thumb cramping.

He started with the census, recording the names of anyone who *might* have lived in the home. The last fifty years were much clearer, and a surge of nostalgia nestled in his bones at the sight of his grandmother's name. An affidavit said she'd won it in a card game.

I didn't think she gambled, Merritt thought with a frown. But there it was in writing.

It was less than comfortable in the city building, so Merritt cracked open the nearest window. He was halfway through the deeds list when he found himself staring down at the city, watching people pass by, taking in the shapes of the surrounding architecture.

His thoughts floated back to Hulda. To the terror that had earlier flashed in her eyes. In that moment she'd seemed . . . younger. Vulnerable. She'd acted like a completely different person on the way to the tram. Quiet. Contemplative. Withdrawn.

An old employer. He tapped his pencil against the side of his nose. *In prison?* Did he have something to do with BIKER? In truth, Merritt knew not a lick about Hulda outside of her profession, except perhaps that she had poor vision and was tidy enough to put a monk to shame. It irked him. He wanted to help, somehow. He wanted to know what ailed her.

"And you'll not find out until you finish this." Merritt glanced at the stack with a sigh. Jotted down another name and another set of dates. By the time he finished the paper, he had to shake feeling back into his hand. He really should learn shorthand.

He moved to the next paper, eyeing the stack with distaste. He should have brought Beth along. She would have fit in the boat . . . if she sat in his lap, perhaps. But that would only create different problems.

Groaning, Merritt leaned his chin into his hand and stared out the window, the faint sound of clopping horse hooves wafting in on the autumn breeze. A woman walked by pushing a pram, followed by a group of adolescents with their heads pushed together, hair stuffed under caps and laughter on their lips. Going the opposite way was a melancholy fellow, shoulders hunched, lips downturned, hole over the left knee of his trousers.

Merritt got an idea. "Hey! Hey, you!"

The man paused and glanced around, taking a few seconds to find the window.

Merritt waved. "I need help scribing something in here, and it's going to take me until midnight if I do it on my own. Can you write?"

The man hesitantly nodded.

"I'll pay you."

The man considered for a moment. Pointed ahead, toward the closest doors. Merritt nodded, and the fellow left, appearing minutes later in the vast records room. He was much taller and broader than he'd appeared out the window.

Merritt waved him over, then shook his hand. "Thank you, my good chum. I need to make copies of all of this." He moved the stack between them as the stranger sat down. "Merritt Fernsby. What's your name?"

"Baptiste," he said, the name spoken in a heavy French accent.

Worried perhaps that he'd called over someone who was only literate in a foreign language, Merritt pressed, "Where are you from, Baptiste? What brings you to Portsmouth?"

Baptiste bent his neck one way, then the other, and it popped loudly. "I am from Nice in France. Been here three months. Had bad luck back home." He shrugged.

Relieved, Merritt said, "Well, hopefully this is good luck today. You take this half"—he handed him several papers—"and I'll take this half." He pulled a second pencil from his shirt pocket. "The quicker and neater you copy them, the more I'll compensate you. Sound fair?"

Baptiste nodded and got to work. His handwriting wasn't perfect, but it was legible, so Merritt set to copying his own papers, drawing out the forks of genealogy and squinting to read smudged names along the tines. He was on his third page when he said, "What do you do for a living?"

Baptiste didn't look up from his work. "Nothing now. Everyone says go farther north for job, but I do not want to work on the railroad or in the steel plants."

"You certainly have the arms for it."

Baptiste merely shrugged and crossed a *T*. "But I do not want to go south, either. I do not like it down there."

"There's lots of work to be had—"

"I do not like it." His tone was final, so Merritt didn't push him. He could easily guess why a person might not want to cross that carefully sketched line that divided the United States.

Merritt copied down another name. "What did you do in France?"

Baptiste sighed, like a long story had disintegrated up his throat and puffed out of him, unintelligible. "I was chef."

Merritt slammed down his pencil, startling the large man. "No! You're joking."

Baptiste finally looked up, his wide forehead wrinkled. "Being chef is funny here?"

"No, not that. I need a chef!" He clapped his hands. "Hulda has been positively pestering me to hire one, and here you are!"

Baptiste leaned away, skeptical, but there was a glimmer of hope in his eyes. "Who is this woman? Your wife?"

Merritt laughed and rubbed the back of his neck. "Ah, no. She's my housekeeper. Or rather, she's someone else's housekeeper but is tending my house on their behalf . . . it's complicated."

Baptiste glanced at the documents, then back up. "You need chef?"

Merritt grinned. "Baptiste, do you believe in ghosts?"

That forehead crinkled even further. ". . . No?"

"Excellent." He slapped the man on the shoulder. "Consider yourself hired."

⁓

Hulda returned to Whimbrel House late; the small fishing boat she'd hired to take her out to the island dropped her off as dusk was starting to settle and the lighthouses sprang to life. There was enough light for her to slip past leathery grape fern and multiflora roses. A path was already starting to form in the long grass, making the way easier. Drawing a deep breath, Hulda absorbed the sweet scent of chrysanthemum and let it fill her, easing the tension of the day. *One thing at a time,* she reminded herself. *Only worry about yourself.* It was advice she had to inculcate often, as she frequently wished she could take control of others' lives for a little while, if only to make the world a more organized place.

As for Silas Hogwood . . . she would do as Myra recommended and sleep on it.

Lifting her skirts, she stepped onto the porch and opened the front door—unlocked, but who else was going to let themselves in? And promptly screamed.

There was a large heathenish man in the reception hall.

He also yelped and nearly dropped a barrel he was carrying on his shoulder. Before Hulda could think to fight or flee, Miss Taylor dashed into the room, both hands reaching toward her. "It's okay, Mrs. Larkin! He's the new chef!"

Hulda clutched the doorframe, waiting for her heart to calm down. Her eyes darted from the large, dark-haired man to Miss Taylor. "I haven't put in for a chef!"

"Mr. Fernsby hired him." Miss Taylor moved slowly toward her, like she was a startled deer. "Met him in Portsmouth."

"I hear that Mrs. Larkin is home!" Mr. Fernsby called from upstairs.

The large man set down the barrel and bowed slightly at the waist. "My name is Baptiste Babineaux," he said in a thick French accent.

Straightening, he glanced around, stiff as the wall itself. "I will go to kitchen now."

Hefting the barrel, he passed into the dining room. The portrait on the wall craned to watch him go, apparently just as curious as Hulda was.

Mr. Fernsby came down the stairs, grabbing the rail tightly as the steps suddenly resized themselves. "Welcome home! Find anything useful?"

Clutching her bag, Hulda stepped in and kicked the door shut behind her. "I thought I was in charge of the hiring?"

"I took initiative! Aren't you proud?" He grinned and jumped the last few steps. "I needed help copying information at the city building, and Baptiste was short a few coins. Turns out he's a chef! From France! Isn't that something?"

Hulda crossed the reception hall to peek into the dining room, but Mr. Babineaux had already passed into the kitchen. Seemed the house was fine with him. "But accommodations—" She'd assumed the chef, if one was hired, would take up her room once she departed.

Miss Taylor whispered, "There's a new room."

She blinked. "What?"

"New room," the maid repeated. "The house made him some space just off the kitchen."

Hulda paused. "A house can't simply make new space."

Miss Taylor shrugged. "Our rooms are a little smaller now."

So it had *moved* space. Hulda considered this for a moment. "I suppose that is fair." Turning her attention to Mr. Fernsby, she asked, "Have you vetted him? Do you have his history?"

Mr. Fernsby shrugged. "He made a very good soup for dinner. He's been in the States three months and wasn't able to find work. I thought I'd give him a chance."

Hulda softened. "I suppose that's kind of you, Mr. Fernsby. We'll have to see to it that he has what he needs. And I will interview him in the morning."

Mr. Fernsby shrugged. "Do as you wish."

Miss Taylor quietly excused herself and started up the stairs. The house didn't challenge her.

Opening her bag, Hulda said, "I have a list of lighthouse workers for the bay, which might line up with previous owners and help us close in on an estimated build date."

"As do I. And I copied as many genealogical charts as I could for potential matches."

Hulda paused. "Oh. That's good." It had always been magical institutions that historically valued genealogy, but their research was useful for local government as well. "We can evaluate them in the morning. Unless you'd like to simply tell us who you are?" She directed the question to the ceiling.

The house didn't respond. Perhaps it was busy haunting Mr. Babineaux.

Glancing over his shoulder, Mr. Fernsby stepped within whispering distance. "Are you all right? After that scare in Portsmouth?"

Hulda drew into herself. "Perfectly fine, Mr. Fernsby. I realized later that it could not possibly have been him—"

"Been who?"

She ruminated for a moment. "Mr. Silas Hogwood. He was my first client after I joined BIKER, and I ended up hiring on to his staff." She stepped around him, to the stairs. Best to see exactly how the house had rearranged her things. "But it's behind me now."

"May I ask," he added with a surprising hesitance, "what he was convicted of?"

Hulda's hand squeezed the railing. *No harm in answering, is there?* "Misuse of magic, to put it simply. He was a very charismatic and diabolical man. His greed for power led him to do unspeakable things."

Twisted bodies, dried out and folded like accordions. A wicked gleam in his eye. Hulda shook the images away.

When Mr. Fernsby didn't respond, Hulda climbed her way up the stairs. She was nearly to the top when he called up to her. "Mrs. Larkin."

She turned around. He'd come to the bottom of the steps. His usual mirth was absent from his face, rendering it long and stern.

"You're safe here. I hope you know that," he offered.

The reassurance pricked her chest. She nodded. "Thank you, Mr. Fernsby."

She walked through the hall, the wizard in residence just missing her when he—or she—made the paint start falling in flashes of purple and yellow. She ducked into her room. It wasn't particularly shrunken; Mr. Babineaux's space had to be relatively small. Did he have a bed, or a pallet on the floor? She'd have to catalog the change in the morning.

Setting her bag on the bed, Hulda shook out her arms, forcing newly tense muscles to ease. She crossed to the small oval mirror on the wall, provided by herself, and peered into it. Took off her glasses, cleaned them on her skirt, and put them back on. *Sleep on it,* she reminded herself, and turned away, plucking hair pins from her scalp. She'd stopped at a street vendor before heading back into the Narragansett, but even then her appetite had been wanting. She needed some rest to clear her head.

With the last pin gone, Hulda shook out her hair, which fell a hand's length below her shoulders—an adequate length for the styles that were currently in fashion. Hulda didn't care much for fashion, but she did want to be presentable at all times, so she had to keep up with it to a degree. The mess was a third straight, a third wavy, and a third curly, from how it had been tucked and pressed. She pulled it back into a braid and crossed to the window, peering out. She couldn't see much. Without city lights, the island got dark as pitch once the sun settled down, the bay around it illuminated only by lighthouses, none of which she could see out her window. A few streaks of dying plum twilight highlighted a passing swallow and a distant elm.

You're safe here. Mr. Fernsby's voice echoed in her thoughts. And she was, wasn't she? Not even her family knew she was out in the middle of nowhere off the coast of Rhode Island; she hadn't written to them yet. Something she should do . . . but perhaps without specifics, until she worked through this morning's scare. The fewer people who could be compelled to provide that information, the better. Besides, there was no need to worry them. There were two men in the house now, as well, one of them more aware than he let on, one of them large enough to join the White House militia. Then again, the right spells could get around size and smarts.

Why would I not concern myself with you?

A smile tempted her. A prick stung her heart.

And almost immediately, mortification overwhelmed her.

"Oh no," she muttered, stepping away from the window. Shaking out her hands. "No, Hulda, we are *not* doing this again."

It was just a little spark, nothing important. But sparks led to embers led to flames, so it had to be snuffed *now*, before her heart again crumbled to ash.

Not only was it inappropriate to indulge in any sort of pining over a client, but Hulda . . . Hulda wasn't made for pining. Not mutual pining, at least. Never in all her thirty-four years had any man, of any station or background, looked at her with any amount of sweetness. And when she got moon eyed over one or the other, it always ended in embarrassment, or heartbreak, or both. She had gotten rather numb to it after all this time, but a silly part of her still squeezed through now and then, and she loathed it more than anything else, including socks by the kitchen sink. A perk of being a consultant for BIKER rather than contracted staff—she usually didn't stay around long enough to form any significant attachment.

Perhaps because Silas Hogwood was on her mind today, her thoughts drifted back to Stanley Lidgett, who had been his steward at Gorse End. Hulda had been only twenty-one at the time, still hopeful and perhaps a little desperate. Although twenty years her senior, Mr. Lidgett had carried himself well, bore a strong jaw, and worked with a logical effectiveness she'd admired. She recalled stupidly curling her hair every morning, cinching her corset a little tighter, always seeking him out to ask after his day or bring him his favorite tarts from the kitchen. Her affections were probably obvious to the man, and he'd addressed her with withering contempt after Mr. Hogwood's arrest. Perhaps he'd known about the magical siphoning, perhaps not—regardless, he was fiercely loyal to his employer and very blatantly disgusted with Hulda.

He'd called her ugly, and a rat. She'd heard the first before. Never the second.

She'd sobbed the entire way back to the States.

Shortly after returning to her home country, she'd overheard another interest of hers mocking her mannerisms at a local restaurant. It was then she'd accepted her old-maid status. Once she resigned herself to it, she was able to focus on more important things, like her work. She'd stopped divining for herself. She'd stopped pinching her cheeks. Stopped adding lace to her dresses.

And she'd done very well for herself. Very well, indeed. She would greatly prefer to continue that trend.

Sitting on the edge of her mattress, Hulda set her spectacles on the side table and dropped her head into her hands. "It is good that you have a kind client," she told herself, enunciating every word. "How very fortunate for you. And it will be equally good to sort out this business with the wizard so you can move on. Do your job, Hulda. No one wants anything else from you."

Resolute with that plan, Hulda stripped off the day's dress, washed her face, and blew out her candle. *Sleep on it,* she admonished.

Something crunched when she laid her head on her pillow. Confused, she reached up to find a small, gauzy parcel she hadn't noticed before. Sitting up, she relit her candle and nearly cried.

There was a gauzy bag of lemon drops on her pillow, tied off with a yellow ribbon.

And only Mr. Fernsby could have left it.

Chapter 17

A few days after hiring Baptiste, Merritt groggily woke to the sun in his eyes—he'd forgotten to close the drapes last night. The remnants of a strange dream clung to the inside of his skull. Something about a giant tree and talking goats and the Mississippi River being a deity, but the more he tried to piece it together, the more disjointed it became, until he felt like he was trying to drink clouds and couldn't remember any details at all.

Rubbing his eye, he propped himself up on one elbow and glared at the window.

Then promptly froze, breath caught halfway up his throat.

That was not *his* window. The drapes were wrong, and so was the carpeting. And that dresser . . . it wasn't his, nor was the mirror above it. His confusion only mounted when he saw his dresser was still here, against the wall closest to him. His wall, his corner, his laundry basket. But beside the laundry basket . . . part of that wall was not his wall. It was white compared to his cream. And the other half of his bed was not his bed. The blankets didn't match, and in fact appeared to have been messily fused with his own.

But more importantly, there was a woman sleeping in them. Specifically, Hulda Larkin.

He gaped at her, alarm running up his navel and refracting off his sternum and into his limbs. He desperately tried to remember last night—

Only, the half of the bed Hulda was in wasn't *his* bed.

He let out a tense breath. The house had shifted again, during the night! Reforming bedrooms, cutting his and the housekeeper's in half and gluing them together!

And he didn't have pants on.

Cool sweat broke over his forehead as he secured the blanket to his hips and tried to figure if it would be better to sneak away or to wake Hulda immediately. Neither could end well.

He scooted toward the edge of the mattress, making a vow to start sleeping fully clothed from now on.

As he pushed his feet over the edge, he glanced back at Hulda, ensuring she was still asleep. She was, probably because she was lying on her side, her back turned to the window. The blanket rested across her ribs, revealing the gauzy sleeves of her nightgown. Her hair fell over one shoulder in a braid that was barely still plaited; most of the walnut locks had freed themselves and waved over her neck and pillow. She didn't wear her glasses, of course.

He'd never noticed her eyelashes before. They were dark and full and splayed across the crest of her cheeks. And the way the morning sun poured from the window . . . she looked almost angelic.

Then he noticed that her nightgown dipped, revealing a good eyeful of milky cleavage.

Admittedly, he stared at that for a few seconds longer than he should have. He ought not to have stared at all. But he was a man, and . . . God help him, she was going to murder him.

It's not *my fault!* his thoughts spat as he sped from the mattress and grabbed yesterday's trousers, pulling them on with impressive speed. He'd determined to sneak away and alert Beth, have *her* wake Hulda, when he turned and saw the portrait from the reception hall was standing upright on the carpet, watching him with an impish smile.

Merritt shrieked. Hulda bolted upright. It took only a few heartbeats for her to shriek as well.

"Where am I?" Her accusing eyes landed on him as she snatched the blanket and shielded herself.

Trying to tamp down his flustered nerves, Merritt managed, "It would seem the house decided two bedrooms should be one during the night." Then, in self-defense, "I only just discovered it myself."

Admittedly, it was fascinating to watch Hulda's face darken to the redness of a high-summer rose.

He backed away. "I'll . . . get Miss Taylor." He nearly knocked over the portrait in his haste to escape, unsure if the ensuing sound of mortification was from the door hinges or Hulda's mouth.

Might be better for the both of them if he didn't find out.

◦

Suddenly Mr. Culdwell back in New York did not seem as bad a landlord as Merritt had always thought him. *He* had never rearranged his things—his furniture, his windows, his *walls*—while he slept. Lord knew he'd had enough of magic to last him the rest of his life.

All the more reason to get on with the exorcism. He buttered a piece of toast. Baptiste had already eaten—he made it a habit to eat before anyone else did, but that might be due to the fact that he woke up before anyone else, including Hulda, who kept a schedule so rigid even the military would be impressed.

Her schedule was, understandably, not so rigid today. She came to breakfast late, her shoulders stiff and her nose high, a folder of papers in her hands.

Merritt perked up. "Do tell me you've discovered who our wizard is."

Pulling out a chair, Hulda sat. "I'm afraid not, Mr. Fernsby. I've only just started sorting through them. Though you'll be pleased to know the house is fixing its second floor."

A snap of wood upstairs punctuated the statement.

The slightest flush could be discerned under Hulda's eyes. Merritt determined he would say nothing more on the matter other than "Thank you," as he assumed it was Hulda's expertise that had convinced this wretched house to put itself back into order.

Setting down his half-eaten toast, he said, "Remind me why a wizard inhabits a house."

"Usually two reasons," she answered without glancing up, pulling out papers from the file. "They've been tethered to it somehow, or their life purpose was unfulfilled in some important way. But a person must have significant magical ability to move their spirit into an inanimate body. Not just anyone can do it, which is why it's becoming a less common phenomenon."

"Could *you* do it?"

She glanced his way. There were flecks of green in her eyes. "No. And I wouldn't want to, besides."

"But what if you knew you were doomed for hell?"

She sighed like a tired nanny. "Really, Mr. Fernsby."

He shrugged. "Just saying." Leaning forward, he looked over his census notes and reached for a paper with dates in the seventeen hundreds. "So if we need a magic fellow, it's likely to be someone further back, before magic diluted."

She peered at his page. "Possibly, but not necessarily. Magic usually subtracts, but with the right parentage—"

"It adds," he finished.

She nodded. "May I?"

He handed the paper to her. She scanned it. "I wish they included more information. But I suppose we weren't a real country yet."

Something like the shattering of glass, but in reverse, echoed from upstairs, making him wonder whether Beth had gotten downstairs before the house's realignment. Just how slowly had the house shifted in the night, so as not to wake anyone? *Sneaky.*

"Does the body . . . have to be close?" He rubbed gooseflesh from his arms. "The wizard's, I mean. Does his body have to be *in* the thing he inhabits?"

"Not *in* it, but one can hardly travel far as a spirit. The wizard would have had to be quite close. On the island itself, I'd say."

Merritt lifted his feet. "You don't think its corpse is under the floor-boards, do you?" A shiver ran down his spine like a hungry spider.

Hulda slammed down the paper. "Of course! Are there any marked graves near the house?"

"No. Well . . ." He glanced out the window. "I've been focused on other things and admittedly haven't toured the entire island. The grass is so long, it could hide just about anything."

"If we can find graves"—excitement leaked into her voice—"that will narrow it down. These documents state who *lived* here, not who *died* here. Very smart, Mr. Fernsby." She stood.

Merritt followed her lead. "Of course. I just . . . wanted you to figure it out on your own."

She was already out the door.

Frowning, Merritt called, "Are we not going to finish breakfast?"

൭

After enlisting Beth's and Baptiste's aid, the four of them ventured outside, Hulda leading the way. Merritt paused near the empty clothesline, adjusting his scarf as he slowly scanned the island. *His* island. That was still such a bizarre thing. For a while, he'd wondered if his grandmother had bequeathed it to him as a curse. But in truth, the place had proven to be a pleasant adventure.

Except for the merging of his and Hulda's bedrooms. And the shrinking lavatory.

Just think how pleasant it will be when the house is just a house again. His stomach tightened a hair at the thought. He saw Beth and Baptiste holding back and called, "Well, let's split up. We're looking for grave markers."

Beth's eyes widened slightly. Baptiste shrugged one shoulder.

"Miss Taylor to the east"—that was the smallest section of land, relevant to the house—"Baptiste south. Mrs. Larkin, do you have a preference for north or west?"

"I will take the west, Mr. Fernsby. The north has been thoroughly trotted from all the traipsing back and forth to and from the boat."

"Only one part of it," he countered.

The four of them split up. Beth walked slowly, running her hands over the top of the grasses, and Baptiste headed for a short hill for a better vantage point. Hulda marched straight ahead, perhaps thinking to start on the beach and work her way back.

Merritt began at the house and walked back and forth through the grass, moving north by a pace every time he turned. Reeds bowed under his feet; weeds crunched. He startled a cottontail on his fifth pass. "Sorry," he offered, though the thing was so quick it likely hadn't heard him.

He squelched around a small pond—more of a large puddle, really—surrounded by common reed. Probably not a good place for a grave. But was anywhere in a marsh a *good* place to bury a body?

What would they do if they came up empty-handed?

How long would it take him to simply cut down eighteen acres?

He was on his twenty-seventh pass when a breeze blew from the Atlantic, rustling the tall grass around his knees. The way it flowed over the meadow made it look like an ocean itself, green and gold. He searched the ripples for a cross, a stone, a break in the plants, but saw nothing. *Where are you, wizard?*

Something pulled his mind northwest. He ignored it, continuing on his back-and-forth path, but it tugged again, as if someone were groggily saying, *Over there.*

He glanced back at the house. He'd wandered some ways from it, but it was still there, perhaps watching all of them. Did it know what they were doing?

Licking his lips, Merritt changed direction and moved northwest, scanning the grass, running his fingers along its tallest tips as Beth had done. A hare watched him warily from behind an elm, ears twitching. A spindly weed as tall as his shoulder swayed with the breeze.

He stubbed the toe of his shoe on a rock.

"Surely not," he said, and parted the grass.

Not was right. It was just a rock.

Sighing, Merritt released the plants, only to spy a sliver of slate through them just as they closed.

Moving over a few feet, he parted the grass again.

There, as high as his shin, was a weathered rock embedded in the ground upright. Years had crumbled away its edges and face, but there was a distinct 7 on it.

He grinned. "I found something!"

Grabbing handfuls of grass, he began yanking it from the ground, clearing space around the stone. By the time Hulda and Beth came running over, he'd found a second similar stone, a little smaller, a few feet away.

Baptiste might not have heard him.

"Brilliant," Hulda said, helping him tug away grass. Beth announced she'd found a third, and bent the surrounding plants at their bases, stepping on their stalks to encourage them to lie flat.

Four stones in all, one clustered near the initial two, one of them fallen over.

Hulda ran her hand over one of them. "Hardly legible. Beth, would you search the area and see if there are any more?"

Nodding, Beth set off walking toe to heel, prowling like a puma.

Merritt had brought out a notebook and pencil from the library; he tore out a page and placed it against the first gravestone, then dragged the edge of the pencil lead back and forth to make a rubbing. The *7* came through clearly, as well as a birthday that said *162*, the last digit of the year consumed by time.

He held up the rubbing to Hulda. "O . . . A-C-E. That's the first name. And M-A . . . E-L."

After tearing out a second paper, Merritt handed it and the pencil over, and Hulda took a rubbing of the second stone. The family name on the fourth stone had been preserved well enough for them to read it in full: *Mansel*. It seemed they were all Mansels.

Merritt snapped his fingers. "Horace." He pointed at the gaps between the letters in the first rubbing. "H-O-R-A-C-E. I bet his name was Horace."

Hulda nodded. "It certainly fits."

The wife's name was indiscernible. But with some sleuthing and guessing, they determined the other two graves belonged to Dorcas and Helen.

"All daughters," Merritt commented. "How terrible for dear Horace. No wonder he chose to stay behind. Needed a break from all the femininity."

Hulda scoffed. "I'm sure." She wrote down the names and what they'd been able to glean of the dates. "This is good. This is a start. The Genealogical Society might have this on record. They're very thorough. Even if these persons weren't magically inclined, they might still have records for them."

Miss Taylor returned, holding up empty hands. "No others around here, Mrs. Larkin."

"Good. That narrows it down more." Standing, Hulda brushed off her skirt. "I think we should still check the rest of the island, but there's seldom reason to scatter the dead, and given the house's history, I doubt we'll find any other grave markers here. Still, best to be thorough."

Merritt stood as well, ignoring his muddy knees. "And what if the Gen Society doesn't know anything?" He blanched. "We won't have to exhume them, will we?"

"I hope not," she retorted, and Merritt's stomach turned.

Miss Taylor asked, "Could we not ask the wizard which one she is?"

"And why would she answer?" Hulda looked sidelong at Merritt and lowered her voice. "Mr. Fernsby wants to exorcise her."

Merritt shrugged. "Can you blame me?"

She glanced down at the rubbings, and a twinge of guilt wormed through his stomach. "I suppose not. It's early enough in the day that I could leave for Boston now." She stood quickly, and Merritt caught a distinct tearing sound. Turning sideways, Hulda clicked her tongue and held up her skirt. Part of the hem was thoroughly torn. "What a bother. But I'm not surprised. I've mended that same spot twice already."

Merritt shifted weight from foot to foot. "Do you want to change before you go?"

She waved away the question with a quick flick of her hand.

"You should see if you can find any communion stones," Miss Taylor suggested. "So we can talk to you when you're away."

Hulda nodded. "I requested them; I'll have to see if they've arrived." New stones were hard to come by, due to the dilution. But not impossible.

Merritt reached into his pocket, though he'd left his wallet in his room. "Do you need fare or anything? Company?"

For some reason, the offer had Hulda stiffening. "Not at all, Mr. Fernsby. This is BIKER work; they will cover the costs. And I am quite used to doing things on my own."

She didn't even look at him when she spoke, which had him thinking back on their conversation and wondering if he'd said something wrong. When he determined he hadn't, he decided Hulda must simply be prickly in the mornings.

"I'll at least walk you to the boat. Work on tramping that path. Beth, would you go collect Baptiste? I very much want to eat whatever he made this morning."

With a dip of her head, Beth marched southward.

 ᘓ

Hulda was grateful to leave Rhode Island.

She had a tendency to overthink things. She knew this about herself. Those closest to her—her family, Myra—knew that about her, too. Sometimes having a mind running as hot as a steamboat had its advantages. It made Hulda productive. She was an excellent juggler of tasks and an expert on many subjects.

But sometimes it tortured her, especially when her thoughts fell outside the comfortable realm of logic. And nothing was more illogical than emotions.

And so, leaning against the side of the speeding kinetic tram on her way to Boston, she found herself analyzing her every interaction with Mr. Fernsby this morning thrice over to ensure she had been strictly professional and nothing more. Only after she finished the third evaluation did she feel comfortable, certain that she'd maintained her decorous position.

She hadn't had any of the lemon drops yet. In truth, she was afraid to, like they might be some sort of ambrosia that would warp both mind and resolve and transmute her into a desperate twenty-year-old again.

She sighed. *Another reason not to read fiction. Really, Hulda.*

She'd telegrammed ahead to the Genealogical Society; they should be expecting her. The kinetic tram had a stop close to their headquarters, so Hulda wouldn't need to hire additional transportation. She should

be excited about the work ahead, for she'd always liked solving mysteries. There was something incredibly validating about sorting through
questions to find an encompassing resolution. In this case, though, she
partially dreaded the answer. Once they had the wizard's identity set, she
would have to exorcise the fellow, leaving Whimbrel House as ordinary
as the next place. Of course, she'd truly have no need to stay after that.
She and Miss Taylor both would be recycled elsewhere. Which was a
good thing.

She ignored the displeasure weighing down her lungs as she strode
from the station and onto familiar Boston streets, her sensible shoes
clacking on the cobbles.

The building for the Genealogical Society for the Advancement
of Magic was impressive; four times the size of the hotel that accom-
modated BIKER's offices. A sculpture of a great tree stood in front of
it, and Grecian columns coddled the doors, which were heavy, Hulda
noted as she pulled one open and slipped inside. The ceiling was high in
the large reception space she entered, which had an enormous half-circle
desk. The man behind it looked frail, though he couldn't have been any
older than forty.

He stood immediately. "Miss Larkin?"

Her title of *Mrs.* didn't exist here. "I am."

"Excellent." He stepped around the desk. "Right this way. Mr.
Clarke took lunch in his office so he wouldn't miss you."

Hulda blinked away surprise. "Very kind of him."

They passed the stairs and took a hallway north, then east, to a
large office without any doors. It had a smattering of bookcases within,
a heavy oak desk, and a large window, the sill of which was completely
covered in various ferns. A taxidermy head of a buck jutted out from
the rightmost wall.

The man on the other side of the desk set down a half-eaten sandwich and stood. He looked to be about sixty, with a nose possibly more
prominent than Hulda's own, though while hers protruded in the

bridge, his stretched forward at the tip. He had dark eyes and white hair. That is, where he still had hair, in a ring above his ears and chops that ran down his cheeks. His smile was pleasant as he came toward her, hand extended. "Miss Hulda Larkin?"

She nodded and shook his hand firmly. "I am. Thank you for taking the time to meet with me, Mr. Clarke, especially at the last minute. In truth, I expected to speak with one of your employees."

He gestured for her to sit, and the secretary discreetly left them. "Perfect timing is perfect timing. I hope your travel was fair?"

Hulda sat, propping her bag on her lap. "Quite, thank you."

Mr. Clarke retook his own chair, sliding his lunch off to the side. "I'm so grateful for your response. It's hard for us to find magically capable women who aren't already spoken for or too old to—"

"Mr. Clarke." Hulda was not one to interrupt, but her cheeks were already flushing at his insinuation, and she did not care to further darken them. "You have mistaken me. In my telegram, I stated I was here to research the Mansel name."

Fortunately, Mr. Clarke did not seem insulted—he merely chuckled. "Ah, yes, so you did." Reaching over, he picked up a small piece of paper, the telegram itself. "I was hoping we'd be able to discuss both things."

Hulda straightened as tall as she could in her chair—sometimes a stiff spine made her flushing recede faster, and there were few things she loathed more than being red in the face, especially in front of a man. "I am still . . . considering the other matter of business. But today I'm here on behalf of the Boston Institute for the Keeping of Enchanted Rooms." Snapping open her bag, she pulled out her list of names, as well as the rubbings of the graves. "I have a possessed house on Blaugdone Island and need to find the identity of the inhabiting wizard. These graves were found nearby." She handed the papers over.

Mr. Clarke pored over the papers for several minutes. Hulda remained silent. She didn't mind silence, especially when there was work being done.

"Very well done, Miss Larkin," he finally said. "Some fifty years ago, we did a survey of early colonial townships—by we, I mean those before me—all the way back to the *Mayflower*." He shrugged. "Could be forty or sixty, with this brain of mine. And with this brain of yours"—he held up one of the rubbings—"you would be an excellent genealogist."

She smiled at the compliment. "Thank you, but I am safely employed for the time being."

Gathering the papers, Mr. Clarke stood, and Hulda followed suit. "Take these out to Gifford—he's the one who saw you in. He'll personally take you down to the files you need. If they're not there, well, then I haven't been doing my job."

Hulda shook the man's hand once more. "You've been a great help, Mr. Clarke."

"Thank you. Do see me when you're finished." Sitting down, he pulled over his lunch. "So I can better explain what my earlier letter didn't."

Hulda nodded, if only to be polite, then left, her steps carrying her a fair bit quicker than they had before.

⁂

In the basement, Mr. Gifford carried the box of Narragansett records to a table for her and lit a second lantern. Hulda pulled her shawl tightly around her shoulders as she sat in the single chair available; it was cold in this vast, earth-scented space.

"Everything should be right there for you," the secretary said. "Do you need help?"

Hulda shook her head. "I shan't keep you from your post. I'm accustomed to file digging."

Mr. Gifford tipped his head. "You know where to find me."

With that, he left her to her box. Lifting a candle, Hulda scanned the handwritten tabs, making sure she could reorder the documents if she had to overturn the whole thing to find what she needed.

However, Mr. Clarke and his predecessors had indeed done their job well, and she found the information she wanted quickly, in a thin folder labeled *Blaugdone, Gould, Hope Islands, 1656–1750*.

She thumbed through a few fragile papers before pulling out one with the Mansel name on it. It was a long parchment, about three feet, folded into thirds. Shifting the box to the ground, she flattened it on the table and brought the second candle closer. A date scrawled in remarkable penmanship on the bottom stated that these records had been created in 1793. Hulda briefly wondered how many gravestones the recorder had had to uncover.

"There you are." She pressed the tip of a well-manicured nail to the name *Horace Thomas Mansel*. His birth, christening, and death dates were neatly printed beneath his name, followed by brief handwritten notes on his calculated magic. His wife's name—Evelyn Peg Turly—was beside his, her information arrayed in a similar manner, though her christening was marked as unknown. These records were made well after the family's passing, so their magical potential must have been estimated. *Ch14* was penned under Horace. *Co6?* beneath Evelyn.

Ch was shorthand for chaocracy, which the house certainly had. *Co* was shorthand for communion, which, thus far, Hulda had not witnessed. However, the question mark suggested uncertainty.

"And a Crisly," she said, following a line to Horace and Evelyn's firstborn child. She and her children had been buried in Baltimore—it appeared she'd gotten married and moved off the island, which explained why her grave marker wasn't with the others. *All daughters, indeed.*

Crisly likely wasn't the wizard of the house, despite her magic mark-ers. Baltimore was too far away. Unless the records had gotten it wrong and Crisly had died and been buried at Whimbrel House. It was a possibility.

Crisly's younger sisters matched the graves: Dorcas Catherine and Helen Eliza, the latter of whom had died at the age of four. She was also likely not the wizard they were searching for; magic typically manifested closer to puberty, though Hulda had begun experiencing flashes of divination when she was ten.

Chewing on the inside of her lip, Hulda traced the family line backward, to their English records. *Here,* she thought, tapping her finger on a great-aunt who had *Al2?* scrolled beneath her name. Alteration, two percent, estimated. The house had alteration. Hulda should attempt a calculation of her own and mail it to Mr. Clarke when this was finished so he could update his records. Either this aunt had possessed a greater amount of magic than was listed or one of the other Mansel ancestors had possessed some, either unknowingly or without any record. It wasn't uncommon for magic to skip generations and remanifest later—it was all a trick of the bloodwork. Regardless, the magic must have originated from somewhere, if their wizard had so much of it.

Both Horace and Evelyn had magic in the blood, which suggested their children might have been stronger than either of them, making Dorcas Hulda's prime suspect. Regardless, she had full names, which meant a successful exorcism. She just needed to purchase the supplies.

"Sorry," she whispered to the faded names before folding up the paper. "But it isn't my choice."

She left the box on the table—heaven forbid she catalog it wrong and have it lost for the next person. As she walked through the darkness toward the stairs, her mind pulled back to Portsmouth.

Yes, sleeping on the matter had calmed her nerves somewhat. But the sighting of that man, that "doppelgänger," still bothered her. She was in town, she had time . . . perhaps she could do some research on the Hogwoods while she was here. If only to find a logical source of comfort. While the Hogwoods were English, the Genealogical Society had imported records from all over, Europe especially, so they might have what she sought.

Hulda returned to the shelves, taking her lamp with her. Her feet felt like anvils as she browsed names, each passing letter sticking to her brain like it was coated in tar. She finally paused at the box she wanted, but instead of taking it to her table, she rifled through it then and there. She sighed in relief when she found the correct line—a great-great-somebody had immigrated to the States in 1745, bringing his records with him.

The Hogwood family line was extensive, their family tree much larger than the Mansels', the writing smaller and more compact. Fortunately, she need only lower her gaze to the past fifty years to find his name: *Silas Hogwood*. He had one brother whom she had never heard of, and his family's magical line was well documented, not a single question mark in the lot.

K12, N24, Al6, Ch6. Kinetic, necromantic, altering, and chaocratic spells were all innate in his bloodline, and there was a chance he had a scratch of augury. A great deal of magic for any one person to have, likely from the purposeful breeding of it. His mother's pedigree certainly focused heavily on necromancy.

Hulda shuddered. A man born so powerful, rendered more so by the clever thieving of others' abilities . . . How had he figured it out? But surely the constable had destroyed all his batteries.

She folded the chart back together. The exercise had made her more uneasy, not less. As though seeing Silas Hogwood's name written on parchment made him more real. She returned the files to the box and the box to the shelf, straightened her spine to the point of pain, and marched on her way. If she feigned confidence long enough, she'd embody it. Eventually.

Upstairs, she thanked Mr. Gifford and started for the doors, and just as she was on the cusp of escape, she heard Mr. Clarke call out, "Miss Larkin!"

She politely turned about near the tree statue, in a sliver of shade cast by its coppery leaves. "Mr. Clarke. I found just what I needed. Thank you for your service."

Mr. Clarke reached up to tip his hat toward her, only to discover he wasn't wearing one. "Not a problem at all! I am, of course, still hoping you'll be using our other services."

Hulda touched cool fingers to the back of her neck and ensured her features were well schooled. "You're a very forward person."

He chuckled. "In this line of work, you have to be. I've got more able men than women, Miss Larkin. You could have your pick."

A flush crept up her neck despite her efforts. "I do believe marriage is a mutual endeavor."

"Of course, of course. But this is for the betterment of society. You seem a very capable woman. I can think of two . . . maybe three who might be suited to your lifestyle, if you'd give them a chance. Well, I suppose it depends on your age preference."

The blush crept over her jaw, but she prided herself on the smoothness of her voice. "That is a bit personal."

"Think about it, Miss Larkin," he pleaded. "I myself don't have a lick of magic in me, but I wish I did. You love yours, do you not?"

The question made her pause. So direct and unexpected. "I . . . do, yes. It's proven very helpful to me." It's what had tipped her off about Silas Hogwood, among many other things.

"Would you not want your children to have that same gift? Or even more of it?" He rubbed his hands together. "Think of how much more we could do if we had more magically capable persons in this country. We'd have more kinetic trams and sustainable energy, healthier crops, better futures, calmer minds, stronger—"

"You've made your point," Hulda assured him. "I will . . . think on it."

Mr. Clarke nodded. "Send me word, and I'll give you information on those beaus I mentioned."

The word *beaus* had her stomach tightening. "Thank you, Mr. Clarke."

He shook her hand again, and she headed back to the refuge of the street. She would head for the post office. She needed to look up some names and addresses, and while she was there, she'd send inquiries to a few constabularies and the warden at Lancaster Castle, the prison where Silas Hogwood was held. With luck, she'd receive confirmation from the warden that Silas Hogwood was still safely behind bars. That all of this worry was, again, the workings of an overthinking mind.

That, and she needed to order at least one new dress.

Glancing up to ensure the road was safe to cross, she thought she saw Mr. Fletcher Portendorfer turning the corner, but he was gone so quickly she couldn't be sure.

Chapter 18

When Hulda returned, Merritt sulkily approached her with a small wheel in his hands.

She paused in the reception hall, an extra bag slung over her shoulder. "What is this?"

Merritt sniffed. He'd had a few hours to come to terms with the transformation, which had led him from wild anger to sadness. Beth and Baptiste were both keeping their distance. "This is my manuscript. Look what the place has done to it!"

Setting her bags down, Hulda took the wheel from him and tilted it toward one of the candles Beth had lit. The sun hadn't quite set, though it was nearly there. "Interesting."

"Interesting!" Merritt grabbed fistfuls of his hair. "That is a month's worth of work!"

She handed the wheel back. "I'm very sorry for it. Hopefully the house changes its mind about it."

He thought his knees might give way. "Can't you fix it? Bully the house like you did before?" He eyed her bags and straightened, a glimmer of excitement bursting in his middle. "Did you find it?"

Hulda didn't look happy when she nodded. "I did. I believe the wizard to be Dorcas Catherine Mansel." She reached for the new bag, briefly explaining the logic among the siblings, most of which Merritt followed. "I brought everything we'll need for the exorcism. If you would assist me with the salt."

"Salt?" Merritt peered into the bag as she fished out a hefty package from it. "What about holy water?"

"It isn't that sort of exorcism, Mr. Fernsby, but I do need the foundation encircled by salt. Best do it now while there's still light."

"And my manuscript?"

She glanced at the wheel. "I'm sure a little goading will do the trick."

Nodding slowly, Merritt slipped outside, glancing up at the purple-tinged sky and the faintest sliver of gold to the west. It really was beautiful, wasn't it? Endless acres of land unspoiled by humans, cradled by clean ocean air, splayed under a flawless sky. He should put something of the sort in his book.

Thoughts of his book had his heart sinking again, so he tore open the package of salt and set to work, nearly stepping on a mouse as he did so. He'd just finished watering the plants in the sunroom—he couldn't leave *everything* to Beth if he still wanted some semblance of independence—and come upstairs to finish a scene he'd been mulling about since that morning. There, on his desk, was this blasted wheel, too small to even be useful for anything. Only the empty reams of paper had been untouched by the spell. He'd choked on his own breath, searched frantically for the manuscript as though he or the others might have misplaced it. But their resident wizard, Dorcas, had alteration magic, and she had used it on his book. Exorcise her, and it would never turn back.

He would never be able to rewrite it the same way. It wasn't possible. He only had the vaguest outline . . . and the thought of starting from the beginning made him sick. He'd already written that part of the story. It would be torture to re-create it!

He'd been pacing relentlessly for Hulda to return, for if anyone could cajole the house into listening, she could. Yet she didn't seem particularly interested in trying.

It was the idea of disenchanting the house that bothered her. He knew it.

Am I doing the wrong thing?

But it was *his* house. He couldn't get by with portraits following him around or his *livelihood* turning into random inanimate objects. He had no desire to return to a cramped apartment in the city, either. He liked it here. The weeping cherries and shorebirds were becoming comforts to him. Even the staff was starting to feel like, well, a strange sort of . . . family. And he hadn't had family for a very long time.

But he was about to lose them, too, wasn't he? Everyone but Baptiste . . .

Finished with the salt—it had taken the entire bag—he returned inside as the sun shrunk beyond the horizon. Beth and Baptiste lingered in the dining room, peeking out as Hulda worked. She'd set out eleven stones, which had to represent the eleven magics. Merritt's eyes flitted from bloodstone to turquoise to a purple one near his foot.

"What is amethyst for?" he asked. He didn't touch it; he knew Hulda wouldn't like her efforts to be interrupted. "Conjury?"

Hulda paused, looking surprised that he even knew what the stones were for. Well, magical or not, he hadn't grown up in a ditch. "Augury, actually."

He nodded.

She gestured for him to join up with Beth and Baptiste, and he noticed the hateful wheel had been moved to the dining room floor. Baptiste murmured, "Is the ghost . . . coming *out*? Should I leave?"

"If it were dangerous, she would have told us," Merritt assured him. Unless Hulda was more frustrated with him than he realized. But surely she wouldn't risk any harm to Beth.

She pulled out a piece of paper. "This is an alteration and wardship spell. The first will change the house to something uninhabitable for the wizard, and the second will counter the spells the wizard used to attach herself. I will perform for Dorcas first; if that doesn't work, Crisly."

"But," Merritt hesitated, "you aren't also an alterist and a wardist, are you?"

"I am not. But these spells were preprepared by wizards who have those talents."

A slight popping sound emanated from behind Merritt. He whirled around to see his manuscript on the floor where the wheel had been. Euphoria filled him from heel to head as he scooped the thing up, hurriedly flipping through pages to ensure it was all there. It was.

"Oh blessed Lord." He hugged the book to himself. "Look, Mrs. Larkin! The house gave it back!"

She nodded sadly. "Probably because the spirit doesn't want to leave."

Merritt frowned. "Well, if that isn't a nail in the reinvigorated fountain of my joy."

Surprisingly, Hulda smiled. Just a small smile, no teeth, but it was there. "Quite metaphorical, Mr. Fernsby. You should be a writer."

She turned to her spells, and Merritt's gut tightened.

It happened very quickly—Merritt had envisioned something long and drawn out, full of shadows and guttural chants and the constant spraying of holy water. But Hulda's reading of the spells was quiet and quick. The stones remained in place. The candles burned with consistency. The house didn't even creak.

Hulda set the paper on the stairs. "Not Dorcas, then." Frowning, she retrieved an identical paper from her bag. One set of spells per exorcism.

Beth shifted her weight, making the floor creak. "It's been excellent working with you, Mr. Fernsby."

His gut tightened further.

The dining room turned black.

"Mrs. Larkin," he began, but he didn't put enough effort into the name. She didn't hear him.

She enacted the spell, using the full name, Crisly Stephanie Mansel. And . . . nothing happened.

Merritt's insides were strange. Anxiety bloomed from his navel. His chest was tight. And yet . . . relief oddly loosened his shoulders.

Hulda shook her head. "I . . . I don't understand it. It couldn't have been the parents. They didn't have the right . . . *mix.*"

Beth said, "Maybe it *is* the youngin."

Hulda sighed. "I did purchase enough for experimentation." She pulled out a third sheet. Enacted the exorcism again, this time for Helen Eliza Mansel.

Nothing happened.

"I know these stones are good!" Hulda stamped her foot, abandoning her post to check the rocks.

Merritt dared to step into the reception hall. "Are you forgetting something?"

"I do not *forget* things, Mr. Fernsby." She finished circling the room, then planted her hands on her hips. "I do not understand it. We'll have to look for more graves. If it is not the children, it must be someone else entirely."

Not one to be thwarted, Hulda attempted it one more time for Horace Thomas Mansel, and then Evelyn Peg Turly. Both were as anticlimactic as the first three.

Baptiste grumbled. Beth said, "Such a bother."

Merritt shrugged. "I suppose things will have to be abnormally normal for another night. Beth, Baptiste, you're welcome to turn in for the evening. Hopefully you wake up where you rested your head and your ceilings don't drip, hm?"

Beth offered a small curtsy. Baptiste looked around curiously before shuffling into the shadows.

As he departed, Merritt turned to Hulda. "He is most excellent with venison. It's a pity you missed it." He took in the hard lines between her brows. "I'm sorry you had to make the trip."

Hulda waved away the apology. "I would be happy for the failure if it didn't seem so utterly illogical." She started, perhaps surprised by her own honesty, and cleared her throat. "Well, since my stay is extending, I'll give you this." She went to her usual bag—the one with all the tricks in it—and pulled out two selenite stones, each about the size of Merritt's fists. They bore the same dark seal of three curved lines, not unlike parentheses, growing in size, transcribed within a caret pointing to the right. Or left, depending on how he held it.

"Are these communion stones?" He'd heard of them—they were quite useful in the revolution—but had never used one himself.

"Indeed. And they're expensive, so please treat them with care. When I leave, I'll need to bring both back to BIKER. If we need to communicate while apart, these will allow it. Press your palm into the seal for about three seconds before speaking. Take your palm off first." She looked at the reception hall like a disgruntled parent might glare at a child. "We wouldn't have needed them if this had been successful."

He passed his stone from hand to hand. "Hardly your fault."

She sniffed. "It literally is my fault." She paused. "I rarely guess wrong."

"But"—he gently prodded her with an elbow—"now you'll get to stay long enough to try Baptiste's venison."

She pulled back from him, and the change of shadows made her cheeks look ruddy. Not wishing to cause her discomfort, Merritt pocketed the stone and said, "If you'll excuse me, I have a scene to finish."

Snatching his manuscript, he tucked it under his arm and ventured upstairs.

He wasn't sure how much the wizard in residence really wanted to stay, because the ceiling dripped on him the entire way to his office.

After breakfast the next morning, Beth and Baptiste set out to find more gravestones, leaving Merritt to draft a letter to his editor and Hulda to organize . . . whatever it was that housekeepers organized. He'd begun to fear she'd gotten very bored with Whimbrel House since it was one of the smaller abodes she'd been assigned to. Which led Merritt to imagine what it would be like to have a new housekeeper. His mind instantly pictured Mrs. Culdwell from his old apartment, and he shuddered. Truthfully, though, when the house was only just a house, he might not need staff at all. There was only himself to pick up after, himself to cook for . . .

There was something invigorating about living alone. A . . . lack of rules, so to speak. Merritt could wash his socks wherever he wanted. He could work at night and sleep during the day. He could pace the hallway and talk to himself out loud, which not only helped him sort out stories, but also helped him understand his own flights of fancy. Being able to talk aloud to someone who always agreed with you could do wonders for the soul.

But there was a sort of hollowness to quiet rooms. One that had been much easier to ignore in a small apartment. Whimbrel House would feel very empty for a lone bachelor. And he feared that if he parted ways with Hulda, Beth, and Baptiste, he might never see them again. That sentiment panged sour in his chest, reminiscent of the barely healed scars that lingered there.

Once his letter was penned and addressed, Merritt listened for sounds of company and found none. He peered out his window, seeing Baptiste's shadow in the distance. Moving into the hallway to another window, he spied Hulda clad in boots and a hat, venturing out to do her *specialty*. She'd likely run herself ragged looking for more graves. Perhaps the bloke in question really was under the floorboards, although he'd seen no sign of a body while he was under the house.

He eyed the floor warily before venturing down the stairs. Halfway through the steps, the stairs suddenly flattened themselves, sending him careening into the reception area on a giant slide. He swayed, stumbled, and fell hard onto his rump.

Wincing, he mumbled, "I suppose I should thank you for not doing that in front of the others."

The stairs righted themselves.

Rubbing his tailbone, Merritt slipped outside and quickly forgot his worries about the house. The weather was utterly perfect. A flush autumn day. The elms were turning golden, and the maples gleamed red. The sun was high, the clouds were few, the sky was a miraculous shade of cerulean that no painter could ever hope to replicate. The temperature was just right for not having a jacket, though once he got moving, he'd surely be overwarm.

Merritt did not have a goal when he started walking, taking first the easy path toward the boat, then wandering in the direction of the weeping cherries, spiraling around clusters of golden aster. He heard the annoyed thump of a hare near some woodland goosefoot, as Beth called them, but didn't see the creature. He stepped carefully where the wild grass thinned, for the ground had loosened with last night's rain. A tantalizing breeze swept through his hair, as though to comment on the unkemptness of it. It carried whispers of salt, and Merritt breathed in deeply, filling his lungs with the scent.

The breeze swept on, rustling the grass and grape fern, filling his head with visions of the Mansels' graves. In his mind's eye, he saw their weathered faces and chipped edges. In his palms, he felt the weight of each stone. Tasted the age on the back of his tongue. His feet changed direction of their own volition, until he found himself standing where he, Hulda, and Beth had cleared out grass.

The Mansels seemed to look at him with distaste. Like he wasn't good enough for them, either.

He crouched before them, hands on knees. "Well? Who is it, then? I'd like to see *you* sleuth it out."

The graves didn't answer.

Frowning, Merritt inched back a bit. "Probably stepping on your heads or something. Sorry."

His gaze shifted from Horace to Evelyn, Dorcas, and finally Helen. *Look.*

He felt tugged southward. Holding his breath at the strange, faint sensation, he stood and shifted that way, peering into the untouched weeds, stepping on a tail of morning glory.

Reaching out, he parted grass one way and then another. Took a step, parted. Stepped, parted. Saw a glimmer of gray against the earth.

Crouching again so his knees would hold back some of the flora, he ran his hand over the unmarked stone. It was small, about the length of his head. Unassuming, dull, flat.

He curled his hands around it and lifted it. A centipede wriggled out from below, along with some beetles.

Merritt swept damp earth from the underside of the rock and saw beneath it the faintest carving of an *O*.

His pulse sped. Kneeling for better balance, he scrubbed his palm over the stone, uncovering a birth date that had broken apart midcentury, leaving just the bottom of a six. Grasping a clump of grass, he gingerly worked away grime, then pressed into the grooves with his fingers to help him read what time had worn away.

O. W. E. L? No, *I.* And it ended with an *N.* It was a Welsh name. *Owein.*

Merritt ran his thumb over the death date. Owein Mansel. Perished at age twelve. Before two of his sisters and both parents.

I don't understand it. It couldn't have been the parents. They didn't have the right . . . mix.

No, Merritt thought. *Not the parents.* Lifting his fingers, he counted. One, Crisly. Two, Dorcas. And three, the youngest, Helen.

He looked at the faded birth date. *Not the youngest.*

Owein was. Born after Helen, though he'd lived eight years longer.

Merritt knew in his gut that this was the wizard. His stone had been dislodged, but his body would be lying beside his family, the location unmarked.

Glancing back to the other graves, a sinking feeling weighed him down. His hands clutched the stone. *Separated from your family, are you?*

Just like he was.

No wonder the boy's spirit clung to the house. He'd died young, so young, and hadn't wanted to lose his family. He had so much more to give . . . and he must have gotten the full brunt of his ancestors' magical abilities, given all the spells he could cast. Come to think of it, the mischief of Whimbrel House very much seemed like the workings of a twelve-year-old boy.

No wonder he'd been so miserable when Merritt arrived! He'd been alone for so long . . . he was likely depressed, hurt, and angry. God knew Merritt would have been. Even the surveyors had separated him from his family—if they'd known about him, he'd have been on that family tree Hulda had found.

Standing, Merritt crossed back to the line of sisters and gingerly set Owein's marker beside Helen's.

He didn't leave. He sat there, crouched in the dirt, staring at that worn gravestone, smaller than all the rest. How long ago had it been misplaced? How long had it been facedown in the muck?

Owein was just an angry little boy trying his best. Trying to remember what it meant to be a part of something.

After some time, grass-crunching footsteps approached. "Mr. Fernsby?" Hulda asked. "Are you ill?"

"Found him." His voice was barely louder than the sparrows' distant calls. He gestured to the stone. "It was turned about, over there."

Hulda gasped and crossed to him, crouching to read the stone for herself. "O . . . Owen?"

"Owein. Owein Mansel."

"Brilliant!" she cried. "I *knew* it had to be one of the children. Fortunately, I have two more spell sheets. I can prepare—"

"Leave him." Merritt rubbed his hands together, flaking off dried mud. Then he stood, blood rushing back into his legs, and started for the house.

After a moment, Hulda hurried after him. "Mr. Fernsby? Leave him?"

Merritt gestured toward . . . nothing in particular. "He's just a boy."

Hulda hesitated. "His spirit is centuries old."

"True." He stepped over a rotting log. "But I understand the lad."

Several seconds passed before Hulda repeated, softer, "Understand?"

He nodded. "Why he'd want to stay . . . He went too soon. Maybe he got sick. Who knows?" He put his hands in his pockets. "But he was separated from his family before he was ready. If one can ever be ready for that. Just like me."

Hulda stopped in her tracks. "Merritt . . . ," she began.

He paused and turned around, leaving about three paces between them. Did she realize she'd used his first name? Any other time, he might have been pleased.

She'd asked after the story before, hadn't she? Merritt was feeling oddly sentimental. He wasn't himself, which was the only reason he said anything at all. "I was eighteen when my father wrote me off. Got a girl pregnant. Or I thought I did."

Hulda's eyes widened.

He rubbed the back of his head. A single, dry chuckle worked its way up his throat. "Goodness, I never tell this story. It sounds so strange out loud."

She swallowed. "You don't have to."

"But you want to know, don't you?" He peered past her to Owein's grave, already hidden by the grass. "I loved her. Got carried away. My father was so wroth with me. He always was, more than my sisters. Never really understood why. He wrote me off there and then. Forbade me from coming home. From speaking to my mother . . ." He felt a lump forming in his throat and coughed to clear it.

"But I was going to make it right, with or without him." He glanced to the eastern horizon. "I got myself a job, even a ring. Not a nice one, mind you, but she seemed happy enough to wear it. And then one morning she was gone. Left for music school, was all her parents told me. That, and she never was pregnant. Just a scare. Refused to tell me where she went. They never did like me."

Hulda didn't respond. He hadn't expected her to. How does one react to that? To learning someone is so wretched that their adolescent sweetheart left him without word?

Without daring to look at her, Merritt added, "Owein stays," and he ventured to the house alone, the wind teasing his hair, the whimbrels crying his arrival.

Chapter 19

Hulda should have been up and about by now. She always strove to be the first one to rise in any house she occupied. No sense in wasting daylight or being unavailable when needed. But her mattress felt very deep this morning, her blankets especially warm, her thoughts particularly insistent.

She was happy the house and its wizard—little Owein!—were intact. And she sensed Whimbrel House was equally content with the arrangement. But that victory was intermixed with thoughts on Merritt's—Mr. Fernsby's—confession. His words had swum around her head the rest of yesterday and even pierced her dreams last night.

Mr. Fernsby had made himself scarce, enmeshing himself in his work and avoiding the staff.

He was separated from his family . . . Just like me.

Hulda rolled onto her side and blew a lock of hair off her face. She only saw her own parents and siblings once a year, usually at Christmas. Her schedule was too busy for more frequent sojourns. But she always had a place there. She couldn't imagine being severed from them for good.

Mr. Fernsby's father's reaction did seem . . . extreme. Many would regard premarital relations very poorly. But to cut him off entirely? From his mother, his siblings? Eighteen was old enough, she supposed . . . but it was an uncomfortable thought. Perhaps they were strict Catholics or Shakers, though Mr. Fernsby didn't seem particularly religious.

Her mind flitted back to the marshland outside the house. The look on his face . . . he'd been smiling, but with such a depth of sadness in his eyes. Like peering down into the deepest part of the ocean, or looking through a ghost.

Thirteen years. This all happened thirteen years ago. Nearly half of Mr. Fernsby's lifetime. A long time to atone for a mistake, and he was hardly a profligate man. She recalled inquiring about spirits when Mr. Portendorfer was visiting. *I avoid things that might get me into trouble.*

The words of a penitent man, or so she thought. It was obvious that he was very careful.

Rolling back, Hulda stared at fine lines in the ceiling. She did have a tendency to be judgmental, as her sister often pointed out. Self-admittedly, she didn't like rule breakers, ruffians, pranksters, and the like. Yet she couldn't find it in her heart or mind to judge Merritt Fernsby. He had a roguish air, yes, but he was kind. A gentleman, really. A gentleman wound through with regret.

Hulda sighed. *How badly did she break your heart?* Surely the loss of a *real* love, someone you had actually shared something with and not merely fantasized about, must be devastating. He'd intended to marry her. This woman could have been the woman of Whimbrel House. Hulda would have been reporting to her instead of him. For a moment, Hulda wondered what her name was, what she was like . . . then chided herself for getting carried away and threw off her covers. Time to get dressed and be useful.

She was certain of one thing: she would not cause Mr. Fernsby any further misery. He'd been punished enough. It wasn't her place, besides.

After donning a dress, pinning up her hair, and cleaning her spectacles, Hulda popped a lemon drop into her mouth and strode from her room with purpose.

❀

Miss Taylor was outside beating a rug. The smells wafting from the kitchen hinted that Mr. Babineaux was near the end of breakfast preparations. Mr. Fernsby was nowhere to be seen, which meant he was shut up in his office or bedroom. Retrieving her ledgers, Hulda took herself to the pantry to update her records of the food stores. Halfway through, she heard Mr. Babineaux in the breakfast room and found him placing a fresh loaf of brioche on the table.

"Smells wonderful," she said, to which he merely nodded. "Are there any supplies we're short on? Anything you need?"

He straightened, tall and foreboding, expressionless. For a moment, Hulda feared he wouldn't answer her. But just as she was turning for the pantry, he said, "Butter. We will always need butter. If we get cow, I will milk her myself."

Hulda blinked. "Noted. Anything else?"

"Is expensive import, but vanilla. And sugar, if you want dessert." He paused. "I am very good at desserts. Especially pastries. For this we need cream *and* butter. If Mr. Fernsby"—he waved his hand, trying to think of a word—"*purchases* a cow, I will take care of her. I will take good care of her."

"I will let him know you are passionate about bovines, Mr. Babineaux. If you think of anything else, please find me." With a nod of her head, she returned to the pantry and finished logging her entries, then moved into the kitchen to finish the task. The pantry was small, so many of their foodstuffs occupied the cupboards.

"Low on flour," she said to herself, and marked it down. She mishandled her pencil, and it toppled to the floor. As Hulda bent to retrieve it, however, she paused, an idea striking her. Straightening, she said, "Owein, dear, would you get that for me?"

A few seconds passed. Then a hole opened up in the floor beneath the pencil—nearly taking Hulda's heel with it—and another opened in the ceiling, dropping the pencil onto the countertop.

Hulda smiled. "Thank you." The nub had broken in the fall, but she certainly wouldn't fault the lad for that. Indeed, he might very well earn himself a place on the staff.

A quick shuffling of the stairs had Hulda's ears perking. Seconds later, Mr. Fernsby's voice said, "Miss Taylor, my pen exploded. I've got ink all over this cravat—" He stepped into the kitchen and spied Hulda. He stopped, a crinkled cravat in his hands with a sizable black stain. "Oh. Sorry. I . . . thought you were Beth."

Had Hulda not been familiar with Mr. Fernsby, she might not have picked up on the awkwardness of his tone—he did a good job at covering it with nonchalance. But she heard it, and it softened her heart. No man should have to feel out of place in his own home, and she didn't wish for this one to feel out of place with her.

She offered him a reassuring smile. "It is hardly beneath me to soak a cravat, Mr. Fernsby. I've had my fair share of ink stains. They are inevitable." She held out her hand.

He hesitated half a second. "I believe you made it very clear that you are not the maid, Mrs. Larkin."

"Then we'd best not tell anyone I secretly wash cravats in my spare time."

He laughed, the sound relaxing parts of her she hadn't realized were tense. Bolstering her spirits. It was a beautiful sound, really.

He handed her the cravat, and Hulda tried and failed not to notice that Mr. Fernsby's shirt was wide open, revealing a good triangle of his collar and chest. The peek of hair there was darker than that on his head—

Averting her eyes, Hulda set the cravat near the sink and forced her thoughts to other things before she could flush. If she did, Mr. Fernsby might misinterpret it as embarrassment related to his recent confession. "Would you like to review a menu with Mr. Babineaux? I wanted to put in a food order for the house."

He kneaded his hands together. "Oh. Well . . . I don't really have a preference. You're welcome to decide."

Hulda nodded and picked up a separate ledger, switching to the page marked with the week's dates. "Then I will see about him planning the venison, since it comes so highly recommended." She wrote down *venison* and *potatoes*, before glancing up to ask Mr. Fernsby if he had—

She suddenly couldn't remember what she was going to say. He was looking at her with . . . curiosity? Incredulity? Interest? She couldn't quite tell. But it caught her off guard. She didn't like the way it made her heart kick. She dropped her eyes to her ledger. *What was I about to say?*

"I was thinking," he said, saving her from a blunder, "about what you said the other day. That you had other things to do in town. Did you visit BIKER again?"

She scrawled something else in the ledger, giving her hands something to do. "It is unnecessary for me to report so often."

He eyed her. Voice lower, he asked, "I know it's none of my concern, but you weren't looking for *him* again, were you?"

Hulda opened her mouth. Closed it. Shut the ledger. "I think breakfast is ready—"

"You know you're safe here—"

"It isn't a matter of my safety," she whispered, glancing toward the breakfast room. She sighed and gestured for Mr. Fernsby to follow her. If he was going to pry, he might as well do it where they were both comfortable.

In truth, the only confidant she really had was Myra, and Myra would likely dismiss her anxieties again. Because that's what they were. Anxieties. Unreasonable thoughts. But . . . she liked assurances. She relied on proof. As soon as she had some, she could logically work her way out of the knot her fears had tied her into, and everything would be fine again.

The first thing she noticed upon entering the living room was that several chairs were sinking into the floor.

"Owein!" Mr. Fernsby called cheerily. "How are you this morning?"

The furniture paused midsink and flashed yellow.

"I think he's feeling rather chipper," he interpreted.

The chairs rose back to the surface, and the floor solidified. Hulda sat on the chair closest to her, smoothing her skirts. "Perhaps because he's no longer being tossed out."

"I have no intention of tossing out any of you," he said, taking up the chair closest to her, with only a small table between them. "I'm already working on my next argument to convince you to stay."

Hulda tried to ignore the fluttering the words started in her gut, and this time she did a fairly good job of it. She had a history of misinterpreting words, and given that she was somewhat emotionally compromised with her client, she knew the likelihood of misinterpretation was high. Besides, she understood precisely how Mr. Fernsby felt about her—he'd said so himself: he was used to her. Humans liked comfort and disliked change as a matter of course.

"I sent inquiries to England," she confessed, listening for Miss Taylor and Mr. Babineaux. While she could use a confidant, she didn't want the entire household nudging into her affairs. "To establish whether he is still imprisoned and ensure that, either way, he hasn't immigrated here. Once I know that, I can put it behind me."

"But if he *were* here," Mr. Fernsby spoke carefully, "he wouldn't find you."

She shook her head. "I doubt it. BIKER wouldn't release such information to a private citizen. Assuming he *did* get out of prison, I'm sure he would prefer to get on with his life than seek me out. He won't have been released, though." She swallowed. "He'll be behind bars for the rest of his days."

"For misuse of magic?"

She sagged into her chair. "You do have a remarkable memory, don't you?"

He shrugged. "When things are interesting."

"I am not a storybook, Mr. Fernsby."

"I never said you were." His tone was completely serious.

She ran her thumb along the groove in her armrest. "Mr. Hogwood had developed some sort of method for extracting the magic out of another person."

Mr. Fernsby stiffened. "You're kidding."

"I wish I were. He has an impressive pedigree. His parents were both members of the Queen's League of Magicians—King's League then. He used some sort of combination of magic to take spells from others. I know he did. He was crazed with it. Secretive. I saw it happen."

Mr. Fernsby paled. "You saw it?"

She lifted her hands, then let them drop to her lap. "I 'saw' it happen in Mr. Hogwood's tea leaves. I watched him take a local hysterian who had *gone missing*, and . . ." She shuddered, suddenly sick to her stomach.

To her shock, Mr. Fernsby reached over and clasped her forearm. His touch was remarkably warm, and the darkness building in the base of Hulda's skull dissipated with it. "You don't have to tell me if you don't want to."

She rolled her lips together. Without pulling up the memories, she explained, "It isn't pleasant, what he can do. It kills the person . . . shrivels them into something unidentifiable. He kept each of the bodies, and I saw the remains with my own eyes."

She cringed. Filled her lungs to bursting. "That said, I just want to make sure it wasn't him—"

A startled *"Oof"* reached their ears.

Mr. Fernsby stood. "What was that?" He passed her an apologetic glance and crossed into the reception hall, Hulda hurrying after him.

The front door was open, Miss Taylor standing just outside of it. She had a small rug rolled up and slung over her shoulder. Her eyes were wide enough to show the whites all around her irises.

"Miss Taylor?" Mr. Fernsby asked.

She tentatively reached her hand toward them, only to have it repelled, as though striking glass.

"What on earth?" Hulda crossed to her, hand out, and met the same "glass." She followed it upward and downward, but it covered the entire door, forbidding her to leave and Miss Taylor to enter.

"Owein, let her in," Mr. Fernsby called.

Unease wound from Hulda's hips to collar. "Owein isn't doing this."

"Pardon?"

She turned to face him. "His abilities lie in alteration and chaocracy. This is wardship."

Brows drawn, Mr. Fernsby joined her at the door and rapped his knuckles upon the invisible shield. "Perhaps he merely hasn't done it until now."

Hulda severely doubted it. As Mr. Babineaux announced breakfast, Hulda stepped back into the living room. "Owein, would you please, I don't know, change the color of the ceiling? To your favorite color?"

The ceiling shifted to a bright blue. Out in the reception hall, the shield remained up.

"He can enchant only one room at a time," she explained.

Miss Taylor asked, "Meaning what?" Her voice sounded like it was underwater.

Hulda dashed up the stairs, hurrying to her room, where she grabbed her tool bag. She returned just as quickly, digging for her dowsing rods. "Meaning Whimbrel House has two sources of magic."

Mr. Fernsby's mouth dropped. "Two? But not the Mansel family—you would have exorcised them."

"It is unlikely the second source is also a wizard in residence. It must be something more subtle. Like enchanted wood." She walked toward the front door with her rods extended. They parted in her hands, then closed again as she moved away. When she entered the living room, they slowly opened again.

"Owein would have to be quite powerful to be doing both. I don't think it's him." She glanced at the blue ceiling. "Owein, would you please drop the shield on the door? Miss Taylor needs to come in."

They were quiet a moment. The ceiling shifted to a darker blue. The shield remained.

Mr. Fernsby's Adam's apple bobbed. "Is it dangerous?"

Hulda moved toward the dining room with her rods. They didn't react. "Highly unlikely."

"Then . . . let's not worry about it." Mr. Fernsby knocked on the shield. "Miss Taylor! Perhaps you could try a window—"

The shield gave way, causing Mr. Fernsby to stumble into Miss Taylor, nearly knocking her over. Fortunately, he caught himself and steadied Miss Taylor with hands on her shoulders, though his elbow smacked into the doorframe, eliciting a hiss, followed by, "Terribly sorry! Mrs. Larkin, I fixed it! Oh goodness, that will leave a bruise—"

Hulda approached the door, her dowsing rods limp in her hands. She hummed to herself, wondering. Magic houses were rarely dangerous, and this second source of magic was mild enough that they hadn't detected it before. Hulda didn't *worry* about it . . . but she wanted to know. Enough questions had gone unanswered in her life that she ached to answer the ones she could. This was her specialty, after all.

Heavy footsteps sounded behind them, followed by Mr. Babineaux's low inquiry, "Is anyone going to eat? It's getting cold." His dark eyes passed over them. "What did I miss?"

Chapter 20

Merritt couldn't wrap his head around how well things were going. Not just with the house, which had been kinder to him ever since he'd learned its name, but . . . Hulda.

The very thing that had made his own father throw him out, she'd barely batted an eye at.

He'd come to terms with it all—his disinheritance, the abandonment—or so he liked to think. He could go days without thinking about it, though when he *did* think about it, it stung like a fresh wasp bite. Ebba, especially. The disintegration of his world had revolved around her. Around their mistake. And yet Merritt had been determined to pick up the pieces, to marry her and raise their child together. To move on as a family. He'd proposed, she'd accepted, and train cars were slowly aligning on the track. So when *she'd* abandoned him, too—apparently with an empty womb—he'd been . . . *shocked* wasn't a strong enough word for it. Words were his business, his trade, and still he wasn't sure an adequate descriptor existed. She hadn't even said goodbye. He'd found out from her parents. There'd been no note, no farewell, no explanation.

She'd left the ring. Fletcher had pawned it on Merritt's behalf.

Merritt's father had always viewed him with disdain, so his abandonment had seemed almost natural. But Ebba had loved him, or so he'd believed. And not knowing *why* she'd ripped him off like a coarse scab still haunted his dreams at night.

And yet.

Merritt sat at his desk, pen in hand, but had not written for several minutes. Twilight was descending, acclimating him to the darkness. He needed to light another candle, but something about the blank wall in front of him magnified the scattered thoughts he needed to sort through.

Finding that forgotten, mud-encased grave had struck a chord within him. A note that still rang, even now. He felt empathetic for a *house*, for the person within its walls that he couldn't see, couldn't really talk to. He felt connected to him, like they were two novels of the same series.

If Owein hadn't reached into his soul so readily, he might not have told Hulda his story. Outside of Fletcher, he'd told *no one*. Fletcher's family knew, of course, but not from Merritt's mouth. And suddenly, thirteen years later, he'd vomited his shame and anguish onto his house-keeper, of all people. He'd truly thought she'd be offended. That he'd wake up this morning to see her bags packed, her replacement already notified.

Instead, she'd offered to wash his cravat and asked for his dinner recommendations.

She was a puzzle. So prim yet . . . utterly unruffled by his delinquencies. By his outcast status. In truth, he'd never met a woman like Hulda Larkin.

Who are you?

He'd been equally surprised by her willingness to talk about this Silas Hogwood. Merritt had a vivid imagination; it had felt as if he were standing beside her as she witnessed those horrors in her vision. The bodies. Surely that had to trouble a person. Surely not even someone as strong as Hulda could shake it off. He'd wanted, badly, to comfort her.

To reassure her. If she hadn't already done so, Merritt would have made his own inquiries regarding the man.

He heard her voice passing by his door with a second set of light footsteps that had to be Beth's. "—not a bother. You're smaller than I am; take the bath first. I'll carry up the water. I need the exercise—"

Merritt wiped his hands down his face before resting his chin in his palms, trying not to let his thoughts wander to the bath. Corsets aside, Hulda was a well-shaped woman, and—

There was some rule against this, wasn't there? Moon-eyeing your staff.

He groaned and leaned back in his chair, filling his eyes—and brain—with the shadowed wall in front of him. There had been plenty of nice women in his life. He'd taken a few to dinner, even. One had gotten awkward around him when she learned he had no family ties, but she'd been a snob, anyway, always wearing mountains of lace even on the hottest summer days. Then there was the mess with Fletcher's sister, who'd turned him down outright, and he'd had to avoid her while living in the same house for months. The woman he'd fancied during his undercover employment at that steel factory had *not* been happy with him when his article put her job in jeopardy.

Sometimes he wondered if his father had placed a curse on him, stripping him of not only his past family, but any chance of a future one as well. He didn't think about it much, but that was because he didn't want to. He'd dug his graves for the loved ones torn away from him long ago, occasionally adding more soil to top them off.

His thoughts drifted back to Hulda. She was so rigid it was comical, but sometimes she softened, showing her humanity as if by accident. When she'd taken his cravat. When he'd mentioned Ebba, the girl he'd been ready to marry. When he'd told her she was safe.

He shook his head. *No.* She was his housekeeper. That would be awkward. And kindness did not equate interest. He was just letting his loneliness get the better of him.

Not that he was lonely.

"I need to work," he growled, pulling a piece of paper in front of him. His characters were undercover with the local crime lords now, and Merritt needed to pull on that imagination of his since he had no desire to do firsthand research. He tapped his pen on the paper, leaving bleeding ink circles like unsightly moles across its face. He wrote, *Elise,* which was the name of his heroine. Thought for a moment, then added, *Elise wasn't fond of dressing like a man.*

He could work with that.

A bubble appeared under the wallpaper of the bedroom, about the size of his head, and moved in lazy circles like some sort of sleepy demon trying to gain entrance.

"Don't go spying on the girls, Owein," Merritt murmured, redipping his pen. "Wouldn't want your soul to rot out of this house, now would we?"

The bubble rippled and sunk as though disappointed. Leaning over, Merritt pet it like it were a cat, and the entire wall rippled.

"Help me out," he said, grateful for the distraction. "If you ran an infamous crime ring, where would you want your headquarters to be? Is beneath the city too dank, or would you be out in the open, maybe in a gambling house?"

The wall pulsed twice.

"Gambling house it is."

And he started writing.

◯◌

Three days after she'd discovered Whimbrel House had a second source of magic, Hulda received a letter via windsource pigeon, which was a rather expensive mode of communication. It required specific spells of elemental magic—air, to enhance flight—and communion magic, which allowed the birds to receive instructions for delivery. In the Middle Ages, the method hadn't been terribly pricey, but in the nineteenth century, it was hard to find people who possessed the right spells to enchant new birds. Thus the people who *could* accomplish it were paid lavishly for their services. But where there was no telegram or appropriately connected communion stones, this was the next best means of communicating quickly.

BIKER's seal was on the letter, so Hulda opened it immediately.

> *Hulda,*
>
> *How is everything going in the bay? I hope your health is still well and you've managed to figure out the possessor. Is Mr. Fernsby still insistent that he or she be expelled?*
>
> *You may be happy to hear I'm reassigning you. To Boston, for now. There's always work to be done at the main office. But our team in Nova Scotia is close to uncovering some interesting finds! I don't think we've sent you there yet, have we? We can discuss in person.*
>
> *Bring your receipts to Sadie; she'll reimburse you and finalize your payroll.*
>
> *Best,*
>
> *Myra*

Hulda's stomach sunk into her pelvis.

She didn't want to leave.

She liked Whimbrel House. She liked the island and the ocean air. She liked working with Miss Taylor and Mr. Babineaux. She liked Mr. Fernsby . . .

Pressing her lips together, she paced the length of her room twice before pulling out a parchment of her own. Her hands trembled as she gripped a pencil. Why were they trembling? She straightened her spine and glared at them, willing them to be reasonable. After a moment, they obeyed.

> *Myra,*
>
> *Thank you for catching up with me. I'm sorry I haven't sent you an update on the house; in truth, I thought I had more time. We did indeed learn the identity of the wizard. He's a twelve-year-old lad named Owein Mansel. Mr. Fernsby determined not to exorcise him, so the house is maintaining its enchanted classification.*
>
> *As there is no immediate need for me outside office work, I would like to request more time at Whimbrel House. You see, I've discovered there is a second source of magic but have not yet determined what. I expect it will prove challenging. Perhaps I will uncover something significant for BIKER or Mr. Fernsby. I will be sure to keep you apprised.*
>
> *Sincerely,*
> *Hulda*

She folded up the paper, sealed it, and affixed it to the windsource pigeon. "Return where you started," she commanded, and the bird ducked out the window and flew north on a sea-scented breeze.

Perhaps I'm being foolish. Truthfully, she didn't really want to travel. She used to love it . . . yet the older she got, the more tiresome it became. And the thought of subjecting herself to menial paperwork in the office instead of being here, searching for the second source of Whimbrel House's magic . . . she didn't savor it. Perhaps she could hire on as a permanent housekeeper here for a while. Like she'd done in Gorse End. So long as she kept her professionalism in place.

"You can't simply *make a slide*!" Merritt shouted from the hall. "You're going to break my ankle next time! If you want a slide, make it *before* I start descending!"

She smiled. How long had it been since Owein had enjoyed good company?

How long had it been for her?

As she pulled away from the window, she noticed a figure in the corner of her eye and glanced back. Miss Taylor stood out there, staring northwest, unmoving. Curious, Hulda slipped out of her room, arriving at the stairs just as Merritt convinced Owein to turn them back into stairs.

He caught her eye and smiled, which made her stupid organs do stupid things that she ignored. He held out his hand to her. "Shall I escort you down this dangerous bluff? One never knows what might happen."

She was about to rebuff him—it was almost automatic for her. But against better judgment, she decided to play along. "Of course, good sir. I have a great need for my ankles today."

He grinned, and she grinned, and she let him take her hand.

It was only thirteen stairs to the main floor, but Hulda felt as though she'd run a mile.

༖

Miss Taylor still hadn't moved by the time Hulda reached her, standing about thirty paces out from the laundry line. The petite woman's eyes were trained somewhere in the deep, grassy meadows of the island, or perhaps just off the visible coast. A breeze swept through, and Hulda noted both the strength of the sun and the quietness of the usual songbirds.

"Miss Taylor?" She approached gingerly. "Are you ill?"

Miss Taylor's eyes snapped to her as though she'd been roused from a daydream. "Oh, sorry. No. I mean, yes, I'm fine." Her gaze drifted back toward the shoreline. "Just thought I saw something queer."

A faint chill crept up Hulda's arms, despite their long sleeves. "What?"

She shrugged one shoulder. "A wolf. But there aren't any wolves on the island, right?"

Rubbing at the uneasiness building in her sternum, Hulda said, "There shouldn't be. Though I thought I saw one once before, too."

A wolf in a library. Her magic had whispered that to her, too. *But what does it mean?*

"Perhaps we'll send Mr. Babineaux out with the musket," she murmured.

Miss Taylor shook her head. "I wouldn't have seen it, I just . . . sensed something. Then it ran away, but not where any real wolf could run. Maybe it's just the shadows."

Hulda nodded. "But I think we'll all feel better if we send a large French man out with a musket, nevertheless." *Mr. Fernsby certainly owns his share of firearms.*

Miss Taylor chuckled. "I did want to ask you, Mrs. Larkin, about taking some time away."

The hopeful glint in her eyes caught Hulda's interest. "There's always the possibility. What have you in mind?"

Suddenly shy, Miss Taylor looked away and pulled down her sleeves. "Well, I saw there was a dance in Portsmouth; some boys were passing out notes about it the last time I went to town to fetch supplies. I thought it might be fun to go. I don't get much opportunity to socialize."

"I can hardly fault you for that." Hulda hadn't been to a dance in . . . over ten years. Thirteen? Fourteen? She'd never felt at place in dance halls. Not because she didn't know the steps, but because she spent most of her time occupying the wall. "When is it?"

"Tomorrow."

"You've certainly earned a night off. And do take the whole night, Miss Taylor. I don't want you trying to navigate these waters in the dark. Do you need a recommendation for a boarding house?"

"My thanks, but I'll be staying with a friend." She smiled, though it looked to be more from nerves than humor. "Well, I don't know how to dance, and I was wondering if you did."

Hulda softened. "Do you need lessons?"

She nodded, eager. "I mean, I know how to dance, but not like they do in Portsmouth. No one danced like that in the South, I mean."

"I'm happy to teach you. And perhaps you could teach me as well." She moved to pull a shawl closer, only to realize she wasn't wearing one. "Tonight after the men go to bed, hm? In my room."

Miss Taylor beamed. "My thanks."

Waving away the gratitude, Hulda merely said, "I could use the exercise."

⌒♋

After dinner, while Mr. Fernsby enjoyed a game of cards with Mr. Babineaux, Hulda went upstairs to compile an official record of her attempts to categorize the house, as well as write up the symptom she believed indicative of a secondary source of magic. Symptom, singular, because she had yet to witness a repetition of the wardship spell, and she'd been testing the doors and windows often. Whatever the source, it was likely small, possibly wavering. Her best guess was a wooden beam or floorboard made from a tree that had absorbed magic during its lifetime. The inconsistency suggested it might be beginning to rot. She had yet to prove the theory correct, however, which rankled her. Seldom had she ever expended so much effort to diagnose an enchanted house, and this one wasn't even particularly large.

Setting down her report, she worked her hands, rubbing growing cramps out of the muscles. Perhaps she should stay up tonight and see if the magic was more active after sundown. Miss Taylor would keep her company for a little while, with this dance practice of theirs, and afterward she could roam the house in her socks, padding around so as not to disturb anyone. She'd been sewing together some charms to tuck into out-of-the-way places in the hopes of finding the wayward spell, and with a little more work, she could be hanging them before dawn.

Deciding to document that undertaking as well, Hulda retrieved her pencil and began writing, only to have the tip snap on her second line. Sighing, she searched for the Lassimonne sharpener, but it wasn't in its usual place. Likely Mr. Fernsby had taken it. Miss Taylor always put things where they belonged, and Mr. Babineaux never wandered upstairs.

Standing, Hulda stretched out her back as much as her corset would allow, then made her way down the hall, pausing at the top of the stairs, where Owein was twisting the carpet downward in the semblance of a whirlpool. Not to bother her, she thought, but because he was bored.

"Evening, Owein," she said, and a narrow path of still carpet stretched across the way, allowing her passage. Nodding her thanks, she crossed the hall, stopping at Mr. Fernsby's office. The door was ajar, the room half-illuminated by orange sunset. Lighting a candle atop a table by the door, Hulda ventured to the cluttered desk. There were *three* cups left there, along with a handkerchief, a smattering of pens and pencils, and a few crumpled pieces of paper, which were not cheap. She'd have to suggest a means of reusing them, for the backsides were perfectly functional. In truth, though, something about the mess was oddly endearing. Beside the crumpled papers sat a blue-jay feather, of all things, a single shoe without laces, a chunk of Mr. Fernsby's manuscript, and, yes, the pencil sharpener.

She noticed his ink vial was depleted. *Hard at work.* She picked up the bottle and slipped back into the library, exchanging it for her own, and then set her mostly full vial beside his papers. As she picked up the sharpener, her candlelight spilled over his manuscript, illuminating, *But a creaking in the dark told Elise she was no longer alone,* on the topmost manuscript page.

Hulda paused. This was not the first page of the book—where that was, only Mr. Fernsby might know. This was midchapter, with a handwritten *102* on the top of the sheet. It was fascinating that a person could just sit down and write an entire novel. That all of these words, and the pictures they painted, had only existed inside his head before he put them to paper. That he could create something from nothing.

She held the candle closer. *She feared to speak; the dark corridor carried sound, so much so she swore she heard echoes of her own breath. She waited, back pressed to the wall, until the creaking happened again.*

"You said they wouldn't look down here." Her voice was barely perceptible. It had to be. Without light, Warren couldn't read her lips.

His response was close enough to her ear to make her jump. Anywhere else, she'd have been embarrassed by the close proximity. But here in enemy territory, it was a comfort. "Don't move."

Hulda lowered herself into the vacant chair. He was rather good, wasn't he? She wasn't sure what she'd expected—if the man made a living off his words, of course he had to be good. She found herself wondering about his first published novel and whether she'd be able to locate and read it. But curiosity gripped her about what was causing the creaking in the darkened corridor, and why these people—Elise and Warren—were there to begin with.

Setting down the candle, Hulda tilted the page toward the light and read to its end, which was midsentence, so she put that page aside and picked up the next. Apparently these two were in a crime lord's lair. Was this the same woman who'd witnessed the robbery Mr. Fernsby had mentioned earlier? Who was the man?

She flipped to the third page. Exhaled sharply. They *weren't* alone. Someone else was down there. Someone who smelled of figurado cigar smoke, which was written like it meant something. Hulda guessed if she'd read earlier pages, she'd know exactly who was following the protagonists, and she had a feeling he wasn't a man of exemplary character.

She turned the page, holding her breath along with Elise as she and Warren ducked into a closet. The man was coming closer. Elise reached for the closet door, but Warren held her back. She squeezed his arm, reassuring him. What did she intend to do?

Good heavens, now she was running out into the hallway in a different direction to distract the cigar man! Hulda turned the page. It was working. He was giving chase. But where would Elise go to escape him?

The same stench from before assaulted her—rot and feces, underlined with old urine. This time she turned toward it, her shoe catching on a divot in the flooring, which nearly sent her toppling. Was that running water? If the canal ran through here, she might be able to escape. Lord knew what diseases she'd pick up along the way, but better a disease than a bullet to the—

"Mrs. Larkin."

Hulda screamed and jumped in the chair, coming very close to ramming her crown into Mr. Fernsby's chin. Her hand rushed to cover her galloping heart. "Merritt, do not creep up on me in such a manner!"

Merritt—Mr. Fernsby . . . goodness, she hadn't called him by his first name, had she?—grinned like a lethargic crocodile and folded his arms. "I did not *creep* in the slightest. You were merely preoccupied."

She glanced to the book and felt her entire body heat. She'd just been caught snooping through his manuscript. "I-I apologize." She simultaneously rose to her feet and slapped the papers back onto their proper stack, but the movement was so emphatic she knocked her spectacles off her nose. They clattered to the floor. "I was coming in for the pencil sharpener and got distracted. I didn't mean to pry."

Mr. Fernsby bent over to pick up the spectacles from the blur of the carpet. "Most people start books from the beginning."

"It won't happen again."

"Mrs. Larkin." He reached forward and set her spectacles upon her nose himself, causing her to flush even more. *God help me, please let the dimness hide it.* But surely his knuckles felt the heat as they brushed her temples. "I am not and will never be upset when someone loses themselves in something I've drafted. Especially considering it's only a draft. Stories are always terrible as drafts."

Stepping away, she smoothed back her hair. "I did not think it terrible. And in my defense, the beginning of the book was not here."

"I dare say that is a compliment, coming from you."

Compliment? She reviewed her words and felt her insides shrink. "I-I didn't mean to say it's not terrible. It's rather good. Very, uh, exciting."

He studied her, and she felt utterly foolish under his blue gaze. "It must be, for my lady's dictionary to be so confounded, considering her usually vibrant vocabulary."

She flushed even more. She must have looked like a ripe tomato.

His expression softened. "I don't mean to embarrass you. In truth, I wouldn't mind a reader. Someone to point out the flaws and such. As long as you give any misspellings some mercy. It *is* a first draft."

Hulda cleared her throat. "Perhaps when the novel is finished. I need to conclude my report to Ms. Haigh at BIKER." She held up the pencil sharpener as if to confirm her alibi. *I can't believe I didn't hear him coming! I can't believe I got so distracted . . . oh, Hulda, you buffoon.*

Adjusting the chair, Mr. Fernsby sat down, allowing Hulda to carefully retreat. "If you insist." He reached for the top-left drawer of his desk and pulled on the handle, but the drawer remained fixed in place. He tugged with more enthusiasm. "Owein, let me open this, would you?"

Glimpsing into the hallway, she saw Owein was still busy swirling the carpet. So rebuilding herself with a stiff spine, pressed-back shoulders, and a lifted nose, she ducked into her room to retrieve a crowbar from her bag. Mr. Fernsby was still working on the drawer when she said, "If I may."

He released the handle. "Are you going to magic it?"

Hulda shoved the tooth of the crowbar just above it. With a little leverage, the drawer popped open.

"It was warm today," she explained. "I believe the wood had merely warped."

"Ah." He glanced from the drawer to her. "You're quite handy. Are you sure you won't stay and read with me?"

The simple, unobtrusive invitation rang through her like a metal spoon running down her ribs. *Stay and read with me.* Stay and spend quiet, peaceful time with Merritt Fernsby. Absorb his work, watch him write, feel a part of it. It was as alluring as the scent of freshly baked rolls at the end of a toilsome day.

She twisted the crowbar in her hands. "I have a report to finish," she said, swallowing her own disappointment.

He nodded. "Good luck."

She set for the exit, feeling neither relief nor accomplishment, but paused before slipping into the hallway. "Mr. Fernsby."

"Hm?"

"What . . ." She felt silly, but a little curiosity was perfectly natural. After all, she did work with the man. "What was the title of your first book? The one already published?"

He grinned. "*A Pauper in the Making.*"

Nodding, Hulda turned away and shut the door firmly behind her.

Chapter 21

The house was quite powerful. It made him reminisce about Gorse End, but this place had a different air. Silas had scouted out the island earlier, confirming there were no other persons occupying the land, no other spells to thwart his intentions, and he'd discovered a special treat along the way.

Silas had collected a good share of psychometry spells over the last three decades, including one that let him sense the magical ability of others. People, things, spells dormant and spells used. This place was strong in chaocracy. Silas had been born with a single chaocracy spell; it's what let him break apart the magic in his donors' blood. But he'd never been able to absorb more. And he wanted more.

He'd planned to begin his work after sundown. But hell and fire, they'd gotten a clairvoyant. Silas *hated* clairvoyants. Their abilities couldn't be avoided by neatness, like with a diviner. He'd never kept any in his company, and for good reason. She'd sensed him, he was sure. Sensed him before he could counter the spell. Silas was powerful, but he possessed nothing magical or otherwise that could mask him from psychic intuition. He would have to plan carefully, so as not to damage other business matters.

His wolf's body bounded farther down the island. He was sure he was out of range of the clairvoyant, but he couldn't take chances. *Chances* made him vulnerable. Chances provided others with opportunities to usurp him, as they had in the past. This was only a minor hiccup, and Silas would overcome it with little effort.

Huffing, he reached the west end of the island and tapped into his alteration spell, mutating his body back from wolf to man. The change made the fingers of his left hand too short, as alteration spells tended to temporarily mutate one's natural body, but they would return to normal within the hour. Then, under the cover of night, he slipped into his boat and sailed for the mainland, avoiding the glow of the lighthouses, mind working through the details as he cut through the currents.

Chapter 22

Merritt wasn't sleeping well.

There were various reasons he wasn't sleeping well. One being that he was too tired. Which sounded silly, but for whatever reason, if Merritt went to bed *too* sleepy, sleep tended to elude him. As though his brain had to stay awake to compensate for the weariness of his body.

Two, he was suffering a bout of creative constipation. He had made good progress on his novel, but now he was somewhat stuck. Merritt didn't really *plan* his stories in advance, so the details had to come out little by little, step by step. He often didn't know how they would end until he got there. And in truth, although he'd made a living with his pen since he was twenty-three, most of it had been newspaper articles and short fiction—his first published novel had been a struggle. So he deliberated over the adventures of Elise and Warren in his head, wondering if they should betray each other (but with what motivation?) or perhaps fall in love.

That train of thought ultimately led him to Hulda. She liked his book. Which meant she liked his brain, didn't it? Which made him consider how nice it would be to have a person to bounce ideas off indefinitely, whether it was midday or midnight. Which also made him think of how nice it would be if there were another body taking up space in this too-wide bed. Someone warm and soft and *there*.

Merritt growled. *Stop it.* He was an independent bachelor who had made a good life for himself with very little help from others. He was content with that life. He'd *made* himself content with it. And every time he tried to expand said contentment to include another person, it always went sour. What was the point of trying?

Rolling over, he folded the pillow under his head and forced his eyes shut. Pretended to sleep for a full minute.

He thought, again, of what it would be like when Hulda left for BIKER. Well, so what? He could overcome infatuation. He had before. But Hulda was like picking up a book with no description, fanfare, or title and discovering it got better and better with each page turned. He wanted to know how her story would read. He wanted to reach the denouement, the end. And he wanted to see if she had a sequel.

It must have been near midnight when Merritt finally groaned, sat up, and ventured out of his blankets to put on trousers. Lying there endlessly obviously wasn't helping. He'd try stretching his legs a bit, maybe get some fresh air. Granted, this far from the cities, it was awfully dark at night, and he was more likely to sprain an ankle strolling outside than he was to relax.

Rubbing his eyes, he padded down the hall, surprised to see light beneath Hulda's door. He heard her voice saying, "Two, three, four, five, six, seven, eight," and wondered at it, but decided to give her privacy and ventured instead toward the stairs. Owein, who did not seem to need sleep, graciously turned the stairs into a giant wooden slide *before* he arrived. With a sigh, Merritt sat and slid down on his rump. The stairs returned to normal a moment later.

Though he was headed toward the front door, he heard a pounding coming from the kitchen, so he ventured through the dining and breakfast rooms, finding Baptiste hunched over the counter in the kitchen, smashing a piece of meat with a little metal hammer.

"I think it's dead," Merritt offered.

The only sign of surprise was a quick flex of the man's shoulders, which he peered over to look at Merritt. "I am . . ." He paused. "Temporizing it."

"Tenderizing?"

"Yes, that." His accent weighed his words more than usual. He had to be tired. "I am making schnitzel."

One of Hulda's choices, no doubt. "I'm sure the meat can be smashed in the morning if you want to get some rest."

The chef shrugged. "Sometimes I do not sleep."

Merritt pulled over a stool and sat. "You and I both. It's something that comes with age. How old *are* you, my friend?"

"I turned forty in August."

"You don't look a day over thirty-seven."

Baptiste snorted. Might have even smiled, but his face was turned toward the meat.

"Pork?" Merritt guessed.

Baptiste nodded.

"What is your favorite thing to cook?"

"Pies," he answered immediately. "Fruit pie, meat pie, cream pie. I am very good at pies."

Merritt's stomach rumbled at the thought of so many pastries. "I will hardly keep you from making pies."

"Need a cellar for the butter. It works better cold."

"Perhaps Owein can dig one for you."

He shrugged. "Give me shovel, and I will dig it myself. And take care of the cow."

That gave him pause. "What cow?"

Baptiste glanced over again. "I talked to Mrs. Larkin about cow. I would like cow. Take good care of her. Have lots of cream."

Merritt wondered what a whole cow's worth of cream would do to his digestion, but his tongue moistened at the idea. "If my novel does well, I will get you—us—a cow. I'll even let you name it."

This time, he thought he caught sight of a dimple on the stoic man's face.

A sudden *thud!* sounded upstairs, followed by a scream.

Both men tensed. Baptiste bolted from the counter, nearly mowing over Merritt as he rushed to his feet. They dashed through the two dining rooms and into the reception hall. Baptiste took the stairs three at a time and reached Hulda's bedroom first, Merritt three paces behind. The chef, still wielding his hammer, barged in so roughly he almost tore the door from its frame.

A million half thoughts rushed through Merritt's mind, centering on Hulda's welfare. Had someone broken in? Was it a rat? Was it—

Hulda in her underthings?

Baptiste was inside the bedroom, but Merritt halted in the hallway, peering over the big man's arm, to where Hulda stood in nothing but her drawers, chemise, and tightly laced corset. Her hands swung up to cover the cleavage spilling over the latter's top, and her face bloomed like a summer hibiscus.

"Get *out!*" she screamed, obviously very hale and unharmed.

Baptiste, equally as red, tripped over himself in his rush to close the door. Slam it, really.

Merritt tried to speak but found he couldn't. He was still trying to catch his breath. Understand what on earth the scream had been about. And why Hulda was trouncing around in her underwear.

His thoughts lingered on that last question, and the visual that went with it.

Baptiste cleared his throat. "We will not speak of this." His long legs carried him to the stairs.

"Indeed," Merritt muttered, confused, and very aware of the woman on the other side of the door.

He certainly would not be sleeping tonight.

Merritt did, eventually, drift off, which lent to a late waking. He scrubbed his face with cold water, brushed his hair and left it loose—he lived on an island, for heaven's sake, no need to concern himself with fashion—and dressed, forgoing the vest because why bother. Beth was polishing the banisters when he came downstairs, and she nodded to him without meeting his eyes, which was curious. Hulda had just finished breakfast and was carrying her dishes to the sink.

Discomfort crept up and down Merritt's esophagus like a colony of termites. "Mrs. Larkin, I'm glad to catch you. I must apologize on behalf of Baptiste and myself; we heard a scream and were rather rash in our discovery of its source."

She set the plates down. "Indeed you were. Or at least, Mr. Babineaux was."

He let out a relieved breath upon hearing her heap most of the blame on Baptiste, suddenly glad the Frenchman was so much quicker than he was. Guilt quickly followed. He wanted to see how the chef was faring after the embarrassment, but Baptiste did not wish to discuss last night's incident.

Wiping off her hands, Hulda turned to face him, every bit as stern and upright as she'd been the day Merritt met her. He'd begun to suspect it was a comforting mask she wore—the utmost professionalism to hide unwanted emotions and discomfiture. Another page turned in her metaphorical book. "I appreciate the apology. I was teaching Miss Taylor some country dances, and in her excitement, she leapt atop my trunk, which was empty. We both toppled over, and she shouted in surprise."

"Beth?" Merritt repeated without thinking.

Her brow furrowed. "I presume you have not yet apologized to her."

"I . . . admittedly, I hadn't noticed Miss Taylor was there as well." His chest warmed. Chuckling, he rubbed the back of his neck to have something to do, realizing he'd just unwittingly admitted his eyes had gone straight to Hulda and never strayed. "I will"—he turned to hide his face—"go do that right now."

"Mr. Fernsby."

He paused.

Hulda scanned the ceiling. "Owein has been very responsive to us, ever since we learned his name."

Merritt relaxed a fraction. "I've noticed the same."

"I recall you were not fond of the idea of hiring employees initially. Perhaps, with some additional training, staff may not be necessary." She offered the information carefully, almost as though it were rehearsed. "Owein's adept at keeping himself orderly, as we saw from the lack of neglect upon your arrival, and he's assisted me in simple chores as well. You needn't worry about Miss Taylor. She will not be short of work so long as she's affiliated with BIKER."

She didn't look at him on that last sentence, but out the window. The streaming sunlight highlighted the flecks of green in her eyes. Why wouldn't she look at him?

Did Hulda not *want* to leave? The thought made his stomach tighten and the termites repopulate. As she was an employee of BIKER, Merritt had little say over her comings and goings. Was it too much to hope she didn't wish for him to follow through on the professional advice she was offering?

Could he convince her to stay? Stay . . . for him?

"Thank you, but my cash reserves are hardly overspent," he offered, coaxing her eyes to meet his gaze once more. And even if they were . . . he wouldn't send any of them away unless they wished to leave. They hadn't been together for long, but a sense of familiarity had begun to settle in the house, a sort of routine that made him think of, well, *home*. He had tried for years not to think of home, for it never left him in a good mood. But Baptiste's quiddities, Beth's quiet presence, and Hulda's restrained banter made him nostalgic in a comforting way. It made him remember the good, not the bad. It felt almost like a family.

"In truth, I like the company. I would like you . . . and Miss Taylor and Baptiste to stay."

A few seconds of silence—which felt like much longer to him—passed between them, gazes interlocked. Still holding his gaze, Hulda said, "I think I—all of us—appreciate that, Mr. Fernsby."

Feeling a little daring, he said, "I still want you to call me Merritt."

She hesitated half a heartbeat, a small smile at the left corner of her mouth. "I know."

With nothing more to be said, Merritt excused himself to offer his apologies to Miss Taylor. And perhaps a raise as well, to sweeten her disposition.

The morning after Miss Taylor's dance in Portsmouth, Hulda sat mending her torn hem in case the two dresses she'd ordered got delayed. She sat across the room from Mr. Fernsby and tried not to pay him much mind as he edited his manuscript, though he had a habit of making strange noises as he did so. Little grunts and inquisitive hums, which Hulda had at first thought were intended to gain her attention. But his eyes never left the pages, and three fine lines were constantly wedged between his eyebrows as he concentrated. He had one pencil behind his ear and another one clenched in his teeth. Oddly enough, Hulda had once made a habit of chewing on pencils herself, but the English instructor at her all-girls school had beaten it out of her when she was a child . . . often using the very pencil bearing her tooth marks.

He had one foot up on the settee upon which he'd perched, the other propped on the table, which once would have driven Hulda mad. Now she found it strangely charming. Which she should not . . . but Merritt's—Mr. Fernsby's—soft words in the kitchen yesterday had softened her resolve. A resolve she heavily starched when alone, yet somehow managed to crinkle whenever she was in his presence.

She liked being in his presence, even if it was quiet. She could be happy with just that—

Her chair inched sideways.

Hulda gripped the armrest with one hand, the other pinching her needle. She glanced around, but nothing seemed amiss. *Odd.* Perhaps she needed to drink some water.

Rolling her lips together, Hulda made one more stitch before the chair shifted again, in the same direction. She paused. The first incident she might have written off as a dizzy spell, but not this one. What on earth—

The chair scooted another inch, toward Mr. Fernsby. Who heard the scraping of its feet, because he glanced up from his manuscript.

It was then Hulda noticed the floor had risen, albeit only the portion beneath her, and the slope was making her chair slide.

Toward the settee where Mr. Fernsby sat.

Nails digging into the armrest, she said, "Owein, stop that."

The floor sloped a little more, scooting her a hand's width, until her chair was touching the settee.

"What's he about?" Mr. Fernsby asked.

Hulda huffed. "Really, Owein. Stop this at—"

The floor bucked upward, tossing Hulda from her seat and propelling her toward Mr. Fernsby.

He dropped his manuscript, sending a few pages flying, and grasped her shoulders, lifting her before she could plop face-first into his lap. Her cheeks burned fiercely, even more so when she started thinking *about* Mr. Fernsby's lap, and she inwardly cursed the fool boy who thought such pranks entertaining.

Finding her feet, she whipped around so sharply her glasses barely held on to her nose. "I swear I will put up enough charms to ward you into the library, Owein Mansel!"

The house stilled.

A few seconds ticked by before Mr. Fernsby said, "It's the last name. Always wields more power than the first, though not as much as the middle." His face dimpled in a way that suggested he found this all very amusing but was trying to be polite. "Do you think he has a middle name? That would really drive it home."

Hulda smoothed her skirt, then snatched her chair and moved it back to its original place. Then a little farther from the settee, as though to make a point she did not care to examine. "Perhaps."

She picked up her mending and plopped down with a childish amount of righteous indignation. Pushing the needle into her torn hem, she dared to glance up at Mr. Fernsby. He caught her eye with a soft, amused smile. She refocused on her work. Three stitches later, she glanced up again, but he was back to poring over his manuscript. Hulda frowned. She didn't *want* to be stared at, after that embarrassing tirade, but . . . perhaps it was silly to want him to notice her more than he did.

Pressing her lips together, she worried she might have muttered some things about Merritt Fernsby aloud once or twice, which little Owein might have overheard . . .

Thank God the spirit couldn't speak to Merritt and embarrass her further.

She glanced up again. Watched him read. Perhaps she should have resituated herself on the settee. A childish thought, and yet . . .

Footsteps outside the door announced Miss Taylor, who stepped inside with a pearly smile on her face and a stack of letters under her arm—she must have stopped by the post office before returning to the island. Upon seeing the stack, Hulda's heart leapt, and she stabbed herself with her needle, eliciting a squeak from her lips.

Mr. Fernsby lowered the papers. "Are you all right?"

He was so absorbed by his work she was surprised and stupidly delighted that he'd noticed. "I haven't pricked myself in years," she said, shaking out the finger. The tiniest welling of blood marked the skin. "Hardly anything serious. Miss Taylor, what are the letters?"

Mr. Fernsby leaned forward to better see the maid. "Miss Taylor! Did you enjoy yourself? I worry you didn't if you're walking so well. I've seen many a dancer bleed and blister their feet on the dance floor."

She beamed. "It was right fun, Mr. Fernsby, my thanks." She nodded at Hulda and pulled out the envelopes. "I've two letters for Mr. Fernsby and two for you, Mrs. Larkin. Plus a package, which I put on your bed."

The dresses, already?

Hulda pulled the needle free of its thread. "Excellent. I shan't have to keep piecing this thing together." Perhaps she could rehem it and send it to her sister, who was shorter than she was . . . but Danielle had much more eclectic taste in fashion and likely wouldn't wear it.

Miss Taylor crossed to Mr. Fernsby first and handed him his letters before shifting toward Hulda.

"Ah! Fletcher." Halfway through tearing open the first letter, he glanced Hulda's way. "He's visiting next week, with luck. I can take care of preparations."

"Need I remind you what staff is for?" She allowed some wryness to creep into her expression, which Mr. Fernsby met with a grin. "Owein could likely make him his own room." Miss Taylor handed her the letters. "Thank you, Miss Taylor."

The envelopes were in such poor condition Hulda wondered if they'd been sent via conjury—transformed into a shape capable of flying across the Atlantic, then restored to their original form upon arrival—instead of a kinetically powered ship. The former was becoming rather antediluvian. Her eyes sailed to the return address. England, both of them.

Her breath hitched. "If you'll excuse me." Draping her torn dress over her shoulder, Hulda headed for the exit. Mr. Fernsby called after her, but she answered only with a reassuring wave as she continued on her way, across carpet that was now pink with large green spots marring it, courtesy of the resident ghost. Hulda barely registered the garishness and arrived at her room with her fingers cold and jittery.

She opened the first letter, from the constabulary of Liverpool. It was brief, the writing little more than chicken scratch.

We've no record of any Hogwoods leaving Merseyside or registering for emigration, but he could have done so at a port city.

She sighed. It was the best she was going to get—few migrants bothered with paperwork, and Mr. Hogwood of all people would hardly wish to leave a paper trail.

Setting the letter aside, she opened the second, from the warden of Lancaster Castle.

> *Miss Larkin,*
>
> *I remember Silas Hogwood, but I pulled up his records to be sure. He was imprisoned here, yes, but passed away on June 14 by an unknown cause. He was still healthy, from what I could tell. Quite peculiar.*
>
> *My apologies if this news brings any distress.*
>
> *Formally Yours,*
>
> *Benjamin Canterbury*

Hulda stared at the letter, not quite comprehending. She read it again, but the words blurred together, so she sat on her trunk and adjusted her glasses before reading it through a third time, top to bottom. Turned the paper over just in case there was something on the back, then read it again.

Distress . . . yes, it *was* distressing. How could a healthy man pass away in a prison, where he would have been routinely monitored, without anyone having a clue as to why? Granted, prisons weren't the most sanitary dwellings . . .

She licked her lips. The letter drooped in her limp grip.

This means he couldn't have been in Portsmouth, she reminded herself. But the information didn't relieve her, only worried her.

Had the warden seen Mr. Hogwood's body with his own eyes? Did they realize what a powerful magic user he was? Perhaps he'd lost many of his spells after those corpses were destroyed . . .

She attempted to quash her unreasonable concerns and take solace that the horrible wizard was gone. And yet, despite the assurance in her hands, those concerns burned bright as a bonfire feasting on her bones.

Chapter 23

October 1, 1846, Blaugdone Island, Rhode Island

Hulda had followed up with the warden the following day, desperate for more information. Nearly a week later, she received his response. This time it was a simple telegram reading, *I'm afraid I cannot disclose more information.*

The missive irked her. Was it truly an issue of privacy, for a man who had been publicly decried, or were his records missing information? *All this fuss over a dead man,* she told herself, yet every time she reasoned herself to stability, a loose thought would send her spiraling into doubt again.

She had *seen* him. She swore she had *seen* him! But why would the prison cover up the release of a repeat murderer? Or the *escape* of one?

The only thing that gave her some comfort was Mr. Fernsby's admonition that she was safe here. And she was. It seemed incredulous that Mr. Hogwood would somehow fake his death, slip out of a high-security prison, and immigrate to America, only to break into BIKER, find her records, and sail all the way out to Blaugdone Island for revenge.

Mr. Fernsby had also been occupied, to the point where Hulda was only seeing him at meals, save for yesterday, when he took a long walk across the island, mumbling to himself as he left the house. He spent almost all his time lucubrating in his office. Had taken dinner there twice. Hulda wondered at it, but it wasn't her place to pry, nor to interrupt. Still, she'd lingered by the door a time or two, listening, and heard nothing within. She'd thought to ask him about *A Pauper in the Making*, which she had taken the initiative to purchase, but with her mind so taken up with the possibilities of Mr. Hogwood, she'd yet to start it.

When Miss Taylor and Mr. Babineaux were occupied with their own tasks and Mr. Fernsby was not around to banter, Hulda quickly got bored. She still had not found the second source of magic and was ready to tear apart the foundation with teeth and nails, if only to occupy her mind with something other than Silas Hogwood.

After Mr. Fernsby took dinner in his office for the *third* time, Hulda volunteered to see to retrieving his tray, telling Miss Taylor she could retire early. Shadows waved to her as she passed through the hallway; Hulda waved back, and the house rumbled in pleasure. She rapped at the closed office door with her first and second knuckle.

"Come," Mr. Fernsby's voice issued from within.

Pressing open the door, Hulda suppressed a sigh at the sight before her. Papers and pencil shavings scattered across the floor, ink smears on the desk, open books by the chair. His dinner tray rested precariously on the corner of the desk. Miss Taylor had cleared out other dishes, but Mr. Fernsby must have shooed away her efforts to do more.

"I'm here for your tray," she offered.

He straightened like she'd trickled cold water down his spine and turned in his chair. "Hulda! I thought you were Beth."

She didn't correct him for not calling her Mrs. Larkin, though her wiser half warned that she should. *Professionalism is protection,* she reminded herself, but now it was too late to make the correction without being awkward about it, so she let it slide. She moved for the tray but paused before picking it up. "Might I ask why you've become a hermit?"

Mr. Fernsby set down his pen and rubbed his eyes with the heels of his hands. "The other letter I got last week was from my editor. I've a meeting with him in a week and a half, and I want to have as much of this damnable thing finished as possible before I see him. I'm worried it won't be as good as the first book."

She glanced over the stacks of paper at his elbow. "I don't know about the first book, but would presenting a synopsis of sorts suffice?"

"I can't write a synopsis."

"Why not?"

"Because then I would have to know the ending, and why would I finish a book when I already know how it ends?" There was mirth in the question, but she sensed his reasoning was entirely serious. "Actually." He turned his chair toward her, and Hulda became very aware of how close his knees were to hers. She could feel heat emanating from them . . . but that was preposterous. Who had hot knees?

She flushed, realizing she'd completely missed what he'd said. "I'm sorry, would you repeat that?"

"Would you help me?" He clasped both hands over his knees, as though hiding them from her scrutiny. Her chest tightened. She hadn't been staring at his *knees* of all things, had she? "Your idea for the beginning unfolded so well. I'd like to pick your brain again, if you have a moment." Suddenly sheepish, he glanced around the room. "I, uh, will clean this up afterward."

She waved the barter away. "I hardly care for the mess considering you're under deadline, Mr. Fernsby." She was grateful for the excuse to talk with him. She felt . . . better . . . around Merritt Fernsby. There was a simple wood chair in the corner, so she pulled it over, ensuring adequate space separated their knees. Fixing her professional self into place, she asked, "For what, precisely, do you need my assistance?"

He pulled over several papers and scanned them. "It's for this blasted romance subplot."

Her warm feelings dissipated, and the professional mask cracked. She stood. "I should go."

"Oh please." He grasped her hand. "Just hear me out."

Her gaze shot to his fingers. He definitely noticed *that*, given how quickly he released her afterward. He cleared his throat. "That is, if the others aren't waiting on you."

Rolling her lips together, Hulda sat, wrists and neck pulsing. "All right." Her upright tone was slipping. "Tell me."

"I've only just started it. I'll go back and allude to it. Longing glances and the like," he replied, and Hulda was grateful his eyes had focused on his papers and not her. "But I've got them alone together at this Quaker's house, and I'm wondering . . . should I do this now? And do what? Though with her being an heiress and him being from Hartford, I intend for them to go their separate ways at the end. But I don't want female readers to think—"

"Mr. Fernsby." *Straight back. Firm voice.*

Pausing, he met her eyes. His looked especially blue when he was tired. "What?"

"I am aware my reading background does not make me an expert on the subject," she went on, "but that is not a romance."

"Sure it is—"

"If you don't intend for the couple to have a happy ending, then don't involve them with each other at all. You'll lose readers. The general populace prefers comedies, not tragedies."

He pondered this for a moment. His nose dipped when he pursed his lips. "So I should have them, what, kiss?"

Hulda fidgeted, trying to ignore the heat creeping up her neck. "I don't know about that. But I'm sure as long as they're together, perhaps married or engaged by the end . . ."

"They have to kiss before they get married. He's a liberal." He winked and glanced at the papers. "Might be too soon for that . . . *unless* I add some tension to this scene where they're hiding in a shed."

"I-It's your book, Mr. Fernsby. I'm sure whatever you think is best will be right." She stood and picked up her chair, meaning to return it to the corner.

"I'm just asking your thoughts." He sounded inquisitive. "Surely you wouldn't kiss a man in a stranger's shed if he hadn't . . . what, held your hand first? Perhaps a declaration is needed? Or am I getting ahead of myself and the kiss should come at the end of the story?"

Her ears were burning. "Everyone is different." She set the chair down with more force than intended, then made the grievous mistake of turning back.

Mr. Fernsby was watching her, his papers forgotten, his right eyebrow raised, his upper lip quirked like a mischievous school boy's.

She felt like she was in her underwear all over again.

"Mrs. Larkin." Two of the usual three lines appeared between his brows. "Have you never been kissed?"

Fire. She was on fire.

"If you'll excuse me." The roughness of her voice only embarrassed her more. She made a beeline for the door.

He stood, papers shuffling. "I'm sorry, it was impertinent of me to ask."

She hesitated at the door.

"I'm just comfortable with you." Regret lightened the words and carried them like candle smoke. "Don't answer. Just . . . forgive me."

Letting out a slow, calculated breath, she glanced back, hardly daring to meet his eyes. Her heartbeat was erratic, but she didn't *want* to leave. "I fear my reaction has already answered it for you."

She expected a jest at her expense, but Mr. Fernsby sat down, set his manuscript aside, and asked, "What's it like to have magic?"

The change in subject was both surprising and appreciated. She released the door handle, cupped her elbows, and took a few paces into the room. "I . . . well, I don't particularly remember *not* having it, except as a little girl imagining being a wizard."

He smiled. "What did you imagine?"

"Psychometry, actually. I wanted to read minds. Know what people really thought of me."

"That would be a terrible spell to have."

"I agree with you. Now, that is." She shrugged. Took another step toward him. "It certainly has been useful. I would hate to be without it. It's akin to a fifth limb."

"Or a sixth sense," he offered.

She nodded. "A more apt metaphor. I suppose that's why you're the writer."

"Or trying to be." He passed a glare at his manuscript. "And you've never been interested in setting up some sort of horoscope shop? They're very popular."

"My great-grandmother had one." Another step. "She was eccentric."

"You don't have to be eccentric to run your own business."

"No," she agreed, "but when you turn yourself into a novelty, you attract a certain kind of person. They see only the novelty, and once they've had their fill, they leave. She had thousands of friends, but none of them were true connections. From what I've been told, at least. She passed away when I was young."

He rubbed his chin. Stubble covered it; he hadn't shaved today. There was something distinctly masculine about the unkemptness, and Hulda briefly wondered how rough it would feel under her fingers. "She sounds like quite a character."

"She was very real."

"Have you ever wondered," he followed up without missing a beat, "if we're all characters in another's book? If all of our actions, whims, thoughts, and desires are being controlled by some omniscient author?"

A strange notion. "By God?"

"If He's writing it, I suppose it would classify as nonfiction."

Hulda laughed. "I would hope so, because fiction would mean none of us were real."

He grinned. It was an appealing grin—genuine and slightly feline, his upper teeth straight. She'd noticed he had two crooked ones on the bottom set.

"Well." He leaned back in his chair. "So long as BIKER is giving you good opportunity to use your gifts."

She studied him for a moment, pushing up her glasses to better do so. He eyed her inquisitively in return. After a moment, she said, "All right. Finish your tea."

"Pardon?"

"You asked me once to do a reading for you." She picked his cold tea up off his tray; the cup was a third full. "I'll do it now."

The expression that washed over his face made him look boyish. "Really?"

She rolled her eyes. "Dawdle, and I'll change my mind." His excitement was palpable; it made her chest flutter that she was the source of it. Besides which, she wanted to know more about Merritt Fernsby, for better or for worse.

He finished the cold tea with only a slight grimace. She took the cup from him and leaned toward a candle, examining the tea leaves. Sometimes it took a moment . . . Perhaps if magic ran thicker through her veins, she'd have more control over the spell—

Her thoughts flashed. Not to a vision this time, but to words and feelings, like she was touching the tip of her tongue to a forkful of food without being allowed to put the morsel in her mouth.

Strife. Confusion. Longing. Betrayal. *Truth.*

It flashed away just as quickly, though Hulda continued staring at the tea leaves afterward.

"It's not so bad, is it?" he asked.

For a brief moment, Hulda forgot where she was. But her augury was so faint, the spell so brief, that the side effect of using magic abated quickly.

Smoothing her forehead, she lowered the cup. A few pretty lies spun beneath her skull. Nicer things to pass on than the discomfort lingering under her breastbone. But Merritt . . . he would want to know.

"Good and bad, I suppose," she managed, setting down the cup. "There's strife in your future . . . but strife that will lead to truth."

"Strife and truth? Sounds religious. I'm not joining the Mormons, am I?"

She blinked. "Who are the Mormons?"

He waved the query aside. Peered into the cup himself. "Well, I see . . . a rabbit. With its ears and tail cut off."

She smiled. "Perhaps Mr. Babineaux can be persuaded to incorporate that into your future as well." Picking up his tray, she turned for the door.

"Does it ever bother you?" His voice trailed in her wake. "Knowing the future all the time?"

Her hands tightened on the tray, and the fluttering in her chest died. "Not at all. Because in truth"—she turned and met his eyes, hoping hers didn't reveal her *own* truths—"I never really do."

⌒⊙

Hulda was up early Saturday morning, determined yet again to make herself useful. There was nothing she was better at than making herself useful. Being *useful* made her feel good about herself, regardless of all the nonsense and trepidation going on in her life.

And so she scoured every inch of the house. Walked every foot of carpet with her dowsing rods. Hung charms and moved charms and wove new charms that provided her with zero useful information. She even took Miss Taylor with her, in case her clairvoyance turned up anything, but alas, it did not.

With nothing else she could do inside, Hulda decided to examine the outside of the house. Mr. Fernsby had already set out for a walk,

Mr. Babineaux was busy in the kitchen, and Miss Taylor . . . well, Hulda hadn't checked to see what currently occupied Miss Taylor. It was as good a time as any. She donned her sturdiest dress and shoes, strapped a sun hat onto her head, and ventured outside, her heavy bag over her shoulder.

She started with the easiest tool to use, the dowsing rods, and walked in a tight circle around the house before taking a step out and walking around it again. Another step out, and this time she moved counterclockwise. She repeated this pattern until she was a good thirty feet from the house. Either there was nothing to detect, or she was in need of a new pair of dowsing rods.

Returning to the house, Hulda pulled out her stethoscope and crouched, placing the drum against the foundation. She heard her own heartbeat from the exercise, and waited a minute until it quieted down. Then she shifted over and listened again.

The stony foundation rippled beneath her touch.

Sighing, Hulda sat back on her haunches. "I'm looking for the second source of magic. Do you have wardship spells, Owein? Maybe one pulse for yes, two pulses for no?"

The house remained still for a few seconds, then rippled twice.

Heaven forbid this be easy. She chewed on her lower lip. "*Is* there a second source of magic? Do you sense it?"

The house shifted slightly, as though shrugging.

That shrug gave her an idea. Placing her hand flat against the foundation, she ran her fingers down to where it connected with the earth. Dug her nails into the dirt, uncovering a sliver more.

"Owein. Do you think you could, hmm, stand up a little straighter? Shift the house up and over a bit, so I can get a look underneath?"

The wall facing her faded to indigo.

"I'm not sure what that means."

The spot just above her hand rippled twice.

Hulda sighed.

It rippled again, one time.

She paused. "Does that mean you're willing to try?"

Instead of answering with their new code, the house began to tremble.

Soaring to her feet, Hulda clamped one hand over her hat as stone cracked and wood bowed. She heard a shriek from inside—Miss Taylor—and immediately felt sorry, but it was hard to schedule one's interactions with a twelve-year-old house-bodied ghost. She would apologize thoroughly in just a moment.

The corner of the house closest to her lifted from the grass, splitting the foundation as it did so—something Owein should be able to fix, if Hulda had guessed correctly about his chaocracy spells. The house looked like a dog relieving itself, one leg in the air.

Fumbling through her bag for a match, Hulda lit it and dropped to her stomach, hesitant to crawl into the newly made cavern. While chaocracy could fix split stone, it could not fix split bone. Not that Hulda had ever heard of, at least.

She slipped her arm inside, coughing at the dust, and peered into the darkness. Stone, stone, dirt, stone. The tail of a fleeing mouse. A disgruntled centipede. And—

Her tiny light glinted off something far off. Something dark and reflective. "Just a moment longer!" she cried as the match burned her fingertips. She dropped it and ignited another. Crawled across the ground, uncaring if she soiled her dress. This would be worth the wash if she were right—

The glassy veins glimmered as she stretched her hand closer.

She grinned wide enough to hurt.

Found you.

Chapter 24

Merritt had thoroughly turned his mind to mud that week, so he decided to spend Saturday in the yard. He tucked his scarf in his shirt, wore an old pair of trousers, rolled up his sleeves, and even tied his hair back, then set to weeding the garden and foundation, leaving a clear trail at the front and west side of the house. If he'd had a scythe, he'd have cut down some of the vegetation elsewhere, but that would have to go at the bottom of the long list of supplies he needed to be a decent homeowner. And here he'd thought his publisher's advance would make him feel wealthy.

Leaves were falling from the island's trees. Merritt walked out to explore them, satisfied with the crunch beneath his boots and the crisp breeze rattling through the branches. He should really have a picnic out here before it got too cold. Right here, under this elm. It was a lovely spot. The autumn scent and color scheme made him nostalgic for something he couldn't quite describe. Perhaps it was simply for childhood autumns, when he hadn't had a care in the world.

For a moment, he thought he heard a cracking, like man splitting stone in two, but when he looked back toward the house, nothing seemed amiss. *Curious.*

Leaning up against the elm, Merritt closed his eyes and breathed in the beauty of the island, letting it unwind the muscles in his arms and shoulders, soothe the lining of his lungs, dance across his lips. Spots of sun glimmered through the tree's thinning crown, driving back goose-flesh raised by the shade. The breeze spun around him, sounding like the whispers of dozens of children, flitting shyly around his ears.

He opened his eyes. The leaves and grasses had gone still, which gave him pause.

No breeze.

No more whispers.

Strange. He glanced back to the house. He must have missed a school of cicadas or some such.

"Merritt!"

Whirling around, Merritt spied a dark figure dressed smartly in gray moving toward him, hand raised in greeting.

He grinned and walked to meet him. "You're late!"

"I'm *late?*" Fletcher repeated. "You live in the middle of Godforsaken nowhere, and you're going to accuse me of being late? Show me your watch."

Merritt patted his side, only to remember he hadn't worn a vest, and he never donned his watch without a vest pocket to slip it into.

Fletcher raised his eyebrows. "And the accused rests his case." He glanced over Merritt's shoulder. "Seems . . . tame."

Merritt embraced him, patting him firmly on the back. "It is, mostly. Thank you for coming out again. I need a break from words."

"Am I allowed to read it?"

"Only if you get bored with our other festivities." They started toward the house.

"Then yes," Fletcher said. "I'll be reading it."

They reached the house; Beth was hanging laundry, so Merritt introduced Fletcher, who tipped his hat to her. Inside, the portrait craned to get a better look at their guest before waving.

"So strange." Fletcher leaned forward to study the animated painting.

Hulda came down the stairs. "Greetings, Mr. Portendorfer. I trust your travel was pleasant. I've your room prepared for you. Any other needs can be addressed to myself or Miss Taylor, our maid."

Merritt, after closing the front door, glanced to Hulda and paused.

Fletcher spoke for both of them when he said, "You look nice, Mrs. Larkin."

She was wearing a new dress, a bright straw-colored thing with a pattern of dark-maroon roses and three-quarter sleeves. Whereas all her other dresses buttoned up clear to the chin, this one had a wider collar, actually exposing her neck and collarbones. Her hair was done up as she usually did it, but . . . there was something different Merritt couldn't quite put his finger on. She looked . . . radiant.

"Indeed," he mumbled, earning himself a curious side glance from Fletcher.

"Thank you, Mr. Portendorfer. I'm afraid the dressmaker mistook my order, but it fits, so I shan't complain about it." Her eyes shifted to Merritt. "In good news, Mr. Fernsby, I believe I've discovered the second source of magic in the house."

"Second source?" Fletcher asked at the same time Merritt said, "Oh?"

"I discovered tourmaline deposits in the home's foundation." She smiled fully at the accomplishment, which only added to her allure. "Tourmaline is a stone associated with wardship. Whimbrel House was used to house necromancers fleeing Salem for several decades; it's very likely some of those women also possessed wardship spells. The tourmaline would be the perfect substance to absorb them."

He nodded slowly. "Makes sense to me."

"Tourmaline, eh?" Fletcher set down his suitcase. "I heard about the whole gemstones and magic connection. My mother used to visit a doctor who used all kinds of stones to cure ailments, saying they linked to the various magics. I didn't believe a lick of it."

Merritt tugged his attention to Fletcher. "I recall that. Why not?"

He shrugged. "The one time I went, I ended up getting hives. Don't you remember? We were fourteen. Took two days off school, and when I went back, the Barrett brothers were relentless about my 'new freckles.'"

"I don't remember, but I really wish I did." Merritt laughed. "Same room as last time; I'm willing to share, but our dear housekeeper thinks it's not hospitable enough. So she's temporarily displaced our maid to her own room. Refuses to hear of anything else."

Fletcher snatched his suitcase again. "Very kind. Let me put this down, and you can show me what you've done with the place." He nodded to Hulda as he made his way to the stairs. Merritt followed, trying not to gawk at her. But he did, and a faint pink arch stretched across her nose.

Before Fletcher could reach the stair rail, however, the stairs began to shift. As did the floor, walls, and ceiling.

Merritt stumbled backward as the floor began to tilt upward, much as it had when Owein had moved Hulda's chair in Merritt's office. Except the incline became much steeper much quicker, and all the floorboards shifted at once.

Managing to stay on his feet, Merritt slid into the back corner between the portrait and the door. When his back hit the wall, he realized the *entire room* was rotating.

"Owein!" Merritt bellowed. "We have *guests*!"

And yet the declaration only incited the ghostly wizard to push his magic harder, and the room bucked to a full forty-five-degree angle. Fletcher dropped his suitcase, which went flying into the dining room, and grabbed the stair rail with both hands. Hulda shrieked, stumbled, and fell back toward the door.

Shoving off the wall, Merritt managed to snag her around the waist before she hit. The impact sent her glasses to the very edge of her nose.

But Owein wasn't finished. The room tilted to fifty degrees, fifty-five, sixty—

Gravity slammed Merritt back into the corner by the portrait. He kept his hold on Hulda, which in turn slammed her into him. He wedged one foot into the doorjamb to keep their place.

"Never fear, Mrs. Larkin." He smiled even as the room continued to churn. "In a moment we may be able to slip into a stationary room."

Fletcher shouted something. Beth's face appeared in the window, but it was difficult to open the door, angled and turning as it was. The room arched enough that Hulda was practically lying on top of him, and his body lit up everywhere she pressed, soft beneath the new dress, hard where the corset hid underneath.

He expected her to berate the house—Owein listened to her above anybody else—but instead she stared at him, her cheeks that lovely shade of pink, her spectacles barely hanging on, a delicate curl drooping over the side of her neck.

They'd reached ninety degrees when she blinked as though waking up and planted both hands on his chest—which he didn't mind—and pushed herself as upright as she could, given the circumstances. "Owein Mansel! The threat of the library still stands!"

The house seemed to sigh around them. And poor Fletcher dangled from the stairway.

"I did say *mostly* tame!" Merritt pounded his fist into the wall behind him. "Come on now, or Fletcher will have to go home."

With a groan, the reception hall slowly began ticking back into place, one degree at a time. Not quick enough for Hulda to be able to right herself with any sort of ease, so Merritt kept one arm encircled around her waist, ensuring she didn't hurt herself.

She tried to straighten her clothes despite the position. "My apologies, Mr. Fernsby."

"Hardly your fault."

"Technically, it is."

"It's a very nice dress," he offered, and she rewarded him with more of that rosy glow. She smelled like rosewater and rosemary . . . and wore roses on her dress. He wondered if she realized what a lovely metaphor she presented.

The room creaked into place. Hulda was slow to pull away from him, and Merritt was slow to let her go. It was not until Beth burst through the door, asking after their welfare, and Fletcher inquired whether the shifting of rooms would be a common occurrence during his stay that Merritt recalled they were not alone in their space, although he wished it were so. His hands fell from Hulda's person. She brushed off her skirt, her hazel eyes dragging slowly from his. What would he have seen in them had her gaze lingered?

She cleared her throat, breaking him from his reverie. "I will ensure it does not happen again, Mr. Portendorfer. Now, as to your room . . ."

⁓

Hulda spent the day finishing her report and assisting both Mr. Babineaux and Miss Taylor; Mr. Portendorfer's second visit was going *much* more smoothly than his first. The scents of dinner were starting to waft through the rooms, the sun was bright, and Owein minded himself after the incident with the stairs, though his spells followed Mr. Portendorfer around like a second skin, as though the boy was trying his best to impress him.

She thought for the dozenth time of Mr. Fernsby's arm snug around her waist, their bodies pressed close enough for her to smell the petitgrain and ink that seemed to emanate from his skin. And for the dozenth time, she pushed the fancy away, though this time it was with more of an internal, desperate pleading to her mind to let it go than a stiff refiling of her thoughts.

She had just finished setting the dining room table when a pecking sounded at the window. Glancing over, she spied a windsource pigeon and wondered if it had flown down here after trying and failing to get through her bedroom window. Hurrying over, Hulda opened the pane and let the weary bird in, took the missive from its foot, and offered it a bread crumb.

She opened the letter, which bore the seal of BIKER. It read, *Hulda, I must insist—*

"What's that?"

Jumping, Hulda turned to see Merritt coming in, and instinctually hid the letter behind her person.

"Is that a windsource pigeon?" He crossed the room to eye the bird, who was unfazed by the closeness of another human. "It is! Look at the seals on its feathers. Been a long time since I saw one up close." He eyed her elbow. "That isn't a letter from your beau, is it?"

The insinuation jolted her. "It is not." She pulled it back out, silently chiding herself for her strange behavior. "It's only a missive from BIKER."

"Oh." His face fell. "I suppose now that you've figured out the tourmaline . . ." He didn't finish the statement, but he didn't need to. *Now that you've found the second source of magic, there's no reason for you to stay.*

Except that there was, however much she fought it.

She shrugged and glanced over the letter—it wasn't long. Couldn't be, if a pigeon were to carry it. It essentially said what the last had, but with stronger verbs and darker punctuation, clear signs of Myra stabbing the paper with her pen. "The director has suggested I return to aid in administrative work, though it is not my forte."

"Soon?"

She folded the paper. "'Soon' is relative. In truth, I'm not sure why she's so adamant about it. I haven't sent in my report yet."

"Then"—his words were careful, and she wondered at them—"you might be able—or willing—to stay a little while longer."

The way he'd spoken—the look in his eyes and his tilted posture— rang faint little bells in her head that she'd silenced so many times before. She pressed her shoulders back. *Professional.* "Perhaps. I *am* an excellent housekeeper."

He smiled. "There is that, too."

The bells clanked and sang. *Ring! Ring! Ring!*

He perked. "That's right, I'm supposed to be borrowing Baptiste's chess board. Do you know where it is?"

Hulda shook her head. "But he's in the kitchen."

Thanking her with a nod, Merritt circumambulated the table, passing back a compliment on how well it looked, and slipped into the breakfast room toward the kitchen.

Sinking against the window frame, Hulda let out a sigh. She hated to assume, but surely a man who cared only for maintaining the status quo wouldn't say such things. Wouldn't care so much about her staying, with her housekeeping as only the *second* reason! She'd heard him correctly, hadn't she? She was formally educated. It wasn't like she didn't understand English.

The thought that Merritt Fernsby might care about her stirred a terrifying hope inside her that had Myra's letter quivering in her fingers. Maybe everything in her past had gone wrong because God or the fates or whatever was out there had known it wasn't yet time for it to go right. Maybe there was something desirable within her after all . . . something a man might want, and not just things she could slap onto a résumé for employers. That *maybe* hurt, but the thrill of it made her feel twenty again.

Don't get ahead of yourself, she chided, but her admonition couldn't dampen the whirlwind of emotions beating against her ribs. Steadying herself, Hulda read through the letter and offered a finger to the pigeon, who stepped onto it obediently. She'd reply in her room, where she could pace and think for a moment. Sort out what she wanted.

She would be clear and concise to Myra. She considered leaving out information about the tourmaline, but she wouldn't subvert her occupation for girlish whims, so she'd send along her full report. And a request to stay on board a little longer.

Just a little longer.

⁓

Merritt and Fletcher resumed their chess game after dinner, playing by the streaks of dying sun through the large multipaned windows, a glass lamp, and half the candles in a modest chandelier overhead. Merritt liked chess well enough, but Fletcher *loved* it, which meant that if a game wasn't drawn out beyond the point of enjoyment, there would have to be another one.

Their game tonight was running long. Merritt's pride alone kept him going. He still had his queen and a rook, which could prove deadly adversaries. Around them, the house had quieted, save for the call of a whimbrel outside and the settling of the house, which could also signify that Owein was entertaining himself in another chamber.

"So you're really going to stay?" Fletcher moved his bishop a single aggravating square. Merritt had caught him up on the exorcisms and such over dinner; Fletcher's own stories had gradually subsided as the man concentrated on the board between them.

"Really." Merritt shifted his rook one square as well, just to see if his friend would notice.

"It's a nice house." Fletcher shifted his last pawn. He'd complimented the house's *niceness* half a dozen times since arriving. Perhaps because he feared Owein would warp the room again. "But I couldn't do it."

"You'd rather keep that room with the parson?"

"I'd rather not have a ghost living in my walls." He watched Merritt shift his queen—only one square—like a hawk. "I'd rather not worry about breaking my leg on the stairs."

"Ankle at worst," he offered.

Fletcher smirked. "At least you're staying positive."

"At least I don't share my lavatory with a family of seven."

He chuckled, studying his pieces. The front door opened, Baptiste's heavy steps announcing him before he passed within sight of the doorway.

There was a skinned foreleg of a buck over his shoulder, and a trail of blood dripping down the back of his shirt.

Baptiste glanced over like a dog caught with a dinner plate.

"Baptiste." Merritt put his heel up on the table, which Fletcher smacked back down. "Can I make you a character in my next book?"

Baptiste stared for a solid three seconds, shrugged, then slipped into the dining room. That shirt would be a nuisance to clean. Merritt would offer his services so Beth didn't get overwhelmed. It'd been a while since he'd scrubbed at a washboard.

"You're my witness that he consented," Merritt chimed.

"I saw nothing." Fletcher's queen crossed the board, venturing close enough to capture Merritt's rook.

He moved it one square.

"Stop doing that." A vein on Fletcher's forehead was beginning to pulse.

"Let me win, and the torture will end."

Laughing, his friend shook his head. "Never. Your move."

Leaning elbows on knees, Merritt studied the board, hoping that a means of victory would magically present itself. *Perhaps I could teach Owein how to help me cheat . . .*

"Merritt."

It was only his name, but it carried a tone Merritt knew well. He glanced up through a lock of hair. Fletcher's attention was entirely on him, not the game.

"Am I about to be scolded?" he guessed.

Fletcher shook his head. "Just thought I should tell you something while we're alone."

"The ghost is always lurking."

"In earnest," he pressed, and Merritt sat up. "I ran into Mrs. Larkin the other day. Well, I saw her. Didn't say anything."

"Oh?" That certainly piqued his interest. "In Boston?"

Fletcher nodded. "She was at that Genealogical Society."

Shrugging, Merritt said, "She had to do research for the Mansels. You know that."

"Sure, sure, they've got records. A veritable library." He scanned the board but didn't make any moves. "But I overheard a bit of her conversation with the director in passing, and—"

"You know the director?"

"Everyone knows Elijah Clarke. All the locals do, anyway. Always very loud come election time."

Merritt waved for him to continue.

He haphazardly moved his queen. "Thing is, the place essentially arranges marriages for wizards."

The muscles around Merritt's stomach tightened. A strange defensiveness rose in him, and he soothed it back down. "Is that so?"

"She was talking to him about it."

"And you heard this clearly?"

"She was talking to him about it," he repeated, enunciating his words. "I see the way you look at her . . . I don't want to make any presumptions."

"You *are* presuming." Even so, a chill braided around his collarbone. Was he so obvious?

"Could be she's only interested in magic folk." Fletcher moved his bishop.

Merritt pointed. "It's my turn."

Fletcher's bishop retreated. Then the man palmed it and brought both fists under his jaw. Low, he added, "I don't want to see you hurt again."

Merritt's muscles tightened, and he leaned back in his chair in an effort to relax them. In an effort to stay nonchalant. "Are you referring to Ebba or the time your sister turned me down?"

"She wasn't right for you. You weren't right for her, either, broken as you were."

That same lock of hair fell into Merritt's face. He blew it away. They sat in silence for a dozen heartbeats before Merritt sighed.

"You know I trust you," he said.

Fletcher replaced his bishop. "I know. I'm not telling you to do nothing, but I am telling you to be careful."

Reaching forward, Merritt forewent his rook and slid his queen up several rows. "Check."

Fletcher cursed under his breath, immediately shifting back into strategy mode. Merritt was grateful. It gave him a moment to sort through his thoughts.

Was Hulda proffering herself to the Genealogical Society? He doubted it. She was too conservative a woman for such things. He even thought—hoped—she might fancy him. Or could learn to. Maybe it would end like all the others. Maybe it wouldn't start to begin with. Maybe he was a fool.

But tomorrow he would turn another page, and see where the story went.

Chapter 25

With a wave of his hand, Silas beckoned water from the enclosed canal down the corridor of his new abode to wash out the grime building there, as well as the few mice and spiders who thought to build homes where they were unwanted. His skin tightened as the water churned and browned. He guided it back down the adjoining hallway and out the pipe again, eyes becoming gritty as he made sure every drop obeyed his command. His luck had cooperated in helping him find this place, but he couldn't stand mildew. The task finished, he massaged his hands and crossed to a pitcher of water, which he gulped down to satiate the unbearable thirst so much magic had wreaked on him. The dry skin and eyes would abate on their own. Soon, he'd leave this place and find a home more suitable to him than this underground lair built by perspiration and magic. But as long as he was hunting, it was better to stay hidden. Oh, how he missed his days of splendor, rife with magic and money in Liverpool. He missed them terribly.

His footsteps echoed against stony walls as he walked to his laboratory, his attention diverted to the alcove carved out of limestone for his treasures. The King's League had destroyed the ones they'd found, but not all. He'd known all this time—he would have felt their losses, and he still possessed their spells. All the donors behind Gorse End's stone were intact. He set his jaw at the memory. The loss of the other bodies felt like missing teeth in his mouth. Once, he could conjure iron, see the future, and control the earth beneath his feet. Such rare spells. So much work and toil lost, because a member of his own staff had betrayed him.

He rested a hand on one of the iron bars protecting his trophies. Ten total, granting him twelve spells he hadn't had before, and augmenting the magic he'd been born with. His gaze pulled, as it always did, to the dolls in the upper-left-hand corner. Their features were less preserved, making them look more like spoiled melons than shrunken, mummified monsters. He'd been so new to his abilities back then, so inexperienced. And yet, they were still with him. Still with him . . .

Silas shut his eyes, the darkness of old memories surfacing. He fought against the tide, pushing it down. He'd already paid his dues for those sacrifices. He'd already suffered the loss. It had nearly broken him. Shredded him, then rebuilt him into something stronger. Something that could conquer anyone and anything. Something that could carry on the legacies of the fallen.

He opened his eyes. If only his father's husk were on these shelves, shriveled and still able to feel pain, so Silas could inflict upon him every ounce of suffering the man had imparted onto him. But his father had played a different part—he'd opened the doorway. Or perhaps God had, and his father was merely a pawn.

Stepping back, Silas shook himself. No time for reminiscing. He knew the island well by now. He was ready for the clairvoyant. Ready to take on his wolf form and live wildly for days until his opportunity came, if that's what it took. Then he would move on. It was almost over. Surely it was almost over, and then he would live in power and peace the rest of his days. Break away from this parasitic life.

For now, though, it was time to add to his collection.

Chapter 26

Mr. Portendorfer stayed the weekend, leaving after dinner Sunday night. The day after his departure, Hulda was forced to consider her predicament. It floated through her mind as she aided Miss Taylor with the day's tasks, even going so far as to scrub wainscoting, wash windows, and repolish silverware. When that wasn't enough to still her thoughts, she combined half-empty vials of ink in Mr. Fernsby's office and swept the carpet. Organized her clothes by color. Ordered herbs in the kitchen by name and took stock again of dwindling supplies. Trimmed her nails.

In the end, though, work could not distract her from an inescapable truth: she couldn't put off Myra forever. So she put her bag over her shoulder that evening and ventured outside, knowing no one would question her goings-on if she had her bag with her. She would appear busy, and it would afford her time to think.

She walked north, winding through weeds and plants that grew low to the ground, following a saltwater brook through the property. The cooling air invigorated her; the sound of birdsong and sight of bright leaves calmed her spirit. Her bag of tools bounced at her hip with every other step.

Yes, she wanted to stay at Whimbrel House. No point in attempting to pother her way out of that one. She would prefer not to resign from

BIKER in order to keep her position, especially since paying her out of pocket would be a drain on Mr. Fernsby's wallet. Neither did she want a demotion. Perhaps she could barter with Myra, do an on-and-off-again position where she spent most of her time on Blaugdone Island but took on an occasional job when a new enchanted structure *was* found and required her attention. Such an arrangement would require her to be gone for weeks at a time, but that was nothing the other staff couldn't handle. Mr. Fernsby would fare just fine with a part-time housekeeper.

Beyond that . . . it wasn't reasonable to think of the *possibilities* beyond that. Hulda *would* get carried away with herself, and that would be no beneficence, especially for her.

Crossing the brook, Hulda allowed herself to stroll and enjoy the open sky, which slowly colored with sun. Sunsets were always prettiest when there were clouds to reflect the light, and the perfect amount of them swam overhead. She went over what she would say to Myra—it would be better to discuss the matter in person and offer a logical argument, something that would conceal her emotional attachments. She could offer to train Miss Taylor in housekeeping. That seemed a viable reason to stay, did it not? And the training wouldn't add a single penny to BIKER's allotted budget for the house. Perhaps she could even offer to survey the other isles in Narragansett Bay. Perhaps there was magic yet to be found—

"Hello, Hulda."

Her body reacted to the low voice before her mind did. It seized, stung by a sudden chill. Her organs drooped as she turned around to meet a dark, penetrating gaze framed by wild, dark hair.

She mouthed, *Mr. Hogwood.* He was there, in the flesh, standing over her, dressed simply and in muted colors, his eyes narrow and mouth pinched. Older than she remembered him. Rougher.

How . . . How was he *here*? He was supposed to be dead!

He grabbed her.

Panic burned through her limbs like fire. She twisted free and bolted away, tall grasses pushing her back, mud sucking at her shoes. Her skirt yanked backward; she fell forward. Her magnifying glass fell from her bag.

Her *bag*.

Kicking at Mr. Hogwood, she fumbled through the satchel, pushing aside dowsing rods and her umbrella, her fingers brushing the selenite communion stone.

Mr. Hogwood's fingers dug into her hair, yanking her back.

She screamed, and the bag fell to the earth, lost amidst the marsh.

~❧~

A scream echoed against the walls of Merritt's bedroom.

He froze, shirt halfway unbuttoned, changing for the night. The hairs on his arms rose. He spun around, confused. That scream . . . It had sounded far away, yet so close.

It had sounded like Hulda.

Blood rushing through his veins, he searched the room, wondering if it was a trick of Owein's, but he'd never done sounds before. "Hulda?" he called, crossing to his dresser.

His eyes landed on his communion stone just as the magic seal on it faded.

His bones shifted to butter. Grabbing the stone, he pressed his thumb into the seal and shouted, "Hulda! Are you there? Hulda!"

He waited for an answer. He didn't receive one.

Rushing through the door, Merritt barreled down the hallway, stone in hand. "Hulda!" He peeked into the library. Turned back and flew down the stairs. "Hulda!"

Baptiste stepped out from the lavatory. "What is happened?"

Merritt held up the stone, as though it could explain everything. "Where is Hulda?"

Baptiste shook his head.

"Mr. Fernsby?" Beth came in from the dining room.

"Where. Is. *Hulda?*"

Beth bit her lip. "I haven't seen her since she went out. I thought to study the tourmaline . . ."

Owein might as well have opened a sinkhole in the floor beneath him.

"Find Hulda." He spun to Baptiste. "Find her *now*. Something is wrong."

He barreled for the door, then paused, letting Baptiste go in front of him. Taking the stairs two at a time, he bounded back to his bedroom and grabbed his rifled musket from the wall, then the Colt Paterson from his drawer. As he tried to leave, however, an invisible barricade slammed into him, striking his head and knocking him off his feet.

"Not now!" He leapt up and rammed the butt of the rifled musket against the wardship spell once, twi—

The shield gave way, and he dashed through the house without second thought. Outside, wind stirred his hair over his face, temporarily blinding him. The sun was a golden tracing on the horizon, nothing more. He cursed. Baptiste's low voice bellowed Hulda's name. Beth bounded toward the gravestones.

"Hulda!" Merritt called. He tried the stone once more, but no one responded. Picking a direction, he started running. "Hulda! Hulda!"

A rabbit hole nearly snapped his ankle in half.

The rifled musket was slick in his hands. "Hulda!"

A cold breeze blew through the vegetation. *Sssssshhhhhhhheeeeeeeeeee,* it whispered.

A shiver coursed up Merritt's neck. "Hello?"

Sssssshhhhhhhheeeeeeeeeeee . . .

"Owein! Where is she?" He trudged through thistles, voice hoarse. "She! Where is she?"

Sssssshhhhhhheeeeee, the air wheezed, and in his head, Merritt saw a coastline far from where he was standing.

He ran.

⁓

Hulda's face pressed into reeds. Her wrists stuck together with nothing but a spell, stronger than any manacles. The sun abandoned her, leaving her to the darkness and Silas Hogwood's hands, one of which stayed at the back of her head, shoving her mouth into mud.

She felt the exact moment a necromancy spell oozed beneath her skin, beckoning her life force away.

She jerked, trying yet again to free herself. Her panic was overwhelming. Suffocating. She couldn't breathe! She writhed, bending her glasses. Managed to buck up one hip.

Mr. Hogwood's grip tightened, pulling hair from her scalp.

"It's not worth fighting. Even without magic, I could overpower you," he murmured. Her muscles heated with his spell, while her skin turned icy. "I should have taken you out first the last time. I'm not making that mistake again."

The statement rang alarms in her head. She tried to talk, to plead, but it only pushed muck against her teeth.

Something buzzed in her blood. Her thoughts flashed to the basement of Gorse End, to the shriveled, blackened bodies of people, no longer recognizable. She screamed. The marsh absorbed the sound.

Mr. Hogwood's knee pressed into the small of her back, sending a wave of pain up her spine. Tears leaked from her eyes. "This takes a while." He was so quiet she could barely hear him over her thundering heart. "But you know that, don't you?"

His nails dug into her scalp. Hot breath brushed her ear before he said, "But do you know *how*? Hm? How I'll suck up your life force, break apart your magic, and move it from this worthless sack of flesh?

I'll make you even uglier than the rest. But your eyes . . . I will try so hard to preserve your eyes. I want you to see how wretched you are."

He leaned onto his knee in her back. Hulda screamed into roots and earthworms as lightning coursed through her body, overwhelming the subtle pull of the spell. Her backbone was going to snap.

"Hardly worth it." He pulled back, unaffected by the sobs shaking her chest and shoulders. She gasped for air and sucked up dirt, barely able to cough it out. She tried to kick, but the spell restraining her wrists also glued together ankles and knees.

She was going to die. *God help me, I'm going to die.*

"I thought about you every day." A new spell jolted through her, one that truly felt like lightning. She cried out as it burned the backs of her thighs. Was this part of the draining, or just a means to torture her? Grit clung to her eyelashes and melded with her tears. "Every day in that Godforsaken place." He shoved her head down again, burrowing her face so deep in the muck there was no air to be had. She struggled, twisted, jerked. "Never thought it would be—"

Thunder exploded. It crashed into Hulda's head and made her ears ring.

Suddenly the unbearable weight on her head and back lifted. Hulda wrenched away, tears streaming down her face. Her arms and legs, unexpectedly free, prickled from lack of blood. She fell back into the grass. Picked herself up again. Her glasses hung off one ear.

Through a single lens, she saw a shadow approaching.

And Mr. Hogwood . . . Mr. Hogwood was gone.

"Show yourself!" The demonic and grating words sounded in Merritt's voice. Thunder ripped through the air again, and Hulda's hands rushed to her ears. Some distant piece of her recognized it wasn't a storm she'd heard, but a firearm.

The shadow rushed across the grass, swinging the butt of a musket like a sword. Heart in her throat, Hulda twisted, searching the marsh for Mr. Hogwood, but it was as if he'd never been there. And with the repertoire of spells that man possessed . . . he could truly be gone.

"Hulda." The edge of the voice dissipated as the shadow dropped down beside her. Her frenzied mind managed to recognize it.

Bloodied lips struggled, "M-Mister . . . Merritt?"

His hands cradled her jaw. It was so dark she could barely see his outline against starlight. He felt so warm against her cold skin, his touch nearly scorching. "You're hurt. You're—"

A rustle in the grass, likely only a hare, but panic shocked Hulda from crown to heel. Merritt leapt to his feet, musket in hand.

Nothing but the wind greeted them.

"Baptiste!" Merritt bellowed. "Baptiste, bring the light! I found her!"

Hulda gawked at him, shaking, teeth chattering, her mind a flurry of disjointed thoughts and fears. Her body still burned from spells.

She didn't see or hear what he did with the gun. But Merritt Fernsby crouched beside her and drew her trembling body into his arms, lifting her from the shallow grave of muck and reeds. Far in the distance, a lantern swung, slowly making its way toward them.

Finally, one thought managed to rise above the others: *Safe*. She was safe.

Hulda turned into Merritt's shirt and wept.

—

Chapter 27

Merritt didn't realize he'd fallen asleep until Beth's hand on his shoulder roused him. His head bobbed up, the hallway outside Hulda's room coming into focus. His posterior ached, as did his back. His knees were propped up to give his arms something to rest on, which had rendered the soles of his feet numb. His trousers and fingernails were still stained with mud.

He'd been there all night.

"She's awake." Beth's timid smile bolstered his spirits. "She's fine, just scrapes and bruises." The smile fell. "A lot of bruises."

He gritted his teeth, the misery of the long night resurfacing again, souring his throat and mouth. If he had been paying better attention . . . He'd promised her she'd be safe here. With a psychometrist and augurist in the house, one would think . . . but Merritt knew better than to lean on those capricious fragments of magic. No one could have predicted this.

Beth offered a small but strong hand to help him to his feet. He had to wait a moment before going in, as the blood in his body reordered its priorities, one of which being his head. Running his hand back through his hair and catching on more than one snarl, he slipped into his housekeeper's bedroom.

Hulda lay on the bed, her blankets pulled up chastely to her shoulders, her arms resting on top of them. Beth had brushed her hair, which splayed out across her pillow in soft waves. Her bent glasses rested on the bedside table, so there was nothing to hide the bruises on her nose and under her eyes. The edge of her bottom lip swelled.

A lot of bruises.

How many did he not see, and how terrible were they?

Her eyes were closed, but when Merritt took up the chair Beth had brought in at the bedside, her eyelids drifted open. The curtains were pulled back, so morning light illuminated them, claiming them as neither brown nor green but hazel, with a dark ring encircling the irises.

Merritt's stomach shrunk on itself, and not because of hunger. "How are you feeling?" he murmured.

Her lips pulled upward—a good sign—until the movement tugged on that swollen bit, morphing the smile into a wince. "Safe," she whispered.

That answer sent gooseflesh up his arms and down his back. He reached for her hand—Beth had scrubbed those clean, too—and squeezed her fingers. "Safe *now*. Baptiste sailed for the constable at first light. I'm so sorry—"

She squeezed his hand. "Don't be sorry. I hardly care for unneeded apologies."

"Whether you *need* one or not—"

"Thank you," she interrupted, eyes drifting closed again, though her warm grip held on. "Thank you for finding me."

Merritt chuckled, though he wasn't sure why. "Thank you for screaming through a rock."

Eyelashes fluttered. "You heard me?"

He nodded. Swallowed. Traced the side of her index finger with his thumb. "Who do you think . . . took you?"

Lines etched her forehead. She turned her neck, faced the ceiling. "Silas Hogwood."

An electric worm zinged up his spine like Baptiste had hammered at it with his meat mallet. "Isn't he imprisoned? He wouldn't have come—"

"He's supposed to be *dead*." With her free hand, she rubbed her brow. "It was him. He . . . spoke to me. He was trying to take my magic."

Merritt's grip on her hand laxed. "Good God."

"It must be a much slower process than I'd assumed. He said . . ." She winced, but whether from the memory or pain, Merritt wasn't sure. The expression tore into his heart all the same. "He said I would be first this time. He was hard to hear, but . . . I'm sure he said that."

Merritt bit the inside of his cheek. "What do you suppose he means?"

"I can think of a dozen terrible things." She tried to sit up, never letting go of his hand, then hissed through her teeth and flopped back down.

Half out of his chair, Merritt said, "You should rest."

She shook her head. "It's my back. Lying like this . . . hurts."

Pulling his hand free, Merritt reached over her for another pillow, then snaked an arm behind her shoulders to help her sit up, noticing for the first time the sore muscles from carrying her across six acres last night. She gritted her teeth hard enough for them to squeak, but together they managed.

Hulda let out a long breath, stirring her hair. "It takes a while. What he does . . . I don't know the specifics. Multiple spells, to pull the magic from a person and place it into himself. He was born with the perfect concoction to do it. If the process were quick . . . I wouldn't be here. Not alive, anyway. He must have thought we wouldn't be interrupted."

Merritt lowered himself to the chair, then pulled it forward until his knees pressed into the mattress. "Did he take any of it?"

"I don't know." She studied her palms. Turned her hands over. "I don't think so . . . but the necromancy must be why I'm so tired."

"Or the trauma of being beaten." His voice had taken on a dark edge. He averted his eyes from the bruises still forming on her face, for the sight of them twisted his insides like taffy. He shouldn't have let this happen.

Her lip twitched. "Or that." This time she reached for *his* hand, and Merritt gladly pulled her fingers against his palm. Without meeting his eyes, she added, "If you hadn't come—"

"I'm a good shot." His thumb caressed her knuckles. "You'd be surprised at how liberating it is to destroy a straw dummy with a firearm." It was a hobby he'd taken up after moving from Fletcher's home. "Much cheaper than a medical professional."

She rolled her eyes—good; her distaste for his humor hadn't been damaged. "That's good. A shot alone wouldn't have scared him off. Mr. Hogwood . . . he would fight back. He has so many spells under his skin. Terrible, damaging spells, and healing spells, too. You must have hit him somewhere vital."

He mulled over that for a moment. It had been too dark to tell. *If I'd missed . . .* What would have happened to Hulda then? To himself?

Bringing up his other hand, he encased Hulda's. "You'll need to tell BIKER. We'll handle the report with the watchmen."

"I will. Or perhaps Miss Taylor will see to it." She winced again.

"I can call for a doctor—"

"Just bruises," she assured him, eyelids heavy. Their gazes interlocked. "Just bruises," she repeated, quieter.

Merritt studied her features for several seconds, memorizing the curve of her jaw and the length of her eyelashes, trying not to growl at the swelling. "You sound less like a dictionary when you're tired," he offered.

She laughed, then winced, free hand cradling her split lip.

"Sorry." He felt like a dog with its tail between its legs.

"I don't mind," she offered once she'd recovered.

Leaning back, Merritt begrudgingly released her fingers. "I should get you something to eat. Then you should rest some more." He stood and pulled the chair back to where it had been.

"Merritt."

God knew he liked the sound of his Christian name on her lips. "Hm?"

She pinched folds of her blanket. "I might like something to read, until I'm hale again."

His ego pranced. "I have three-fourths of a most excellent story, if you're interested."

She smiled very carefully, so as not to hurt herself. Then squinted at her glasses on the bedside table. "I . . . that is, if you don't mind—"

"Would you like me to read to you?" he offered, and the slightest bit of pink glowed under her bruises. "I do voices."

She chuckled, again holding her lip so it wouldn't stretch. "I would like that very much."

Nodding, he slipped out of the room. Breakfast first, reading second. And he didn't mind the tasks in the slightest.

At this point, he'd do anything she asked of him.

⁃

Word of Silas Hogwood had been hastened to England, and the household and the local authorities had scouted the island, though the only significant find was Hulda's bag. A week after the terrifying ordeal, Hulda had regained enough strength to slip into normalcy again. She dressed herself, choosing her corded corset instead of the whalebone one, pinned her hair, and carefully straightened the wires of her glasses. She'd look into getting a new pair next time she was in town, which would be tomorrow, as Myra had sent a panicked windsource pigeon in response to Miss Taylor's telegram about the attack. Hulda had assured her she was fine and would speak to her in person imminently. For now, she'd have to ignore the scratches haloing the lenses of her spectacles. Her vision wasn't quite good enough for her to go without them.

Hulda worried she wouldn't have a leg to stand on in her inevitable debate with her employer regarding her extended stay at Whimbrel House. But despite what had happened, she still ached to stay, now more than ever.

A faint *chop* sounded through her window. Pulling aside the curtain, she watched as Merritt set a narrow half log on a chopping block, then swung an axe around to split it into two. He'd tied his hair back for the exercise. After splitting a second one, he set the axe down and shook out his hands. Pulled a splinter from his palm. His shirt was open and sweat-soaked. Safe behind the drapes, Hulda didn't feel the need to look away. Though the longer she stared, the snugger her midsection became, as though her corset were tightening all on its own.

It's too late now, she thought, biting the inside of her healed lip. *I can't persuade myself out of this one.* She was in too deep. All these days she'd been abed, tucked and secure, but in truth she'd been falling. Falling into a depth that couldn't be measured—falling further every time Merritt came to check on her, every time he read to her, every time he subverted Beth and brought her the dinner tray himself. Every time he held her hand . . .

A shuddering breath escaped her. She was in love with him. She'd only known him a little over a month, but she loved him.

And she thought, with a daring, stinging hope, that he might love her, too.

Clasping her hands together, she felt his touch in memory. His thumb tracing patterns across her knuckles. It was utterly terrifying to make such assumptions, no matter what the evidence . . . but she wanted it so badly. Was it so wrong to want something, just one thing, that couldn't be bought in a store or persuaded via résumé? Hadn't she waited long enough? Hadn't she paid her dues to society, watching all her friends, family, and acquaintances grasp that *one thing* she had always wanted, yet strived to convince herself that she *didn't* want?

Oh, it hurt. It hurt in such a curious, singular way.

Dropping the drape, Hulda checked her hair once more in her mirror, then pinched her cheeks, grabbed her shawl, and set out into the house, quietly closing her door behind her. The carpet undulated like the ocean on a breezy day, brightening in yellow spots around her feet.

She laughed. "Hello, Owein. It's nice to see you, too."

The spirit had been absent from her room, as far as she knew, during her recovery. She wondered if he'd been fearful to bother her, or if Merritt had demanded he let her rest.

The spots of color followed her to the stairs, where she paused, hand on the railing. Something that had been bothering her resurfaced in her mind. How *had* Mr. Hogwood found her? How had he known where she was stationed, let alone when she would be out? There were a handful of spells that could aid him in the discovery, but he would have first needed to narrow it down to at *least* the Narragansett Bay area, and the place was so underpopulated, it seemed an unlikely place for him to start his search. True, he would assume she'd kept her employment with BIKER, but their files were confidential, and she was almost always stationed elsewhere.

She'd worked the question over and over in her mind the last few days, never coming up with even a fragment of an answer. Nor had she any notion of how Merritt had found her. A communion stone only relayed sound, not location.

Owein popped into the portrait in the reception hall, changing the woman's hair to match the style Hulda wore. She smiled at him before stepping outside, the autumn chill quick to greet her.

Merritt's back was turned toward her. He split another log, adding it to a sizable pile. Either he preferred a very warm house in the winter, or he was taking out some sort of physical frustration on the trees.

Which gave her another pause. *Strife and truth.* Had that premonition been about Mr. Hogwood? It had certainly been *strife filled* for all of them, but the incident felt more personal to Hulda than to him. Had the reading already come to pass, or was it yet before them?

Merritt dropped the axe and turned, wiping his forehead with his sleeve. His expression brightened upon seeing her, which created the sensation of a hundred hatching butterflies in her stomach. "Hulda! You look well!"

She touched the side of her nose, where she knew a yellowing bruise still resided. "Well enough, I suppose."

"Better than me, surely." He glanced down at himself before self-consciously buttoning up his soiled shirt. "Not off for a walk again, are you?"

She warmed at the unsurety in his voice. "Any walks I take for the time being will be accompanied ones, I assure you. Fortunately, the turning of the season is upon us, and it will be much less pleasant to exercise out of doors."

He smiled. "And what exercise do you have planned for within doors?"

It shouldn't have made her blush, but she did, anyway, blasted cheeks. But Merritt simply chuckled, which eased her embarrassment.

He reached for the axe, then crossed the yard to lean it against the side of the house, giving the logs a break for a moment. "I'm happy to escort you, though I fear I smell like a boar."

She picked at the end of her shawl and walked closer, until there was but a pace between them. She made a show of tilting her head. "I do not smell anything except the marsh."

The smile he gave her was lopsided, like that of a mischievous boy. Still, he straightened his shirt and brushed back his hair, making himself as presentable as he could, before offering up his elbow. Biting the inside of her cheek to keep her expression smooth, she took it, letting the heat of his arm seep into her fingers.

She *could* smell him, as a point of fact, but it wasn't a foul odor. Hardly. He smelled masculine, with a hint of cloves and orange twigs from that cologne of his, mixed with freshly chopped wood. She was entranced by it, so much so that she didn't speak for the beginning of the walk, merely took in his scent and the crisp air and the glimmer of sun on her shoulder.

Merritt broke the silence, though his tone was easy. "Baptiste has been beside himself that we're out of eggs. Now he wants a henhouse in addition to the cow."

She grinned. "Well, we—you—certainly have the space for it."

Merritt surveyed the island stretching before them. "Never built a henhouse before, though my mother kept them. Should be simple enough." He glanced back. "If I leaned it up against the house, that'd be one fewer wall for me to set."

They pushed through some reeds to a new trail, one Hulda suspected Baptiste had worn into the land. There was still some tightness in her back, but the walk eased it. She noted that Merritt crunched through the grasses off the trail so she could take the easier path, and it relaxed her stride even further.

"Mer—Mr. Fernsby," Hulda said, "if I may solve a mystery with you."

He glanced at her. Did he look to her lips? "Which mystery?"

Which, indeed. "That night, with Mr. Hogwood. How . . . did you find me? It was dark, and I was far from the house."

He blew out a long exhale and rubbed the back of his neck. "You have Owein to thank for that one. He pointed me in the right direction."

That was not the answer she'd been expecting. "Owein?"

He shrugged. "He's tall. Must have seen it for himself."

Hulda peered in the direction of the incident. It had been far off . . . even a person atop the house's roof would not have seen it without some sort of spyglass. "How would he have told you? Did he . . . write it?"

"Uh, no." His nose crinkled as he tapped into his memory. More likely than not, Owein was illiterate, given his upbringing. "I just . . . I was outside, calling for you. And he said, 'She,' like he was referring to a woman. To you." He met her eyes. "And then he . . . pointed, I suppose. But without pointing."

Hulda drew back, slowing their pace, but kept her hand in the crook of his elbow. "I-I'm not sure such a thing is possible. Owein . . . his 'body' is Whimbrel House, not the island. His magic is trapped within those walls." She gestured to the building. "He has no jurisdiction outside of it." Unless the tourmaline ran deep . . . but those were wardship stones. Nothing that would empower him to speak.

Merritt appeared chagrined, and Hulda wished she had presented the information in a softer manner. "I'm honestly not sure, then," he confessed. "Perhaps it was just luck. Or divine intervention."

She nodded, accepting the answer for now. "Either way, thank—"

"Mrs. Larkin." His voice was firm, his lips mischievous. "Thank me again, and I'll feel compelled to behave in a very knave-like manner in order to restore balance to the universe."

She was tempted to play along. To ask, *And what knave-like manner would that be?* But such impulsivity was not natural to her, and she gave him a simple nod instead. "If you insist."

Reaching over, Merritt guided her arm through his, pulling her closer until their elbows locked, simultaneously sending the butterflies in her stomach fluttering to her extremities. They continued their walk at a leisurely pace, Hulda occasionally picking up her skirt when it snagged on weeds. Lifting her head, she saw a figure shifting in the distance and tensed.

Merritt's other hand covered hers. "It's a watchman. They've been here all week. Never more than one; we're a little out of the way for the constabulary. But they're either on the island or boating through the bay."

Hulda relaxed. "Kind of them."

"Hulda." He paused. "Would you tell me about your family?"

She wondered at the change in subject. He didn't look at her but at his feet, leaving her eager to see into his mind, to pry apart what he was thinking at that moment. Why inquire as to her family? Then again, he didn't really have one of his own. Or he did, but they weren't . . . his, anymore. The reminder sat like a wet sandbag in her chest.

"I've both my parents still," she explained, "and a younger sister. Her name is Danielle. She lives in Massachusetts with her own family."

"She's married?"

"Yes, to a lawyer." It had been a bittersweet day, Danielle's wedding. Hulda had been happy for her sister, truly, but it was hard watching a sibling four years her junior win the game of love and matrimony when she herself had no prospects. Many of the guests had seen fit to comment on that fact. A soft chuckle passed Hulda's lips when she said, "We don't look much alike. I take after my father. She takes after my mother." As she said it, she self-consciously touched her nose.

Feeling Merritt looking at her, she dropped her hand. Quietly, he asked, "Do you think taking after your mother is connected to her being married?"

Suddenly embarrassed, Hulda tried to mask the discomfort with a shrug. "She and my mother are both pulchritudinous," she murmured, finding comfort in the intellective and overly specific word.

"Pardon?" he asked.

A twig crunched under her foot as she walked, her feet in perfect rhythm with his. "Beautiful," she simplified.

"You know, the interesting thing about writing," he said, changing the conversation once more, "is actually the readers. Novels critically acclaimed by one person are detested and even burned by another. When I wrote for the paper, the press would occasionally get letters either commending my points or criticizing them. Sometimes we'd get both for the exact same article. Especially the one I did on the steel plant."

She studied his profile.

"The point being"—he stepped over a fallen tree branch—"subjectivity is inescapable. If I've learned one thing in my line of work, it is no two minds are alike, and there is nothing *wrong* with that. Some people like mysteries, some prefer histories. Baptiste likes fennel, and I've never been a fan of it. But that doesn't make fennel wrong."

Hulda swallowed. "I'm not sure I follow."

"I think you do." He offered her a flicker of a smile. "Some people prefer women who look like their mothers, and some prefer women who look like their fathers. Beauty is just like a book. Some will not bother to look beyond the cover; others will find the entire tome utterly captivating."

Her heart pumped with renewed vigor at the statement. Did that mean what she hoped it did? Did Merritt Fernsby truly think she was . . . beautiful? Or was it simply a reassurance for the sake of being kind?

She desperately wanted him to continue, to speak plainly, to tell her all those things she direly wanted to hear.

But he did not. He was careful with his words, just as she was careful with hers, and the conversation shifted to the trip they needed to take into Boston tomorrow, the work Hulda wanted to catch up on, and how Miss Taylor and Mr. Babineaux were faring. Gradually, Hulda set her hopes and disappointments aside and settled into the security of Merritt's arm and enjoyment of his companionship, absorbing as much of the beauty of the moment as she could, fearing that someday it would only exist in memory.

Merritt stayed alert the next day as he and Hulda took the enchanted boat across the bay toward Portsmouth. He searched the coastlines of the islands, peered at fishing vessels, listened to the air. But nothing appeared to be out of the ordinary. Not a blade of grass or wandering fish seemed out of place.

"You'll tip the boat, rigid as you are," Hulda said, one hand on her hat to keep the wind from seizing it. One downside to their convenient method of transportation, though Merritt liked the way the breeze tugged at Hulda's meticulous curls, like it wanted to force the ever-calculated woman to loosen up a bit.

But she had been doing that on her own, more and more. Since before the odd attack, even. At first, her moments of relaxation had seemed like slipups. She'd catch herself being too casual and button up immediately, until she was more proper and strict than she'd been before. But those moments had grown so frequent that they were just as common, if not more so, as the guarded ones. Which was part of why Merritt felt "rigid" about this outing, though he was trying to relax. Not merely for Silas, but for the woman in the boat with him. Because of what he was planning to do, and how she might receive it.

Truth was, Merritt was in the real meat of the Hulda story now, and he didn't want to stop reading. Hers was a story he didn't want to end. But how many pages would she let him turn? What was her ending—their ending—going to be like?

His knotted emotions only made him warier of their surroundings. If this dogged Mr. Hogwood had struck once, who was to say he wouldn't strike again? He could, Merritt was certain. Because if Merritt had shot something *truly* vital, there would have been a body. And he wasn't sure how much the watchmen could do against a man like Silas Hogwood, or how long the constable would be willing to lend out his officers.

Maybe they should move back inland for a little while. He didn't savor the idea of abandoning Owein for long, but . . .

Hulda leaned forward. "What are you thinking about?"

Blinking, Merritt steered the boat for a moment, ensuring they stayed on course. "He who shall not be named."

Hulda nodded solemnly, then looked out across the bay.

They docked and took a tram into Boston, which let them off on Market Street. From here, their individual errands would take them different directions—Merritt to his editor to discuss the book hanging in a satchel off his shoulder, and Hulda to the Boston Institute for the Keeping of Enchanted Rooms to check in with her boss, Myra Haigh, and do whatever it was enchanted-house keepers did. Hopefully not get transferred.

They passed a group of rowdy men in the Union Oyster House. Once they'd distanced enough for easy conversation, Merritt drew himself up and swatted away the nerves that clung to him like flies. He couldn't remember the last time he'd been so nervous.

"Hulda." He'd been calling her that more and more, and she never corrected him, which was one good sign of many. When she glanced up at him, he found it hard to meet her eyes. *You're thirty-one years old,* he reminded himself. *Act like it.*

He cleared his throat. "After our errands today, I'd . . . like to speak with you privately." Perhaps he should have done it on the boat, where the only thing that could overhear him was a dragonfly, but if it had gone wrong, well, he'd have been trapped in a small boat in a large bay with his rejection.

"Oh? About what?" They stepped apart to let a child and his dog slip through.

"Just to . . . talk." *Imbecile.* He paused at the junction he knew she needed to take to head north.

"Oh." Was that recognition dawning on her face? Since when had Merritt struggled to read people? "I would . . . like that. Before we head back to Blaugdone?"

He nodded. Peered up the street, where his eyes caught on a set of stone pillars. "Meet me at Quincy Market? Would six be enough time?"

She fidgeted with the hems of her sleeves. "I think so, yes." She smiled. God, she was pretty when she smiled. Why had he not noticed how pretty she was when she first knocked on his door? Hadn't he likened her to, what, a schoolmarm?

She was a little older than he was, but not by much. The older people got, the less age mattered, in truth. Was it awkward that she was his housekeeper? But she wasn't *his* housekeeper; she was BIKER's. And if his confession that he direly wanted to court her was unsuitable, they could go their separate ways easily, no harm done.

Would she turn him down? But the way she'd held on to his arm for their entire walk yesterday—and it had been a long walk—whispered that she wouldn't. The way she smiled more easily and chuckled at his attempts to be funny. The way she looked at him . . .

That was, he *thought* she looked at him in a certain way . . .

He cleared his throat. "I'd best be going or I'll be late."

"Six, then," she said.

He nodded. Hesitated. Awkwardly tipped a hat he wasn't wearing and turned on his heel. His publisher wasn't too far; the walk might do him good.

He glanced back when he reached the next street, catching just a flash of Hulda's skirt as she boarded a cab.

∞

"Excuse my lack of professionalism," Myra said midpace, "but are you out of your bloody mind?"

Hulda would have taken a step back, were she not seated in a chair across from the director's desk. It took her a few heartbeats to collect herself. "Should I excuse it?" In all the scenarios she'd concocted of how this conversation would go, none had contained such vitriol. "I'm hardly asking—"

She paused as Myra turned away and grumbled in Spanish, so quickly Hulda could not discern one word from the next. When she turned back, eyes ablaze, she said, "You were *attacked*, Hulda! By a

255

wayward ruffian! Almost *killed*, and you want to *stay*? You're no longer needed! You said so yourself." She scooped up Hulda's report from her desk and threw it back down again.

"I did not say I wasn't *needed*, only that I'd confirmed a second source of magic . . . and it wasn't *some ruffian*, Myra. It was *Silas Hogwood*."

"So Miss Taylor said." Myra paced, paused, and punched her hands into her hips. "Are you sure—"

Hulda stood, her bag toppling to the ground. "I could not possibly be more sure. I've already given his name to the authorities. I don't know how he fooled everyone into thinking he was dead, but it *was* him."

The older woman pinched the bridge of her nose and collapsed into her chair. "I want you to move on, Hulda. I wanted you to move on *before* your life was in jeopardy, and now I want you off that island even more."

Hulda frowned, relaxing a fraction, but refused to sit. Her employer was being relentless, and she didn't understand why. Normally, Myra was much more amenable. Certainly, her attitude would make sense if she knew the truth, but Hulda knew Myra too well to fear her employer would invade her mind without permission. There was too much respect between them. Too much trust. So she couldn't know that while Hulda wanted to stay for the coast and the air and little Owein, she also very much wanted to stay for the love of a man. A man who wanted to *speak* with her later in what sounded to be a very specific manner.

Her pulse quickened at the idea of it, and she swiftly banished the thoughts, fearful they'd be so strong Myra would hear them without trying. So she studied, very hard, the grain of the desk before her, picking out abstract pictures and shapes, and asked, "Are you lonely?"

Myra shook her head. "I'm fine, really." Myra was also single, albeit a divorcée. Her entire world was BIKER, though as a psychometrist possessing the spell to read minds, she could easily find employment in dozens of fields. Her dark eyes lifted. "I am. But there is work to be done—"

"In Nova Scotia?" Goodness, Hulda had adopted a terrible habit of interrupting, hadn't she?

Myra's face fell. "Not . . . yet, for Nova Scotia. But." She hesitated. "There are a few fundraisers I've been planning, plus some extensions into the west. And the east."

"Which I would love to stay and hear about, if you've the time," Hulda pressed. "But otherwise, *outside* of the issue with Mr. Hogwood, I would like to stay until something new is prepared."

Myra's nail scratched into the desk hard enough it would start pulling up splinters at any moment. "Hulda, I don't understand why—"

A knock broke the question, and Miss Steverus poked her head in. "Ms. Haigh, I just received a notice from Mr. Maurice Watson. He wants an appointment today."

Hulda tipped her head. *Maurice Watson.* Why did that name sound familiar? She searched her thoughts but couldn't pinpoint it.

Myra cleared her throat. "I'll address it myself momentarily. After lunch." Myra met Hulda's eyes. "Do you have time for lunch?"

Smiling, Hulda nodded. "Always, for you."

∽

The meeting with Merritt's editor, Mr. McFarland, had gone better than expected. He was an amiable fellow Merritt's age, who had a dark sense of humor and a severe widow's peak. They'd spent a long time together . . . because Mr. McFarland had been reading Merritt's sample pages. Silently. Many wouldn't understand this, but often the lack of compliment—and critique—was a very good thing. It meant a person was engrossed. And engrossed was the best thing a reader could be.

He'd left the mostly finished manuscript with Mr. McFarland, eager to hear what he thought of the rest of the story, and if he'd like the twist that Hulda had helped him brainstorm while on bedrest. He supposed he had Silas Hogwood to thank for the inspiration—having the corpse his protagonists had spent half the novel searching for turn up *alive* was an excellent turn of plot, though it would mean changing the ending he'd begun to piece together, not that he minded. Another reason why planning ahead was a bad idea.

Speaking of planning ahead . . . he was almost to Market Street, which marked the cusp of the *conversation* he'd alluded to earlier with Hulda. Perhaps she'd forget about it. But there was little point in procrastinating. In truth, the anxiety in waiting for something was often worse than the thing itself.

Merritt thought he might be casual about it. Casual was safe. Just ask her to have dinner with him, *not* at the house. Night was descending, which meant the travel home would be dark regardless, so they could go tonight. If she was strange about it, he could blame an empty stomach, which was not a falsehood. He was rather famished.

But if she says yes, it could be due to her own famishment, he thought, then wondered if *famishment* was a word. He'd have to look it up later. Perhaps slip it into his novel so his editor would do the research for him.

He slipped around two old men prattling on the side of the street and came around the corner of Quincy Market, which glowed with a display of bright lanterns no doubt intended to attract straggling guests before its doors shut. He found Hulda quickly, near the far side of the market, standing close to a lantern as if to keep herself warm.

Merritt picked up his pace to reach her. "Were you waiting long?"

She perked up. Good sign. "Not at all. Five minutes at most."

"How was BIKER?"

"It was . . . interesting. I'll be at Whimbrel House for a little while longer." Her eyes peeked over the silver rims of her glasses and searched his. "I also visited an optometrist and filed my own report with the city marshal, so I've kept busy."

"For Hogwood?" he asked.

"It certainly wasn't for you."

He chuckled. "That's a relief."

She rolled her lips together. Merritt thought back to the conversation they'd had about the romantic subplot in his titleless book. *Never been kissed.* It had been a while since he'd kissed someone himself. Did he still remember how? Would those lips be warm to the touch, or cold from the evening chill?

"And your editor?" she asked.

He blinked to clear his thoughts. "Oh. He's fine. I mean . . ." He slipped his hands in his pockets. "It went well. He seemed to like the book."

Her eyes brightened. "Good!"

"Indeed, for I do not have the patience to rewrite it." Someone exiting the market bumped into his shoulder, forcing him to sidestep. The man rushed an apology before hurrying on his way. Merritt pressed a hand to the wall to gain his balance, and his thumb landed beneath a familiar name. One that shot lightning up his spine.

"You mentioned," Hulda spoke quieter, "wanting to talk to me about something?"

The earth shifted beneath his feet, until the outer wall of the Quincy Market was *down*, with gravity yanking him toward it.

Mullan, the name read. Merritt moved his thumb. *Ebba C. Mullan.*

His pulse quickened until his rapid heartbeat was the only sound inside his skull. He exhaled shakily, and suddenly he was eighteen years old again, standing in the middle of the street after a heavy rain with nowhere to go. No family to take him in, no fiancée to soothe his hurt, no child to take his name, no promises left to keep—

"Can't be," he breathed, taking in the entirety of the poster pasted to the wall of the market. Trying to remember how to read. To think. It advertised a concert in Manchester, Pennsylvania, which would pay tribute to the great German musicians. Small print on the bottom third of the page listed the members of the orchestra. Fate had glued his hand right to her name: *Ebba C. Mullan, flutist.*

Ebba Caroline Mullan, *his* Ebba, had played the flute. She'd been devoted to it. At that moment, he could hear it ringing through his memories: her playing in the front room while he read a book, chiding him for not listening—

"Merritt?" Hulda asked from somewhere very far away.

One of the scars crisscrossing his heart began to bleed. He'd never found out what had become of her. Only that she hadn't wanted him, just as his father hadn't wanted him. He'd never gotten any closure, even from her family—

"Merritt?"

He forced air into his lungs. Tried to anchor himself to reality. "Ebba," he wheezed. He pointed to the name. "This is . . . Ebba."

Hulda pushed up her glasses. He tried so hard to focus on her, but something had ruptured in his mind. Something he had locked and buried and poured shovelful after shovelful of dirt onto. Something he had shot up dummy after straw dummy to mask, to hide.

"Who is Ebba?" she asked.

It spread like a sickness, seeping into his arteries, veins, capillaries. "The one . . . the reason my father . . ."—he swallowed—". . . disowned me."

Another *something* ruptured at the thought of his father, but he shoved it down with a hard swallow.

And Ebba . . . She'd been all he'd had left until she wasn't. She'd vanished as swiftly as the snapping of two fingers. Shattered his world in an instant and left him to pick up the splintered pieces. He still didn't know *why.* That question plagued him more than anything else, even the heartbreak. He'd stepped up, ready to make it right, to take her to the nearest church and work two, three jobs if needed to provide for their family. She'd accepted what he had to offer. Until she vanished. No letter. No word. No trace.

And here she was. In Manchester.

His mind yawned and gaped, stretching the wound wider, until it bled. He was over it. He'd been so good at pretending it didn't affect him—

The performance was tomorrow night. If he left now, booked a hotel, got up when the kinetic tram got running . . . yes, he could make it, if the show wasn't sold out. He didn't care how much the ticket cost. He could finally *know*. He could finally glue together at least a few of these broken pieces . . .

Hulda's gloved fingers brushed his wrist. "You look sick."

He shook his head. "I-I'm fine." Stepping back from the poster, he ran a hand through his hair. "I'm fine." The lie came so easily, for he'd spent the last thirteen years practicing it. "I . . ." *I need to talk to you.* But he was unraveling. He couldn't announce his intentions to Hulda when he was unraveling. She wouldn't *want* him if he was unraveling, just as Ebba hadn't wanted him—

He cleared his throat. Desperately tried again for an anchor. "I . . . I'll see you back to the boat. Wait, no." He didn't want Hulda traveling home on her own in the dark, not with the attack so recent. Squeezing his eyes shut, he did some silent calculations. Yes, he could manage. Return her to the island and sail back here. "We need to head back now. I need to—" Flustered, he gestured to the poster. "I need to do this."

Hulda, stiff, glanced between him and the poster. "But it's in Manchester."

"I know. I know." He rubbed his eyes. "But I have to . . . I have to see her. I have to *know*." He could take Hulda with him, but then she'd see all his broken pieces. She'd see the broken things pushing out of the darkness, slicing him open, turning him to mulch—

He turned from the poster and started for the dock. His thoughts had devolved into bees, his skull the hive, and sticky honey coated everything. It couldn't be coincidence! Her family had refused to speak to him. Not then, not in the letters he'd written to them in the ensuing years. He'd never understood it, but now he could. *Now he could.*

Hulda wasn't with him. He turned back. "Hulda? Please, I need—"

She shook her head. "You see, Myra invited me to dinner. At the Oyster House."

Jittery and cold and lost, Merritt glanced down the road. Tried to form a coherent sentence. "The Oyster House?"

She nodded. "Yes. BIKER business. Many of us are meeting . . . to discuss Nova Scotia."

His blood pumped fast, eager to get him moving. He had time. He could mask his agitation well enough to see her taken care of. And once he was better, once the mystery was resolved, then he could talk to Hulda. Then he could tell her what he wanted to tell her. "Let me take you there."

"It's only three blocks."

"Hulda—"

"I actually see Miss Steverus now." She waved to someone in the distance. "Please, *Mr. Fernsby.*" She smiled tightly. "You're in a hurry. Don't let me hold you up."

Merritt's gut clenched. His gaze shifted once more to the Oyster House. His brain nailed itself to that poster. "You're sure? It's no trouble."

"Please. I would prefer it."

The statement was like a dart burrowing into his chest, like he was drunk on laudanum and could only half feel it. *Prefer* it?

The concert poster seemed to pulse over her shoulder.

"But going home—"

"I'll take a hired boat and have Myra see to me. I'm not incapable just because I'm a woman."

He hesitated.

"Please." She cleared her throat. "Or I'll be late."

Merritt sighed through his teeth. Why was he so cold? Or . . . maybe the cold wasn't the reason he was shaking. *Think.* "Do you have the communion stone?" Its companion weighed down his pocket. He slipped his hand in and grasped it, if only to have something solid to clutch.

She patted her bag.

"Use it as soon as your dinner is done." God help him, he was already losing it. "When you're on the boat. On the island, and when you're back at the house."

She looked like she wanted to fight, but the cold was getting to her, too, judging by the reddening around her eyes. She nodded.

A headache was forming behind his forehead, amplifying his erratic pulse. "Thank you, Hulda."

But she was already heading down the street, the ends of her shawl catching on the breeze.

Chapter 28

October 13, 1846, Boston, Massachusetts and Blaugdone Island, Rhode Island

One of the hardest things Hulda had ever done was to sew up the guise of self-sufficient old maid and keep a straight face through her conversation with Merritt. Ignoring his obsession with that poster on the front of Quincy Market. Walking briskly to the docks, passing stranger after stranger. Acting as if her insides hadn't been scooped out. And she did a bloody good job of it, too.

Until she got to the boat.

Once she activated the kinetic spell and propelled the boat into the bay, once she got far enough from the voices and city lights, her guise shattered completely.

Idiot, idiot, idiot. She held back the tears as best she could but still had to remove her glasses to wipe her eyes. How. Had. She. Not. Learned? How many times did this have to happen before she *learned*?

She fumbled through her bag for a handkerchief, then hurriedly steered the boat where it needed to go, guided by the lighthouses on nearby islands. She'd thought—she had actually, *stupidly* thought—that he cared for her. That he wanted her around for his own gratification. That he even *returned* her feelings . . . ha! And had she really been fool enough to think he'd asked for a private word because he meant to *confess* something of the sort to her? Pah! Likely he'd wanted the menu changed, or he'd changed his mind about the steward, or he'd decided to take a more active role in the running of his property. *Stupid, stupid, stupid.*

Strife and truth. She'd foreseen this, hadn't she? But the premonition was more closely tied to her fate than she'd imagined. *And the truth is that you're nothing to him.*

Her chest felt like it was cracking in two, like old, dry scabs were pulling apart fiber by fiber.

Because she had watched him drop everything to pursue another woman. An old love. A person he had intended to marry once. An accomplished musician, no less.

An intolerable sob worked its way up her throat. She was overreacting. She repeated that over and over, scolding herself like a grizzled headmaster would. It did nothing to quell her tears, which only frustrated her more.

She made it to Blaugdone Island with zero fanfare. Tried to pull on her mask again, but now that the proverbial dam had broken, it didn't fit anymore. Like she was trying to shove a lamb shank into a sausage casing. At least the air was cold. That would help with the swelling and give her an excuse for the redness.

Tromping across the plashy ground, she paused once at a stirring sound, but it was only a grouse. She let herself into the house, purposefully ignoring the portrait on the wall. She could hear Mr. Babineaux moving about the kitchen. Rushing up the stairs, she darted for her room before Miss Taylor could witness her humiliation.

The closed door at her back was a comfort. She tossed her spectacles onto the bed and lit a candle. Crossed the room and opened the window as wide as it would go, beckoning in a hiemal breeze. She still had water in her pitcher, so she poured it into a bowl and splashed her face. Loose tendrils of hair stuck to her forehead.

Sidestepping to her mirror, she leaned in to better see herself. A chuckle rough as rusted nails tore up her throat.

She was a histrionic mess. Her crying had made her eyes even smaller. Her jaw was too wide to be feminine—she'd seen those sharp lines work on other women, but not on herself. And her nose . . . her nose was the sort of thing authors put on storybook villains. Authors like Merritt Fernsby.

She stared at herself as new tears brimmed her eyelashes. No, her portrait would never rest in a frame on a lover's bedside table or be pressed into a wallet or pocket watch. Her body would never know the touch of a man or the weight of a child. She was an augurist, after all. Her talent lay in knowing the future.

The most hateful thing of all was that she *knew* this, and she had *accepted* it years ago. She had *made her peace*, truly. She had been content with her achievements, her career, and her colleagues before coming to this blasted house.

She turned away, blinking rapidly, pulling her hairpins free with little grace. A tear fell to the floor. She ignored it. Tore a button from her dress, trying to free herself of it, and cursed. Cursed again. Spat out every foul word she knew, just because she could. It made her feel a little better. A little.

She chucked her corset across the room, nearly sending it out the window, but gravity pitied her and tugged it to the floor. She was a little more careful with her nightdress. She didn't need two articles of clothing to repair, especially since she'd be leaving imminently.

She paused at the thought. Sunk into her mattress. Mouthed the words. Yes, she had to leave. For her own sanity and wellbeing, she could not remain in this house. Her rejection was raw and fresh and would certainly not heal with Merritt Fernsby walking the same halls, sharing the same jokes, wondering why she was such a mess. And heaven help her, if he brought this Ebba Mullan home to be lady of the house . . .

Hulda pressed her palms to her eyes as humiliation washed over her, rancid and prickly. *Fool. You always have been.*

Myra had known about her preposterous attraction. Somehow, she had known. That's why she'd worked so hard to pull her from Whimbrel House. Or perhaps it had all been an act of God, to spare her this internal beating. And yet, it would seem she'd needed to learn the painful lesson again, so next time she would be stalwart in her resolutions. So her heart would stay in the cold, steel cage where it belonged.

She wiped her eyes with the back of her hand as a new ache pushed up from her navel and spread through her chest. "Why couldn't this have happened two weeks ago?" she whispered.

Then, she could have written Mr. Fernsby off as an infatuation. But she'd gone and fallen in love with him, his clever words, his gentle hands, his uplifting laugh. Curse Miss Mullan for having her name on that damnable poster!

Slouching, she cradled her head. It was her fault, she knew. No one had asked her to form an attachment. But it felt better, for a moment, to pin the blame on others. Anger was an easier pill to swallow than this sopping remorse.

A light rapping sounded at her door. Hulda forced a swallow, then fanned her face with her hands. Said nothing; hopefully Miss Taylor would assume she'd retired for the evening and leave her alone.

Another soft tap. "Mrs. Larkin? Do you want to talk about it?"

She managed to keep the next curse within her throat. Had she been so conspicuous?

The door cracked. "Mrs. Larkin?"

Hulda released a shuddering breath. "I suppose if I haven't h-hid it well enough, th-there's no point in turning you away, is there?"

Miss Taylor slipped into the room, closing the door soundlessly behind her. She held her own candle and set it on the bedside table. Concern pulled at her expression as she sat beside Hulda and touched her sleeve. "Whatever is the matter?"

Hulda smiled. She didn't know why. Relocated her damp handkerchief and dotted her sore eyes. "It's n-nothing, really. I'm leaving, is all. Tomorrow, I think. No, the day after . . . it will take me a m-moment to get everything in order with BIKER"—another swallow—"and get my things packed. But it's for the best."

Miss Taylor frowned. "Ms. Haigh is pulling you? Why?"

Hulda twisted the handkerchief in her hands. A sore lump was building in her throat.

Hesitant, Miss Taylor said, "Is it . . . Mr. Fernsby?"

A most unpleasant shock shot up her spine. "What makes you say that?"

"He didn't come home with you." She put a hand on her knee. "And he must be the reason you don't want to leave."

Hulda shook her head. "Nonsense."

"I know I'm overstepping," she went on, "but I see the way you two are around each other."

New embarrassment made Hulda too warm in her skin. "How *I* behave around *him*, I suppose." She felt even more imbecilic than before, hearing she'd been so obvious.

"Nah, the both of you." She offered a smile. "He cares about you, Mrs. Larkin."

Hulda pinched her lips together, but could not stop another wave of tears. She buried her face in her handkerchief and chewed on a sob so it would come out in dainty spurts instead of one ugly heaving. Miss Taylor rubbed her back, patiently waiting for her to find an ounce of control.

"Th-Then we're both fools," she whispered. "Mr. F-Fernsby has not returned b-because he's seeking out his ex-fiancée, Miss Mullan. H-He is pursuing h-her."

Miss Taylor's hand stilled. "Oh."

Hulda lowered her handkerchief and sniffed. Several tense seconds sat in the room like bricks.

"I'm sorry," Miss Taylor whispered. There was nothing else she could say.

Hulda nodded. "So am I, my dear. So am I."

∽৯

It was dark again when Merritt reached Manchester City Hall, where the concert was to be held. He pulled his frock coat closer around him, wishing he'd brought gloves, but there was nothing to be done about that now. His nerves felt exposed to the outdoors. Every clop of a horse hoof or peal of laughter aggravated him, as though someone were raking a cheese grater up and down his skin, hard enough to rattle his bones.

Hulda had *not* chimed in on their stones as she had promised. He'd beleaguered her past midnight over and over, until finally Beth had answered, saying yes, Mrs. Larkin was home and well, just asleep. She must have forgotten. Which only served to make Merritt feel even more jilted than he already did. He retraced his words, wondering if he'd offended her, but he'd never gotten the chance to say his piece, so how could he have managed such a thing?

She was safe, though, and Merritt had another thing drawing in his focus, sucking away his thoughts like a newly born tornado, leaving only anxiety in its wake.

The city hall was lined with carriages and boys tending to horses. The windows glowed from within. The concert was starting any minute; he could hear violins tuning their strings.

He filtered inside behind an older couple dressed far finer than he was attired; he hadn't particularly considered such matters when purchasing a ticket for the event. But he stopped before entering the performance room. Stopped and shook his knee, peering through the open door, where a security man of some sort eyed him.

He couldn't do it. He couldn't sit through two hours of music and watch her, unable to say anything, sandwiched between strangers caging him in. It sounded like torture. He preferred the cheese grater.

And so Merritt slipped back outside, choosing instead to walk laps around the building to keep his legs warm. He thumbed the communion stone, careful not to activate its spell, wishing to speak with someone but having no idea what he could possibly say. His thoughts were too incoherent to form words. So he walked, and walked, and walked.

The concert began; he could hear the music as he traipsed the south side of city hall, but it shifted to silence as he came around the north, stopping once to help a lad get a blanket on an impatient mare. He recognized most of the songs. He was grateful the tall windows were too high for him to peer through.

He grew chilly, so he slipped inside the building halfway through the concert, showing someone his ticket so he wouldn't get in trouble for loitering, though that's exactly what he did. Loitered in the foyer, catching his breath, working out what he would say, changing his mind every few minutes. When his legs grew jittery again, he slipped outside once more and circled the building in the opposite direction, strides as long as he could make them.

It was then that he noticed the larger carriages in the back—they had more cargo space than the others, but less finery. After speaking with a driver smoking a pipe, he confirmed that these were the musicians' coaches, and a plan emerged in his mind. Merritt didn't have to go in and hear the music, filter through the crowd, and catch Ebba's attention. He just needed to wait by these doors for her to exit. If nothing else, it offered a semblance of privacy.

The next few songs seemed eternal, but when they finally finished and applause filled the building, Merritt forgot all about the autumn chill.

When the doors opened, his nerves coalesced into a ball, rushing up his torso before dissipating like feral dogs throughout his chest and arms. His pulse was hard, his veins stiff, his mouth dry. But he would not yield. He would not have this chance again.

The first musician to exit was a portly fellow carrying a massive black case that had to hold a tuba or some such in it. He held the door for a much slighter man towing identical luggage. Dozens of string players poured out after them. Some were focused on their carriages, but most conversed in tones of excitement. A couple of yawns came from a clarinetist. Merritt stood on his toes, searching the building crowd, all dressed in black. Most of them were men, which made his job a little easier . . . unless their bulk hid the women who traveled among them. If she reached her carriage before he saw her—

His bones and blood froze painfully, sending a rush to his head, when a familiar face slipped from the building. Pale, slight, long dark hair pulled up with careful elegance. She looked the same and yet entirely different. More mature, with slimmer cheeks. She spoke to another flutist briefly before waving goodbye and setting out for her carriage.

Old aches bubbled in Merritt's gut. He shoved them down and strode toward her, matching his pace to hers so that they reached the carriage door at the same time.

He chose formality. "Miss Mullan, if I might have a word."

She turned, smiling, and said, "Yes? I've only a moment—"

The smile faded as recognition—and *horror*—bloomed on her face.

With that single expression, Merritt understood that *she* knew exactly what she had done. Exactly why he was here.

Her breath clouded when she murmured, "M-Merritt?"

"In the flesh." He tried to make it sound light, but the words came out heavy.

She pulled away, obviously uncomfortable. "I-I'm surprised to see you here."

"So am I. I need to speak with you. Now." He didn't have much time.

She rolled her lips together. Glanced around as though she needed to be saved.

"Really, Ebba." His tone morphed to pleading. "I only want to talk. I need to know what happened. I'm not here for you. Only for answers."

Still, she shied away, one hand gripping the handle of her flute case, the other moving to her hair. "I-I don't think that's a good idea."

"Not a *good idea*?" he repeated, heat rising from his lungs.

"This bloke bothering you?" one of the clarinetists asked, tailed by a man without an instrument.

No. Not now. "I'm an old friend," he said in his defense.

Ebba turned toward the clarinetist. "Oh, yes, but I'm tired and ready to go home."

"Ebba," Merritt pressed, but the clarinetist slipped between him and Ebba, while the second man opened the carriage door. Ebba stepped inside.

Merritt's hands formed fists so tight his nails cut into his palms. "Ebba, I deserve to know!"

She paused.

The clarinetist put a hand on Merritt's shoulder. "You heard her. She's done for the night. Move on."

Merritt shrugged the man off. "I'm not going to hurt her. Stay, if you must, but—"

"It's all right."

All three men turned as Ebba came out of the carriage, her flute still on the seat. She pulled her cloak around her shoulders. "I . . . I *do* need to speak to him. Just for a moment."

Her friends glanced at each other, uncertain. "If you insist . . . but we'll be just over there. Won't leave till we see you boarded."

Ebba nodded to them, then jerked her head toward city hall. Steeling himself with a breath, Merritt followed her to the wall, far enough from the doors that they couldn't easily be overheard.

"Thank you." His words were clouds on the still night air.

She finicked with her cloak hem, much the way Hulda busied herself with the end of her shawl. She looked everywhere but at him, trying to get her thoughts together—she'd always done that when discussing something uncomfortable. It brought up an odd sense of nostalgia.

He waited.

"I didn't think I'd ever see you again," she finally said.

He nodded. "I dare say you planned it that way."

She pressed her lips together.

Merritt leaned against the stone wall, despite its frigidity. "Why did you leave? No word, no letter . . . if you left one, I never saw it—"

"No letter," she whispered.

"Your parents said nothing except that you'd gone to school. They wouldn't even say where." Like they'd shared his father's desire to be rid of him.

She swallowed. "Oberlin." Her voice was no louder than a falling leaf. "Oberlin College."

He could have tracked her down, if he'd known that. Perhaps it was better that he hadn't. He scraped his brain for something to say. "That's . . . good. You'd always wanted the education."

Ebba lifted her chin, but she still didn't meet his eyes. The lights from the windows highlighted tears on her lashes.

He thought to reach out to her but kept his hands in his pockets. "Ebba—"

"I left because I was ashamed." Tears leaked into her voice. "Because I didn't know how else to do it."

Merritt shook his head, not understanding. "I said . . . we were going to move, remember? Where no one knew us—"

"Not because of that." She dabbed her eyes with the hood of her cloak. "But you're right. You deserve to know. And it can be off my conscience, after tonight."

One of the drivers called out. Ebba waved an arm but didn't turn.

"Your father paid for me to go to Oberlin," she confessed.

Merritt leaned back like he'd been pushed. "My father? Why?" And why hide it?

She drew in a deep breath. Found a spot on Merritt's shoulder and pinned her gaze to it. "It was a bribe, Merritt."

He still didn't understand.

Her jaw worked. "It was a bribe. Not all of it. I did . . ." She cleared her throat. "I did *care* for you then. But he hated you. Said you always reminded him . . . that you were a 'symbol' of your mother's unfaithfulness . . ."

Merritt stepped back and brought up his hands. "Wait. *Wait.* What do you mean, my mother's *unfaithfulness*?"

Now she met his eyes. Her lips parted. The driver called.

"You don't know?" she asked.

"Know what?" His head was throbbing. "Know *what*?"

"That you're a *bastard*, Merritt!"

The silence of the night seeped around him like oil after the outburst. His ears rang. His skin pimpled. Nausea curled in his bowels.

She wiped her eyes again. "I-I'm sorry. I don't have time—"

"He disowned me because I'm not . . . his?" he murmured.

Her eyes glistened.

He couldn't process it. "Then whose am I?"

"I don't know." She glanced back to the carriages. Her cheekbones became pronounced as she pressed her lips together, readying to deliver another blow. "He offered to send me to Oberlin if I . . . if I faked a pregnancy."

Merritt's stomach sunk. He felt transported back thirteen years. Ebba had been awfully forward that night . . .

"I never was pregnant."

He swallowed. "I-I know. Your parents said . . ."

"You were eighteen. That's the only reason I can think for why he approached me then. You were old enough to go off on your own. He faced no legal repercussions for cutting you off."

Ice to the marrow, he shook his head, although not in disbelief. The driver called.

Ebba turned away.

"And you didn't think to *tell* me?" Venom burned his tongue. "You didn't think to tell me that my father played me like . . . like a chess pawn?"

Tears ran down her cheeks. "I promised not to say a word."

"Promised?" He was shouting now. "You also *promised* to marry me! You said you loved me, and then you pulled . . . this?"

She was readily crying now. The clarinetist and his crony were quickly approaching. "I'm sorry, Merritt. I had to make a choice."

"And you did," he spat. "You made that choice at *my* expense. I lost *everything*, Ebba. I haven't seen or spoken to my mother and sisters in *thirteen years*. You lied to me and tore my heart out for what, a flute?"

"It's not like that," she countered. "You could never understand."

"You're right, I couldn't." He jutted an accusing finger at her. "I could never understand the selfishness of a person like you."

She was openly sobbing now, but Merritt couldn't bring himself to care. The clarinetist put a hand on her shoulder. "Come on, Miss Mullan. Let's be done with him."

Ebba let the man pull her away. Halfway to the carriage, she turned back and had the decency to mouth, *I'm sorry.* Merritt received it like a stone wall. He watched her slip into her carriage. Watched the coaches pull away, until the street was bare and the city hall was dark.

It was oddly reminiscent of his time in the root cellar. He stood there, staring at nothing, until his fingers and toes went numb, wishing his heart and thoughts would follow suit.

Rather than go numb, they burned bright, a long pyre on a dark Pennsylvania street, consuming Merritt, alone.

Chapter 29

October 15, 1846, Blaugdone Island, Rhode Island

Merritt was exhausted when he came home the next morning. He'd managed to find a bed at a local coach house around eleven last night, which he'd shared with two men who snored louder than firing cannonballs. He'd then emptied his wallet to get back to Blaugdone Island. His body was sore, his eyes were dry, and everything else was . . . wrung out and still wringing. He needed to . . . he wasn't sure. Run until he couldn't move another inch, only so he could sleep for a week and force his mind to work out these new revelations in his dreams. Wouldn't that be nice.

Bastard. Could it be true? What reason would she have had to lie about it? It worked with the events as they'd transpired, but . . .

Bury, bury, bury.

For now, he'd have to settle for staring at a wall. Perhaps Hulda knew of some sort of tea or tincture that would settle him down enough to get some rest. If only it were as simple as sleeping it off.

She'd taken his boat, after all, so he'd hired a driver to cross the bay. As he handed over his last coins, he noticed a new boat tied about two hundred feet east—larger than his, big enough for maybe eight people. He squinted at it awhile, until the driver of the boat he stood on asked, "Um. Could you get off?"

Merritt forced his feet to step into eight inches of water, eyes still on the unknown sea vessel. Who was visiting? Not Fletcher . . .

Slapping himself twice on either cheek, Merritt forced wakefulness into his person and trudged through the wild grasses and reeds toward the house. At least he had this quiet place for refuge. At least he could wrap himself up in normalcy while he reordered the story of his life and determined what to do next. At least he could depend on Beth and Baptiste to keep the days going, and Hulda . . .

He still needed to talk to her. He wanted to, as soon as he got his head around all of this—*bastard*—and stuffed it away like he always did. It took time and tears, and a few unfortunate trees would bear the brunt of his target practice and likely his fists, but he would piece himself back together, and they would talk. There could still be a silver lining to the mess of his life. God grant him just one silver lining.

That hope buoyed him. His porch grumbled under his weight—Owein was either happy to see him or anxious about something. The boat, perhaps? Concerned, Merritt quickened his step and opened the front door.

He tripped over a trunk sitting just behind it.

Hulda's trunk.

"What on . . ." He left the door ajar and stepped around the trunk. There was a suitcase sitting beside it. He grasped its handle and lifted it—full.

What was going on?

Two men came down the stairs just then, complete strangers dressed in work attire. They nodded to him before pushing past, taking up either end of the trunk and hauling it outside—

Beth stepped out from the living room and started upon seeing him. "Mr. Fernsby! Are you . . ." She took him in—he undoubtedly looked a mess—and finished weakly, ". . . well?"

"Hardly." He hefted the suitcase. "What's all this?"

Beth bit her bottom lip.

Hulda came down the stairs, not noticing him until she'd reached the third to last. She paused, her overlarge bag—which also appeared to be very full—slung over her shoulder. She blanched upon seeing him.

"What the hell is going on?" He brandished the suitcase. His freshly painted mortar cracked. He might as well be standing outside Manchester City Hall yet again.

Hulda lifted her chin and descended the final stairs. He thought her lip quivered for an instant, but the mark of uncertainty vanished the moment she spoke. "As you know, Mr. Fernsby, BIKER has been requesting my return to Boston."

He stared at her incredulously. Beth backed out of the room.

"BIKER?" His tone was more forceful than he meant it to be. "I thought you spoke with them already. You're staying on."

"You are misinformed." She cleared her throat. Stood even taller. "Which is a blunder on my part. However, seeing as you were out of the house—"

"With a communion stone you failed to use," he interjected.

She pressed on, "I have taken matters in hand. I am departing today, but a new housekeeper will be appointed to you within the fortnight, if you choose to hire a replacement."

He gawked at her. Set down the bag, then kicked the door closed and whirled on her. "So you're moving out, without so much as a note?" *No letter. No word. No trace.* Something sharp and hard formed in his chest. "You said you were staying."

She huffed. "What I said is not relevant. I am BIKER's employee, not yours—"

His heart bled acid. "This is because of that consarning Genealogical Society, isn't it?"

She looked taken back. "What do you mean?"

Lies, lies, and more lies. Why did everyone *lie* to him?

"You know exactly what I mean." He closed the distance between them, and Beth all but fled. "I know you've been meeting with them.

Don't lie to me. You're leaving because this house is tamed, and I'm not some fancy wizard. There's nothing fun in your boring life anymore, so you're quitting."

Hulda's eyes widened. Cheeks tinted carmine. "How *dare* you make such asinine assumptions! And how dare you judge *me*, when you just spent the last thirty-six hours chasing some hussy across New England!"

"Hussy? *Hussy?*" The acid blazed into fire, melting his fingertips and choking out his air. "If she's a hussy, then what does that make me?"

Hulda flushed darker. Pressed her lips into a hard line.

"Huh, Hulda?" he pushed. "Because I'm every bit as guilty as she is."

Gripping the strap of her bag, Hulda pushed past him and scooped up the suitcase. "I don't have to listen to this. I've no contract with you."

"Contract!" he barked. "Why don't I help you with your self-righteous tirade, eh? I'm a bastard, too! An unemployed, sex-mongering, unmagical bastard. Hardly good enough for the likes of a pretentious housekeeper, if I say so myself."

She spun on her heel. "You insolent, horrible man! Don't pin your shortcomings on me or anyone else in this house!" With that, she marched for the door.

"Leave, then!" he bellowed after her. "Leave, just like everyone else does!"

She slammed the door.

The pyre burned hot and cold. He felt like a loaded and cocked gun; he needed somewhere to fire. Spinning, he punched the wall hard enough to crack it . . . and to send white-hot pain racing up his arm.

The portrait behind him *tsked*, and the wall resealed itself.

Pinching his nose, Merritt dropped onto the first stair and sunk his elbows onto his knees. "Just like everyone else does," he whispered, and squeezed his eyes closed so tightly no tears could escape.

Hulda could not remember the last time she'd been so *angry*.

It was embarrassing to have been caught in her escape by Merritt—*Mr. Fernsby*, that was—but why should she have to explain herself? It was no lie that BIKER wanted her return. Myra had pushed for it more than once. And what did he care? Heaven forbid something disrupt his comfortable life! *I've just gotten used to you,* he'd said once. A person wasn't entitled to service merely because he was "used to" it.

And his assumptions about her and the Genealogical Society . . . how utterly crude. He knew she'd gone there to get information for *him*. His words had been vile and confusing. What had fueled him to act in such a savage way? *Just his true colors, perhaps.*

In an odd way, she was grateful for the argument. Anger was easier than dolefulness, humiliation, despondency. She clung to anger.

She managed to dial her mood down to simmering by the time she arrived at BIKER; the moving company would deposit her things in her temporary apartment, until Myra sent her to Nova Scotia. Lugging her bag up the stairs, Hulda was relieved to see her friend standing over Miss Steverus's desk, looking through a file. The secretary herself was away at the moment.

Myra glanced up at her approach, then jumped from her chair, a grin splitting her face. Hulda couldn't help but return the smile. *Oh, to be appreciated.* It was a cool balm to her wounded soul.

"You're back!" She eyed the bag. "Are you here to stay?"

Hulda nodded, a gesture that gave her the utmost satisfaction. "You'll be pleased to know I considered what you said and decided you were right. I'm ready for whatever assignment you need me for, even filing." Anything to keep her busy.

Myra clapped her hands before embracing Hulda. "I'm so glad. Oh, it will be good to have you around, if only for a little while. I'm expecting news from London any time now." She paused. "Hulda, are you all right? I'm reading—"

"Please, don't." Hulda put up a stalling hand while scrambling her thoughts, tucking away the sore ones and replacing them with meticulous descriptions of the office. "I know you can't help picking up on strong thoughts, but please . . . I'll explain later."

Myra frowned. "Of course, if that's what you want."

Relief tickled beneath her skin. "It is."

Myra collected the folder. "I need to compare this to some findings. It should only be a minute. Do you mind waiting?"

"I might see to unpacking." Hulda patted her bag.

"Of course. I'll come to you." Myra squeezed her arm, sympathy coming through her countenance—an expression Hulda was all too familiar with, from all too many people. Myra ducked into her office, taking her pity with her.

Switching the heavy bag to her other shoulder—carrying a crowbar, among other things, across state lines took a physical toll—she started for the stairs, trying to ignore the frustrating ache over her diaphragm. She just needed to get engaged in her work. Occupy herself. She prayed for a lot of filing—

"Mrs. Larkin!" Miss Steverus hurried down the adjoining hallway. "Just my luck! I ran off to send you a telegram, but here you are!"

Hulda paused, confused. "Telegram about what?"

"Your report." She motioned for Hulda to follow, then slipped behind her desk and dug through a stack of papers there, pulling out the letter Hulda had sent via windsource pigeon. "It's just, I was copying this, and, well, I studied metaphysical geology for a time before taking this job." She looked up through her lashes sheepishly. "And you mentioned tourmaline, and I thought . . . well, I went and looked it up to be sure, and I don't think . . . that is, it's not my place to correct—"

Hulda didn't have patience for pandering, not today. "Just spit it out, Sadie."

"Right. Right." She set the paper down. "It's just that tourmaline can only hold a magical charge for about a week before it diffuses."

Hulda took a few seconds to work that out. "You're sure?"

Miss Steverus nodded.

"But that makes no sense." She adjusted her bag. "The only thing that could recharge the tourmaline is the wizarding spirit, and he doesn't possess wardship abilities. He's never exhibited them, and his genealogical records have no such recordings."

Miss Steverus shrugged. "I can show you the research if you want to see it, but *if* the tourmaline is producing magic, it's pulling it from another source."

Hulda shook her head. "Yes, I'd like to see it."

"One minute." The secretary bounded back down the hallway she'd come from.

Hulda tapped her fingernails against the desk's surface. It made no sense. Perhaps Hulda had somehow missed something, or the Mansel records were incomplete, or . . .

A memory surfaced—the wardship shield disintegrating after Merritt knocked on it. Before that she'd been telling him about Mr. Hogwood. Wardship was a protective discipline, and if Merritt had been feeling protective . . .

He pointed me in the right direction . . . He said, 'She,' like he was referring to a woman. To you . . . He pointed, I suppose. But without pointing.

Hulda's body went so slack her bag dropped to the floor.

It couldn't be . . . *Merritt* . . . could it?

She had to know. The urge to *know* burned within her like a blacksmith had hooked bellows to her lungs and shoved iron down her throat. Securing her bag, Hulda rushed for the stairs, essentially tripping over them, her feet moved so quickly.

Sadie Steverus called out after her, but Hulda had her own research to perform.

Mr. Gifford stood from his desk as Hulda swept into the Genealogical Society for the Advancement of Magic's office, her skirt inches from getting caught in the closing door.

"Miss Larkin! How are you to—"

"I need to see your records immediately. I do not require an escort. It's BIKER business. Do I need to fill anything out before I go down?"

The man choked on his words. "N-No, let me just write down your name—"

She sped past him, grabbing a lantern and taking the winding stairs down to the basement library. She managed to get it lit before touching down on the main floor. The smells of mildew and old parchment wafted over her like the tide. She wove through shelves until she found the box that would contain records for the surname Fernsby. Grabbing it, she found the same table she'd used before and set to work.

The file was larger than the Mansel one had been, and after spreading it out on the table, she took a full five minutes to find his name. Merritt Fernsby, listed second under Peter Fernsby and Rose Fernsby. He had two sisters—the elder was named Scarlet and the younger Beatrice. Her heart panged reading the names of family who had left him behind—family he avoided speaking of—but ravelment overtook her as she scanned up the family line.

No magic notes. No estimates or wizarding markers of any kind.

She leaned back, confounded. If not Merritt, then what—

Why don't I help you with your self-righteous tirade, eh? I'm a bastard, too! An unemployed, sex-mongering, unmagical bastard.

"Bastard," she repeated, that pang hitting harder this time as his self-deprecating anger pushed to the front of her memory, still fresh, still stinging. If Merritt *was* a bastard, then this lineage wouldn't be correct . . .

She paused. She hadn't unpacked yet. Reaching down, she shuffled through her black bag until she found the BIKER file on Whimbrel House. The file that included the short list of past inhabitants.

She spread it out. Found the name of the previous owner, Anita Nichols—Merritt's maternal grandmother, if she remembered right. She had apparently won the house and land in a game of chance, from Mr. Nelson Sutcliffe, who'd inherited it from his father, who'd taken it from his brother. None had ever inhabited it.

Hulda knocked over her chair in her hurry to get to the shelves, then retrieved the Mansel file and brought it over. She spread it on top of the Fernsby file. Found Horace and Evelyn and their daughters—Owein's sisters. She traced their lines down until . . .

There! There was a Mary Mansel in Crisly's line that married a Johnson, and her third daughter married a Sutcliffe! The families *were* connected.

She chewed on her lip. Pondered. Grabbed her lantern and ventured upstairs.

"Mr. Gifford," she said to the frazzled clerk, "is there a means to look up genealogical records by location?"

"Um. Yes, there is . . . Allow me." He set a few papers straight and escorted her back into the dark, taking up a lantern of his own. He led her deeper into the basement, to another set of shelves. "These are by location. Do you know what you're looking for?"

Hulda snapped her fingers, trying to think of it. Merritt's birthplace hadn't been included in the Whimbrel House file, but Mr. Portendorfer had mentioned it before. "New York. New York . . . Cow, no, that's not it. Cattle something . . ."

"Cattlecorn?" Mr. Gifford supplied.

"Yes! Yes, Cattlecorn."

He passed by a few shelves, then took his time studying the different files, leaving Hulda to force patience into restless limbs. When he finally pulled a bin free, Hulda snatched it, rushed a thank-you, and hauled it over to her table.

She opened up the files to the newest entries. "Sutcliffe," she murmured, drawing her finger down. "Sutcliffe, Sutcliffe . . ."

Sutcliffe, Nelson. No magic markers, though his grandfather had *W10* written on his name, and a great-uncle had *Co12*. There was a smattering of other magic markers going up the line.

So Nelson Sutcliffe lived in Cattlecorn and had the magic markers Hulda was searching for . . . If this man was Merritt's biological father, then it *was* Merritt causing those spells. He must have used communion to find her the night of the attack! She laughed, disbelieving. All this time, Merritt had been adding to the enchantments . . .

And he didn't know. He *didn't know.*

"Oh dear." She fished out her communion stone.

"Miss Larkin?"

She jumped. "Oh, Mr. Gifford. I forgot you were here."

He glanced to the mess she'd made on the table. "Can I help you sort anything?"

"I . . . No. But I need to make some copies. Please."

He nodded. "I'll get you a pencil and paper."

She waited for him and his lantern to vanish up the stairs, then activated the selenite. "Merritt?" she asked. "Merritt, I've found something very important."

She paused, the stone heavy in her hands. If this was all true . . . Merritt was related to Owein. She'd trace that line in just a moment.

No answer.

"Merritt, it's Hulda. I know you're angry, but I need to speak with you! It's about the house. About Owein, and *you.*"

No answer.

"Impertinent man," she mumbled. She'd make her copies and try again. If he still didn't answer, well . . . she'd go back to Blaugdone Island herself and make him.

If nothing else, she needed the exercise.

⟋⟍

Merritt sat at the head of the dining room table, the room dimly lit with a smattering of candles, the shutters drawn closed against the twilight. He slouched in his chair and propped his forehead halfheartedly on his palm. Both elbows were firmly planted on the table, but this was his house. He could put his joints wherever he wanted.

He felt Beth and Baptiste watching him as he speared and respeared a pea with his fork, over and over until it resembled a shucked oyster, then moved on to mutilating another. He never did manage to take that nap. His body felt heavy yet hollow, his brain fuzzy, his innards numb. But numb was good. He tried very hard not to think about anything, as thoughts disrupted apathy. He was weary of thinking, besides. Perhaps, if he never slept, he would never think. Wouldn't that be something?

He was beginning to regret the lack of liquor in the house.

Beth murmured, "I'll take your plate."

Merritt glanced up, though she'd been addressing Baptiste. Both he and the maid had finished their dinner. Merritt's was growing cold and being slowly massacred by silver prongs.

Sighing, he set the weapon down. "I'm sorry, Baptiste. It's nothing you've done. In truth, meat pies are my favorite food."

Baptiste frowned. "I know."

Merritt perked a little. "You do?" He couldn't remember mentioning it.

The cook shifted an uneasy glance to Beth. "Er . . . the menu is Mrs. Larkin's task. She chose it."

Merritt wilted. "Oh." So much for apathy. A bitter screw began twisting its way up his middle. He stared at the golden-brown crust before him. Picked up his fork and attacked it, but couldn't bring himself to eat.

Perhaps tomorrow Baptiste would make soup so Merritt could drown himself in it. Though he really should eat something. He'd only feel worse if he didn't. Lifting a tiny morsel to his lips, he chewed, barely registering the flavor.

Wiping her hands on her apron, Beth said, "I've some chamomile tea, if you'd like."

Ah, chamomile. Calming, sleepy chamomile. "As strong as you can manage it, please. Thank you."

Beth nodded and walked toward the kitchen, but came to a sudden halt after three steps. Turned back to Merritt—no, the window.

Merritt sat up. "What's wrong?"

Beth pursed her lips. "I sense something. Something bad—"

The glass shattered, raining shards over Merritt's head and back, blowing out half the candles.

Beth screamed.

"Get down!" Merritt shouted, dropping from his chair and slipping under the table. An earthquake? But the ground wasn't moving—

The table jerked; a thick something slammed against the far wall, followed by a deep grunt. Heart in his throat, Merritt crawled under the table to see Baptiste slumped against the far wall, a streak of blood leading to his head.

"Baptiste!" Merritt dove for the man, but not before a giant, unseen hand wrapped around him, turning him about.

A shadowy figure stood in the dining room, a black cloak billowing around him, a high, white collar pressed against his face. He was a tall man, broad shouldered, with dark hair swept to one side. Long sideburns marked his cheeks.

And there was a dog, some sort of terrier, on a leash beside him, whimpering.

"Mr. Fernsby, we have not been properly introduced," he said in an English accent.

Beth, standing from the ground, said, "You're Silas Hogwood."

Merritt's stomach sank.

The Englishman growled. "And you are a pain in my side."

The spell holding Merritt released, dropping him several feet to the ground. He landed sideways on his foot, which sent a sharp pain racing up his leg as he collapsed to the floorboards. The same spell took hold of Beth and pinned her to the ceiling.

The house shuddered, and the far wall came alive, jutting forward and slapping Silas in the back, nearly knocking him off his feet. He let go of the mongrel, who scurried into the reception hall with its tail between its legs.

"Oh don't worry." Silas scowled and planted his hand on the wall. "I've plans for you."

Something sparked—Merritt tasted it on the back of his tongue—and the house went still.

"What do you want?" Merritt forced himself to stand, favoring his right leg. He glanced to Baptiste, whose head lolled to one side. His chest still moved, thank God. "She's not here!"

"I'm aware." A gust of wind collided with Merritt's back, blowing him toward the taller man. But as Silas reached for him, his hand struck an invisible wall, and the wind cut out.

The wardship spell again. The tourmaline?

Merritt backpedaled, grabbing a chair to keep balance. His heart was the size of his entire torso and pulsed with the power of a hurricane. He searched frantically for a knife. Baptiste moaned again—a good sign.

Silas chuckled, tapping a gloved knuckle against the shield. "Very clever. I sensed your magic when you came for her. A two-for-one deal. Very generous."

That gave Merritt pause. "Magic?" He didn't have any magic. What he needed was help—his guns were all the way upstairs. Baptiste's eyelids fluttered. He crouched by the man and tried to help him up.

"You know what another wardship spell is, Mr. Fernsby?" Silas asked. "Spell-turning."

He waved his hand, and the shield disappeared. In four long strides, the Englishman reached Merritt and grabbed him around the throat. A feeling like lightning jolted from his neck down to his heel. His body spasmed. His lungs gasped for air.

"I always learn from my mistakes." Silas's dark eyes found Beth, still bound to the ceiling. "And I don't like snitches." He raised his other hand.

"No!" Merritt screamed.

Beth fish-mouthed like she'd been punched in the gut. The spell holding her vanished, and she fell hard to the floor, unmoving.

"No!" Merritt grabbed Silas's arm, almost breaking his hold, but that blasted spell from before overtook him, freezing him in place. He could barely blink, let alone fight.

"Nor do I like loud cargo," he sneered as the distant gleam of a lighthouse reflected off the window.

Noise built up in Merritt's brain, a thousand different sounds calling over one another, filling his thoughts, blocking out everything else. He fell limp to the floor, just barely registering the whimpering of that dog.

And he finally got to sleep.

Chapter 30

October 15, 1846, Blaugdone Island, Rhode Island

Hulda didn't get to Blaugdone Island until after dark, but she was becoming so used to its shadows she didn't mind. She tipped her boat driver handsomely and took a lantern with her, hurrying down the path from Merritt's enchanted vessel to the house. Light glowed from the dining room window, and she focused on it, not realizing until she reached the porch that the glass had been completely shattered, the door left ajar.

Panic seized her and sent a thorny rush into her crown. Grabbing her skirts, she hastened into the house, seeing first Mr. Babineaux slumped in a chair, holding a rag to the back of his head. Miss Taylor, on the floor, held her middle with one hand and carefully sipped water. Her eyes widened at the sight of Hulda. "Mrs. Larkin!" She tried to stand, then winced and dropped to her knees.

"Good heavens, what happened?" She rushed to Miss Taylor, inspecting her.

The woman winced and pushed her hands away. "B-Broken ribs, one or two," she ground out.

Hulda turned to Mr. Babineaux, who murmured, "Is just a little blood."

She took the man's face in her hands and brought a candle closer, watching his pupils. "You hit your head, didn't you? You have a concussion."

"He took Mr. Fernsby," Miss Taylor wheezed.

Hulda's skeleton turned to jelly, which sent her heart down to her navel. "Wh-What? Who?"

"Silas Hogwood."

The jelly morphed to ice. *Strife and truth.* Was this what she'd foreseen?

"I sensed him like I did before." Miss Taylor carefully leaned herself against the wall, still holding her middle. "He left just . . . fifteen minutes ago."

"Maybe half hour," Mr. Babineaux grumbled. "Tried to follow but . . . too dizzy." He slumped even further.

Hulda's eyes burned. Her limbs shook like she'd *run* all the way from Boston. "H-He's gone?" A pick chiseled through the center of her chest.

Miss Taylor nodded, face screwed like she was holding back tears. "He saved my life. Hogwood . . . he meant to kill me. But I felt Mr. Fernsby's spell touch me first. A shield like before."

Shivers coursed down Hulda's arms. "Then you know it's him. *He's* the second source of magic."

"That's what Mr. Hogwood said." She took a careful breath.

Panic bubbled up Hulda's throat. So Silas Hogwood knew, too. Was that what he meant, by Hulda being the first? Had he already planned on taking Merritt, too? "All right. All right." She breathed deeply. *In, out. In, out.* "Which way did they go?"

Miss Taylor winced. "Don't know."

"God help us." On her feet, Hulda rushed to the window and peered out into the night. "Owein! Owein, did you see? Do you know anything?"

The house didn't respond.

Hulda knocked on the wall. "Owein!"

Nothing.

Think, Hulda! Mr. Hogwood wouldn't still be on the island. The transference took a long time—that's what the police report had said back in Gorse End, and her own experiences lent to that theory. Using so much magic would surely leave a man sick as well. Vulnerable. Mr. Hogwood wouldn't risk getting caught again, like he had with Hulda, which meant he must have left the island. He'd want to avoid witnesses, too, so he wouldn't have a hotel room, or anything in a big city. Where, then? There were more remote places in the United States than anyone could ever count!

She shook her hands, trying to attenuate the nerves burning her like bug bites. She searched the room, eyes landing on the shattered glass. She stared at it hard, trying to connect the patterns . . . but it told her nothing. Either Mr. Hogwood's earlier spells on her had affected her augury or his future was too convoluted for her magic to see.

"I have to go to BIKER." She didn't know where else to turn. They had no neighbors on this island or the neighboring ones, and she didn't know where the Portsmouth constable lived, or if he'd be available. "I have to go to BIKER and ask Myra for help. If she knows someone with communion spells, the plants and birds can tell us where to find him." But would that take too long?

It doesn't matter. I have to do something*!* And to think of the way she and Merritt left things . . .

She spun back to Miss Taylor and Mr. Babineaux. Grabbed her lantern. "I'll send a doctor for you straightaway. Can you hold on a little longer?"

Miss Taylor nodded. Mr. Babineaux grunted.

Good enough. Grabbing her skirt, Hulda flew from the house and ran down the trail, holding the light ahead of her so she could avoid rabbit holes and wayward tree roots. She barely felt the effort of the run; panic was wonderful like that. It was a good fuel.

"Hold on, Merritt." She set the lantern in his boat and shoved it into the water, uncaring that her stockings got soaked in the process.

She activated the kinetic spell on the boat and pleaded with it, "As fast as you can."

The boat sped off into the night.

⌒୨

Hulda used her key to unlock the front door of the Bright Bay Hotel in Boston, not bothering to keep her footsteps quiet as she rushed through BIKER's headquarters to the room where its director slept. She threw open the door, and Myra sat upright in bed with a gasp.

"Who—Hulda!" She rubbed her eyes. Immediately stood, the skirt of her nightgown swishing around her ankles. "What are you doing here at this hour?"

"Silas Hogwood has attacked Whimbrel House!" Hulda set her lantern on a short bookshelf. "Merritt Fernsby has been captured. I don't know how to track them!"

Myra stared at her, openmouthed, for several seconds, then shook her head, her loose hair bobbing about her shoulders. "Surely . . . Surely not." She lowered herself back onto the bed as though standing had become too much of an effort.

"You cannot continue to deny it." Hulda marched over and grabbed the bed post. "He nearly killed Miss Taylor and our chef! Miss Taylor confirmed his identity."

"He wouldn't have left witnesses."

"Mr. Fernsby is a wizard, Myra!"

The woman's breath hitched.

"Yes," Hulda pressed. "I researched it myself. That's why I left. The second source of magic wasn't the tourmaline, but Mr. Fernsby! Through his paternal side." She crouched to better see Myra's face. "Mr. Hogwood must have figured it out . . . he may have psychometry spells. Perhaps he sensed it when he attacked me." She shuddered at the thought of Merritt pinned down, suffering the same—no, worse—fate. They were running out of time. "At the least, Mr. Fernsby has both communion and wardship spells in his blood. He warded Miss Taylor."

Myra shook her head yet again. "Too soon. Not like this."

"Not like *what*, Myra?"

Myra stood, forcing Hulda to do the same so she wouldn't be stepped on. "Maurice would never—"

"Maurice?" Hulda repeated. "Myra, are you awake? I'm talking about *Silas Hogwood*!"

But then she stopped short. She *knew* that name. Maurice. Maurice Watson.

She remembered Merritt holding a letter. *A Watson fellow is inquiring about purchasing the house.*

Miss Taylor had chimed in, *Odd feeling about this one. Can't explain what, but . . . doesn't sit right with me.*

And there was Miss Steverus's interruption the other day. *I just received a notice from Mr. Maurice Watson. He wants an appointment today.*

Hulda had augured premonitions about a wolf on Blaugdone Island *and* at BIKER. And with an alteration spell, any wizard could take a beastly form.

Hulda was talking about Silas Hogwood.

But so was Myra.

Merritt . . . Merritt had always been the target.

Hulda backstepped. "You knew." Her hand went to her chest. "You knew the whole time that Silas Hogwood was alive. That he was *here*. That's why you tried so hard to assure me otherwise."

Myra paled. "It's not what you think—"

"How is this not what I think?" Hulda was shouting now. "You . . . You traitor!"

Myra rushed for the door and slammed it closed. "Keep your voice down."

Hulda's tone darkened as the shadows when she said, "Tell me one reason why I should."

"I had *nothing* to do with your attack," she hissed, but her energy puffed away, leaving her face drawn and shoulders slouched. "I was sick, Hulda."

Hulda gaped. "What do you mean . . ." She paused. "That was years ago, Myra."

Myra nodded. "I know. But it wasn't simply a passing illness. I didn't want to tell you, or Sadie, or anyone." She kneaded her hands. "But I was sick, and Mr. Hogwood is a powerful necromancer."

Hulda's breath caught. "He healed you."

Myra nodded. "I bartered with him. I would help break him out of jail, out of England, in exchange for the cure."

"You helped him." She felt light-headed. "You used your powers . . . *BIKER* . . . to falsify those records."

Myra waved the accusation away. "I knew he would keep his word. I read his thoughts. He was trustworthy."

Hulda closed the space between them and grabbed Myra's shoulders. "He. Is. A. *Murderer!*"

Myra tugged free. "Because of him, I survived. And so did BIKER." She looked away. Rubbed a chill from her arms.

"Tell me everything," Hulda pressed. "I can't read your mind, Myra. Tell me, or else I'll—"

"Don't." She cut off the threat. "Don't." Rubbing her temples, Myra paced the length of the room and back.

Hulda stamped her foot. "I do not have time for this. Merritt is in *danger*. I'll never forgive you if he dies. I will never—"

"New favors came up," Myra croaked. "My sister got sick, too. A friend of mine, her husband was a drunk . . . She needed wardship to protect herself. I knew Maurice—Silas—could do it all. I knew he would always hold up his end of the bargain. He's a man of his word."

Hulda scoffed.

"So I went back to him a few times. Always in exchange for something. A new identity, new papers . . . and BIKER was on the brink of ruin."

Hulda pulled off her glasses and rubbed her eyes. "You never said anything."

"We were losing funding. Magical houses are increasingly rare, especially in the States. Silas agreed to travel around and infuse high-potential dwellings with spells so we could stay in business. So *you* could stay here."

Hulda slapped her glasses back on. "Do not pretend you did this for me."

Myra waned. "For his next payment, he wanted Whimbrel House. I don't know how he knew about it. He must have read *my* mind, or dove into our records."

Now Hulda paced. "Why?"

"It has magic he wants."

She whirled on the director. "So you knew he was back at it again. You *knew* he was taking magic."

"From a house, Hulda!"

"From Merritt!" she countered. "From *me*!"

"You were supposed to leave!" Myra screamed, voice echoing. Both of them froze from the outburst for several seconds. Regaining composure, Myra said, "Why do you think I tried so hard to pull you from that house? I refused to sign it over until I could make sure you were safe! He even tried to purchase it!"

"And a bloody good job you did! However *trustworthy* you might think that . . . that *criminal* is, he is a selfish, power-lusting horror that *you* unleashed on us!"

Tears brimmed Myra's eyes. She sank to her bed. "I know," she whispered, weeping. "I know. I'm sorry."

"Tell me where he is. You owe me that."

"He'll kill you."

"Tell me where he is," she pressed. "Surely you weren't so naïve as to help him without plucking that information from his mind."

Myra cradled her head. Sniffed.

Hulda crouched before her again. "Myra. I am running out of time."

"Marshfield," she whispered. "He's outside of Marshfield in a run-down house with a gambrel roof."

An image pushed its way into Hulda's mind—an image Myra had no doubt stolen from Mr. Hogwood. Hulda saw the dilapidated three-story house clearly, the large oak tree outside it, the surrounding fields.

She could find it.

"If you care for my life at all, you'll wake the city watch and send them," she said. "Because I *am* going. And I'm taking your horse."

Standing, Hulda snatched her lantern and hurried from the room, not leaving so much as an ounce of gratitude in her wake.

Chapter 31

The farther Hulda rode from the city, the denser the forest grew. Cedars, birches, and oaks crammed together. In the daylight, their autumnal crowns would have appeared lovely, restful. In the dark, they were shadows, walls, and obstacles, terrorizing both her and Myra's gentle mare.

Hulda never would have found the place had Myra not pressed the images into her mind. Images Myra never should have had in the first place, but Hulda would save her indignation for later. She was in a race against the clock. A race in which she hopefully had the upper hand, as she wasn't dragging a captive along with her.

The poor horse was exhausted when Hulda neared the house in question. It was an early 1700s building in ill repair, barely distinguishable from the narrow dirt road leading near it. Its walls were dark and slightly bowed in, its windows unlit, its roof sloping as though a heavy snowfall might make the entire thing collapse. She pulled the mare off the road some distance from the house, not wanting to be overheard, though the running of a nearby shallow canal helped muffle her footsteps. Whispering an apology to the mare, for she would not be able to tend to her just yet, Hulda balled her skirts in her hands and crept toward the house.

It appeared abandoned. There was no sound of humans whatsoever, only the mild babbling of the canal waters. Sourness built in her stomach. Had Myra led her astray? Surely she hadn't turned so far from goodness . . . and surely Hulda could not have beaten Mr. Hogwood to his hidden residence.

Then her toe hit what felt like a very stiff rock, but was in fact a warding wall, much like the one Merritt had accidentally made that day at Whimbrel House.

Pursing her lips, Hulda ran her hand over the spell. It seemed to surround the entire house. Something so large could be cast only by a powerful wizard, which indicated this, at least, was the right place. Stepping lightly, she followed the ward to see if it got any closer to the house. It connected with the canal and stretched on from there. Moonlight reflected off the water.

A dog barked somewhere far off. Hulda stiffened, listening, and reached into her bag for something to defend herself with. A second bark made her pause. It wasn't distant, but *stifled*. A third bark, fourth. Kneeling, Hulda pressed her ear to the earth just as a *yip!* ensued, and the animal fell quiet.

Underground, she thought. Mr. Hogwood had built his lair underground, away from detection. Just like in Gorse End. With as many spells as he'd stolen, he'd likely been able to dig it out quickly.

Certainty thrummed through her bones. Finding the entrance would prove tricky in the dark, though, and she didn't have *time*. That, and if Hogwood had other wards more lethal than invisible walls, she could be in a lot of trouble.

Think, Hulda. She dug into her bag. She had no firearms—she barely knew how to use them, and she was hardly going to wander the streets of Boston at night in an attempt to secure one. The only offensive objects she possessed were a letter opener and her crowbar, for what good they would do. At least she had some dice in here—if she could read her own future, she might see *how* she got into the house, thus saving herself precious minutes. Inching closer to the moonlight, she was about to pull the dice free when her eyes landed again on the canal.

And the grate in its side, leading toward the house.

She swallowed. Highly unlikely that was the *front* door, but . . . Hogwood was a tidy person. He'd want means of disposing of his messes . . . or at least a second exit to save himself from being cornered again, like he had been eleven years ago in his own home.

Hulda blew out a puff of air that stirred the mess her hair had become. After retrieving the charms she'd hung at Whimbrel House to prevent the wardship wall from restraining her, she pushed her bag to the back of her hip and carefully lowered herself into the canal, gritting her teeth when cold water climbed up her calves, knees, and paused mid-thigh. Her dress floated atop it, ballooning where air had been trapped. The grate wasn't screwed in, but the way was tight, wet, and rank. She wouldn't be able to do it in this dress. Even if she made it through, she'd drip an ocean once she was inside, and the clothing would easily quadruple in weight, further hindering her.

She peered back up to the house. She could wander in there and find an actual door . . . but would Hogwood hear creaking wood under her feet? Was the door even *there*, or elsewhere?

She eyed the grate and sighed. "He's already seen you in your underthings, so it hardly matters." Still, as she hurriedly stripped from her dress and tossed it against the side of the canal so it wouldn't float downriver, her courage waned. This was a job for the town watchmen, whom Myra was hopefully contacting. What could she hope to do?

Then she thought of the blackened, shriveled bodies at Gorse End. She couldn't let that happen to Merritt. She simply couldn't. So she heaved the grate from its place, clutched her bag to her chest in hopes of keeping it dry, and crawled down the long, grimy pipe, trying very hard not to think of what the slime at her hands and knees consisted of.

She crawled for some time, until her knees and shoulders ached and she'd gotten used to the smell, before she reached a second grate.

This one had a hinge, thank the Lord, so it wasn't quite so loud when she slid under it into a dark, stony cellar. She couldn't see a thing, but feeling in the dark, she touched meat hanging by string, jugs, and wine bottles. Foodstuffs. Purchased or stolen? Hardly mattered.

Concealed by darkness, Hulda did her best to wring out her drawers so she wouldn't leave a trail of drips wherever she went. Feeling along the wall, she passed a shelf and a stack of burlap bags and clanked her nails against a lantern. Pulling it off the wall, she retreated, rump smacking into another shelf, and rummaged through her bag until she found a match to light it.

The dim light burned her eyes. A short door made of two planks of wood strapped together with leather sat ahead of her. If she couldn't see light coming in, Hogwood likely wouldn't see light going out.

All right, Hulda. Use what you have. She reached for her dice again, then paused. She had more than temperamental divination in her arsenal. She *knew* Silas Hogwood. She'd lived with him for two years. She'd managed his staff, his kitchen, his house.

So what did that tell her?

She tapped one of the embedded stones on the ground. Hogwood hated filth. He was an immaculate person—the majority of the tiny staff he'd kept at Gorse End were maids; the cleanliness had made it impossible to divine his future when Hulda's suspicions began. This lair was out of sight and out of mind, his main goals, surely, but he still wanted to minimize the dirt. This place was likely reinforced with rock and wood all over, if only to protect it from earth. Which might mean it wasn't terribly large, because Hogwood also wasn't in favor of manual labor. At least not manual labor he had to perform himself, magic or no. On top of being a wizard, a murderer, and a convict, he was also an aristocrat.

Hogwood was not the sort of person who would live like a pauper anywhere, including prison. So Hulda guessed this lair would be, perhaps, half the size of Whimbrel House.

What else . . . She flew through memories of Gorse End. Oh! His living and sleeping areas would be at the farthest point from the entrance, wherever that may be. He was a very private person. He had not liked anyone but his steward venturing into his wing, and he'd despised unsolicited visitors.

But where is the door? Gingerly lifting the lantern and turning it as low as it would burn, Hulda crept to the exit of the cellar and creaked it open. Dim light flowed down a low but long corridor straight ahead. Immediately to her right was an adjoining hallway, and to her left, a set of stairs leading up to a door.

Front of the "house," she determined. She hoped that dog would bark again, if only as a distraction.

She was stepping out of the cellar when she noticed muddy boot prints on the makeshift cobblestones, veering down the corridor. Still wet—recent. Hogwood would only have tracked mud into this place if he were in a hurry. He must have taken Merritt that way, which was . . . north, she believed.

A pulse of fear thudded in her chest. She swallowed.

Hogwood wouldn't want to be cornered. Not after losing his freedom before. There had to either be a second exit—which could be the canal route, though Hogwood would have a harder time using it in human form—or another way around.

Lifting her lantern, she peered down the short way to the right, which was entirely dark. Illuminated a set of dog prints mingled with the boot prints. Looked to be a medium-sized dog. Could Hulda over-power a medium-sized dog if need be?

Without a skirt in the way, certainly.

Cheeks warm, she closed the cellar door behind her. Slipped into the passageway. Paused and turned back to the mud.

She scooped up a handful of it and tossed it down again, grit splattering.

In her mind's eye, she saw Merritt flying back through the air, colliding hard onto a stone floor.

Shuddering, she pulled back and wiped her hand on her corset, focusing to keep any forgetfulness at bay. She couldn't change the future. Her visions took everything into account, including any attempts to alter it. What she saw was what would come to pass. Still, she needed to hurry.

Footsteps sounded in the long corridor going north. Hulda quickly toed her way east, around the next bend, letting the shadows envelop her. Frozen, she listened for the footsteps to come closer. They didn't.

Down the corridor, the dog yipped.

Shifting her joints one at a time, Hulda crept across the stone. She didn't have to go far before finding another room, more of a large cubby, really, with a hanging sheet instead of a door.

Pushing the sheet aside, she choked on a sigh. "Merritt."

The space was barely large enough for a man to lie down, and certainly not tall enough for him to stand up. Merritt lay in the middle of it, tied up in enough rope to hinder a bull. It made sense that Hogwood wouldn't use a spell when a rope would do. Spells cost. But why was he waiting?

Shuddering, she hurried inside as he rolled over, blinking at her. One of his eyes was swollen. There was nothing else in the room but a jug in the corner.

"Hulda?" he rasped.

"Shh." She ran her hands over his bindings, trying to find the end of the rope. Of all the useful things in that bag of hers, none of them bore a blade.

He still blinked at her, confused. "Did he capture you, too?"

"No. Be quiet." Fear was starting to leak into her hands, making her fingers tremble. She pushed him over to find his wrists. He released a relieved sigh as she loosened the expert knot there.

"How'd you find me?" he whispered.

"Augury." Truth enough.

A pause. "Doesn't *he* have that, too?"

Hulda hesitated half a second. "I don't know." If he did, had he fore-seen Hulda's arrival? Was he waiting for her? Her heart pumped quicker, which made her fingers tremble more. Still, she managed to unravel the first knot. Merritt flexed his hands and hissed through his teeth.

She followed the rope to the second knot and tugged. Merritt held still to let her work, but being quiet was not in his repertoire. "I need to apologize—"

"*Later*, Merritt." She jerked another portion of rope free, then rolled him to his back to get at a knot over his stomach.

A few seconds passed. "You're in your underwear."

She gave him a scathing look.

He rested his head back. "I have to—ow!"

She paused. "What?"

"He socked me there."

Sympathy calmed her irritation. She tugged at the knot with a fraction more gentleness.

"I have to apologize."

She shook her head. "We can talk when we're not in danger of homicide."

"My point, though. What if one of us dies down here, and I never get the chance?"

She tugged the third knot free. Sitting up with a stifled grunt, Merritt shook his arms free and helped her work on his legs and feet.

"I was very . . . unkind . . . at the house," he said without looking at her. "I didn't understand. I should have asked for an explanation."

Hulda hated that they had to discuss this *now*. "I hardly care, Merritt. We need to hurry."

"I am hurrying." He tugged more rope from his thighs. "I'd just learned that my father bribed Ebba to seduce me so that he could dis-inherit me—"

Hulda's hands stilled. "What?" It was as close to a yell as one could get without using her actual voice.

"It's all very dramatic." The words were meant to be humorous, but the delivery was anything but. "Perhaps that *is* something to be discussed if and when we survive," he continued as Hulda freed his feet. He shimmied out of the rest of the rope. "But I am sorry for it. I saw you leaving . . . You were going to leave just like she did, without a word or letter—"

Face hot but hidden by darkness, Hulda said, "I was leaving because I didn't want to be present when you returned with another woman." Strife *and truth.* That had been, by far, the most meaningful and utterly useless premonition she'd ever had.

He stared at her. "I hardly intended to proposition her. I'm . . . rather fond of *you*, Hulda."

Blood rose to the skin in her neck and chest, but all she could think to say was "Oh."

He tried to stand, knees shaking, so Hulda grasped his upper arm and helped him right himself. Clamoring for the lantern, she said, "Merritt, *you* are the second source of magic at Whimbrel House."

He rubbed his wrists. "I've sorted that out, considering my abduction by a murderous wizard."

"Yes, of course. And . . . I think I know who your father is. Your biological father, that is."

He paused. "Now *that* you can tell me later. I'm still working through the abduction at the moment."

Grabbing his hand, she whispered, "There's a canal just this way. I'm going to blow this out. Be quiet—"

He tugged her back from the hanging sheet. "We can't leave without Owein."

Her breath caught. "Pardon?"

"Owein. He has Owein."

She stared, confused.

"He . . . took him somehow," he rushed to explain. "He took his spirit out of the house and put him into a dog."

Her lips parted. *The barking. The footprints.* The house hadn't responded to her, either. Was Hogwood so powerful a necromancer that he could move spirits? Such a thing hadn't been done since Edward III's time . . .

The dog had cried out moments ago. Was Mr. Hogwood hurting Owein? Had he already begun?

"We need to hurry." Merritt took the lantern from her. "Beth and Baptiste—"

"Are fine enough. A doctor should be reaching them by now." She shook her head at his hopeful look. "Later. Where's Owein?"

He pointed north. "Around there, I think." He paused, head cocked. "There are . . . others. I hear voices." He winced, shook his head. "I don't understand, I—"

His lips moved, but his voice cut out.

Hulda pressed a thumb to his lips. Any other time, the gesture might have sent a wave of red through her body, but her nerves were otherwise occupied with the situation at hand. "You're using communion." She barely put any air into the words, keeping them hushed. Muteness was a side effect of communion—he must have unknowingly been pushing the spell hard to have already garnered a side effect, though it should last only seconds.

Lines dug between his brows, but he removed his shoes and crept down the corridor in perfect silence, shielding the lantern light with his body. Hulda shouldn't have been surprised by his presence of mind—this was just like something out of his novel. Whether they'd get a happy ending remained to be seen.

Biting the inside of her cheek, she hugged herself to keep her fear localized and followed him.

As they neared the end of the passageway, that same light Hulda had noticed earlier spilled into view. Her heart pounded at the back of her skull, warning her. If it came to her versus Hogwood . . . any of them versus Hogwood . . . they would lose.

Passing back the lantern, Merritt poked his head into the adjoining room. Holding her breath, Hulda spied under his arm.

The space was relatively large, about one and a half times the size of the living room at Whimbrel House. Shelves stacked with ropes, chains, and all sorts of tinctures, potions, and bandages took up the walls. Two barrels sat in the corner, near an iron grate that—

Oh God. Hulda's stomach clenched. Behind it were the shrunken, mutated victims . . . but she didn't have long to study it, for her eyes fell onto a straight bench in the center of the room. The dark terrier strapped to it convulsed silently as Mr. Hogwood pressed both his palms into it, enacting the slow-moving spells that would suck the animal—*Owein*—of his power and turn him into one of the pruney dolls that had haunted Hulda's dreams for eleven years.

But Mr. Hogwood hadn't noticed them yet.

Hulda grabbed Merritt's elbow—what was their plan?—but Merritt didn't budge. He stood there, stiff as granite, his eyes not on Mr. Hogwood or Owein, but on the shriveled monsters behind the iron bars.

And he trembled.

༄

Moans. Cries. Screams.

They filtered through Merritt's head like a gentle winter wind. The suffering felt very far away yet omnipresent, and it came from that corner, where the masses that looked like old, dehydrated cacti sat on shelves behind bars. Heaven help him, were they still *alive*? Alive and suffering, pleading for death—

Owein whimpered.

The magic cut off abruptly, leaving Merritt in blissful silence. He blinked his eyes, trying to reorient himself—

A wall of fire burst to life behind him and Hulda.

Silas Hogwood had risen from his macabre spell-winding. He glared at Merritt and Hulda with dark, furious eyes. His hand extended toward them, his fingertips . . . *frosty*? Owein whined but tilted his head to see. He was still all right. He was still alive.

But Merritt had a feeling he and Hulda soon would not be.

"You think you can thwart me?" Silas's dark gaze slunk from Merritt to Hulda. The fire behind them burned hotter, forcing them into the revolting laboratory. "Nobody will have power over me. Not family, not BIKER, not even the Queen's League."

He eyed Hulda up and down, sneering, then flung out a hand, sending her flying across the room. Merritt burst forward, but not quickly enough to catch her. She slammed into the shelving on the wall opposite the mutated dolls, ripping free a wooden plank, knocking over half a dozen bottles that shattered when they hit the stone floor. Merritt dropped to his knees at her side, picking her up. Blood from several shallow cuts smeared his fingers.

Anger and fear warred within him. "We don't want power over you," he spat. "We want nothing to do with you. Just let us go."

Silas's mouth split into a foul smile, parting to release a chuckle. "Release you? No. Chaocracy has such beautiful enchantments, and I've craved them for a long time. The one thing that could make me truly untouchable." His lips curled. "Even for the royal family. And you two are rife with it."

Merritt blanched. Two? Owein and . . . *him*? *Chaocracy*? "You're mad." He still struggled to believe he had any magic, even though he'd seen and heard evidence. But chaocracy?

Hulda pushed herself upright. Her eyes flicked to the dolls.

Merritt's gaze followed but didn't linger. *The dolls.* They were important. Hadn't Hulda said Silas got his magic from the people he did *that* to? So if they could destroy them . . .

Hulda stood; Merritt rose next to her. Owein writhed, his straps slowly turning into glass marbles . . . a sluggish chaocracy spell to free himself. Merritt pointedly kept his gaze on Silas so as not to give the dog away.

"Mr. Hogwood, *please*," Hulda begged. "I know you can be reasonable. Let me strike a deal with you, just as Myra did—"

"Don't be so *hysterical*." He flung out his fingers.

Hulda retreated into Merritt, then doubled over shaking. Her skin turned cool and clammy beneath his touch. "Hulda!"

What was this? Another spell? *Hysteria?*

Merritt grasped her shoulders, trying to shake her out of it—

The pattering of marbles hitting the floor sounded just before a vicious growl tore through the air. Owein, free, ran for Silas and leapt, clamping his teeth down on the man's forearm. A gasp escaped Hulda as Silas lifted Owein from the ground and flung his arm outward, slinging the dog toward the fire.

"No!" Merritt reached for the animal.

Owein collided with an invisible wall erected before the flames. He yelped and fell to the stone.

Merritt gave himself half a heartbeat to marvel at the shield he'd managed to put up. Then he turned about and charged the Englishman himself.

∽

Still shaking off the fear spell, Hulda dashed again for the dolls, nabbing a shard of glass on her way. Merritt cried out. Hulda winced. Ran. Collided with the bars.

And stabbed the glass shard into the center of the closest doll.

Hogwood roared and arched like a gargoyle coming to life, throwing Merritt off his back. The fire extinguished, but she couldn't be sure whether he'd lost his hold on the spell or lost it forever because the stabbed doll had been giving him that power.

Lifting her arm, she stabbed the next doll—

An unseen force slammed into her, knocking her into the wall, tearing both the air from her lungs and the glass shard from her hand. Moving stiffly as a side effect of the kinetic spell, Hogwood hunched, turned back to Merritt, and picked him up off the ground with the same spell, shoving him toward the plank with the leather straps nailed to it. As his shoulder blades hit, Merritt said, "I can hear them."

Hogwood hesitated.

"Your dolls," Merritt rasped as Hogwood's knuckles pressed into his throat. "I can hear them screaming."

A stone slammed into Hogwood, right below his neck. Merritt dropped.

Owein barked, his magic ripping another stone from the floor and hurling it in Hogwood's direction. Hogwood used wind spells to shift that stone, then another, and another, away from him. Spells that left him gasping for air. His left hand crooked up, and the air popped as lightning came down from the ceiling and struck the dog.

"Owein!" Hulda cried, trying to push herself up. But Merritt, recovered, was faster, darting to the dog's side.

Hogwood shifted to wolf form and barreled after him. Panic flooded Hulda's limbs. She flew to her feet. The wolf bit down on the back of Merritt's trousers, sending him crashing into the torn-up floor. But as Hogwood pounced, Merritt reared and flung up a protection spell that sent the wolf crashing into another invisible wall.

Merritt winced and hissed through his teeth. The side effect of wardship was physical weakness—he would be feeling his bruises acutely.

Hulda searched for a weapon. Moved for another glass shard—

Her blood dripped onto stone and earth, forming an uneven pattern that pushed an image into her mind. It was *her*. She ran to the doll cage. Hogwood shot a kinetic spell after her to crush her—

The future.

Ignoring the glass, Hulda turned around and bolted for the dolls.

She heard the popping as Hogwood shifted back into a man. The spell was coming. She was almost to the cage—

Hulda dropped to her stomach, bruising her knees and hips as she did so, nearly breaking her nose against the floor. The kinetic spell she'd foreseen flew overhead and struck the cage, so powerful the iron bars groaned and snapped. Two of the dolls toppled to the ground.

"No!" Hogwood bellowed. He crawled along the floor toward her. The shock of losing more magic had to be reverberating through his body.

Owein barked, and to Hulda's horror, the dolls began jumping off the shelves, bobbing about on their mutated, bulbous limbs as though trying to escape. Hulda screamed and reeled back before one could touch her.

Owein whimpered and shook his head. *Of course!* He'd used a spell, just like the one that set the books dancing in the Whimbrel House library. Chaocracy spells caused confusion—Owein wouldn't be used to suffering side effects, after having an ability to cast without cost for two hundred years.

With the dolls spreading out, Hogwood couldn't protect them all at once.

Charlie N. Holmberg

"The dolls, Merritt!" Spinning on her hip, Hulda smashed her foot into a small one, sending it into the wall.

"I will *kill you*!" Hogwood leapt to his feet. Shot out a hand. Nothing happened.

Whatever spell he'd planned to use was gone.

It was working.

He shot out his other hand. Hulda's corset began squeezing in on her, its size shrinking with an alteration spell that threatened to snap her ribs.

Merritt leapt onto Hogwood's back. Her corset released, but a kinetic spell rippled out from Hogwood's body, striking all three of them. Merritt, the hardest. He flew backward into a narrow alcove in the wall. He didn't move.

"Merritt!" Oh God, what if they didn't escape this?

Owein, limping, snatched one of the vile dolls in his mouth and shook it until something snapped.

Hogwood faltered. Another burst of lightning hit Owein's hind leg. The dog yipped and collapsed.

Hogwood whirled around, fiery countenance focused on her. He moved toward her with stiff legs, his kinetic spells having sucked the mobility from his knees and hips. Lifting an equally stiff arm, he reached his hand toward her. A larger, unseen hand scooped her up, gluing her knees together and pinning her arms to her sides. A tendril of lightning pierced the back of her neck and needled to her ankles. Her body seized with the pain of it. A second followed, setting her limbs on fire, and the strain frosted the tips of Hogwood's hair.

"I would love to make you suffer, little canary, but I've work to do." He squeezed her tighter. Shuffled toward her, growling at the scattered dolls that no longer danced. "Give my best to that little maid of yours when you reach the other side."

312

The fingers closed in, cutting off her air. Blood pooled in her face. Her head felt like an expanding balloon. Her bones bent and—

A dense *whap!* echoed through the chamber. Hogwood's face slackened. Hulda dropped, landing on her feet but falling forward onto her knees. She coughed. Gasped for air. Looked up just as Hogwood teetered to one side and collapsed in a great heap on the stone.

Behind him stood Merritt, shoulders heaving, his mess of hair netting over his face.

And in his grasp was her crowbar.

They held their positions for several seconds. When Hogwood didn't move, Merritt gradually straightened. Blew hair from his face. Looked down at his weapon.

"That *is* handy." He turned the metal rod over.

A painful laugh rang up Hulda's throat, but it died on her lips. "Owein."

Dropping the crowbar, Merritt sped to the dog. Knelt at his side. "He's all right. Breathing." He stroked the mutt's fur. "Hey, boy, can you hear me?"

Snatching a broken bottle, Hulda shakily rose to her feet and approached Hogwood. Stepped over a deformed doll. Hogwood's chest moved slightly with his breaths. She knelt by his head, pushing the glass against his cheek should he wake—

Silas Hogwood drew in a fluttering breath, then released it.

His body remained still.

Hulda gaped. Dead. *Dead.* Too hurt to even heal himself . . . She couldn't internalize it. Like her brain had disconnected from her body and sat in one of those jars on the shelves.

Her tormentor . . . gone. And all his magic with him.

Sounds came from overhead—footsteps, creaking floorboards, a few shouts.

Merritt stood, Owein filling his arms, and looked up. "Please don't say those are his accomplices."

313

Hulda tilted her head, listening. "I believe it is the local watchmen."

"Ah." He glanced at the heap that was Silas Hogwood, then at her. He hefted the dog. "Do you want to hold him?"

Hulda gave him an inquisitive look.

He merely tipped his head toward her. Hulda looked down . . . at her underthings.

Sighing, she held out her arms. "Yes, please."

At least the animal would give her some sense of modesty when the patrol made their way downstairs.

Chapter 32

BIKER was more powerful than Merritt had given it credit for.

Watchmen had poured into the strange basement hovel that Silas had built for himself, like any true villain would, followed shortly thereafter by a Ms. Myra Haigh, an attractive woman in her late forties. Hulda and Merritt were separated—Hulda still using Owein as a modesty shawl—and thoroughly questioned, which really wasn't a problem, as Merritt had nothing to lie about. In the end, Ms. Haigh stepped in and covered everything, assisting law enforcement, cleaning up the mess, ridding them of the . . . body. By dawn, after the strangest and most dangerous night of his life, Merritt and Hulda were free to go.

Which was how he ended up in Boston midmorning, stifling a yawn as he leaned against a whitewashed brick wall of Bright Bay Hotel, where BIKER was supposed to be clandestinely tucked away. He picked absently at the bandage around his forearm, where Silas had burned him with a handy streak of lightning. Owein danced nervously around his feet, taking in the sights of the city, sniffing people as they passed by. He wondered how much of the creature's mind was mutt and how much was boy. He certainly heeled well.

Owein perked, his floppy ears lifting. Merritt turned just in time to see Hulda slip out of the back door, her trusty bag ever on her shoulder, all her bandages covered by a modest dress with a collar snug against her chin. Despite the long and arduous night, she managed not to look exhausted, though her hair looked like someone had taken her to bed in a very passionate manner. Merritt bit down on a grin and did not share the simile.

When she reached him, she held out a file. "Here."

He straightened and took the papers, flipping over the first one. "What's this?"

She rolled her lips together. "This is the information on your father. That is, who I believe your father to be."

Merritt lowered the papers without reading them. "I see."

"When you're ready." She rubbed her hands together like she wore gloves that didn't quite fit. "If I'm right, then Owein is your great-great-great-great-great-great-great-great-uncle. Give or take."

The papers felt like steel sheets in his hand. He glanced at the dog, who barked at his side, tail wagging.

"Thank you." Unsure what to do, he tucked the file under his arm. Lingered. Frowned.

"Are you well?" Hulda asked.

He shook his head. "Are either of us?" Hulda shrugged, and he added, "I should feel bad about it, shouldn't I?"

She studied him. "About what?"

"Killing him," he said, softer. "I killed a man last night. But I . . . I don't feel bad about it. Shouldn't I feel bad? Guilty, perhaps?"

Hulda drew in a shuddering breath. "Mr. Hogwood was not a good man. You did what you had to." Her shoulders relaxed. She lifted a hand toward him, then dropped it. "You saved me. No one could hold you accountable for it."

"I believe *you* saved *me*."

Her lip quirked. "Regardless."

He nodded slowly, letting the absolution roll over him. "All right, then. Shall we?"

He stepped onto the street, but when Hulda didn't follow, he paused.

She sighed. "I don't know, Merritt. My position with BIKER is . . . tenuous." She'd whispered Ms. Haigh's involvement as they rode over in the back of a patrol wagon. "I don't even know whether I'm employed anymore . . . and all my things are here. But I do not want to stay here."

He shrugged a shoulder, hope building in his chest. "You could pack a bag. Send for the rest."

A small smile flickered on her mouth. "I'm not sure that would be . . . appropriate, given the circumstances."

He deflated. "Of course." He glanced to the hotel. "Then where will you go?"

Rubbing the back of her neck, she said, "My sister's, I suppose. She lives not terribly far from here. Until things . . . sort."

He shifted his weight to his other leg. "And when will they sort?"

She picked at her hem. "I'm not sure."

An open carriage rolled by.

"Do you still have your communion stone?" he asked.

She patted her bag. "Of course."

He nodded, unsure what else to say, or what to do with his hands. "Well then."

She checked her posture. "I should . . . get my things together before Myra returns."

"Probably a good idea."

"But I'll leave a note."

He smiled. "Also a good idea."

They stood there awkwardly for another moment before Merritt finally turned away, taking the road toward the dock. He glanced back once. Hulda was still watching him.

Is she not coming back? asked a youthful, clipped voice in his head.

He started. A man on horseback was coming his way, so he quickly crossed the road, Owein following at his heels. It took him a second to identify the voice as the dog's. "Um." He wasn't sure what to do with this magic business. He wasn't sure he believed it. Perhaps he would be persuaded by the contents of this file . . . a file he had no desire to read. Yet. But despite the strangeness of the conspicuous second voice in his head, heaviness replaced surprise. He glanced back a second time, but didn't see her.

"I don't know, Owein," he admitted. "I don't know."

⁓

It took three days for Merritt to open the file Hulda had bequeathed him. The first bit was a family tree, with the name Nelson Sutcliffe underlined.

Merritt stared at it. Cattlecorn was a decent-sized place; he'd half expected not to know the man. But he knew Sutcliffe. Constable Sutcliffe, that was. He had a wife and three sons younger than Merritt. His . . . brothers?

He looked at the notes underneath; it took a minute for him to figure out they were magic markers. If this was taken from the Genealogical Society for the Advancement of Magic, the markers made sense. His eyes scanned the branches, noting the *Ch*s, the *W*s, and, in one line, *Co*s. Communion. That seemed to be the most prevalent in the family line. It was communion that had led him to Owein's grave marker. Which meant . . . what? That the grass and reeds were speaking to him? He'd had the same experience when looking for Hulda in the dark. And then those mutated *things* in Silas's laboratory . . .

Merritt shuddered and pulled his mind back from the unpleasant memories, refocusing on the pedigree. Sure enough, Nelson Sutcliffe's paternal line traced back to the Mansels, though Owein's name wasn't recorded on this document. He took a moment to pen it in.

Merritt's eyes dropped back to Nelson Sutcliffe. "Let me get this straight," he said to the page. "You had an affair with my mother, who had me, and my father knew about it. Which was why he was such a boor to me all my life, but either because of social pressure or perhaps some semblance of conscience, he waited until I was eighteen to *bribe my sweetheart* to seduce me and fake a pregnancy, but in the meantime you, what, looked up my grandmother and gave her this house to make amends?"

He threw down the papers and sat back in his chair. The door to his office creaked, and the sound of sniffing told him it was Owein. Unless Baptiste had gotten hit in the head harder than he thought.

"I should write a memoir," he said to the dog. "Though no one would believe it was true."

What's a memoir?

He still wasn't used to the voice in his head. It was happening more and more frequently, which meant *somehow* Merritt was getting the hang of a communion spell trapped in his blood. "It's an autobiography with oomph," he answered.

From what Merritt understood, Owein would stay a dog indefinitely . . . until he died, in which case he could inhabit the house again, so long as he passed away on Blaugdone Island. Not that Owein was eager in the slightest to inhabit the house—he enjoyed having a body again, smelling, touching, tasting things, which he couldn't do in a frame of wood and brick. That, and Merritt's communion spells only worked on plants and animals—if Owein were to transfer back to the house, they'd lose that outlet of communication.

Merritt rubbed his eyes. On top of the mess of discovering he was a *wizard* at thirty-one, he needed to go back to New York. He needed to confront Nelson Sutcliffe *and* Peter Fernsby. At least one of them would not be happy to see him.

He glanced to the communion stone sitting quietly at the edge of his desk. "One thing at a time." Opening a drawer, he pulled out his ever-growing manuscript.

Right now, it was very crucial that he finish his book.

It'd been just over a week since Hulda had come to stay with her younger sister, who'd received her most graciously, considering Hulda had been unable to send word ahead. Danielle Larkin Tanner lived in Cambridge, northwest of Boston, in a nice home she shared with two children and her husband of ten years, who was a lawyer hailing from a family of the same profession. Which was excellent, for they had room to spare for Hulda and her things, and room for her to wander about and sigh wistfully and be generally aoristic about her life.

She hadn't heard from Myra. She hadn't heard from Merritt. Miss Taylor had contacted her once through the stone, which was nice. Then again, perhaps someone else had tried and Hulda hadn't been around to hear it. She'd forbidden herself from carrying the stone around, knowing it would lead only to sulking. Admittedly, though, she'd spent a good amount of time staring at it. She'd tried to work up the courage to activate it, even written down possible phrases she could use to open a conversation, but her courage was shaken, presuming she'd ever had any to begin with. In truth, every night she played with a variety of ideas for reaching out to Merritt, but by morning her strictly trained rational side dismissed every last one.

Now, belly full of a luncheon she had no hand in preparing, Hulda sat in the seat of a multipaned window, watching her nephews and brother-in-law run around outside, bright orange and red leaves flying about their feet. It was cold enough now for hats, scarves, and gloves, and the trees were half-naked, but the sun remained bright. Pushing up her glasses, Hulda smiled at the scene, feeling wistful again, and a little sad. But that was becoming the norm for her.

"Miss Larkin?" Her sister's only hired staff, Miss Canterbury, approached with a broom under one arm and a brown-paper package in her hands. "This just came for you."

Hulda blinked. "For me?" Who even knew she was here? Only Myra had the address. Was this some sort of apology? "Thank you."

She took the package—it felt like a book—onto her lap, and Miss Canterbury gave her some privacy.

Unwrapping the parcel, she found it was not a book, but a stack of papers in familiar handwriting, atop which sat a note:

> *Hulda,*
> *I thought you might like to know the ending.*
> *Sincerely,*
> *Merritt Fernsby*
> *PS: Sadie Steverus is very kind and not hardly secretive enough to be of your acquaintance.*

Hulda smiled, though in truth she wished the note were longer. She read it again, slower, and set it beside herself on the window seat. The papers in her hand picked up exactly where Merritt had finished reading to her while she was recuperating from Silas Hogwood's *first* attack. She was surprised he'd remembered the place so precisely.

"This is it." She turned the ruby-studded cross over in her hands, gilt glinting in the candlelight. "Red Salvation."

The priest hunkered into his oversized robes, getting comfortable. A warm smile lit his face, one that reminded Elise of her father. "I haven't heard that name in a long time."

Warren bent over, holding up the magnifying glass. "But you know what this is, don't you?"

The priest's expression was unwavering. "Aye, I know. I've forgotten many things, but I know that."

"Must be worth a fortune." Warren held out his hand, and Elise placed the crucifix against his palm like it were a newborn babe. "I can easily see how this could bring a man happiness."

"Then you see nothing at all." Father Chummings clicked his tongue. "Do you know Latin?"

"I do," Elise offered.

He dipped his head. "Then read the inscription on the back, child. Aloud, for your partner's sake."

Hulda put the page aside, curious. However, the story changed completely on the next page.

Once upon a time, there was a lonely old (but not really very old) rogue who lived in a dingy (but not that dingy, let's be honest, he's not a pauper) apartment in New York, who suddenly received a call from a very polite lawyer about a house in the middle of nowhere that was his. By the way, this house was haunted. Fortunately, the rogue did not believe in ghosts at the time, so he went anyway.

Hulda smiled. Something warm and strange ballooned in her chest.

The house was utterly terrible, as one can expect a haunted house to be. But fortunately for the rogue, someone competent came by. Competence claimed she was sent by a special organization with a truly terrible acronym, but truthfully her visit had been arranged by divine intervention.

The house (which later became a talking dog, but that is a story for another day) gradually settled down under her hand, and so did the rogue. In fact, the rogue found he no longer slept in and made pastries the highlight of his day; he woke (relatively) on time just to see Competence chewing absently on her lip while she was nose deep in a book, or chattering with the staff, or admiring the sunset when she thought no one was looking.

The balloon swelled. Rings of heat formed around Hulda's eyes. She turned the next page, covering the second half with her hand, terrified she would read ahead and ruin it all.

Competence helped the rogue write what was likely a terrible novel, hired help who would become his friends, and provided him with conversation that was both amusing and deep. Very soon, the rogue found that he wanted nothing more than to share that house with her forever, though there was the tricky business of her refusing to use his Christian name.

Hulda laughed. A tear pooled in the corner of her eye.

The rogue, of course, was a rogue for a reason. He had a less-than-savory past, involving a contumelious (Competence would appreciate the complexity of that word) father and a tricksy belle, which had left him with some heavy thoughts and (mostly) without an inheritance. Plus, unfortunately, both the rogue and Lady Competence shared the trait of being very poor communicators when it came to important and uncomfortable things.

A second tear formed. Hulda wiped it away with her thumb. Smudged her glasses, but didn't bother to clean the lenses.

And so it was that the rogue went on a mission to uncover the truth of his labyrinthine (there's another word for you) past when he had intended to tell Competence that he was falling madly in love with her.

A sob tore up her throat. Hulda clapped a hand over her mouth, fearing Miss Canterbury would hear it, and continued reading through increasingly foggy spectacles.

Competence, in turn, determined to move out immediately. Which the rogue very much hoped was a way of dealing with heartbreak because, if so, that meant Competence likewise might be falling in love with him. Or, at the very least, strongly tolerated him.

She laughed. A teardrop fell on the paper and smudged the penned *likewise*. She felt like her ribs were pulling apart in the most fascinating way. Her heart pumped like it was skipping rope. Pleasant prickles danced across her scalp.

And so, after some nonsense with a supernecromancer that is hardly important to the story, the rogue determined to tell Competence how he felt in the hope she'd return to him someday. He lucked out in that he got to do it in a very strangely arranged letter, as he always was a better writer than speaker.

Take your time, Hulda. I've kept the communion stone in my pocket.

Absolutely Yours—Merritt.

Speechless, Hulda turned the page, only to see the continuation of Elise and Warren's story. And yet she couldn't bring herself to read it. Not now.

Collecting the papers together, she clutched them to her chest and hurried from the window seat, out into the hallway. Her sister was playing the pianoforte in the front room, so she ran to see her, uncaring that her eyes were probably red.

"Danielle!" she burst out, causing her sister to pause midmeasure and swivel on her bench. "Danielle, I need to leave immediately. Could you take me to the tram station?"

∽

Hulda hadn't been away for even a fortnight, yet the island seemed different when the dinghy driver banked to drop her off. The place was filled with color, hues of yellow, orange, red, and brown. The green in the reeds and grass was slowly fading with the promise of winter. Songbirds still trilled in half-bare trees. Frost glimmered where the branches cast shade.

Taking a deep breath, Hulda pulled her shawl close and made her way to Whimbrel House. Nothing hung on the line, though perhaps it had been too cold to dry much of anything today. No one chopped wood, though the axe protruded from the stump in the yard. There was a faint smell of rosemary and sage wafting from the kitchen window, which served to bolster Hulda's spirits and calm her nerves. She knew the house had changed, but she *felt* it, too, in a way she couldn't quantify. As though a sense outside of the five—or perhaps six—that she possessed whispered it. And yet it still very much felt like home.

She paused at the front door, wondering if she should knock. Wondering if she wanted to have this conversation at the threshold instead of sequestered in a private room. Remembering that her contract had not yet terminated, she deemed it appropriate to open the front door and slip inside. The portrait on the wall took no notice of her; the painted woman merely stared ahead as she'd been created to do, depleted of magic.

A dog barked upstairs. Within seconds, the terrier mix darted into view and sprinted down the stairs, its paws losing purchase as it hit polished hardwood. It slipped to its rump, earning a laugh from Hulda, but recovered quickly, rushing to her and planting its front paws on her knees.

"You look like you're convalescing well." She rubbed Owein's ears and allowed him to lick her chin. "Glad to see you. Where's the man of the house?"

"Hulda!" Miss Taylor swept in from the dining room and rushed to her, hugging her with the utmost gentleness. "You're back!"

"Are you well?" Hulda pulled away to survey her friend for injuries.

"Doing better every day," Miss Taylor assured her. "Just can't lift anything heavy or reach too high. Mr. Babineaux has taken up dusting."

Heavy steps announced Baptiste arriving to investigate the noise. He made no physical reaction to Hulda's presence. "You look well," he said.

"I am, thank you. And you?"

He shrugged. "I'm preparing chicken."

"I'm sure it will be wonderful." She glanced back to the stairs, hoping to see Merritt appear atop them. "Is he working?"

"Mr. Fernsby went out for a walk about half an hour ago," Miss Taylor explained, a small smile on her face. "West. I'm sure you'll find him. He's begun to wear a path."

Hulda nodded, nerves igniting anew. "If I can leave my bag here."

"Of course. I'll put it in your room."

Her room. She thanked her and slipped back outside. Owein tried to follow, but Miss Taylor called him back, whispering something Hulda didn't catch. On reflection, perhaps it was better she hadn't heard it.

Sure enough, a narrow path marked by trampled grass and goosefoot wound behind the house and westward. How often had Merritt walked this way since her departure? She followed it, rubbing her hands together, though it was more anticipation than the weather that chilled her fingers. The sun encouraged her, leaving a warm spot on the side of her head. A whimbrel called nearby.

She'd been walking about a quarter hour when she saw him near a weeping cherry, staring toward Connecticut with his arms folded and hair loose as always, wearing his coat, though by the fit of it, she could tell it was unbuttoned. The crunching of grass hardly made her approach quiet, but Merritt must have been lost in thought, for he turned around only when she was roughly six paces from him. His eyes, blue as the deepest parts of the bay, widened slightly, and his jaw went lax. "Hulda. I . . . wasn't expecting you."

She stopped at a good four-pace distance and lifted her nose. "You invite me to return and then say you weren't expecting me?"

The corner of his lip twitched. "You have me there." He reached into his vest pocket to pull out his watch, checking it. "The mail was much more timely than I gave it credit for. I was not expecting you to receive said invitation for another two days."

She shrugged. "I was in Massachusetts, not France."

"I ate an apple once that looked suspiciously like France." Returning the watch, he closed the distance between them by two paces. Hulda's heartbeat echoed in her ears. "Did you . . . like the book?"

She pressed her thumb into her palm. "I admit I haven't finished it yet."

"Oh?"

"I was rather distracted by a scene that did not fit the narrative in the slightest."

Merritt glanced down and pinched the watch chain between his fingers. "And what did you think of it?"

"Competence is a very apt name. I would have preferred it over Hulda, as a child."

He met her eyes again. "Truly?"

She tilted her head to one side. "It would have given me something to aspire to."

Keeper of Enchanted Rooms

The half smile that formed on his face was mesmerizing. "I hardly think you needed encouragement."

She drew in a steadying breath. "Unfortunately, I often need encouragement."

He took another step, leaving a single pace between them. "Is that so?"

She nodded. Swallowed. Glanced at his lips.

When Merritt took another step, her pulse resonated down to her knees. He took her hand, driving back the chill there. "And what did you think of the rest?" His voice lowered to just above a whisper.

Her cheeks flushed, which didn't surprise her in the least. "I liked it very much."

He leaned forward and pressed his forehead to hers. Closing her eyes, Hulda relished the weight of it. The warmth wafting off him, enveloping her with spring when she was surrounded by winter.

He squeezed her hand. She heard him smile when he asked, "Do you need more encouragement?"

Opening her eyes, she met his penetrating gaze. Held it for several seconds. "No."

Tilting her head, she inched forward enough to brush her lips against his. Her nerves exploded like a flock of sparrows taking flight. Merritt's free hand came up to cup her jaw and pull her a little closer, enough to truly, softly, and blissfully kiss her.

In that moment, despite the patterns of light dancing across her eyelids, she pushed her augury away.

She didn't need magic to see a bright and joyous future for the both of them.

ACKNOWLEDGMENTS

Well. This was a wild ride.

And wild rides come with safety bars and seat belts, and I have a lot of metaphorical safety bars and seat belts to thank for this!

He's always first, so don't be surprised—thank you to my spouse and partner in crime, Jordan Holmberg. Books wouldn't happen without you. Thank you for supporting me and our babies, for being a sounding board, an alpha reader, and an enthusiast. Love you a million.

Many thanks to my agent, Marlene, even though she made me do another BIG edit on this book. This thing has been through so. Many. Edits. But it's better for it in the long run. And thank you to Jeff Wheeler, who helped me with said BIG edit. You are wise and smart and kind.

Thank you to my early readers! Tricia Levenseller, Rachel Maltby, and my podcast cohost, Caitlyn McFarland. Y'all don't realize the absolute word sludge they have to suffer through. And I cannot forget Whitney Hanks and Leah O'Neill, who are the speediest beta readers ever and wield fine-tooth combs like swords.

Many thanks to the team that makes my manuscripts readable, including Adrienne Procaccini, Angela Polidoro, Karah Nichols, Laura

P., Ariel, and all the copyeditors/proofreaders/cold readers/designers who go unsung year after year.

Huge thank-you to my readers. You are the air in my flotation device and the yeast in my bread. I owe you guys so much.

Lastly, many hosannas to God in Heaven, who tolerates me and guides me through all my stories, literal and not.

Cheers.

ABOUT THE AUTHOR

Charlie N. Holmberg is a *Wall Street Journal* and Amazon Charts bestselling author of fantasy and romance fiction, including the Paper Magician series and the Numina Trilogy. She is published in more than twenty languages, has been a finalist for a RITA Award and multiple Whitney Awards, and won the 2020 Whitney Award for Novel of the Year: Adult Fiction. Born in Salt Lake City, Charlie was raised a Trekkie alongside three sisters who also have boy names. She is a proud BYU alumna, plays the ukulele, and owns too many pairs of glasses. She currently lives with her family in Utah. Visit her at www.charlienholmberg.com.